J. Durand, H. Taine

Italy, Florence and Venice

J. Durand, H. Taine

Italy, Florence and Venice

Reprint of the original, first published in 1871.

1st Edition 2022 | ISBN: 978-3-36812-504-2

Verlag (Publisher): Outlook Verlag GmbH, Zeilweg 44, 60439 Frankfurt, Deutschland
Vertretungsberechtigt (Authorized to represent): E. Roepke, Zeilweg 44, 60439 Frankfurt, Deutschland
Druck (Print): Books on Demand GmbH, In de Tarpen 42, 22848 Norderstedt, Deutschland

ITALY

FLORENCE AND VENICE

FROM THE FRENCH OF

H. TAINE

BY

J. DURAND

NEW YORK
LEYPOLDT & HOLT
1871

Stereotyped by LITTLE, RENNIE & Co.,
645 & 647 Broadway, New York.

CONTENTS.

BOOK I.

PERUGIA AND ASSISI.

CHAPTER VI.

CHAPTER VII.

BOOK II.

FLORENCE.

CHAPTER I.

CHAPTER II.

CHAPTER III.

BOOK III.

THE FLORENTINE SCHOOL OF ART.

CHAPTER I.

CHAPTER II.

CHAPTER III.

CHAPTER IV.

CHAPTER V.

CHAPTER VI.

BOOK IV.
FROM FLORENCE TO VENICE.

CHAPTER I.

CHAPTER II.

CHAPTER III.

CHAPTER IV.

CHAPTER V.

CHAPTER VI.

BOOK V.

VENICE.

CHAPTER I.

CHAPTER II.

PAGE

ANCIENT VENICE.—PROLONGATION OF THE MUNICIPAL SYSTEM.—
ORIGINALITY AND RICHNESS OF INVENTION IN SMALL FREE
STATES.—THE RENAISSANCE OF ARCHITECTURE.—SAN MARCO.
—IMPORTATION AND TRANSFORMATION OF THE BYZANTINE
STYLE.—MOSAICS AND SCULPTURES.................... 231

CHAPTER III.

SAN GIOVANNI E PAOLO.—I FRARI.—THE MAUSOLEUM OF GUAT-
TEMALATA.—MONUMENTS OF THE DOGES.—THE SPIRIT OF DI-
VERSE CENTURIES AS STAMPED ON SCULPTURE.—THE MIDDLE
AGES, THE RENAISSANCE, THE SEVENTEENTH CENTURY, AND
THE MODERN EPOCH.—"ST. PETER MARTYR," BY TITIAN.—TIN-
TORETTO.................... 242

CHAPTER IV.

PROMENADES.—SANTA-MARIA DELL' ORTO.—SAN GIOBBE.—LA GUI-
DECCA.—I GESUATI.—I GESUITI.—MANNERS, CUSTOMS AND
CHARACTERS.—MISERY.—PUBLIC SPIRIT.—IDLENESS AND REV-
ERIE AT VENICE.................... 251

CHAPTER V.

THE LATTER DAYS.—EPICUREANISM.—CANALETTI, GUARDI, LON-
GHI, GOLDONI AND GOZZI.—THE CARNIVAL.—LICENSE.—THE
LIDO.—THE SEA.—THE TOWER OF SAN-MARCO.—THE CITY, THE
WATER AND THE SANDS.................... 262

BOOK VI.

VENETIAN ART.

CHAPTER I.

CLIMATE.—TEMPERAMENT.—ART, AN ABSTRACT OF LIFE.—MAN IN
THE INTERVAL BETWEEN HEROIC AND DEGENERATE ERAS.. 272

CHAPTER II.

THE EARLY PAINTERS.—JOHN BELLINI.—CARPACCIO.—VENETIAN
SOCIETY IN THE SIXTEENTH CENTURY.—UNRESTRAINED VO-
LUPTUOUSNESS.—DOMESTIC ESTABLISHMENT OF ARETINO.—
SENTIMENT OF ART.—COLOR INSTINCTS.................... 281

CHAPTER III.

CHAPTER IV.

CHAPTER V.

BOOK VII.

LOMBARDY.

CHAPTER I.

CHAPTER II.

CHAPTER III.

CHAPTER IV.

CHAPTER V.

ITALY.

BOOK I.

PERUGIA AND ASSISI.

CHAPTER I.

FROM ROME TO PERUGIA.—THE ROMAN CAMPAGNA.—THE APEN-
NINES.—SCENERY.

I LEFT Rome at five o'clock in the evening; I had
not yet seen this portion of the Campagna, and I will
never see it again for my own pleasure.

Always the same impression—that of an abandoned
cemetery. Long monotonous hillocks succeed each other
in interminable rows, like those seen on a battle-field
when the great trenches are covered over in which the
dead lie heaped. Not a tree, not a stream, not a hut.
In two hours I saw but one round cabin, with a pointed
roof, like those found amongst the savages. Even
ruins are wanting. On this side there are no aque-
ducts. At long intervals we encounter an ox-cart;
every quarter of a league the sombre foliage of a
stunted evergreen bristles up by the roadside, the
sole living object, a forlorn straggler lost in the solitude. The only trace of man is the fences bordering
the highway and traversing, far and wide, the undulating verdure, in order to confine the flocks during the
season of pasturage. At present, however, all is barren,

and the sky expands its divine cupola over the funereal waste with mournful, ironic serenity. The sun declines, and the fading azure, growing more limpid, tinges its crystal with an imperceptible hue of emerald. No words can express this contrast between the eternal beauty of the sky and the irremediable desolation of the soil. Virgil, in the midst of Roman pomp, already first indicated the merciful contemplation of the gods, who, under Jupiter's roof, looked down amazed upon man's miseries and strifes.*

I cannot rid my mind of the impression that here is the sepulchre of Rome, and of all the nations she destroyed — Italians, Carthaginians, Gauls, Spaniards, Greeks, Asiatics, barbarian populations and enlightened cities. All antiquity, indiscriminately, lies buried here under the monstrous city which devoured them, and which died of its surfeit. Every verdant undulation of the soil is, as it were, the grave of a distinct nation.

Daylight is gone. In the moonless night, the miserable post-houses, with their smoking lamps, appear suddenly, like the dwellings of the watchers of the dead. Heavy stone walls, begrimed arcades, shadowy depths with lank forms of horses vaguely discernible in them, strange, bronzed, sallow visages circulating around the harness and clanking chains, their gleaming eyes lit up with fever—all this fantastic disorder and grimacing in the midst of the darkness and chilly dampness falling around it like a pall, imparts to the nerves and heart a long sentiment of horror. The ghastly vision is completed by a lugubrious postilion, who, in an old tattered cap, eternally jumps about in the yellow light. The rays from the lantern fall on his back with a spectral tint. He is constantly writhing

---

* " Di Jovis in tectis iram mirantur inanem
Amborum et tantos mortalibus esse labores."

and twisting around in order to beat his nags, and you can see the fixed leer, the mechanical contraction of his meagre jaws.

On awakening, at early dawn, a river appears meandering beneath its morning exhalations; then ravines and bald slopes confusedly intermingled and riven by innumerable fissures, with courses of whitened stones rolled down into the hollows and on the declivities and, in the distance, lofty, dark, striated mountains. The frontier is passed, and the Apennines commence. A bright sun illumines the sharp crags of their summits; the lungs breathes healthy atmosphere; the land of pestilence is left behind. We have now come to a meagre soil, but one favorable to existence; the country has a rigorous aspect, with grand and striking features, serving to stamp on the minds of its children noble and definite images without the body becoming sensualized by a too gross and abundant nourishment. Heaths, barren rocks, with here and there a strip of rich aromatic pasturage, some stony fields, and olives everywhere—you might imagine yourself in Provence. Everything, even these pale olive-trees, adds to the austerity of the landscape. Most of these trees have burst asunder, their trunks having split and separated into fragments, the parts being held together only by a suture: one might regard them as the damned in Dante undergoing the penalty of the sword, cleft in twain, and hewn and hacked on every side from crown to heel and from heel to crown. Their tortuous roots cling to the rocks like despairing feet; and the bodies, tormented with their wounds, writhe and recoil in their agony: distorted or distended they still live, and no declivity, or rock, or flood of winter, triumphs over their struggles and vitality. Toward Narni the aspect changes; the road runs winding up the mountain, the face of which is completely covered with evergreens: these have sprung up

everywhere, even in the hollows and on inaccessible
heights; only a few walls of perpendicular rock have
opposed their invasion. The mountain thus rises,
round from the torrent below to the sky above, like a
magnificent summer bouquet intact in the midst of winter. After leaving Narni the landscape becomes still
more beautiful. It is a fertile plain; fresh grain, elms
wedded to vines, an extensive smiling garden, and all
around high hills of a graver hue; beyond, a circle of
blue mountains fringed with snow. *Soave austero* is a
phrase frequently recurring to one in the landscapes
of Italy: the mountains impart nobleness to them,
without, however, being too lofty; the imagination is
not overwhelmed by them; they form amphitheatres
and backgrounds to pictures, and are simply a natural,
architecture. Beneath them, varied cultures, numerous fruit-trees, and terraced fields, compose a rich and
orderly decoration which soon renders one oblivious of
our monotonous fields of grain, our still more monotonous vegetation, and every northern landscape which
seems to be a manufactory of bread and meat.

We see, passing, numerous little carts with young
couples in them, a man and a girl; the latter is gayly
attired in bright colors, and has her head bare: she looks
as if she was accompanying her lover. Many are the
signs here of a voluptuous and picturesque contentment. The young girls bind up their hair in the latest
fashion, with puffs over the brow, and wear silk handkerchiefs, pendent ear-rings, and gilded combs. In Rome,
some superb and charming heads projected out of the
dirtiest of rookeries. A little while ago, in passing
through a small town, I observed, in a dull and gloomy
street, leaning half-way out of an obscure window, a
black velvet bodice, and above it, large dark eyes,
flashing like lightning. Elsewhere, they raise their
shawls over their heads, and stand ready draped for the
painter. We cross before a cart in which eight peasants

are packed—all of them singing, each taking a part in
a grave noble air, as in a choral. Indifferent objects—
the form of a head, a garment, the physiognomies of
five or six lads in a village auberge proffering gallantries to a pretty girl—all indicate a new world and a
distinct race. In my judgment, the characteristic trait
by which they are distinguished is the regarding of ideal
beauty and sensuous happiness as one and the same
thing.

The road ascends and the carriage advances slowly,
with a re-enforcement of horses over the precipitous parts
of the mountain. A meagre stream alternately winds
and tumbles, and loses itself beneath the bed of rocks
rolled down by it during the winter. The white skeleton of the mountain pierces through the brown mantle
of its bare forests. I have never seen mountains more
racked by upheavals; the uplifted strata sometimes
stand perpendicular like a wall. All this mineral
framework is shattered and seems to be dislocated, so
cracked and so full of crevices is each layer. Patches
of snow, on the summit, marble the carpet of fallen
leaves. The north wind moans sad and cold. The contrast is a strange one, when one regards the radiant sky
where the sun shines in full force, and the delicious
azure with its tints fading in the distance. On passing the Apennines, low hills and rich plains appear
well framed in and laid out, as on the hither slope.
Here and there is a town stacked on a mountain; a
sort of round mole, and an ornament of the landscape,
as we find them in the pictures of Poussin and Claude.
This is the Apennines, with its bands of bastions extending along a narrow peninsula, and imparting its
character to the entire Italian landscape : no long
rivers or grand plains, but narrow valleys, noble forms,
plenty of rock and sunshine, with aliment and sensations to correspond. How many individual and historic traits bear the imprint of this character !

CHAPTER II.

PERUGIA, *April* 3.—This is an old city of the middle ages, a city of defence and of refuge, situated on a craggy plateau, commanding a view of the entire valley. Portions of its walls are antique; several of the gate foundations are Etruscan, the feudal epoch having added to them its towers and bastions. Most of its streets are sloping, and arched passages in them form sombre defiles. Oftentimes a house strides over the street, the first story prolonging itself into that which faces it; vast walls of red brick, without windows, seem to be remnants of fortresses.—Innumerable fragments suggest to the imagination the feudal and republican city ;—the black entrance of San Agostino, a huge stone donjon, so scathed and corroded that it might be called a natural cavern ; and, on the summit, a terrace, supported by pretty little columns, which are Roman, and so many delicate forms, the first ideas of elegance and of art that flourished amid the dangers and enmities of the middle ages ;—the *Palazzo del Governo*, massive and severe, as was essential for street fights and seditions, but with a graceful portal, entwined with stone wreaths and cordons of sculptured figures, simple and sincere ;—Gothic forms and Latin reminiscences ; cloisters of superposed arcades, and lofty brick church-towers, blackened by time ; sculptures of the early renaissance, of the thirteenth and fourteenth centuries, the most original and animated of all ; a fountain by Arnolfo di Lapo, by Nicolas and by John of Pisa; a tomb of Benedict XI., again by John of Pisa (1304). Nothing is more charming than this first flight of an active invention, and of modern thought half-emerging from gothic tradition. The pope lies on a couch in a marble alcove, of which two cherubs withdraw the curtains : above, in an ogive arcade, stand the Virgin and two saints, to welcome his soul. Language cannot express the surprised, tender, and childlike air of the Virgin : the sculptor had seen some young girl weeping at the bedside of a dying mother, and, wholly mastered by the impression, freely, without thought of the antique, unrestrained by any school, he expressed his sentiment. It is these spontaneous utterances which make a work of art a thing of eternity. They are heard athwart five centuries of time as distinctly as at the first day : man at length speaks across feudal and monastic tyranny, and we listen to the personal exclamation of an independent and complete spirit. The most trifling productions of this early age of sculpture arrest one's steps and fix one to the spot : it seems as if one caught the tones of an actual vibrating voice. After Michael Angelo, types are established ; no change is made but to arrange or purify a prescribed form. Before him, and even into the middle of the fifteenth century, each artist, like the citizen, is himself : genius and character are not subordinated by fashion and conventionalism ; every man stands erect before nature with a sentiment of his own, and figures emerge as diversified and as original in the arts as in life.

The chanting of a mass in the cathedral prevented me from seeing more than a bishop's tomb near the entrance. Beneath the recumbent bishop are four women holding two vases, a sword, and a book, admirable in ·their breadth and simplicity, with ample figures and magnificent luxuriant hair, but realistic nevertheless, and only a nobler imprint of the model employed by veracious nature. To be one's self through one's self, alone and without reserve, to the very end, is there any other precept in art and in life? Through this precept and this instinct the modern man has made himself and unmade the middle ages. Such are the reveries that occupy one's brain while wandering through these quaint, steep, and rugged streets, in these rude passages paved with brick and crossed with foot-props, amidst these strange structures where the eccentricity and irregularity of the municipal and seigneurial life of ancient days bursts forth scarcely tempered by the few restorations of a modern police. Perugia, in the fourteenth century, was a democratic and belligerent republic, contending with and overcoming its neighbors. The nobles were excluded from office, and one hundred and fifty of them plotted the massacre of the magistrates: they were either hung or banished. One hundred and twenty castles stood on its territory, and there were eighty fortified villages. Gentlemen *condottieri* maintained their independence in these and waged war against the city. In Perugia there were gentlemen *condottieri:* the principal one, Biordo de Michelotti, assuming too great authority, was assassinated in his own house by the Abbé de St. Pierre. Besieged by Braccio de Montone, the Perugians sprung from the top of their walls, or let themselves down with ropes, in order to fight hand to hand with the defiant soldiers below. In the midst of such usages the souls of men are kept alive, and the soil is well prepared for the growth of the arts.

Painting: Fra Angelico and Perugino.—But what a contrast between these arts and these usages! In the Pinacotheca is a collection of the pictures of the school of which Perugia is the centre. It is mystic throughout; it seems as if Assisi and its seraphic piety governed all intellects. In this barbaric era she was

the one centre of thought; there were but few of them
during the middle ages, and each extended its rule on
all sides. Fra Angelico da Fiesole, driven from Florence, came and lived near here for seven years, and
likewise worked here. He was better off here than in
his own pagan Florence; and it is to him that the eye is
first attracted. It seems, on contemplating him, as if
one were reading the "Imitation of Jesus Christ;"
pure and gentle figures on golden backgrounds breathe
a mute repose, like immaculate roses in the garden of
Paradise. I remember an "Annunciation" by him, in
two frames (Nos. 221, 222). The Virgin is candor
and gentleness itself: she has almost a German physiognomy—and how beautiful the two hands so piously
clasped! The angel with curling tresses kneeling before her seems like a little smiling maiden, somewhat
simple, who is about to leave the maternal home.
Alongside of this, in the "Nativity," before the delicate
infant Christ with dreamy eyes, two angels in long
robes offer flowers; they are so youthful, and yet how
grave! These are the delicate touches which subsequent painters are not to recover. A sentiment is an
infinite and incommunicable thing; no research and no
labor can reproduce it in its integrity. In true piety
there is a certain reservation, a chasteness, and consequently, arrangement of drapery and a choice of accessories which the cleverest masters, a century later,
will know no more.

For example, in an "Annunciation" by Perugino,
which is quite near this, the picture represents, not a
small private oratory, but a grand court. The Virgin
is standing, frightened, but not alone; there are two
angels behind her, and two others behind Gabriel. Is
this chasteness to be reproduced later? Another picture by Perugino exhibits St. Joseph and the Virgin
kneeling before the infant: behind them, a slender portico profiles its light columns in the open air, and three

shepherds, at intervals, are praying. This great void enhances the religious emotions; it seems as if one heard the silence of the country.

In like manner Perugino's features and attitudes express an unknown and unique sentiment. His figures are mystic children—or, if you please, adult souls kept infantile by the schooling of the cloister. None of them regard each other; none of them act, each being absorbed in his own contemplation; all look as if dreaming of God; each remains fixed, and seems to withhold the breath for fear of disturbing the vision within. The angels especially, with their downcast eyes and bended brow, are true adorers, prostrate, steadfast, and motionless: those of the "Baptism of Jesus" have the humble and virginal modesty and innocence of a nun communing. Christ himself is a tender seminarist, who, for the first time, leaves the house of his good uncle the curé, never having raised his eyes to a woman, and receiving the host every morning in serving the mass. The only heads at the present day which give you any idea of this sentiment, are those of peasant girls reared, quite young, in a convent. Many of these at forty years of age have rosy cheeks without a wrinkle. From their placid look it seems as if they had never lived, while on the other hand they have never suffered. In like manner, these figures stand motionless on the threshold of thought without crossing it—without, indeed, attempting to cross it. Man is not arrested, he arrests himself: the bud is not crushed, but it does not open. No similarity here is there to the mortifications and excesses of ancient Christianity, or of the catholic restoration; the end in view is not to stifle thought, or to subdue the flesh; the body is beautiful and in perfect health. A youthful St. Sebastian, in green and gold bootees, an amiable young virgin almost Flemish and gross, besides twenty others of Perugino's fig-

ures, are not the subjects of an ascetic regimen. Their
slender legs, however, and inert eye, denote that they
are still the inhabitants of the sleeping forest. What
a singular moment!—The same with Perugino as with
Van Eyck : the bodies belong to the renaissance, and
their souls to the middle ages!

This is still more apparent in the *Cambio*, a kind of
exchange or guildhall of the merchants. Perugino was
intrusted with its decoration in the year 1500; and he
has placed here a "Transfiguration," an "Adoration
of the Shepherds," Sibyls, Prophets, Leonidas, Socrates,
and other pagan heroes and philosophers, a St. John
over the altar, and Mars and Jupiter on the archway.
Alongside of this is a chapel wainscoted with sculptured wood and gilded and painted, the Eternal in
the centre, and diverse arabesques of elegant nude
women on the cruppers of lions. Can the confluence
of two ages be better realized, the intermingling ideas,
the bloom of a fresh paganism underneath a decrepit
Christianity? — Merchants in long robes assembled
on the wooden seats of this narrow hall; before opening their deliberations, they proceed to kneel down in
the little adjoining chapel to hear mass.—There Gian
Nicola Manni has painted on the two sides of the
high altar the animated and delicate figures of his
"Annunciation," an ample Herodias, some charming
erect young women, graceful and slender, which make
one realize the spirit and richness of corporeal vitality.
While joining in the droning hum of the responses,
or following the sacred gestures of the officiating priest,
more than one of the faithful has let his eyes wander
up to the rosy torsos of the little chimeras crouched on
the ceiling, executed, as is said in the town, by a young
man of great promise, the favorite pupil of the master
Raphael Sanzio d'Urbino.— The service is over ; they
return to the council-chamber, and there, it may be
presumed, a debate ensues on the payment of three.

hundred and fifty crowns in gold promised to Perugino for his work. This is not too much; he has
devoted seven years to it, and his fellow-citizens comprehend sympathetically, through mental similarity,
the two phases of his genius, the old and the new,
the one christian and the other semi-pagan.

First comes a "Nativity," under a lofty portico,
with a landscape of slender trees, such as he loved. It
is an aerial meditative picture, calculated to make one
appreciate a contemplative life. One cannot too highly
commend the modest gravity, the mute nobleness of the
Virgin kneeling before her infant. Three large serious
angels on a cloud are singing from a sheet of music;
and this simplicity bears the mind backward to the
times of mysteries. But one has only to turn his head
to see figures of an entirely different character. The
master has been to Florence, and antique statues,
their nudities, the imposing action and spirited in-
flexions of figures new to him, have revealed another
world, which he reproduces with some restriction, but
which entices him away from the road he first followed.
Six prophets, five sibyls, five warriors and as many pagan philosophers stand erect, and each, like an antique
statue, is a masterpiece of force and physical nobleness. It is not that he imitates a Grecian type or
costume, for complicated casques, fantastic coiffures,
and reminiscences of chivalry, are oddly intermingled
with tunics and nudities; but the sentiment is antique.
They are powerful men satisfied with existence, and
not pious souls dreaming of paradise. The sibyls are
all blooming with beauty and youthfulness. The
first one is advancing, and her bearing and form are
of royal grandeur and stateliness. Just as noble and
grand is the prophet-king who faces them. The seriousness, the elevation of these figures is incomparable. At this dawn of the imagination, the face,
still intact, preserves, like that of Greek statuary, the

simplicity and immobility of primitive expression.
The changes of the physiognomy do not efface the
type; man is not broken up into petty, varying, and
fleeting thoughts; the character is made prominent
by unity and repose.

On a pilaster to the left is a bloated countenance,
quite vulgar, with long hair under a red cap, which
might be taken for an ill-humored abbé: the expression is one of irritability, and even of craftiness.
This is Perugino, painted by himself. He was at this
time much changed. Those who have seen his other
portrait, also painted by himself some years before at
Florence, have some difficulty in recognizing it. There
is in his life as in his works two contrary sentiments,
and two distinct epochs. No mind furnishes better
evidence, through its contradictions and its harmonies,
of the great transformation that was going on around
him. He is, in the first place, religious: no one can
doubt this when for so long a time, and even in the
heart of pagan Florence, he is seen repeating and
purifying figures so religious—painting gratuitously, to
obtain by prayers the oratory of a confrerie situated
opposite to his home; painting and retaining in his
house fourteen banners, in order to loan them to processions, and living and developing himself in the
pious convents of Umbria.* He is a creator in sacred art, and a man creates only after his own heart.
It is not, again, pushing conjecture too far to represent
him at Florence as an admirer of Savonarola. Savonarola is Prior of the convent which he is decorating;
Savonarola causes pagan pictures to be burnt, and
suddenly excites Florence up to the highest pitch of
ascetic and christian enthusiasm. The first words of
one of Savonarola's sermons are inscribed on a paper
in the hand of the portrait which Perugino then made

* Rio, *Histoire de l'Art Chrétien*, vol. ii. p. 218.

of himself; and he purchases a plot of ground on
which to erect a house for himself in the reformer's
city. Suddenly the scene shifts: Savonarola is burnt
alive, and it seems to his disciples that Providence,
justice, and divine power, are engulphed in his tomb.
Several among them have retained to the end in their
souvenirs, wholly corporeal and highly colored, the image of the martyr, betrayed, tortured, and reviled at
the stake by those whose salvation he secured. Is it
this great shock, joined to the epicurean teachings of
Florence, which overthrew the faith of Perugino?
At all events, on his return he is no longer the same
man. His countenance, ironically distrustful, bears the
marks of inward brooding and depression. His religious works are less pure; he dispatches them finally
by the dozen like a manufacturer; he is soon charged
with caring no longer for any thing but money.* He
undertakes in the Cambio pagan subjects, and in their
treatment assumes the style of the goldsmiths and
anatomists of Florence. He paints, moreover, allegorical nudities,† Love and Chastity, meagerly and
coldly, like a laggard libertine who poorly compensates
himself for the severities of his youth. He seems to
have become a common atheist, embittered and hard-
ened like all those who deny in hate and in mockery,
through deception and chagrin. "He never could,"
says Vasari, "bring himself to believe in the immortality of the soul. His iron brain could never be turned
to good works; he centred all his hopes in the goods
of fortune." And a contemporary annotator adds:
"Being at the point of death, he was told that it was
necessary to confess himself.' He replied: 'I want
to see what a soul which has not confessed, will be
in that place!' And he steadily refused to do otherwise." Such an end, after such a life, does it not

---

* Vasari.   † Gallery of the Louvre.

show how the age of St. Francis becomes the age of Alexander VI.?

Others were more fortunate—as, for example, Raphael. It is here, in this atelier, before these landscapes, that he was formed; and many times have I here dwelt on his pure, happy genius; on his clear, open landscapes; on the precision, somewhat dry, and the exquisite simplicity of his early works. This sky is of perfect serenity; the light transparent atmosphere allows one to see the fine forms of the trees a league away. A hundred yards from San Pietro, an esplanade, planted with evergreens, advances like a promontory; below, spreads the campagna, a vast garden scattered with trees where the foliage of the olive imprints its pale rays on the verdure of the fresh-growing grain. The magnificent blue cupola glows sparkling with sunshine; and the rays sport at will in this grand amphitheatre, through which they dart unimpeded by any obstacle. Toward the west rise gilded mountain-chains, one above the other, clearer and clearer as they approach the remote horizon, the last one as exquisitely delicate as a silken veil. Meanwhile their ridges meet, mingling together lights and darks until, finally descending and expanding, they diminish and are lost in the plain. Light, relief, and harmony—the eye marvels at and revels in so broad an expanse, so lovely in composition, of such perfect distinctness of form. But the chilly atmosphere from the mountains will not let the body lose sight of itself in a too voluptuous contentment: one feels that the infertile rock and winter are near at hand. Yonder winds a long precipitous broken crag, sharp against the sky, which pales to the hue of steel above fields of snow that seem to be slabs of marble.

CHAPTER III.

ASSISI.—VILLAGES AND THE PEASANTRY.—THE THREE CHURCHES
—GIOTTO AND DANTE.—CONCORDANCE OF CHRISTIAN MYSTI-
CISM WITH GOTHIC ART.—AN ENTHUSIASTIC IMAGINATION COM-
PATIBLE WITH BARBARISM.

ASSISI, *April 4th.*—A stroll on foot of four hours to
see the peasantry.

A well-cultivated and charming country; the green
grain is coming up profusely, the grapevines are budding, and every vine clings to an elm; clear streams flow
through the trenches. On the horizon is a belt of
mountains, and the brilliant, immaculate snow blends
with the satin of the clouds.

Carts abound, with peasants in them singing. It is a
great sign of prosperity, these little vehicles; they show
that there is a class elevated above hard labor and the
grosser necessities of life. Madonnas are numerous,
and, for three *ave*, promise forty days of indulgence.
This is Italian religion. Otherwise, the villages resemble ours, and indicate about the same degree of cultivation. It is Sunday; the people wear heavy shoes and
passable clothes—no rags. They are very gay, and
laugh and chat together in the open square; some are
pitching quoits; others are playing ball; and others
morra. The inns and houses are not dirtier nor worse
furnished than in France. Heavy beams support the
ceiling; there are chairs, tables, sideboards of polished
wood, and a bottle-dresser provided with a couple of Madonnas. In the entrance-hall two large casks, encircled
with heavy planks, stand permanently; and I can testify that the wine is not dear. Quarters of meat hang
suspended on iron hooks. In a fertile country that
consumes its own products, prosperity is natural. The

inn begins to fill up, and the young lady of the house
enters with her mother, gaudily dressed, with a black
veil on her head and a sweet smile on her lips. She is
gay, brilliant and coquettish; and the young men begin to hover around her with that tender complacency
and ravished voluptuous air which is peculiar to the
Italians.

On the summit of an abrupt height, over a double
row of arcades, appears the monastery; at its base a
torrent ploughs the soil, winding off in the distance between banks of boulders; beyond is the old town prolonging itself on the ridge of the mountain. We ascend
slowly under the burning sun, and suddenly, at the end
of a court surrounded by slender columns, enter within the obscurity of the edifice. It is unequalled: before
having seen it one has no idea of the art and the genius
of the middle ages. Append to it Dante and the "Fioretti" of St. Francis, and it becomes the masterpiece
of mystic christianity.

There are three churches, one above the other, all of
them arranged around the tomb of St. Francis. Over
this venerated body, which the people regard as ever
living and absorbed in prayer at the bottom of an inaccessible cave, the edifice has arisen and gloriously
flowered like an architectural shrine. The lowest is a
crypt, dark as a sepulchre, into which the visitors descend with torches; pilgrims keep close to the dripping
walls and grope along in order to reach the grating.
Here is the tomb, in a pale, dim light, similar to that of
limbo. A few brass lamps, almost without light, burn
here eternally like stars lost in mournful obscurity.
The ascending smoke clings to the arches, and the
heavy odor of the tapers mingles with that of the cave.
The guide trims his torch; and the sudden flash in this
horrible darkness, above the bones of a corpse, is like
one of Dante's visions. Here is the mystic grave of a
saint who, in the midst of corruption and worms, be-

holds his slimy dungeon of earth filled with the supernatural radiance of the Saviour.

But that which cannot be represented by words is
the middle church, a long, low spiracle supported by
small, round arches curving in the half-shadow, and
whose voluntary depression makes one instinctively
bend his knees. A coating of sombre blue and of reddish bands starred with gold, a marvellous embroidery
of ornaments, wreaths, delicate scroll-work, leaves, and
painted figures, covers the arches and ceilings with
its harmonious multitude; the eye is overwhelmed by
it; a population of forms and tints lives on its vaults;
I would not exchange this cavern for all the churches
of Rome! Neither antiquity nor the renaissance felt this
power of the innumerable: classic art is effective through
its simplicity, gothic art through its richness; one
takes for its type the trunk of a tree, the other the tree
entire with all its luxuriance of foliage. There is a
world here as in an animated forest, and each object
is complex, complete like a living thing: on one hand
is the choir-stalls, surcharged and sown with sculptures; yonder a rich winding staircase, elaborate railings, a light marble pulpit and funereal monuments,
the marble of which, fretted and chased, seems the
most elegant jewel-casket: here and there, haphazard,
a lofty sheaf of slender columns, a cluster of stone
gems whose arrangement seems a phantasy, and, in
the labyrinth of colored foliage, a profusion of ascetic
paintings with their halos of faded gold: all this vaguely
discernible in a dim purple light, amidst dark reflections from the wainscotings, whilst, at the entrance, the
setting sun radiates myriads of golden darts like the
peacock displaying its splendor.

On the summit, the upper church shoots up as brilliant, as aerial, as triumphant, as this is low and grave.
Really, if one were to give way to conjecture, he might
suppose that in these three sanctuaries the architect

meant to represent the three worlds; below, the gloom of death and the horrors of the infernal tomb; in the middle, the impassioned anxiety of the beseeching christian who strives and hopes in this world of trial; aloft, the bliss and dazzling glory of paradise. The latter, uplifted in the air and in the light, tapers its columns, narrows its ogives, refines its arches, mounts upward and upward illuminated by the full day of its lofty windows, by the radiance of its rosaces, by the stained glass, and golden threads, and stars, which flash through the arches and vaults that confine the beatified beings and sacred passages with which it is painted from pavement to ceiling. Time, undoubtedly, has undermined them, several have fallen, and the azure that covers them is tarnished; but the mind immediately revives what is lost to the eye, and it again beholds the angelic pomp such as it first burst forth six hundred years ago. Cathedrals do not have this splendor; a detached chapel is necessary in order to prefigure to man the last of the stations of the christian life. As in the *Sainte Chapelle* of our Louis IX., man here found a tabernacle; the gravity and the terrors of religion were effaced; he could see nothing around him but celestial brightness and ecstatic raptures. Beneath this vault which, like an aerial dais, seems not to rest on the earth, amidst golden scintillations and floods of light transfigured by the windows, in this marvellous embroidery of forms confusedly intermingling and intersecting each other as in a bridal robe, man felt as if he were translated alive into paradise. We can neither reproduce nor depict these festivals. They have been depicted for us, and I silently repeated these stanzes by Dante:

> And lo! a sudden lustre ran across
> On every side athwart the spacious forest,
> Such that it made me doubt if it were lightning.

And a delicious melody there ran
Along the luminous air . . . . .

. . . .

While mid such manifold first-fruits I walked
Of the eternal pleasure all enrapt,
And still solicitous of more delights,

In front of us, like an enkindled fire
Became the air beneath the verdant boughs
And the sweet sound as singing now was heard.

A little farther on, seven trees of gold

. . . .

Far brighter than the moon in the serene
Of midnight, at the middle of her month.

. . . .

Then saw I people, as behind their leaders,
Coming behind them, garmented in white,
And such a whiteness never was on earth.*

Everything is in keeping; Dante's friend Giotto has painted similar visions in the second church. His pupils and successors, all imbued with his style, have tapestried the other walls of the edifice with their works. There is no christian monument where pure mediæval ideas reach the mind under so many forms, and which explain each other by so many contemporary masterpieces. Over the altar, enclosed within an elaborate iron and bronze railing, Giotto has covered an elliptic arch with grand, calm figures, and with mystic allegories. There is Saint Francis receiving Poverty as spouse from the hands of Christ; Chastity vainly besieged in a crenelated fortress, and honored by angels; Obedience under a canopy, surrounded by saints and kneeling angels; Saint Francis, glorified, in the gilded mantle of a deacon, and enthroned in the midst of celestial virtues and chanting cherubim. This Giotto, who in the north seems to us simply unskilful and barbarous, is already a perfect painter; he

---

* Purgatorio, canto XXIX, Longfellow's translation.

composes groups and appreciates airs of the head; whatever rigidity still remains with him does but augment the religious seriousness of his figures. Too powerful relief, too great human action would disturb our emotion; too varied or too animated expressions are not necessary for angels and symbolic virtues; all are spirits in ecstatic immobility. The vigorous and splendid virgins and muscular archangels, which are to follow two centuries later, reconduct us back to earth ; their flesh is so tangible that we do not believe in their divinity. Here the personages, the grand and noble women ranged in hieratic processions, resemble the Matildas and Lucias of Dante; they are the sublime and floating apparitions of a dream. Their beautiful blonde tresses are gathered chastely and uniformly around their brows; pressing close to each other they meditate; grand white or blue tunics in long folds depend around their forms ; they crowd around the saint, and around Christ in silence, like a flock of faithful birds, and their heads, somewhat melancholy, possess the grave languor of celestial bliss.

This is a unique moment. The thirteenth century is the term and the flower of living christianity; henceforth there is only scholasticism, decadence, and fruitless gropings after another age and another spirit. A sentiment which previously was only forming, Love, then burst forth with extraordinary power, and Saint Francis was its herald. He called water, fire, the moon and the sun brothers ; he preached to birds, and ransomed lambs on their way to market with his own mantle. It is stated that hares and pheasants sought refuge under the folds of his robe. His heart overflowed toward all living creatures. His first disciples dwelt like himself in a sort of rapture, " so that oftentimes for twenty and even thirty days they lived alone on the tops of high mountains, contemplating all celestial objects." Their writings are effusions. " Let

no one rebuke me if love forces me to go like a mad-
man! No heart can resist, none can escape from such
love . . . For heaven and earth declare aloud and
repeat to me, and all those whom it is my duty to love,
address me : 'Cherish the love which hath made us in
order to bring us near to Him' . . . O, Christ, often
hast thou trodden this earth like a man intoxicated!
Love led thee, like a man that is sold. In all things
thou showest only love, never art thou conscious of
thyself . . . . The arrows poured down in such flights as
to overwhelm me with agony. He launched them
forth so powerfully that I despaired of warding them
off, overcome not by a veritable death, but by excess
of joy." It was not merely in the cloisters that such
transports were encountered. Love became sovereign in
laic as well as in religious life. In Florence associa-
tions of a thousand persons clad in white traversed
the streets with trumpets, led by a chief who was
called the Lord of Love. The new language growing
into life, fresh poesy and fresh thought, are devoted
to describing and exalting love. I have just re-read
the " Vita Nuova," and a few cantos of the "Paradiso ;"
the sentiment is so intense that it fills one with fear :
these men live in the burning realm where reason
melts away. Dante's account of himself, like his poem,
shows constant hallucination : he swoons, visions assail
him, his body becomes ill, and the whole force of his
thoughts is given to the recalling of or commenting
on the agonizing or divine spectacles under which he
has succumbed.* He consults various friends about
his ecstasies, and they reply to him in verses as mysterious and as extreme as his own. It is clear that at
this moment all the higher culture of the mind is centred around morbid and sublime reveries. The in-

---

* Compare the " Aurelia" of Gerard de Nerval, and the " Inter-
mezzo" of Heine.

itiated use an apocalyptic language, purposely obscure; their words imply double and triple meanings. Dante himself lays it down as a rule that each subject contains four. In this state of extremes everything becomes symbolic : a color like green or red, a number, an hour of the day or of the night, is of peculiar significance ; it is the blood of Christ, or the emerald fields of paradise, or the virginal azure of heaven, or the sacred cypher of divine personages which thus becomes present to the mind. Through catalepsies and transports the brain labors, and an overcharged sensibility thrills with paroxysms which exalt it to supreme delight or precipitate it into infinite despair. Then do the natural boundaries between the diverse realms of thought become effaced and disappear. The adored mistress is transfigured into the likeness of a celestial virtue. Scholastic abstractions are transformed into ideal apparitions. Souls congregate in etherial roses, "perpetual flowers of eternal joy which, like a perfume, make perceptible all odors at once." Brute tangible matter, and the entire scaffolding of dry formulas melt and evaporate on the heights of mystic contemplation, until nothing remains but a melody, a perfume, a luminous ray, or an emblem ; this remnant of terrestrial imagery never having any value in itself, other than to prefigure the unfathomable and ineffable *beyond*.

How did they support the anguish and constant excesses of such a condition—the nightmare visions of Hell and Paradise, the tears, the tremors, the swoons, and other alternatives of such a tempest?* What were the nerves that resisted all this? What fecundity of soul and of imagination fed it? All has since degenerated ; man then was more vigorous, and remained

---

* *E caddi, come corpo morto cade.* Many similar instances almost equal to this one are to be found in the Divine Comedy.

young a longer time. I glanced lately over the life of
Petrarch, written by himself. He loved Laura fourteen
years. Now, the youth of the heart, the age of great
discontents and great reveries, last five or six years;
after this one craves a comfortable house and a respectable position. I imagine that a body tempered by war
was more resistant, and that the rude, semi-barbarous
regimen which destroyed the weak, allowed only the
strong to subsist. But it is especially necessary to consider that melancholy, danger, monotony of life without diversion, without reading, and ever threatened, developed a capacity for enthusiasm, sublimity, and intensity of sentiment. The security, comfort, and elegancies of our civilization divide us and belittle us; a
cascade is converted into a marsh. We enjoy and suffer through a thousand daily, petty sensations; in
those days, sensibility, instead of evaporating, became
choked up, and accumulated passion burst forth in
eruptions. In a Russian romance, Tarass Boulba, a
young Cossack chief, on leaving the camp with his
senses blunted by the foulness of nomadic life, the
odors of brandy and of the stable, and through daily
contact with ferocious and brutal beings, perceives a
beautiful and delicate maiden in handsome attire; he
is intoxicated, kneels down, forgets father and country,
and thenceforth contends against his own kindred. A
similar crisis prostrated Dante before a child of nine
years.

Let us dwell a moment on the surrounding condition of things. It was an epoch of pitiless wars and
of mortal enmities. People in Florence proscribed
each other, and fought from house to house, and from
quarter to quarter. Dante himself was condemned to
the stake. The torments invented by the Romanos
were still rife in men's imaginations, and a régime
worse than our Reign of Terror had taken root between family and family, caste and caste, and city and

city. Out of this bristling precinct the mind issued
free for the first time after so many centuries, and it
entered on an unexplored field. It did not follow its
natural bent, as formerly at a similar crisis in the
small republics of Greece ; a powerful religion seized
upon it at its birth and diverted it off. The supreme
good tendered to it was not an equilibrium of moderate
sensations and the healthiness of active faculties, but
transports of infinite adoration and the raptures of an
over-excited imagination. Happiness no longer consisted in a consciousness of strength, wisdom and
beauty ; in being the honored citizen of a glorious
city ; in dancing and singing noble hymns ; in talking
with a friend under a tree on a serene day. These
pleasures were declared inadequate, low and criminal ; appeals were made to feminine sentiments, to
nervous sensibility, and man had held out to him
ecstatic contemplation, indefinable raptures and delights to which the senses, language and the imagination never attain. The sterner life was, the more exalted were these assurances. The vastness of the contrast multiplied the charms of the promised bliss, and
the heart with all its youthful energy rushed through
the issue opened to it. Then was seen that strange
incongruity of a laic life similar to that of the Greek
republics, and a religious life similar to that of the
Soufis of Persia—on the one hand, free ·citizens, practical men, combatants and artists, and on the other,
cloistered ascetics, preachers wandering about half-
naked, and penitents offering themselves to the·lash ;—
furthermore, the two extremes met in one person, the
same spirit harboring the most virile energy and the
most feminine gentleness ; the same man magistrate
and mystic ; a practical politician filled with hatred,
corresponding in enigmas on the languors and halluci-
nations of love ; the chief of a party and the father
of a family absorbed with the worship of a dead child,

and diffusing over actual landscapes and contemporary
figures, over positive interests, local resentments, and
the technical science of his country and century, the
monstrous or divine illuminations of ecstasy and of
horror.

A monk conducted me into the refectory, and then
through a series of halls to a square interior court
where a two-story portico, supported by delicate little
columns, forms an elegant promenade. Pavement, columns, walls and cisterns, all are of stone ; above, like
a frame, runs a roof of reddish tile. The blue sky, like
a round dome, overspreads the white square ; no one
can imagine the effect of such simple forms and colors.
All around the convent winds a second promenade under ogive arcades of rough stones turned brown by
the sun ; from this the eye embraces the beautiful valley and its diadem of snow-clad mountains. The poor
monks of the "Fioretti," through impoverishing their
life, ennobled it ; two or three sentiments absorbed it
entirely, but these were sublime. Whoever abandoned
the brutal herd was compelled to become a great poet ;
when he had not become a kneeling machine, he ended
in appreciating the serenity and grandeur of scenes
like this. "Brother Bernardo lived in contemplation on the heights like a swallow: for this reason
Brother Egidio declared that he was the sole one to
whom was awarded the gift of nourishing himself in
flying like the swallow. . . . . And Brother Currado having performed his orisons here, there appeared
to him the Queen of Heaven with her blessed infant
in her arms, in great splendor of light, and, approaching Brother Currado, she placed in his arms the
blessed infant, which Currado having received and very
devoutly kissed, and embracing it and pressing it to his
bosom, melted away and wholly dissolved in divine
love with most inexpressible consolation."

On the plain below is a large church containing the

saint's house; but it is modern, with a pompous pagan cupola. Overbeck's frescoes are imitations. In striving to be gothic he shows himself awkward, giving twisted necks to his angels, and to the figure of God the pitiful expression of a man whose dinner disagrees with him. You hasten away from them; after genuine devotion nothing is more disagreeable than its counterfeit.

CHAPTER IV.

April 8.—Numerous conversations every day with people of every class and opinion; but the liberals predominate.

The diplomats, they say, are ill-disposed toward the unity of Italy; they do not regard it as substantial. According to the two clever men with whom I have travelled, one an officer and the other an *attaché* to an embassy, the capital trait of the Italians is weakness of character and richness of intellect, quite the opposite of the Spaniards, who with a strong will have narrow and obdurate brains. They dispute about the number of volunteers under Garibaldi in 1859; some carry it up to twenty-five hundred, and others to seven thousand,—in any event a ridiculously small number. The Emperor Napoleon led the foreign legion with almost empty regiments; nobody came forward to fill them up. It seems very hard to the Italian to quit his mistress or wife, to enlist and to undergo discipline; the military spirit died out a long time ago in the country. According to my friend the officer, who served in the late campaign, Milan furnished in all but eighty volunteers, and the peasantry rather sided with the Austrians. As to either the middle class or the nobles, they were very enthusiastic and made speeches, but their enthusiasm evaporated in words, none of it extending to risking their lives. Generosity, true feeling, and ardent patriotism were only to be found among the women. After the peace of Villafranca some Frenchmen, lodging near Peschiera, said to their hosts, "Ah, you remain Austrians—what a pity!" The daughter of the family did not at first comprehend them, but when she understood their meaning she raised both hands, and, with flaming eyes, asked her brothers if they had no guns and if they called themselves men; "Never," said the officer, "have I seen an expression so ardent and so sublime!" Her brothers shook their heads and replied with the discreet patience of the Italian, "What is there to do?"

This lack of energy contributed a good deal toward precipitating peace. The Emperor Napoleon stated to M. Cavour, "You promised me two hundred thousand men, sixty thousand Piedmontese and one hundred and forty thousand Italians. You give me thirty thousand; I shall be compelled to call for one hundred thousand more of the French." If the protected do not aid themselves the protector becomes uneasy and discouraged, and the war suddenly droops. Accustomed to yielding, the Italian has lost the faculty of resisting; if you get angry he is astonished, becomes alarmed, yields and regards you as crazy, (malto). Such is the process by which the fiery M. de Merode obtained an ascendancy over the Sacred College. Now, when a people knows not how to fight, its independence is only provisional; its life depends on grace or on accident.

This is why, they say, Piedmont did wrong to yield to opinion in the taking of Naples. It has made itself so much the weaker; its army is the worse for recruiting its regiments with poor soldiers. If, to-day, it is master there, it is the same as with Championnet, Ferdinand, Murat and their predecessors: with ten thousand soldiers one can always be master of Naples; but let any sudden crisis occur, and the government falls to the ground, this one running the same risk as those that have gone before it. It has just committed a serious blunder in abandoning the convents to municipal rancor; a lot of miserable monks and nuns are turned out of doors, which only excites scandal, and provokes resentment, as in la Vendée. Now religion here is not abstract or rational as in France; it is based on the imagination and is so much the more sensitive and vivacious; some day or other it will inevitably turn against liberalism and Piedmont. Besides, the unity of the country is against nature; Italy, through its geography, its races and its past, is divided into three sections; the most it can do is to form a federation. If it is kept together to-day, it is through an artificial power, and because France, on the Alps, stands sentinel against Austria. Should a war occur on the Rhine the Emperor will not amuse himself splitting up his forces, and then Italy will break up into its natural divisions.

I reply to this that the revolution here is not an affair of race, but one of interests and ideas. It began at the end of the last century, with Beccaria for instance, in the propagation of French literature and philosophy. The middle class, the enlightened are those who diffuse it by leading the people along with them in their wake, as formerly in the United States during the war of independence. It is a new force, superior to provincial antipathies; unknown a hundred years ago; inherent, not in the nerves, in the blood and in the habits, but in the brain, in study and in discussion; of vast grandeur, since it brought about the American and French revolutions, and growing in grandeur since ceaseless discoveries of the human mind and multiplied ameliorations of the human condition daily contribute to augment it. Will it suffice to sustain Italy? That is a problem of moral mechanics, and is not to be solved, for lack of the means by which to estimate the power of the lever in relation to the resistance of the mass. Meanwhile, let us examine a few simple facts ready at hand : it is the only way to arrive at any approximate value of forces which we can see but which we cannot measure.

Conscripts are passing along the road in gray vests, soldiers in uniform, and frequently handsome officers in blue with a gay and spruce air. Every small town has a national guard :—you will see these guards sitting on stone benches in the sunshine at the entrance of town-halls ;—the streets bear the names of Victor Emmanuel, Garibaldi and Solferino. People are intoxicated with their recent independence, and talk of themselves vain-gloriously. A Roman who is going to Switzerland, remarks that " we have four hundred thousand soldiers and six hundred thousand national guards ; in two years Italy will become united, and we shall then be able to whip the Austrians."—The exaggerations of patriotism and of hope are spurs of great utility.

On the frontier the chief of customs, a Piedmontese and formerly a soldier in the Crimea, stormed and railed in the middle of the night in his wooden shanty against Antonelli and Merode, " those brigands and assassins." He descanted on the rights of nations and the duties of citizens. " The atmosphere here is unhealthy four months of the year, the country is gloomy, living is dear and life solitary,—but I serve Italy, I have already served her in the ranks, and I trust that next year there will be no frontier."—You will note that the comrades of Hoche, a sergeant in 1789 in the French guards, uttered substantially the same words and in the same tone.

At Foligno, in a small café, I offer *baiocchi* in payment ; the proprietor refuses them ; " No, Signor, that money has no value here—we want nothing Roman. Let the Pope and the priests clear out and go to

Heaven! It's the best thing they can do for us! He is ill now—the sooner it is over the better!" And all this coarsely, amidst the jeers of his wife and of five or six laborers there.—This is a veritable Jacobin household as with us in 1790.

Yesterday in a public vehicle I had three hours' conversation with my two companions, one a brass-lamp maker of Perugia and the other a peasant and tile-maker. The former is a well-to-do mechanic; he went to Turin as one of a deputation to Victor Emmanuel, and is a passionate partisan of Italy. His son who had completed his studies and become a painter, enlisted and is serving as a sergeant against the Calabrian brigands. The tile - maker had ten nephews in the army. They were not disposed to be reserved and gave me innumerable details.

According to these men every thing is going on well. Out of twenty persons, fifteen are for the government, four for the pope and one republican. The republicans have entirely lost ground; they are regarded as fanatics (fantastici). The peasantry are daily coming round to the government; they are already hunting out refractory conscripts (renitenti) and bringing them back. The conscription was a sore trial to them, but they are getting used to it. In the army the young men eat good food, return home strong and active, and with a martial spirit; the effect is wonderful on the young girls, and consequently on the young men, and yet again on their parents and neighbors. Taxes are unquestionably more onerous; but everybody works and doubly profits by it. People are building and repairing. Spoleto is completely renovated; gas has been introduced at Perugia; the railroad to Ancona progresses and there is great excitement everywhere. "The farthings circulate!" (Tutti i quattrini lavorano.)

The entire middle class is enthusiastic in this sense

In a population of 82,000 at Perugia there are 1400 members of the national guard, including merchants, shop-keepers and prominent, well-established people. They do patrol duty with the soldiers, drill, subject themselves to inconveniences, and contentedly. "I have made sacrifices for my country," said my banker, "and am willing to make still greater ones." There are no more municipal or provincial rivalries; Florence has sent back to Pisa in token of fraternity the chains of its harbor which she had formerly captured. I point to an officer passing and ask if he is not a Piedmontese. "No more Piedmontese—we are all mixed up in the army—nobody now but Italians!"

They have all the confidence and illusions of 1789. On remarking that the Italian army had not yet demonstrated its capacity:— "We fought at Milan in 1848, and in three days, drove off alone the Austrians. We fought also at Perugia, against the Swiss, who massacred the women and children;—I was then in the cavalry. There was a fortress against the town,— look, that is all there is left of it;—we are converting it into a museum. No, no, we have no fear of the Austrians. We had seventy thousand volunteers against them in 1859. In two years more the peasantry will rise to a man and we will drive them out of Venice." (Seven thousand volunteers have become seventy. But the people are poetic; the more they magnify, the more they exalt themselves.)

There is the same anti-ecclesiastic rigidity as in our revolution. According to my two companions "the priests are scamps *(birbanti);* the government does right in confiscating the property of the monks; it ought to drive away every rascal who openly agitates against it. Before 1859 they were all-powerful and meddled in domestic matters; they were tried by a special tribunal and never punished. Now they lower their heads; two of them have lately been condemned

for crimes and everybody rejoices. They did nothing
but harm. The beggars, children, and adults, who
beset us at Assisi are of their providing, physically
as well as morally. They corrupted women, encouraged idleness through their mendicity, and maintained a state of ignorance; but now instruction is
everywhere diffused, each commune having its own
school;—there are thirteen in Assisi, which has but
three thousand inhabitants." A beggar attached himself to our vehicle. "Be off, you knave! go to the
monks—among them you will find your father!" The
beggar with his obsequious, sly Italian smile replied,
"No, signor, I do not belong to this part of the country, give me a little something."

Many trifling circumstances bear witness to this
resentment against the clergy. Lately, at Foligno, in
a masquerade, the pope and the cardinals were trav-
estied in the streets with shouts, laughter and universal excitement.—In Perugia, alongside of San Domenico, stands a blackfriar's convent converted into
a military barracks. The soldiers, on entering it,
pierced the frescos of the inner wall with their bay-
onets. The lacerated figures are now falling off in
fragments; one can scarcely distinguish, here and
there, the forms of some of the personages. The
smoke of a soldier's kitchen suffices to destroy the
finest group.—A quarter of an hour after this, at San
Pietro, a priest informed us with a sad look, that on
entering that place they had also torn away paintings
in another chapel. He uttered this with a melancholy,
humiliated aspect; the ecclesiastics here do not speak
in the same tone as at Rome.—These outrages are
similar to those of our revolution: the layman and
military barracks are substitutes without transition
for the ecclesiastic and the monastery. This antag-
onism provokes thought; there is little probability of
its ending; it has never ended in France; the revolu-

tion and Catholicism still remain under arms and in battle array. Protestant peoples, the English for example, are more fortunate. Luther has there reconciled the Church and society. Marrying the priest, making of him by education and habit a sort of more serious layman, elevating the layman to reflection and criticism by giving him the Bible and an exegesis, suppressing the ascetic portion of religion and infusing into society the conscience as moral guide, is the greatest of modern revolutions. The two spirits harmonize in Protestant countries; they remain hostile in Catholic countries and, unfortunately, to their hostility one sees no limit. Another merchant, an officer, and my purveyor with whom I chat entertains me with similar views. What an animated and complete understanding these Italians have! Here is a domestic who tells me all about himself, his marriage and his views of life, who reasons and judges like a cultivated man.— A miserable guide, half beggar, in a shop at Assisi expressed well-connected opinions and explained to me, skeptically, the state of the country. "The peasantry hunt after the conscripts," he said "because they are jealous; their sons have been taken and they wish to have the sons of others caught. The rich always eat up the poor while the poor never eat up the rich." There is a great readiness of conception and promptness of expression; such a people is always prepared for political discussion; you notice it in the cafés; the ardor and copiousness of discussion are surprising, and likewise its good sense. In the upheaval of a general revolution and of a vacillating government every town is self-administered and self-supporting.

They agree generally in this, that the liberal party is progressing. According to my friend the young officer the number of the refractory diminishes every year; this year some borough near Orvieto, where he is in garrison, no longer possesses one. At Foligno, where he

has lived, only two or three old papal families are named;
they are avaricious and behind the age, one being related to a cardinal; the rest of the town is for Victor
Emmanuel. Ecclesiastical property is rented at low
rates to the peasantry, which reconciles them to the
government; the result will be a sale of it to them and
then they will become openly patriotic. In short the
enemy of the new order of things is the clergy,
monks who are reduced to fifteen cents a day and
priests who advise young men to avoid the conscription, and to pass over the Roman frontier.—Finally, like
almost all the Italians I have seen, he is Catholic and a
believer; he blames the "*Diritto*" a violent jacobin
journal, and thinks that religion may accommodate itself
to the civil government. What he disapproves of is
the temporal authority of the clergy; let the priests
confine themselves to their functions as priests, admin-
ister the sacraments and set an example of good be-
havior; once under proper restraint they will become
better. At Orvieto, where he lives, many of the children
in the town are attributed to the monks, which is an
evil. He admires our clergy, so correct, and never provoking scandal; he approves of the prescribed costume of our priests,—in Italy they are only required
to dress in black. He ridicules those Roman *monsig-
nore*, set to watch over morals and superintend the
theatres, who enter the box of the leading *danseuse* in
order to forbid her to indulge in caprices. According to him such an order of things excites people against
religion itself. At Sienna, in the shop-windows, we
have just seen a translation of "le Maudit," and the
"Vie de Jésus," the last work of Strauss, and an engraving representing Truth overwhelming obstinate and
hypocritical priests.

My impression of the country between Perugia and
Sienna is that it is similar to France. The villagers are
about as well clad as our own; they have more horses,

and many among them are landowners. The aspect of the villages and of the small towns reminds one of our South. The country is of the same structure—small valleys and moderate elevations—the soil seeming to be as well cultivated. The garrison anecdotes which my friend the officer relates to me and the interiors of the inns and of the middle-class tenements with which I glance recall trait for trait a journey I made last year in the middle and south of France. To complete the resemblance soldiers are everywhere seen on the road, on furlough, or proceeding to join their regiments; the people are as gay and their conversation as animated as with us. The boroughs and small towns wear that provincial aspect, somewhat dull and tolerably clean, which we are so familiar with. It might be called a backward France, a younger sister that is growing and "catching up" with the elder. If we consider the contending parties, on the one side the nobles and clergy, and on the other the middle and commercial class, people of education and the liberal professions, and between the two the peasantry which the revolution is trying to emancipate from traditional influences, the resemblance becomes striking. To complete it, it is evident by their conversation, that their model is France; they repeat our ancient ideas and confine themselves to reading our books. Slightly cultivated people know French and scarcely ever English or German : our language is the only one like theirs, and besides, they, like ourselves, require gayety, wit, the agreeable and even license; one finds in their hands not only our good authors but our second-class romances, our minor newspapers and low-class literature. Their great reforms all take place in the same sense; they have imitated our coinage and our measures; they are organizing a salaried church without private property, primary schools, a national guard and the rest.

I am aware of the drawbacks to our system,—the suppression of all superior ranks; the reduction of all ambitions and of all mind to the commonplace ideas and enterprises of life; the abolition of the proud and lofty sentiments of one brought up in command, the protector and natural representative of those around him; the universal multiplication of the envious, narrow-minded, insipid *bourgeois* as described by Henri Monnier; all the wear and tear, vileness and impoverishment of head and heart from which aristocratic countries are exempt. Nevertheless, such as it is, their form of civilization is passable and preferable to many others, and natural enough to Latin populations; and France, which is now the first of Latin nations, takes the lead with its revolution and its civil code among its neighbors.

This social structure consists in this : a great central government with a powerful army, heavy imposts and a vast corps of functionaries restrained by honor and who do not peculate ;—a small portion of land to each peasant, besides schools and other facilities to enable him to mount upward to a higher class if he has capacity ;—a hierarchy of public offices open to the ambition of the middle class, all unfairness being limited through the organization of examinations and competitions, all aspiration being kept within bounds and satisfied by promotion which is slow but sure ;—in short the almost equal partition of all desirable things so that every one may have a share—nobody a very large one—and almost all one of small or mediocre proportions; and, above all, internal security, a fair sum of justice and of fame, and national glory. All this goes to make up a partially instructed, very well protected, tolerably regulated and very inert *bourgeois*, whose sole thought is to pass from an income of two thousand francs a year to one of six thousand. In a word a multitude of the half-cultivated and the half-rich, twenty or thirty millions of individuals passably contented, carefully penned, drilled and restrained, and who, when necessity calls, can be launched forth in a single body. Taking things in gross it is about what men have thus far found to be best; nevertheless we must wait a century to see England, Austria and America.

CHAPTER V.

FROM PERUGIA TO SIENNA.—ASPECT OF SIENNA.—TRANSITION FROM
A REPUBLICAN TO A MONARCHICAL SYSTEM.—MEDLÆVAL MONU-
MENTS.—THE CATHEDRAL.—ITALIAN–GOTHIC ARCHITECTURE.—
NICHOLAS OF PISA.—EARLY SCULPTURE.—APPRECIATION OF FORM
IN THE RENAISSANCE.

SIENNA, *April* 8.—The country becomes flat between
Chiusi and Sienna; we enter Tuscany; marshes in
the distance spread out their dingy and sickly verdure.
A little farther on there are low hills and then gray
slopes covered with the black twisted sprouts of the
vine; it is a meagre and flat French landscape. An
old city surrounded with brown walls appears at the
left, on a hill, and we then enter Sienna.

It is an old republic of the middle ages, and often on
the maps of the sixteenth century, I had contemplated
its abrupt silhouette, bristling with bastions, crowded
with fortresses and filled with evidences of public and
private contention. Public wars against Pisa Florence
and Perugia, private wars among the bourgeoisie the
nobles and the people, street combats, massacres in the
town-hall, violations of the constitution, exile of all nobles capable of using arms, exile of four thousand artisans, proscriptions, confiscations, wholesale executions,
plots of the exiled against the city, popular insurrec-
tions, despair carried even to the surrender of liberties
and submission to a foreign yoke, sudden and furious
rebellions, clubs similar to those of the Jacobins, asso-
ciations like those of the carbonari, a desperate siege
like that of Warsaw, and systematic depopulation like
that of Poland,—nowhere has life been so tragic.
From two hundred thousand inhabitants the population of the city fell to six thousand. The enmities re-

quired to exhaust a people of such vivacity cannot be
told. Of all human creatures the feudal Italian was
the most richly endowed with an active will and concentrated passions, and he bled himself, and was bled,
to the last drop in his veins before sinking down into
the bed of monarchical tranquillity. Cosmo II., in order to remain master, destroyed by starvation, war and
executions fifty thousand peasants. At this epoch we
see in engravings, defiling on the republican *piazza*,
pompous cavalcades, mythological chariots, reviews
and the livery of the new prince. The artist indulges
in interminable adulation on the margin of his picture.
Servile manners, somnolency, worn out gallantry and
universal inertia become established. Sienna is reduced to a provincial town, visited by tourists. I am
told by an ecclesiastical acquaintance that when he
came here in 1821 the lifelessness and ignorance of the
place were complete. Two days in a vettura were
necessary in order to go from Sienna to Florence. A
noble before setting out on his journey confessed himself and made his will. There was not a library, not a
book. One day my clerical friend, who is liberal and intelligent, subscribes to two French newspapers. Some
one pays him a visit; "What, have you a French newspaper!" The visitor takes hold of it and feels the
miraculous godsend. Twenty minutes after this the
ecclesiastic goes out for a walk. The first person he encounters exclaims, "Is it true that you have a French
newspaper?" and then another who utters the same
thing, the report having spread instantaneously like a
ray of light in a chamber closed for a century.

A town thus preserved is like a Pompeii of the middle
ages. You ascend and descend steep narrow streets
paved with stone and bordered with monumental
houses. A few still retain their towers. In the vicinity
of the *Piazza* they succeed each other in rows, forming
lines of enormous bosses, low porches and curious

masses of brick pierced with occasional windows.
Several of the palaces seem like bastions. The *Piazza*
is surrounded with them; no sight more aptly suggests
to the imagination the municipal and violent customs of
ancient times. This square is irregular in shape and
in surface, and is peculiar and striking like all natural
objects that have not been deformed or reformed by administrative discipline. Facing it, is the Palazzo Pub-
lico, a massive town-hall adapted to resist sudden attacks and for the issue of proclamations to the crowd
assembled in the open square. Frequently have these
been cast from these ogive windows and likewise the
bodies of the men killed in the seditions. The cornice
bristles with battlements; defence in these days is
often encountered under ornament. To the left of this
the symmetrical form of a gigantic tower with its
double expansion of battlements rises to a prodigious
height; it is the tower of the city which plants on its
summit its saint and its standard and speaks afar to
distant cities. At its base the Gaja fountain which in
the fourteenth century, amid universal acclamation,
brought water for the first time to the public square,
stands framed in by one of the most elegant of marble
baldachins.

It was growing late and I entered the cathedral for
a moment. The impression is incomparable; that of
St. Peter's at Rome does not approach it : a surprising
richness and sincerity of invention, the most admirable
of gothic flowers—but of a new gothic that has
bloomed in a better clime, in the midst of genius of a
higher culture; more serene, more beautiful, more religious and yet healthy, and which is to our cathedrals
what the poems of Dante and Petrarch are to the songs
of our trouvères; a pavement and pillars with stones of
alternate courses of white and black marble, a legion
of animated statues, a natural combination of gothic
and roman forms, corinthian capitals bearing a laby-

rinth of gilded arcades and arches panelled with azure
and stars. The declining sun streams in at the door
and the enormous vault with its forest of columns sparkles in the shadow above the crowd kneeling in the naves
and chapel, and around the columns. The multitude
in the profound darkness swarms indistinctly up to the
foot of the altar, which, all at once, with its bronzes
and candelabra and the damask copes of its priests and
the prodigal magnificence of its jewels and tapers, rises
upward like a bouquet of light of magical splendor.

April 8.—I passed half of the day in this church;
one might easily pass a whole day there. For the first
time elsewhere than in engravings I find an Italian-
Gothic, the earliest of two renaissance periods, less
pure than the other but more spontaneous.

A grand portal decked with statues projects above its
three entrances three pointed pediments, over these
pediments three pointed gables, around these gables
four pointed spires and all of them crenelated with
openings; but the arch of the doors is Roman : the
façade, in spite of its elongated angles, has latin reminiscences : the decoration is not of the filagree order
and the statues are not a multitude. The architect
loves the up-springing forms derived from the north,
but he likewise loves the solid forms bequeathed to
him by ancient tradition. If, in the interior, he masses
columns together in piers, if he spins out and surrounds
the windows with trefoils and mullions, if he curves the
windows into ogives, he suspends aloft the aerial rotundity of the dome, he garlands his capitals with the corinthian acanthus and diffuses throughout his work an
air of joyousness and strength through the firmness
of his forms, an appropriate distribution of light and a
lustrous assortment of marbles. His church is christian,
but of a christianity other than that of the north, less
grandiose and less impassioned, but less morbid and
less violent, as if the sprightliness innate in the Italian

genius and the early impulse of laic culture had tempered
the sublime phrensy of the middle ages, and preserved
for the soul a hope on earth by leaving to it an issue in
heaven. Of what avail are rules? and how insignifi-
cant are the barriers of the schools? Here are men
who stood with one foot in the renaissance and the other
in the middle age, diverted both ways, so that their
work could not fail to miscarry and contradict itself.
It does not miscarry, and its contradictions harmonize.
And for this reason, that, in their breast, both sentiments
operated energetically and sincerely; that suffices for
good work; life begets life.

You enter. The same marriage of ideas reappears
in all the details. On each side of the door they have
set up two admirable corinthian columns, but they have
appropriated the Greek column by clothing the shaft
with a profusion of small nude figures, hippogriffs, birds,
and acanthus leaves interlaced and winding about to
the top.—Three paces farther on are two charming
holy-water fonts, two small columns decked with grapes,
figures and garlands, each bearing on its top a cup of
white marble. One, they say, is antique; the other
must be of about the beginning of the fifteenth century. The heads and torsions of these small figures
remind one of Albert Durer; the feet and knees are somewhat salient; they are naked females with their hands tied
behind their backs; the artist in order to obtain true
action does not fear to slightly disfigure the breast.
Thus is developed between Nicholas of Pisa and
Jacopo della Quercia an entire school of sculpture, a
complete art, already perfect like a healthy lively child
struggling in its catholic swaddling clothes.

Finally, there is the celebrated pulpit of Nicholas of Pisa, the renovator of sculpture (1266). What can be more
precious than these early works of the modern mind?
Our true ancestors are here, and one craves to know
the way in which, at this early dawn, they compre-

hended man as we of to-day regard him; for, when
an artist creates a type, it is as if he expressed by flesh
and bones his conception of human nature; and this
conception once popular, the rest follows. I have no
words to express the originality and richness of invention displayed in this pulpit. It is as peculiar as it is
beautiful. The pedestals consist of lionesses, each
holding a lamb in its jaws, or sucked by its young; the
quaint symbolism of the middle ages is here apparent;
but from the bodies of these lionesses spring eight
small, pure white columns expanding into a rich cluster
of leaves, entirely original in taste, and which join together in trefoils supporting a sort of octagonal arch
or coffer of the simplest and most natural form possible. On the entablature of each column sits a woman;
several wear the crowns of empresses, and all hold infants that are whispering to them in their ears. One
loses sight of their being of stone, so animated is their
expression; it is more decided than in the antique. In
this joyousness of primitive invention the new conceptions so suddenly obtained are dwelt on to excess; it is
a pleasure to perceive, for the first time, a soul, and the
attitude which manifests that soul! Ideas did not
abound in those days, and they clung all the closer to
those they had. Through a striking innovation the
body, neck, and head, somewhat too large, have a sort
of Doric heaviness; but this only adds to their vigor.
Leaving behind him the meagre, ascetic saint, the artist, in imitation of the antique bas-reliefs, already constructs the firm bony framework, fine, well-proportioned
limbs, and the healthy flesh of renaissance figures. In
northern sculptures, the physiognomies and attitudes of
northern artists, when their genius blooms out in the
fifteenth century,* are delicate, pensive, emotional, and

* See the sculptures of the church of Brou, of Strasbourg cathedral,
and the tomb of the Duke of Brittany at Nantes.

always ingeniously personal. These, on the contrary, display the simplicity, breadth, and gravity of ancient pagan heads. It seems that the Italian, as he at this moment first opens his mouth, resumes the grave, manly discourse arrested twelve hundred years before on the lips of his brothers of Greece and of his ancestors of Rome.

On the panels of the pulpit a labyrinth of crowded figures—a long octagonal procession, the Nativity, the Passion, and the Last Judgment,—envelop the marble with their marble covering. Apostles and virgins stand or sit on the angles, uniting and separating the diverse incidents of the legend. The margins are filled with a delicate and rich vegetation of marble intertwined with arabesque and with foliage, a most luxurious display of light and complicated ornaments. One recoils astonished at this richness, and then perceives that he is walking on figures. The entire floor of the church is incrusted with them ; it is a mosaic of characters seemingly traced with a pencil on the broad slabs. There are some of all ages, from the birth of art to its maturity. Figures, processions, combats, castles, and landscapes ; the feet tread on scenes and men belonging to the fourteenth and the two following centuries. The most ancient, indeed, are rigid, like feudal tapestries: Samson rending the lion's jaw, Absalom suspended by his hair, with large, open, idiotic eyes, and the murdered Innocents,—reminding one of the manikins of the missals : but, as one advances he sees life animating the limbs. The grand white sibyls, on the black pavement display the nobleness and gravity of goddesses. Innumerable heads impress one with their breadth and firmness of character. The artist as yet sees nothing in the human organism but its *general framework ;* he is not distracted as we are by a multiplicity of gradations, by the knowledge of an infinity of spiritual modifications and innumerable changes of physiognomy.

For this reason he can produce beings who, through their calmness, seem to be superior to the agitations of life. A primitive soul creates primitive souls. In the time of Raphael this art is complete : and the greatest of the three niello artists on stone, Beccafumi, has covered the space around the high altar and the pavement of the cupola with his designs. His half-naked Eve, his Israelites slain for espousing the Midianite women, his Abraham sacrificing, are superb figures of a wholly pagan conception,—often with torsos and attitudes like those of Michael Angelo, but yet simple. It is only at that time that they knew how to make bodies.*

The great man himself has worked here : they attribute to him an admirable little chapel in which small figures appear, ranged above each other in shell niches amongst light arabesques and winding over the white marble. His predecessors, the most glorious restorers of art, keep him company ; under the altar, in a low chapel, a " St. John " by Donatello, and vigorous figures with knotted muscles and contorted necks impress one with their energy and youthfulness. To see this pavement, these walls, these altars thus filled and crowded, these files of figures and of heads ascending on the efflorescences of the capitals, extending in lines along the friezes and covering the entire field of view, it is evident that the arts of design were the spontaneous language of this epoch, that men spoke the language without effort, that it is the natural mould of their thought, that this thought and this imagination, fecund for the first time, blossomed outwardly with an inexhaustible generation of forms, that they are like youths whose tongues are unloosed and who say too much because they have not spoken before.

Too many beautiful or curious things is a constantly

---

* See the cartoons in the Institute of the Fine Arts at Sienna.

recurring remark here; for example the *Libraria* extending to the cathedral and built at the end of the fifteenth century. Here are ten frescoes by Pinturicchio, the history of Pius II., several figures of females very chaste and very elegant, the work however being still literal and dry. The painter preserves the costumes of the time, the emperor being represented in a gilded robe with the exaggerated display of the middle ages Pinturicchio employed Raphael on his cartoons; here the passage from the old to the new school is apparent; from master to pupil the distance is infinite, and eyes that have just left the Vatican are fully sensible of it.

CHAPTER VI.

THE ORIGIN OF PAINTING AT SIENNA AND PISA.—CREATIVE ENERGY
IN SOCIETY AND IN THE ARTS.—DUCCIO DA SIENNA.—SIMONE
MEMMI.—THE LORENZETTI.—MATTEO DA SIENNA.

THIS Sienna, so fallen, was the early instructress in,
and mistress of, the beautiful. Here and at Pisa we
find the most ancient school. Nicholas of Pisa is Sien-
nese by his father. The revivor of mosaic art in the
thirteenth century is Jacopo da Turrita, a Franciscan
monk of Sienna. The oldest Italian painting that is
known is a crucified Christ with lank limbs and drooping head in the church at Assisi by Giunta, a Pisan.*
Here, even, at San Domenico, Guido of Sienna painted
in 1271 the pure sweet face of a Madonna which already
far surpasses the mechanical Byzantine art. This corner of Tuscany had freed itself from feudal barbarism
before the rest of Italy. Already in 1100, Pisa, the first
of maritime republics, traded and fought throughout the
Levant, creating a school of architecture and building
its cathedral. A century later Sienna attained to its
full power and, in 1260, crushed Florence at the battle
of Montaperto. They were so many new Athens, commercial and belligerent like the ancient city, and genius
and love of beauty were born with them as with the
old city in contact with enterprise and danger. Confined to our great administrative monarchies, restrained
by the long literary and scientific traditions of which
we wear the chain, we no longer find within us the force
and creative audacity which then animated mankind.
We are oppressed by our work itself; we limit with our

---

* 1236. He wholly acquired his art here, about 1210.

own hand our own field of action. We aspire to contribute only one stone to the vast structure which successive generations have been erecting for so many centuries. We do not know what active energies the human heart and intellect can generate, all that the human plant can put forth of root, branch and flower on encountering the soil and the season it needs. When the State was not a lumbering machine composed of bureaucratic springs and only intelligible to pure reason, but a city evident to the senses and adapted to the ordinary capacity of the individual, man loved it, not spasmodically as at present, but daily, in every thought, and the part he took in public matters exalting his· heart and understanding, planted in him the sentiments and ideas of a citizen and not those of a bourgeois. A shoemaker gave his money in order that the church of· his city might be the most beautiful; a weaver polished his sword in the evening determined that he would be not the subject but one of the lords of a rival city. At a certain degree of tension every soul is a vibrating cord; it is only necessary to touch it to make it utter most beautiful tones. Let us picture to ourselves this nobleness and this energy diffused through every strata from top to bottom of a civic community; let us add to this an established, increasing prosperity, that self-confidence, that sentiment of joy which man experiences in a consciousness of strength; let us banish from before our eyes that load of traditions and acquisitions which to-day embarrass us, as well as our wealth; let us consider man free and self-surrendered in that desert due to degeneracy and we will then understand why here, as in the time of Æschylus, the arts arose in the midst of public affairs; why a fallow soil, bristling with every political brier produced more than our well-tilled and registered fields; why partisans, combatants and navigators at the height of their perils, their preoccupations and their ignorance, created and revived beautiful forms with an instinctive certainty, a fecundity of genius to which the leisure and the erudition of the present day cannot attain.

Slowly and painfully, beneath sculpture and architecture, painting develops itself; this is a more complicated art than the others. Time was necessary in order to discover perspective; a more sensual paganism was necessary in order to appreciate color. Man, at this epoch, is still quite christian; Sienna is the city of the Virgin and places itself under her protection as Athens under that of Pallas; with an entirely different moral standard and different legends the sentiment is the same, the local saint corresponding to the local divinity. When Duccio in 1311 finished his Madonna the people in its joy came and took him from his studio and bore him in procession to the church; the bells rang and many of the crowd carried tapers in their hands. The painter inscribed under his picture, "Holy Mother of God, grant peace to the people of Sienna; grant life to Duccio since he has thus painted thee!"* His virgin testifies to a still unskilful hand, resembling the painting of missals; but around her and the infant she holds in her arms are several heads of saints already singularly beautiful and calm. Twenty-seven compartments, the entire story of Christ placed in the chapel facing it, accompany them. The sky is of gold and golden aurioles envelop the small figures. In this light the figures, almost black, seem like a remote vision, and when formerly they were over the altar, the kneeling people, who caught distant glimpses of their grave grouping, must needs have felt the mysterious emotion, the sublime anxiety of christian faith before these human apparitions profiled in multitudes in the brightness of eternal day.

---

* Mater sancta Dei, sis causa Senis requiei
Sis Ducio vita, te quia pinixit ita.

At the Institute of the Fine Arts are the pictures of Duccio and of his contemporaries and successors, the entire series of the old masters of Sienna, and almost all taken from convents. In these pictures the nuns have scratched out the eyes of the demons and marred the faces of the persecutors with their nails and scissors. There is but little progress apparent; the picture is yet an object of religion rather than of art, as may be well conceived by these thoughtless mutilations. It is at the hotel-de-ville of Sienna that this art is the most expressive. A gallery is always a gallery and works of art, like the productions of nature, lose half their spirit when removed from their *milieu*. They must be seen along with their surroundings on the great wall whose nudity they covered, in the light of the ogive windows which illuminated them, and in the halls where the magistrates sat attired like their own personages. One might pass a couple of months in this palace studying feudal manners and customs without exhausting the ideas it provides : figures, costumes, youthful cavaliers and veteran men-at-arms, lines of battle and religious processions. Colorless, grave, sombre even, rigid and stiff, such are the terms that enter the mind before this art. The fourteenth century is incarnated in these paintings ; we feel the constant presence of strife, the forced adhesion to the breast of danger, the abortive aim at more blooming beauty, and a freer harmony. This is the epoch of horrible intestine wars, of condottieri and the Visconti, of deliberate torments and atrocious tyrannies, of a tottering faith and a crumbling mysticism and of the half-visible, experimental and fruitless renaissance. With his tragic, skeptical, sensual tales clad in Ciceronian periods, Boccaccio is the faithful image of it.*

---

* Compare his " Bride of the King of Garbe " with that of La Fontaine.

In these are the characters and aspirations of the time.
Simone Memmi, the painter of Laura and the friend of
Petrarch, has painted in the great council chamber a
Virgin under a canopy surrounded by saints, grave
and noble heads in the style of Giotto; and a little
farther on, Guido Ricci, a captain of the day, on a
caparisoned horse—a realistic personage; in these we
see painting becoming laic.* One of the Lorenzetti
has heaped up near this conflicts of armor and combats
of people; and Spinello Spinelli, in the prior's hall, has
represented the victory of Alexander II. over Frederic
Barbarossa, the emperor lying stretched on his back
before the pope,† also naval combats and processions
of troops;—art here is taking a historic and realistic
turn. Ambrogio Lorenzetti, in the hall of archives,
has portrayed good and bad government,‡ a defile of
grand personages beneath a reclining female, already
beautiful, draped in white with a laurel branch over her
blonde tresses, all this according to that Aristotle so
denounced by Petrarch, and so dear to the liberal-
minded now multiplying;—it seems as if painting was
running into a philosophical vein. I pass many others
in which the taste for actual life, for local history, and
for the antique—everything approaching the renaissance—is visible; but it is in vain—they fall short,
merely standing on its threshold. A St. Barbara by
Matteo da Sienne, in 1478, in the Church of St. Dominic, soft and pure but without relief and surrounded
by gold, is simply a hieratic figure. And Leonardo da
Vinci is already twenty-six! How comprehend so long
a halt! How comes it that after Giotto, among so
many groupings, painters do not succeed in putting on
their canvases one solid form of flesh with life in it?
What stopped them half-way in spite of so many trials,
after such a universal and happy early inspiration?

---

* From 1816 to 1828.   † 1400.   ‡ 1340.

The question becomes irresistible when one contemplates in this same palace, in the Institute of the Fine Arts, and in San Domenico, the frescoes of a complete artist, Sodoma, one of Raphael's contemporaries, and the first master of the country. His scourged Christ is a superb nude torso, animated and suffering like an antique gladiator; his "St. Catherine in Ecstasy," his two male saints and female saint between them under an open portico, all his paintings, force the others back at once into the indeterminate region of incomplete, defective beings incapable of life. Once more why, having discovered painting, did men pass a hundred and fifty years with closed eyes without seeing the body? We must see Florence and Pisa.

CHAPTER VII.

FROM FLORENCE TO PISA.—SCENERY.—PISAN ARCHITECTURE.—THE
DUOMO, LEANING TOWER, BAPTISTERY AND CAMPO-SANTO.—
PAINTINGS OF THE XIV. CENTURY.—PIETRO D'ORVIETO.—SPI-
NELLO SPINELLI, PIETRO LORENZETTI, AND THE ORCAGNA.—
RELATIONSHIP OF THE ART OF THE XIV. CENTURY TO ITS
SOCIETY.—WHY ARTISTIC DEVELOPMENT REMAINS STATIONARY.

FLORENCE, *April* 10.—I passed my first day in the
Uffizi :—but you do not require me to dwell on it now.
I must not dissipate my impressions ; I have already
had trouble enough to render them.

On the following day I, accordingly, visited Pisa
absorbed by the question which occupied me in quitting Sienna. It is only such matters that fill up time
in travelling. One moves along wrapped up in one's
ideas and other matters are let go. It seems to me that
a man divides himself up into two parts : on the one
hand a lower animal, a sort of necessary mechanical
drudge who eats, drinks and walks for him without his
knowing it, settles down comfortably in inns and in
carriages, endures without letting him perceive it disagreeable, petty annoyances, the platitudes of life, and
attends to all that pertains to his ordinary condition ;
on the other hand a mind that is excited and strained
all day by a vehement curiosity, stirred and traversed
by germs of ideas, discarded and revived, in order to
comprehend the sentiments of great men and of ancient epochs. What made them feel in this way? Is
it true that they did feel in this way? So from question to question, at the end of a week, one listens to
them and sees them face to face, forgetting the drudge,
who becomes awkward and does his duty negligently.
It is all the same to me—and to you :—but I am talking
at random,—we are going to Pisa.

A Tuscan landscape, agreeable and noble. The

grain, in blade, glows with freshness; above it run files
of elms, loaded with vines, bordering the channels by
which they are irrigated. The country is an orchard
fertilized by artificial streams. The waters flow co-
piously from the mountains and wind about limpid and
blue in their too capacious bed of boulders. Signs of
prosperity everywhere. The mountain slopes are dot-
ted with thousands of white spots, so many villas and
summer resorts, each with its bouquet of chestnut,
olive and pine trees. Marks of taste and of comfort
are evident in those that we observe in passing; the
farm-houses have a portico on the ground-floor, or on
the first story, wherein to enjoy the evening breeze.
All is productive; cultivation extends far up the mountain and is continued here and there by the primitive
forest. Man has not reduced the earth to a fleshless
skeleton; he has preserved, or renewed its vestment of
verdure. As the train recedes, these terraces of soil,
each with its own tint and culture, and farther on, the
pale, vapory bordering of mountains, encompass the
plain like a garland. The effect is not that of a grandiose beauty, but harmonious and regulated.

For the first time in Italy I see a true river in a true
plain; the Arno, yellow and turbulent, rolls along between two long ranges of dingy houses. A mournful,
neglected, meagrely populated, lifeless city, calling to
mind one of our towns in decay, or set aside by a wandering civilization, like Aix, Poitiers or Rennes;—such
is Pisa.

There are two Pisas: one in which people have
lapsed into ennui, and live from hand to mouth since the
decadence, which is in fact the entire city, except a remote corner; the other is this corner, a marble sepulchre where the Duomo, Baptistery, Leaning Tower and
Campo-Santo silently repose like beautiful dead beings.
This is the genuine Pisa, and in these relics of a departed
life, one beholds a world.

A renaissance before the renaissance, a second budding almost antique of antique civilization, a precocious and complete sentiment of healthy, joyous beauty,
a primrose after six centuries of snow—such are the
ideas and the terms that rush through the mind. All
is marble, and white marble, its immaculate brightness
glowing in the azure. Everywhere appear grand, solid
forms, the cupola, the full wall, balanced stories, the
firmly-planted round or square mass ; but over these
forms, revived from the antique, like delicate foliage refreshing an old tree-trunk, is diffused an invention of
their own in the shape of a covering of delicate columns
supporting arcades that render the originality and
grace of this architecture, thus renovated, indescribable.

The most difficult thing in the arts is to discover a
type of architecture. The Greeks and the middle ages
produced one complete ; Imperial Rome and the sixteenth and seventeenth centuries produced one half-
complete. In order to find other types we are obliged
to abandon Europe and European history and consider
those of Egypt, Persia, India or China. Usually they
testify to a completed civilization, to a profound transformation of all instincts and of all customs. Really,
to change any conception of a thing so general as form,
what a change must be effected in the human brain !
Revolutions in painting and in literature have been
much more frequent, much easier and much less significant. Figures traced on canvas, and characters
portrayed in books will change five or six times with a
people before its architecture can be changed. The
mass to be moved is too great, and in the eleventh
century, in the times of our first Capet kings, Pisa
moves it without effort.

There was a dawn then, as in Greece in the sixth
century before Christ. Everything then burst forth
radiantly like light at the first hour. " The Pisans,"
said Vasari, " being at the apex of their grandeur and
3*

of their progress, being lords of Sardinia, Corsica and the island of Elba, and their city being filled with great and powerful citizens, brought from the most distant places trophies and great spoil." At Byzantium, in the Orient, in ancient cities still filled with the ruins of Greek elegance and of Roman magnificence, among Jews and Arabs their visitors and their customers, in contact with foreign ideas, this young community started up and elaborated its own conceptions as formerly the Greek cities in contact with Phenicia, Carthage, the Lydians and the Egyptians. In 1083 in order to honor the Virgin, who had given them a victory over the Saracens of Sardignia, they laid the foundations of their Duomo.

This edifice is almost a Roman basilica, that is to say a temple surmounted by another temple, or, if you prefer it, a house having a gable for its façade which gable is cut off at the peak to support another house of smaller dimensions. Five stories of columns entirely cover the façade with their superposed porticoes. Two by two they stand coupled together to support small arcades; all these pretty shapes of white marble under their dark arcades form an aerial population of the utmost grace and novelty. Nowhere here are we conscious of the dolorous reverie of the mediæval north; it is the fête of a young nation which is awakening, and, in the gladness of its recent prosperity, honoring its gods. It has collected capitals, ornaments, entire columns obtained on the distant shores to which its wars and its commerce have led it, and these ancient fragments enter into its work without incongruity; for it is instinctively cast in the ancient mould, and only developed with a tinge of fancy on the side of finesse and the pleasing. Every antique form reappears, but reshaped in the same sense by a fresh and original impulse. The outer columns of the Greek temple are reduced, multiplied and uplifted in the air, and, from a support have become an ornament. The Roman or Byzantine dome is elongated and its natural heaviness diminished under a crown of slender columns with a mitre ornament, which girds it midway with its delicate promenade. On the two sides of the great door two corinthian columns are enveloped with luxurious foliage, calyxes and twining or blooming acanthus; and from the threshold we see the church with its files of intersecting columns, its alternate courses of black and white marble and its multitude of slender and brilliant forms, rising upward like an altar of candelabra. A new spirit appears here, a more delicate sensibility; it is not excessive and disordered as in the north, and yet it is not satisfied with the grave simplicity, the robust nudity of antique architecture. It is the daughter of a pagan mother, healthy and gay, but more womanly than its mother.

She is not yet an adult, sure in all her steps,—she is somewhat awkward. The lateral façades on the exterior are monotonous; the cupola within is a reversed funnel of a peculiar and disagreeable form. The junction of the two arms of the cross is unsatisfactory and so many modernized chapels dispel the charm due to purity, as at Sienna. At the second glance however all this is forgotten, and we again regard it as a complete whole. Four rows of corinthian columns, surmounted with arcades, divide the church into five naves, and form a forest. A second passage, as richly crowded, traverses the former crosswise, and, above the beautiful grove, files of still smaller columns prolong and intersect each other in order to uphold in the air the prolongation and intersection of the quadruple gallery. The ceiling is flat; the windows are small, and for the most part, without sashes; they allow the walls to retain the grandeur of their mass and the solidity of their position; and among these long, straight and simple lines, in this natural light, the innumerable shafts glow with the serenity of an antique temple.

It is not, however, wholly an antique temple, and hence its peculiar charm: in the rear of the choir a grand figure of Christ in a golden robe, and the Virgin, and another saint, smaller in size, occupy the entire concave of the absis.* His face is serene and sad; on this golden background, in the paleness of the dim light, he looks like a vision. Countless paintings and structures of the middle ages assuredly correspond to ecstatic yearnings.—Other fragments indicate the decadence and utter barbarism out of which they sprung. One of the ancient bronze doors still remains covered with rude and horrible bronze bas-reliefs. Behold what the descendants of the statuaries preserved of antique tradition, what the human mind had become in the chaos of the tenth century, at the time of the Hungarian invasions of Marozzia and of Theodora: sad, mournful, dwarfed, dislocated and mechanical figures, God the Father and six angels, three on one side and three on the other, all leaning at the same angle like the figures scribbled by children; the twelve apostles ranged in file, six in front and six in the intermediate spaces, are like those round rings with holes in them for eyes and long appendages for arms which boys scrawl on the covers of their copy-books. On the other hand, the entrance doors, sculptured by John of Bologna (1602), are full of life: leaves of the rose, the vine, the medlar, the orange and the laurel, with their berries, fruits and flowers, amongst birds and animals, twine around and make frames for energetic and spirited figures and groups of an imposing aspect. This abundance of accurate living forms is peculiar to the sixteenth century: it discovered nature the same time as it discovered

---

* By Jacopo Turrita, the restorer of mosaic art.

man. Between these two doors occurs the labor of five centuries.

Nothing more can be added in relation to the Baptistery or the Leaning Tower; the same ideas prevail in these, the same taste, the same style. The former is a simple, isolated dome, the latter a cylinder, and each has an outward dress of small columns. And yet each has its own distinct and expressive physiognomy; but description and writing consume too much time, and too many technical terms are requisite to define their differences. I note, simply, the inclination of the Tower. Some suppose that, when half constructed, the tower sank in the earth on one side, and that the architects continued on; seeing that they did continue this deflection was only a partial obstacle to them. In any event, there are other leaning towers in Italy, at Bologna, for example; voluntarily or involuntarily this feeling for oddness, this love of paradox, this yielding to fancy, is one of the characteristics of the middle ages.

In the centre of the Baptistery stands a superb font with eight panels; each panel is incrusted with a rich complicated flower in full bloom, and each flower is different. Around it a circle of large corinthian columns supports round-arch arcades; most of them are antique and are ornamented with antique bas-reliefs : Meleager with his barking dogs, and the nude torsos of his companions in attendance on christian mysteries. On the left stands a pulpit similar to that of Sienna, the first work of Nicholas of Pisa (1260), a simple marble coffer supported by marble columns and covered with sculptures. The sentiment of force and of antique nudity comes out here in striking features. The sculptor comprehended the postures and torsions of bodies. His figures, somewhat massive, are grand and simple ; he frequently reproduces the tunics and folds of the Roman costume ; one of his nude person-

ages, a sort of Hercules bearing a young lion on his
shoulders, has the broad breast and muscular tension
which the sculptors of the sixteenth century admired.
What a change in human civilization, what an accelera-
tion of it, had these restorers of ancient beauty, these
young republics of the twelfth and thirteenth centuries,
these precocious creators of modern thought been left
to themselves like the ancient Greeks? had they followed their natural bent, had mystic tradition not
intervened to limit and divert their efforts, had laic
genius developed amongst them as formerly in Greece
amidst liberal, rude and healthy institutions, and not, as
two centuries later, in the midst of the servitude and
corruptions of the decadence?

The last of these edifices, the Campo-Santo, is a
cemetery, the soil of which, brought from Palestine, is
holy ground. Four high walls of polished marble surround it with their white and crowded panels. Inside,
a square gallery forms a promenade opening into the
court through arcades trellised with ogive windows.
It is filled with funereal monuments, busts, inscriptions
and statues of every form and of every age. Nothing
could be simpler and nobler. A framework of dark
wood supports the arch overhead, and the crest of the
roof cuts sharp against the crystal sky. At the angles
are four rustling cypress trees, tranquilly swayed by
the breeze. Grass is growing in the court with a wild
freshness and luxuriance. Here and there a climbing
flower twined around a column, a small rosebush, or
a shrub glows beneath a gleam of sunshine. There is
no noise; this quarter is deserted; only now and then
is heard the voice of some promenader which rever-
berates as under the vault of a church. It is the
veritable cemetery of a free and christian city; here,
before the tombs of the great, people might well
reflect over death and public affairs.

The entire wall of the interior is covered with

frescoes; the pictorial art of the fourteenth century
has no more complete charnel-house. The two schools
of Florence and Sienna here combine, and it is a
curious spectacle to observe their art halting between
two tendencies, arrested in its powerlessness like a
passive chrysalis no longer a worm and not yet a
butterfly. The ancient sentiment of the divine world
is enfeebled, and the fresh sentiment of the natural
world is still weak. On the right of the entrance
Pietro d'Orvieto has painted an enormous Christ,
which, except the feet and the head, almost disappears
under an immense disk representing the world and the
revolving spheres; this is the spirit of primitive symbolism. Alongside, in his story of the creation and of
the first couple, Adam and Eve are big, well-fed,
plump, realistic bodies, evidently copied from the nude.
A little farther on Cain and Abel, in their sheepskins,
display vulgar countenances taken from life in the
streets or in a fray. Feet, legs and composition
remain barbarian, and this incipient realism goes no
farther. On the other side, and with the same incongruities, a grand fresco by Pietro Lorenzetti represents ascetic life. Forty or fifty scenes are given in
the same picture: an anchorite reading, another in a
cave, another roosting in a tree, here one preaching
with no other clothes on than his hair, and there one
tempted by a woman and flogged by the devil. A few
large heads with gray and white beards show the rustic
clumsiness of ploughmen; but the landscapes, the
accessories, and even most of the figures, are grotesque;
the trees are feathers, and the rocks and the lions seem
to belong to a five-franc menagerie. Farther on Spinello d'Arezzo has painted the story of St. Ephesus.
His pagans, half Romans and half cavaliers, wear
armor arranged and colored according to mediæval
taste. Many of the attitudes in his battles are true, as,
for instance, a man overthrown on his face, and another

seized by the beard. Several are figures of the day,
for instance a pretty page in green holding a sword,
and a trim young squire in a blue pourpoint with
pointed shoes and well-drawn calves; observation and
composition, an attempt to impart interest and dramatic
variety, begin to appear. But it is only a beginning, it
is simply a pasteboard sketch. Relief, flexibility,
action, the rich vitality of firm flesh, a feeling for a
balanced organization and the innumerable laws which
maintain natural objects is still remote; we have
imagery striving after, but which does not yet attain
to art.

Nothing more clearly illustrates this ambiguous
state of minds than a fresco placed near one of the
angles called the " Triumph of Death," by Orcagna.[*]
At the base of a mountain a cavalcade of lords and
ladies arrives; these are the contemporaries of Froissart: they wear the hoods and ermines and the gay variegated robes of the time, and have falcons and dogs
and other appurtenances such as Valentine Visconti
went to find at the residence of Louis of Orleans. The
heads are not less real: this delicate trim chatelaine
on horseback, and veiled, is a true lady, pensive and
melancholy, of the mediæval epoch. These gay and
powerful ones of the century suddenly come upon the
corpses of three kings in the three degrees of corruption,
each in his open grave, one swollen, the other gnawed
by worms and serpents, and the other already exposing
the bones of his skeleton. They halt and tremble:
one of them leans over his horse's neck to obtain a
better view, and another stops his nostrils; this is a
"morality" like those then given in the playhouses.
The artist aims to instruct his public, and to this effect
he masses around the principal group every possible
commentary. On the summit of the mountain are

---

[*] Deceased about 1876.

monks in their hermitages, one reading and another
milking a fawn, and, in their midst, are beasts of the
desert, a weasel and a crane. "You good people who
gaze on this, behold the Christian, contemplative life,
the holy living disdained by the mighty of the earth!"
But death is present who restores the equilibrium: he is
advancing in the shape of an old graybeard with a
scythe in his hand in order to cut down the gay, the
voluptuous, the young lords and ladies, fat and
frizzled, who are diverting themselves in a grove.
With a sort of cruel irony he is mowing down those
who fear him, and is avoiding those who implore him;
a troop of the maimed, of cripples, of the blind, of
beggars vainly summon him; his scythe is not for
them. Such is the way of this frail lugubrious,
miserable world; and the end to which it is tending is
more lugubrious still. This is universal destruction, a
yawning abyss into which all, each in turn, are to be
confusedly ingulphed. Queens, kings, popes and
archbishops with their ministers and their crowns lie
in heaps, and their souls, in the shape of nude infants,
issue from their bodies to take their place in the terrible eternity. Some are welcomed by angels, but the
greater number are seized by demons, hideous and base
figures, with bodies of goats and toads, and with bats'
ears and the jaws and claws of cats—a grotesque pack
gambolling and capering around their quarry: a singular commingling of dramatic passion, morbid philosophy, accurate observation, awkward triviality and
picturesque impotence.

The fresco next to this, "The Last Judgment," is
similar. Many of the faces bear an expression of despair, and of extraordinary stupor,—for instance, an
angel in the centre, crouched down, and, his eyes
opened wide and rigid with horror, gazing on the
eternal judgments; another, a hairy recluse thrown violently backward, with outstretched arms appealing to

Christ the mediator, and a condemned woman clinging convulsively to another. All these personages, however, are simply figures cut out of paper; the forms are arranged mechanically, in rows like onions, five stories high, the souls issuing from square holes like trap-doors in a theatre stage; the art is as inadequate as the sentiment is profound, and, so soon as the sentiment begins to decline this inadequacy becomes platitude and barbarism.

We realize this right alongside in the " Hell" of Bernardo Orcagna, which completes the work of his brother Andrea. It is a grave in compartments, arranged so as to frighten little children. In the centre, a huge green Satan of glowing metal with a ram's head is roasting souls in a furnace inside of himself, from which they are seen to issue through the fissures. Around him in a confused medley of flames and serpents, appear naked dolls in the hands of hairy little devils who are flaying, disembowelling and dismembering them, tearing out their tongues and spitting them like chickens, the whole forming a great kitchen stew.—A poetic world from which all poetry is abstracted, a sublime tragedy converted into a parade of executioners and a workshop of torture is what this talentless Dante has depicted on these walls. The great era of Christian faith terminated with the scandals of the Avignon popes and the convulsions of that schism; scholasticism dies out and Petrarch ridicules it. A few paroxysms of morbid fervor,—the flagellators of France, the white penitents of Italy, the visions of Saint Catherine and the authority of St. Bernard at Sienna, and later the evangelical dictatorship of Savonarola at Florence,—indicate at most the rare and violent palpitations of a departing life. The heretics of Germany and England undermine the church; the Averrhoëists of Italy undermine religion, while, on all sides, the mysticism which had supported religion and ennobled the church becomes decrepit and falls. Petrarch, the last of the Platonic worshippers, views his sonnets as amusements, devoting himself to reviving antiquity, to discovering manuscripts, and to writing latin verses and prose, and with him we see commencing that long succession of humanists who are about to introduce pagan culture into Italy. Popular literature, meanwhile, changes its tone; practical historians, amusing story-tellers in prose,—the Villani, the Sacchetti, the Pecoroni and the Boccaccios—substitute merry or ordinary converse for a sublime and visionary poesy. The serious declines, for people are disposed to be gay; Boccaccio's poesy consists of gallant and descriptive novels of adventure, and around him, in France and in England, is displayed in poets and chroniclers, an interminable string of chivalric cavalcades, of princely sumptuousness and of amatory discourses. There is no longer any grand, austere idea to excite the enthusiasm of men. In the midst of the wars and the disastrous dislocations which counter-check or dismantle governments those who look beyond seigneurial pomp and revelry see nothing with which to control man but Fortune, " a monstrous image with a cruel and terrible face, and a hundred arms, some elevating men to the high places of worldly honor, and others rudely grasping them in order to hurl them to the ground;" alongside of her is blind Death " who grinds all into dust, kings and cavaliers, emperors and popes, many lords who live for pleasure and lovely ladies and mistresses of knights who cry aloud and sink in anguish." * These expressions of a contemporary seem to describe the fresco of Orcagna. The same impression, indeed, is there found stamped on all hearts; a bitter sentiment of human instability and misery, an ironical view of passing existence and of worldly pleasure, the liberation of laic opinion freed at

---

* Piers Plowman.

last from mystic illusion, the intemperance of long-bridled senses in quest of enjoyment—do we find aught else in Boccaccio? He places death side by side with voluptuousness, the atrocious details of the plague side by side with the frolics of the alcove. Such is truly the spirit of the time; and here I imagine we at last arrive at the cause which for so long a time retarded the progress of painting in Italy. If, during a hundred and fifty years, painting, like literature, remained passive after the vigorous advance of its early progress, it is owing to the public mind having remained inactive likewise. Mystic sentiment becoming less fervid it was no longer adequately sustained in order to express the pure mystic life. Pagan sentiment being only in embryo it was not yet far enough advanced to portray the broad pagan life. It was abandoning its first road and still remained at the entrance of the second. It was abandoning ideal faces, innocent or ravished physiognomies, the glorious possessions of incorporeal souls ranged like visions against the splendor of divine light. It descended to the earth, delineating portraits, contemporary costume, interesting scenes, and expressed common or dramatic sentiments. It no longer addressed monks but laymen. These laymen however still had one foot in the cloister, and many long years were necessary before their admiration and sympathies, clinging to the supernatural world, could rally in combined force and effort around the natural world. It was necessary that the terrestrial life should gradually ennoble itself in their own eyes even to appearing to them to be the only true and important one. It was necessary that a universal and insensible transformation should interest them in the laws and actual proportions of things, in the anatomical structure of the body, in the vitality of naked limbs, in the expansion of animal joyousness and in the triumph of virile energies. Then only could they comprehend, suggest and demand accurate perspective, substantial modelling, brilliant and melting . color, bold and harmonious form, all parts of complete painting, and that glorification of physical beauty which demands sympathetic spirits in order that it may attain to perfection and find its echo.

They devoted a century and a half to this great step, and painting, like a shadow accompanying its body, faithfully repeated the uncertainties of their advance in the slowness of its progress. In the middle of the fifteenth century Parro Spinelli and Lorenzo Bicci faithfully copy the grotesque style; Fra Angelico, nurtured in the cloister like a rare flower in a conservatory, still succeeds in the purest of mystic visions; even with his pupil Gozzoli, who has filled up the whole side of a wall here with his frescoes, we detect, as in the confluence of two ages, the last flow of the christian tide beneath the fulness of the pagan flood. During these two hundred years innumerable paintings are produced to clothe the nudity of churches and monasteries; this period having elapsed they are regarded with indifference; they fall off along with the plaster, the masons scratch them away, they disappear beneath whitewash, the restorers make them over afresh. The remains we now have of them are fragments, and only in our day have interest and attention been again directed to them; antiquarians have dug down to the geological stratum which bore them and we now see in them the remains of an imperfect flora extinguished by the invasion of a more vigorous vegetation.—The eyes, again turning upward, rest on the four structures of ancient Pisa, solitary on a spot where the grass grows, and on the pallid lustre of the marbles profiled against the divine azure. What ruins, and what a cemetery is history! What human pulsations of which no other trace is left but a form imprinted on a fragment of stone! What indifference in the smile of the placid

firmament, and what cruel beauty in that luminous cu-
· pola stretched, in turn, like a common funereal dais
over the generations that have fallen! We read similar
ideas in books, and, in the pride of youth, we have considered them as rhetoric; but when man has lived the
half of his career, and, turning in upon himself, he
reckons up how many of his ambitions he has subdued,
how much he has wrung out of his hopes, and all the
dead that lie buried in his heart, the sternness and
magnificence of nature appear to him as one, and the
heavy sobbing of inward grief forces him to recognize
a higher lamentation, that of the human tragedy which,
century after century, has buried so many combatants
in one common grave. He stops, feeling on his head
as upon that of those gone before, the hand of inexorable
powers, and he comprehends his destiny. This humanity, of which he is a member, is figured in the
Niobe at Florence. Around her, her sons and her
daughters, all those she loves, fall incessantly under
the arrows of invisible archers. One of them is cast
down on his back and his breast, transpierced, is
throbbing; another, still living, stretches his powerless
hands up to the celestial murderers; the youngest conceals his head under his mother's robe. She, meanwhile, stern and fixed stands hopeless, her eyes raised
to heaven, contemplating with admiration and horror
the dazzling and deadly nimbus, the outstretched arms,
the merciless arrows and the implacable serenity of the
gods.

BOOK II.

FLORENCE.

CHAPTER I.

A CITY complete in itself, having its own arts and edifices, lively and not too crowded, a capital and not too large, beautiful and gay—such is the first idea of Florence.

One wanders along carelessly over the large slabs with which the streets are paved. From the Palazzo Strozzi to the Piazza Santa Trinita there is a humming crowd constantly renewing itself. In hundreds of places we see the constantly recurring signs of an agreeable and intellectual life : cafés almost brilliant, print-shops, alabaster *pietra dura* and mosaic establishments, bookstores, an elegant reading-room and a dozen theatres. Of course the ancient city of the fifteenth century still exists and constitutes the body of the city; but it is not mouldy as at Sienna, consigned to one corner as at Pisa, befouled as in Rome, enveloped in mediæval cobwebs or plastered with modern life as if with a parasite incrustation. The past is here reconciled with the present; the refined vanity of the monarchy is perpetuated by the refined invention of the republic; the paternal government of the German grand-dukes is perpetuated by the pompous government of the Italian grand-dukes. At the close of the last and the beginning of this century Florence formed a little oasis in Italy, and was called *gli felicissimi stati*. People built as formerly, held festivals and conversed together; the social spirit had not perished as elsewhere under a rude despotic hand or through the

respectable inertia of ecclesiastical rigor. The Florentine, as formerly the Athenian under the Cæsars,
remained a critic and a wit, proud of his good taste,
his sonnets, his academies, of the language which gave
law to Italy, and of his undisputed judgments in
matters of literature and the fine arts. There are
races so refined that they cannot wholly degenerate;
mind is an integrant force with them; they may
become corrupt but never be destroyed; they may be
converted into dilletanti and sophists but not into
mutes and fools. It is then, indeed, that their under-
lying nature appears; we recognize that with them, as
with the Greeks of the Lower Empire, intelligence
constitutes character, since it persists after this has
deteriorated. Already under the first Medicis the
keenest enjoyment is that of the intellect, and the
leading mental characteristics are gaiety and subtlety.
Gravity subsides; like the Athenians in the time of
Demosthenes the Florentines care only for amusement,
and, like Demosthenes, their leaders admonish them.
" Your life," says Savonarola, " is passed in bed, in
gossiping, in promenading, in orgies, and in debauchery." And Bruto the historian adds that they infuse
"politeness into slander and gossip, and sociability
into criminal complaisance;" he reproaches them for
doing "everything languidly, effeminately, irregularly,
and of accepting indolence and baseness as the rule of
their life." These are severe expressions. All the mor-
alists use the same language, and elevate their voices
in order to make themselves heard. It is clear, however, that, toward the middle of the fifteenth century,
the trained and cultivated senses, expert in all matters
of pleasure, ostentation and emotion, are sovereign in
Florence. We realize this in their art. Their renaissance has in it nothing of the austere or tragic. Only
old palaces built of enormous blocks bristle with
knotty bosses grated windows and obscure angles,

indicating the insecurity of feudal life and the assaults
they have undergone. Everywhere else a taste for
elegant and joyous beauty declares itself. The principal buildings are covered with marble from top to
bottom. *Loggia*, open to air and sunshine, rest on
corinthian columns. We see that architecture emancipated itself immediately from the gothic, abstracting
from it only one point of originality and of fancy, and
that her natural tendency from the first led her to the
light and simple forms of pagan antiquity. You walk
on and you observe the apse of a church peopled with
intelligent and expressive statues; a solid wall where
the pretty Italian arcade is inlaid and developed into a
border; a file of slender columns whose tops expand in
order to support the roof of a promenade, and, terminating a street, a panel of green hill, or some blue
mountain top. I have just passed an hour on the
square of the "Annunziata," seated on a flight of
steps. Opposite to me is a church, and on either side
of this, a convent, all three with a peristyle of light
half-ionic, half-corinthian columns, terminating in arcades. Overhead are brown roofs of old tile intersecting the pure blue of the sky, and, at the end of a street,
stretching away in the warm shadow, the eye is arrested
by a round mountain. Within this frame, so natural
and so noble, is a market; stalls protected by white
awnings contain rolls of drygoods; countless women
in violet shawls and straw hats come and go and are
buying and chatting; there are scarcely any beggars or
ragged people; the eyes are not saddened by spectacles of misery and savage brutality; the people seem
to be at their ease and active without being excited.
From the middle of this variegated crowd and these
open airy stalls rises an equestrian statue, and near
this, a fountain empties its waters into a basin of
bronze. These contrasts are similar to those of Rome;
but instead of clashing they harmonize. The beautiful

is as original but it inclines to the pleasing and harmonious and not toward disproportion and enormity. You turn back. A beautiful stream of clear water, spotted here and there with white sandbanks, flows by the side of a magnificent quay. Houses seeming to be palaces, modern and yet monumental, form a bordering to it. In the distance you observe trees donning their spring verdure, a soft and pleasing landscape like those of temperate climes; beyond, rounded summits and hillsides, and still farther on, an amphitheatre of barren rocks. Florence lies in a mountain basin like a statuette in the middle of a vast fountain, and its stone lacework becomes silvery under the bright lustre of the evening reflections. You follow the course of the river and reach the Cascine. Fresh green and the delicate tintings of distant poplars undulate with charming sweetness against the blue mountains. Tall trees and dense evergreen hedges protect the promenader from the north wind. It is so pleasant, on the approach of spring, to feel one's self stirred by the fresh warm sunshine! The azure of the sky glows magnificently between the budding branches of the beeches, on the pale verdure of the ilex, and on the blue-tinted needles of the pine. Everywhere between gray trunks animated with sap are blooming tufts of shrubbery that have not succumbed to winter's sleep, and fresh blossoms, combining with their youthful vivacity, to fill the avenues with color and fragrance. The light laurel profiles its grave tops against the river-bank, as in a picture, while the broad Arno tranquilly expands its ruddy gleaming waves in sunset glow.

You leave the city and ascend an eminence in order to embrace it and its valley in one view in the rounded vase in which it lies : nothing could be more charming! Comfort and prosperity are apparent on all sides. Thousands of country-houses dot the surface with their white spots, rising above each other from slope to slope even to the mountain heights. On every declivity the tops of the olive-trees cluster together like sober grazing flocks. The soil is supported by walls and forms terraces. Man's intelligent hand converts all to profit and at the same time into beauty. The soil, thus disposed, assumes an architectural shape; gardens are grouped together in stories amongst balustrades, statues and fountains. There are no great forests, there is no luxuriance of abundant vegetation; it is only northern eyes that need to feast themselves on the universal softness and freshness of vegetal growth; the grouping of stones suffices for the Italians, and the neighboring mountain furnishes them, according to fancy, with beautiful white or bluish blocks, sober and refined in tone. They arrange them nobly in symmetrical lines; the marble fronts of the houses glisten in the transparent atmosphere, accompanied with a few grand trees always green. One can here enjoy sunshine in winter and shade in summer, while the eye idly wanders over the surrounding landscape.

Afar, in the distance, a gateway is seen, a campanile and a church. This is San Miniato, situated on a hill and developing its façade of variegated marbles. This is one of the oldest churches in Florence, belonging to the eleventh century. On entering it you find an almost latin basilica, capitals almost grecian, and light polished shafts bearing round arcades. The crypt is similar. There is nothing lugubrious about it or overburdened; ever the upspringing column terminating in harmonious curves. Florentine architecture from the very first derives or resumes the antique tradition of light and solid forms. Early historians call Florence "the noble city, the daughter of Rome." It seems as if the melancholy spirit of the middle ages had only glided over it. She is an elegant pagan, who, as soon as she first thought, declared herself, at first timidly and afterward openly, elegant and pagan.

CHAPTER II.

VISITS AND EVENINGS AT THE THEATRES.—There are
eight or ten theatres, which shows great fondness for
amusement. They are convenient and well ventilated;
a wide passage surrounds the parquette and the orches-
tra; the audience is not stifled as at Paris; several of
the houses are handsome, well decorated and simple:
good taste seems to be natural in this country. In
other respects it is different; seats are at such low
rates that the managers have difficulty in making both
ends meet, and as to the scenery, supernumeraries and
the mechanical department they manage as they best
can; for instance, at the Opera, the *figurantes* get from
two hundred and fifty to three hundred francs for the
season, which lasts two months and a half; they provide themselves with shoes and stockings, the rest
being given to them; most of them are grisettes. In
addition to this the *figurants* and *figurantes* are rather
unmanageable. If a fine is imposed on them for being
late or for any other cause they leave the manager in
the lurch. Their service in the theatre is simply so
much extra; they obtain a living elsewhere; this or
that journeyman mason, a druid or musketeer in the
evening, comes to the rehearsal in his working pantaloons, his knees still plastered with lime. A large capital, and lavish expenditure of money are necessary to
lubricate the wheels of a modern theatre: they occasionally creak and get out of order, as is sometimes
seen at the performances. Centralization and a com-

plete national life are likewise necessary in order to
supply dramatic ideas; here they translate our pieces.
I have just heard "Faust," the prima-donna of which
is a French lady. At the Nicolini theatre the "Mont-
'joie" of Octave Feuillet is performed, and, to make it
more intelligible, it is entitled *Montjoie o l'Egoista.* On
another day we have *Geloisa*, which is "Othello" arranged as a domestic melodrama;—it is impossible to
remain,—I leave at the third act. A few novels are
produced like *Un prode d'Italia* and *Pasquale Paoli*,
great historical machines in the style of Walter Scott,
written in declamatory language and with frequent al-
lusions to the present time. One of my friends, a cultivated person, admits that the literature of the day in
Italy is bad; politics absorb all the sap of the tree,
other branches proving barren. In a historical line
there are only monographs. Writers resemble provin-
cialists thirty years behind the capital on account of
their remoteness from it; a good deal of time is requisite to acclimate a clear concise style, based on facts
and free of exaggerations. They have not even a fixed
language; all the Italians born outside of Tuscany
are obliged, like Alfieri, to resort to it in order to
purify their dialect. Besides this, Tuscans and Italians,
are all expected to avoid French turns of expression,
so contrary to the genius of their language, to painfully
unlearn them, and purge their memories of them.
Now, as France, for a hundred and fifty years, has
furnished Italy with books and ideas you may judge of
the difficulty of doing so. In this particular, many
writers fall into classic pedantry and superstitions;
they nourish themselves on the standard authors of the
sixteenth century, and, as purists, go farther back, to
the fourteenth ;—but how express modern ideas in the
language of Froissart, or even in that of Amyot?
Hence they are constrained to interlard their antique
style with contemporary terms; these incongruities

torment them; they can only walk with shackled feet, embarrassed by souvenirs of authorized forms and of a precise vocabulary. A writer confessed to me that this obligation put his mind to the rack. This abortive result is, again, an effect of the past; its causes are at once perceptible, namely, on the one hand, the interruption of literary traditions after the seventeenth century, in the universal decadence of studies and of intellects, and, on the other, the want of centralization and a capital essential for the suppression of dialects. The history of all Italy is derived from one circumstance: she could not unite under a moderate or semi-enlightened monarchy in the sixteenth century at the same time as her neighbors.

To make amends politics are now in full blast; one might compare it to a field suffering with a long drought, reinvigorated by a sudden shower. You see nothing but political caricatures of Victor Emmanuel, Napoleon and the Pope. They are coarse in conception and in execution: the Pope is a skeleton or a rope-dancer; death, playing at bowls, is knocking him and the cardinals down. They are without wit or finesse; the aim is to express the idea forcibly, and to make a sensational impression. In like manner their journals, almost all penny-papers, talk loud and high rather than justly. They seem like people who, after a certain time, are released from their fetters and gesticulate vigorously and strike out in the air to stretch their limbs. Some, meanwhile, la Pace, and the Milan Gazette, reason closely, appreciate differences, refuse to be considered for De Maistre or for Voltaire, laud Paolo Sarpi, Gioberti and Rosmini, and strive to revive their Italian traditions. People so spiritual and so nobly endowed will finally hit upon some moderate tone and a medium course of things. In the mean time they are proud of their free press and ridicule ours. To tell the truth we, on this point, make a sad figure

abroad; after reading in a café the "Times," "Gali-
gnani," the "Kœlnische or "Allgemeine Zeitung,"
and a French paper is taken up, one's pride suffers.
A cautious or commonplace political paragraph, a
vague or too complacent editorial, scanty correspondence always got up, very little precise information and
sound discussion, a good many phrases of which some
are well written, such is the substance of a French
newspaper; and this is poor, not merely because the
government interferes, but again and especially, because intelligent readers capable of serious attention
are too few in number. The public does not insist on
being furnished with facts and with proofs; it requires
to be amused, or to have a ready-made idea clearly
resifted. A few cultivated minds at the most, a
Parisian coterie with small provincial branches, detects
here and there an allusion, a bit of irony or of malice,
at which it laughs and is satisfied. If our journals are
politically defective it is because the whole country is
defective in political aptitude and instruction. Here,
it is asserted, the Italians have naturally an instinct
and talent for political affairs;—in any event they are
passionately fond of them.

Many persons in a good position to observe, often
tell me that if France posts its sentinels ten years
longer on the Alps in order to prevent an Austrian invasion the liberal party will have doubled: the schools,
the journals and the army, every accumulation of prosperity and of intelligence contributes to increase it.
Provincial or municipal jealousies are no obstacle
whatever. In the beginning there was some disaffec-
tion apparent in Tuscany, and some resistance; this
section of the country was the most contented and the
best governed in Italy; there was some hesitation in
submitting to Turin, and in taking risks; but the
Marquis Gino Capponi, the man the most respected in
the Tuscan party, declared in favor of the union as

there was no other means for maintaining an existence in modern Europe. All the great Italians, moreover, since Machiavelli and Dante have urged in their writings the importance of being able to resist Austria. To-day all are united and fused together; we already see in the army a kind of common language which is a compromise between the various dialects.

Two traits distinguish this revolution from ours. In the first place the Italians are neither levellers nor socialists. The noble is on a familiar footing with the peasant, he converses with the people in a friendly manner; the latter, far from being hostile to their nobility, are rather proud of it. All property is subject to the metayer system,* and the division of products establishes a sort of companionship between the owner and the farmer. This farmer is often on the *podere* (manor) two hundred years, from father to son, and consequently is a conservative adverse to innovations, and inaccessible to theories; the system of cultivation is the same as under the Medicis which was much advanced for those times, but far behind for these. The proprietor comes in October to superintend his harvest and then departs;—not that he is a "gentleman farmer," for he has an agent, and often possesses seven or eight villas, in one of which he resides; with no moral or political authority over the peasantry as in England he yet lives on good terms with them. He is not scornful, insolent or a "citadin," like our ancient nobles; he loves economy and, formerly, sold his own wine. For this purpose every palace had an opening through which customers passed their empty bottles and received them full on paying the money; suppressed vanity leaves to human benevolence a much larger field of action. The master "lives and lets live."

---

* An equal or relative division of products of land between the cultivator and the proprietor.

There is no pulling and hauling; the meshes of the social web are relaxed and they do not break. Hence the ability of the country to govern itself since 1859. In this respect it is more fortunate than we are. It is a great feature in the organization of a government or of a nation not to feel your feet resting on communistic instincts and theories.

In the second place they are not Voltairians. Bérenger's commercial traveller, philosopher and student is not with them a frequent or popular character.* They do not approve of the violent language of the "Diritto." They are too imaginative, too poetic, and besides that, are endowed with too much good sense; they are too conscious of social necessities, too remote from our logical abstractions to desire to suppress religion as we did in 1792. They are educated to see processions, sacred paintings and pompous or noble churches; their catholicism forms a part of the habits of their eyes, their ears, their imagination and their taste; they need it as they need their beautiful climate. Never will an Italian sacrifice all this, like a Frenchman, to an abstraction of the reasoning brain; his way of conceiving things is quite otherwise, much less absolute, much more complex, much less adapted to sudden demolitions, much better accommodated to the world as it is. And still another substantial support is this, they build on a religion and a society that are intact, and are not obliged, like our politicians, to guard against grand convulsions.

Other circumstances or traits of character are less favorable. There is a greater lack of energy in Tuscany than elsewhere. In 1859 the country furnished twelve thousand men against the Austrians,—six thousand belonging to the old army, and six thousand volunteers,— and many came back. They boast of a few heroes,

---

* See the apothecary Homais in " Madame Bovary" by G. Flaubert

individuals like M. Montanelli, always in quest of
bullets; but as to the masses discipline annoys them;
the strictness of military life takes them by surprise;
they miss their cup of coffee in the morning. In
Florence, society for the past three hundred years has
been epicurean; nobody feels uneasy on account of his
children, his relatives or anybody else; people love to
gossip and lounge about; they are *spirituel* and ego-
tistical. On getting a small income a man wraps himself up in his cloak and goes to a café to chat away the
time. On the other hand the tyranny of habit and of
the imagination is an obstacle to the formation of any
definite religious opinions. They do not see clearly
into the catholic question. No one conceives beforehand a positive personal symbol as in France in the
eighteenth century, or as in Germany in the time of
Luther; reason and conscience do not speak loud
enough. They say vaguely that catholicism should accommodate itself to modern necessities, but without
precisely defining the concessions it ought to make or
be forced to make; they do not know what might be
exacted or abandoned. They committed a grave mistake in 1859 in not instituting the civil marriage, and
in not returning to the Leopoldian laws. The Pope,
by his perseverance, had undermined or transformed
them; he could not endure by his side a true laic government. Now, with such an adversary confronting
them, it is important to decide, apart from one's self
and in advance, what one will yield if necessary and
what will be insisted on at all hazards; for his imperceptible encroachments are tenacious like those of the
ivy, and irresolution is always mastered by obstinacy.
Add to this that a notable part of the clergy, most of
the prelates, are for him; one of these, the cardinal of
Pisa, possesses all the rigidity of the middle ages and
is *papabile.*—The Italians to sum up, are in a strait.
They would like to remain good catholics, keep the

capital of the christian world amongst them, and yet
reduce the Pope to the position of the Grand Llama
without being able to see that, once despoiled, he becomes forever inimical; it is like "wedding the Grand
Turk to the republic of Venice." These are their two
weak points, a lack of the military spirit and irresolution in religious matters. Things must be left to time
and to necessity, which may strengthen one and define
the other.

CHAPTER III.

IN a city like this one wanders about for the first few
days without any plan. How can you expect one in
this medley of works and of ages to attain at once to a
definite idea? It is necessary to turn over the leaves
before reading.

. Our first visit is to the Piazza della Signoria; here,
as at Sienna, was the centre of republican life; here as
at Sienna, the old town hall, the Palazzo-Vecchio, is a
mediæval structure, an enormous block of stone pierced
with occasional trefoil windows, with a heavy cornice
of projecting battlements and flanked with a similar
high tower, a veritable domestic citadel calculated for
strife and a beacon, on the defensive near by and
visible afar off, a perfect panoply crowned with a
visible crest. It is impossible to look at it without
being reminded of the intestine wars described by
Dino Campagni. Times in Italy were rude during the
middle ages; we only had a war of castles, they had
the warfare of the streets. For thirty-three successive
years, in the thirteenth century, the Buondelmonti on
the one side with forty-two families, and the Uberti,
on the other, with twenty-two families, fought without
ceasing. They barricaded streets with chevaux-de-
frises and fortified the houses; the nobles filled the
city with their armed peasants from the country.

Finally, thirty-six palaces, belonging to the vanquished were demolished; and if the town-hall has an irregular shape, it is owing to the furious vengeance which compelled the architect to leave vacant the detested sites on which the destroyed houses stood. What would we say in these days if a battle in our streets, like that of June, lasted, not merely three days but thirty years; if irrevocable banishments deprived the nation of a quarter of its population; if the community of exiles, in league with strangers, roamed around our frontier awaiting the chances of a plot, or of a surprise, to force our walls and proscribe their persecutors in turn; if enmities and fresh strife intervened to irritate the conquerors after a victory; if the city, already devastated, was forced to constantly add to its devastations; if sudden popular tumults arose to complicate the internecine struggles of the nobles; if, every month, an insurrection caused the shops to be closed; if, every evening, a man on leaving his house, dreaded an enemy in ambush at the nearest corner? "Many of the citizens," says Dino Campagni, "having assembled one day on the square of the Frescobaldi, in order to bury a deceased woman, and, as was customary on such occasions, the citizens sitting below on rush mats and the cavaliers and doctors above on the benches, the Donati and the Cerchi sitting below facing each other, one of these, in order to arrange his mantle, or for some other reason, arose to his feet. His adversaries, suspecting something, sprang up also and drew their swords. The others did likewise, and they came to blows." Such a circumstance shows how high strung spirits were; burnished swords, ever ready, leaped of themselves out of their scabbards. On leaving the table, heated with wine and words, their hands itched. "A party of young men in the habit of galloping together, being at supper one evening in the kalends of May, became so excited that they resolved to engage

the troop of the Cerchi, and employ their hands and
arms against them. On this evening, which is the
advent of Spring, the women assemble at the halls in
their neighborhood to dance.* The young men of the
Cerchi encountered accordingly, the troop of the
Donati, which attacked them with drawn swords. And
in this encounter, Ricoverino of the Cerchi, had his
nose cut by a man in the pay of the Donati, which
person it was said was Piero Spini; ...... but the
Cerchi never disclosed his name, intending thus to
obtain *greater vengeance.*" This expression, almost
removed from our minds, is the key of Italian history ;
the *vendetta*, in Corsican fashion, is a naturalized, permanent thing between man and man, family and family,
party and party, and generation and generation. "A
worthy young man named Guido, son of Messire
Cavalcante Cavalcanti, and a noble cavalier, courteous
and brave but proud, reserved and fond of study, at
enmity with Messire Corro, had frequently resolved to
encounter him. Messire Corro feared him greatly because he knew him to be of great courage, and sought
to assassinate Guido while he was upon a pilgrimage
to St. James, which attempt failed......... Guido,
thereupon, on returning to Florence, stirred up some
of the young men against him, who promised him
their aid. And one day being on horseback with some
of the followers of the house of Cerchi and with a
javelin in his hand, he spurred his horse against
Messire Corro, thinking that he was supported by his
party, and, passing him, he threw his javelin at him
without hitting him. There was with Messire Corro
Simon, his son, a brave and bold young man, and
Cecchino dei Bardi, and likewise many others with
swords who started in pursuit of him, but not overtak-

---

* See the first act of Romeo and Juliet. Shakespeare has imagined and portrayed these customs with admirable fidelity.

ing him, they launched stones after him and also flung
them out of the windows on him so that he was
wounded in the hand." In order to find similar
practices at the present day we have to go to the
placers of San Francisco, where, at the first provoca-
tion, in public and at balls or in a café, the revolver
speaks, supplying the place of policemen and dis-
pensing with the formalities of a duel. Lynch law,
frequently applied, is alone qualified to pacify such
temperaments. It was applied now and then in
Florence, but too rarely, and in an irregular manner,
which is the reason why the custom of looking out
for one's self, of ready blows and honored and honorable
assassination prevailed there up to the end of and
beyond the middle ages. To make amends this
custom of keeping the mind always on the stretch, of
constantly occupying it with painful and tragic sentiments, rendered it so much the more sensitive to the
arts whose beauty and serenity afforded such contrasts.
This deep feudal stratum, so ploughed and broken up,
was essential in order to provide aliment and a soil for
the vivacious roots of the renaissance.

The little book in which these stories are narrated is
by Dino Campagni, a contemporary of Dante; it is
about the size of the hand, costs two francs and can be
carried about with one in the pocket. Between two
monuments, in a café, under a *loggia* one reads a few
passages—an affray, a council, a sedition—and the
mute stones speak.

But when the eye passes from the Palazzo-Vecchio
and turns to neighboring monuments there appears on
all sides a joyous aspect and a love of beauty. The
Loggia de'Lanzi on the right presents antique statues,
bold, original figures of the sixteenth century—a
"Rape of the Sabines" by John of Bologna, a
"Judith" by Donatello, and the "Perseus" of Cellini.
The latter is a Grecian ephebos, a sort of nude Mercury

of great simplicity of expression. The renaissance statuary certainly revives or continues the antique statuary, not the earliest, that of Phidias, who is calm and wholly divine, but the later, that of Lysippus who aims at the human. This Perseus is brother to the Discobulus and has had his actual anatomical model: his knees are a little heavy, and the veins of the arms are too prominent; the blood spouting from Medusa's neck forms a gross, full jet, the exact imitation of a decapitation. But what wonderful fidelity to nature! The woman is really dead; her limbs and joints have suddenly become relaxed; the arm hangs languidly, the body is contorted and the leg drawn up in agony. Underneath, on the pedestal, amidst garlands of flowers and goats' heads, in shell-shaped niches of the purest and most elegant taste, stand four exquisite bronze statuettes with all the living nudity of the antique.

I try to translate to myself this term *living*, which I find constantly on my lips, on contemplating renaissance figures. It just came into my mind on looking at the fountain of Ammanati from the other side of the palace, consisting of nude Tritons and graceful Nereids, with heads too small, and grand elongated forms in action, like the figures of Rosso and Primaticcio. Art, of course, degenerates and becomes mannered, exaggerating the prancing and the display of the limbs, and altering proportions in order to render the body more spirited and elegant. And yet these figures belong to the same family as the others, and are living, like them ; that is to say they freely and unconsciously enjoy physical existence, content in spreading out and in lifting up their legs, in falling backward and in a parade of themselves like splendid animals. The bestial Tritons are thoroughly jovial ; there could not be more honest nudity and greater effrontery without baseness. They rear up, clutch each other, and force out their

muscles ; you feel that this satisfies them, that that fine
young fellow is content to take a spirited attitude and
to hold a cornucopia ; that this nymph, undraped and
passive, does not transcend in thought her condition of
superb animality. There are no metaphysical symbols
here, no pensive expressions. The sculptor suffers his
heads to retain the simple, calm physiognomies of a
primitive organization; the body and its pose are
everything to him. He keeps within the limits of his
art ; its domain consists of the members of the body,
and he cannot after all do more than accentuate torsos,
thighs and necks ; through this involuntary harmony
of his thought and of his resources he animates his
bronze and, for lack of this harmony, we no longer
know how to do as much.

Desirous of seeing the beginnings of this renaissance
we go from the Palazzo-Vecchio to the Duomo. Both
form the double heart of Florence, such as it beat in
the middle ages, the former for politics, and the latter
for religion, and the two so well united that they
formed but one. Nothing can be nobler than the
public edict passed in 1294 for the construction of the
national cathedral. "Whereas, it being of sovereign
prudence on the part of a people of high origin to
proceed in its affairs in such a manner that the wisdom
no less than the magnanimity of its proceedings be recognized in its outward works, it is ordered that Arnolfo
master architect of our commune, prepare models or
designs for the restoration of Santa Maria Reparata,
with the most exalted and most prodigal magnificence,
in order that the industry and power of men may
never create or undertake anything whatsoever more vast
and more beautiful ; in accordance with that which
our wisest citizens have declared and counselled in
public session and in secret conclave, to wit, that no
hand be laid upon the works of the commune without
the intent of making them to correspond to the noble

soul which is composed of the souls of all its citizens united in one will." In this ample period breathes the grandiose pride and intense patriotism of the ancient republics. Athens under Pericles, and Rome under the first Scipio cherished no prouder sentiments. At each step, here as elsewhere, in texts and in monuments, is found, in Italy, the traces, the renewal and the spirit of classic antiquity.

Let us, accordingly, look at the celebrated Duomo,— but the difficulty is to see it. It stands upon flat ground, and, in order that the eye might embrace its mass it would be necessary to level three hundred buildings. Herein appears the defect of the great mediæval structure; even to-day, after so many openings effected by modern demolishers, most of the cathedrals are visible only on paper. The spectator catches sight of a fragment, some section of a wall, or the façade; but the whole escapes him; man's work is no longer proportioned to his organs. It was not thus in antiquity; temples were small or of mediocre dimensions, and were almost always erected on an eminence; their general form and complete profile could be enjoyed from twenty different points of view. After the advent of christianity men's conceptions transcended their forces, and the ambition of the spirit no longer took into account the limitations of the body. The human machine lost its equilibrium; with forgetfulness of the moderate there was established a love of the odd. Without either reason or symmetry campaniles or bell-towers were planted, like isolated posts, in front or alongside of cathedrals; there is one of these alongside of the Duomo, and this change of human equipoise must have been potent, since even here, among so many latin traditions and classic aptitudes, it declares itself.

In other respects, save the ogive arcades, the monument is not gothic but byzantine, or, rather, original; it is a creature of a new and mixed form like the new and mixed civilization of which it is the offspring. You feel power and invention in it with a touch of quaintness and fancy. Walls of enormous grandeur are developed or expanded without the few windows in them happening to impair their massiveness or diminish their strength. There are no flying buttresses; they are self-sustaining. Marble panels, alternately yellow and black, cover them with a glittering marquetry, and curves of arches let into their masses seem to be the bones of a robust skeleton beneath the skin. The Latin cross, which the edifice figures, contracts at the top, and the chancel and transepts bubble out into rotundities and projections, in petty domes behind the church in order to accompany the grand dome which ascends above the choir, and which, the work of Brunelleschi, newer and yet more antique than that of St. Peter, lifts in the air to an astonishing height its elongated form, its octagonal sides and its pointed lantern. But how can a physiognomy of a church be conveyed by words? It has one nevertheless; all its portions appearing together are combined in one chord and in one effect. If you examine the plans and old engravings you will appreciate the bizarre and captivating harmony of these grand Roman walls overlaid with oriental fancies; of these gothic ogives arranged in byzantine cupolas; of these light Italian columns forming a circle above a bordering of Grecian caissons; of this assemblage of all forms, pointed, swelling, angular, oblong, circular and octagonal. Greek and Latin antiquity, the Byzantine and Saracenic orient, the Germanic and Italian middle-age, the entire past, shattered, amalgamated and transformed, seems to have been melted over anew in the human furnace in order to flow out in fresh forms in the hands of the new genius of Giotto, Arnolfo, Brunelleschi and Dante.

Here the work is unfinished, and the success is not

complete. The façade has not been constructed: all that we see of it is a great naked, scarified wall similar to a leper's plaster. There is no light within: a line of small round bays and a few windows fill the immensity of the edifice with a gray illumination: it is bare, and the argillaceous tone in which it is painted depresses the eye with its wan monotony. A "Pieta" by Michael Angelo and a few statues seem like spectres; the bas-reliefs are only vague confusion. The architect, hesitating between mediæval and antique taste, fell only upon a lifeless light, that between a pure light and a colored light.

The more we contemplate architectural works the more do we find them adapted to express the prevailing spirit of an epoch. Here, on the flank of the Duomo, stands the Campanile by Giotto, erect, isolated, like St. Michael's tower at Bordeaux, or the tower of St. Jacques at Paris; the mediæval man, in fact, loves to build high; he aspires to heaven, his elevations all tapering off into pointed pinnacles; if this one had been finished a spire of thirty feet would have surmounted the tower, itself two hundred and fifty feet high. Hitherto the northern architect and the Italian architect are governed by the same instinct, and gratify the same penchant; but whilst the northern artist, frankly gothic, embroiders his tower with delicate mouldings and complex flower-work, and a stone lace-work infinitely multiplied and intersected, the southern artist, half-latin through his tendencies and his reminiscences, erects a square, strong and full pile, in which a skilful ornamentation does not efface the general structure, which is not a frail sculptured bijou but a solid durable monument, its coating of red, black and white marble covering it with royal luxuriance, and which, through its healthy and animated statues, its bas-reliefs framed in medallions, recalls the friezes and pediments of an antique temple. In these medallions Giotto has symbolized the principal epochs of human civilization; the traditions of Greece near those of Judea, Adam, Tubal-Cain and Noah, Dædalus, Hercules and Antæus, the invention of ploughing, the mastery of the horse, and the discovery of the arts and the sciences; laic and philosophic sentiment live freely in him side by side with a theological and religious sentiment. Do we not already see in this renaissance of the fourteenth century that of the sixteenth? In order to pass from one to the other, it will suffice for the spirit of the first to become ascendant over the spirit of the second; at the end of a century we are to see in the adornment of the edifice, in these statues by Donatello, in their *baldness* so expressive, in the sentiment of the real and natural life displayed among the goldsmiths and sculptors, evidence of the transformation begun under Giotto having been already accomplished.

Every step we take we encounter some sign of this persistency or precocity of a latin and classic spirit. Facing the Duomo· is the Baptistery, which at first served as a church, a sort of octagonal temple surmounted by a cupola, built, doubtless, after the model of the Pantheon of Rome, and which, according to the testimony of a contemporary bishop, already in the eighth century projected upward the pompous rotundities of its imperial forms. Here, then, in the most barbarous epoch of the middle ages, is a prolongation, a renewal, or, at least, an imitation of Roman architecture. You enter, and find that the decoration is not all gothic: a circle of corinthian columns of precious marbles with, above these, a circle of smaller columns surmounted by loftier arcades, and, on the vault, a legion of saints and angels peopling the entire space, gathering in four rows around a grand, dull, meagre, melancholy, Byzantine Christ. On these three superposed stories the three gradual distortions of antique art appear; but, distorted or intact, it is always antique art. A significant feature, this, throughout the history of Italy: she did not become germanic. In the tenth century the degraded Roman still subsisted distinct and intact side by side with the proud Barbarian, and Bishop Luitprand wrote: "We Lombards, as well as the Saxons, Franks, Lorranians, Bavarians, Suabians and Burgundians, so utterly despise the Roman name that, when in choler, we know not how to insult our enemies more grievously than to call them Romans, for, in this name we include whatever is base, whatever is cowardly, whatever is perfidious, the extremes of avarice and luxury, and every vice that can prostitute the dignity of human nature." *

In the twelfth century the Germans under Frederick Barbarossa, counting upon finding in the Lombards men of the same race as themselves, were surprised to find them so latinized, "having discarded the asperities of barbarian rudeness and imbibed from sun and atmosphere something of Roman finesse and gentleness, preserving the elegance of diction and the urbanity of antique customs and imitating, even to their cities and the regulation of public affairs, the ability of the ancient Romans."† Down to the thirteenth century they continue to speak latin; St. Anthony of Padua preached in latin; the people jargoning in incipient Italian, always understand the literary language‡ the same as a peasant of Berri or Burgundy whose rustic patois is no obstacle in the way of his comprehending the purer discourse of his curé. The two great feudal creations, gothic architecture and chivalric poesy, appear among them only at a late hour, and through importation. Dante states that, even in 1313, no Italian had composed a chivalric poem; those of France were translated, or were read in the Provençal

---

* Quoted by Gibbon. † Otho of Freysingen.
‡ *Litteraliter* and *sapienter* opposed to *materialiter.*

dialect. The sole gothic monuments of Italy, Assisi and the Duomo of Milan, are constructed by foreigners. Fundamentally, and under external or temporary alterations, the local latin structure remains unchanged, and in the sixteenth century the christian and feudal envelope is to drop off of itself in order to allow the reappearance of that noble and sensuous paganism which had never been destroyed.

There was no need of waiting until that time. Sculpture, which, once before under Nicholas of Pisa, had anticipated painting, again anticipated it in the fifteenth century; these very doors of the Baptistery enable one to see with what sudden perfection and brilliancy. Three men then appeared, Brunelleschi, the architect of the Duomo, Donatello, who decorated the Campanile with statues, and Ghiberti, who cast the two gates of the Baptistery,* all three friends and rivals, all three having commenced with the goldsmith's art and a study of the living model, and all three passionately devoted to the antique; Brunelleschi drawing and measuring Roman monuments, Donatello at Rome copying statues and bas-reliefs and Ghiberti importing from Greece torsos, vases and heads which he restored, imitated and worshipped. "It is impossible," said he in speaking of an antique statue, "to express its perfection by words. . . . It has infinite suavities which the eye alone cannot detect; only the touch of the hand discovers them!" And he alluded sorrowfully to the great persecutions through which under Constantine "the statues and paintings that breathe such nobleness and perfect dignity were overthrown and broken in pieces, besides the severe penalties which threatened all who undertook to make new ones, which led to the extinction of art and of the doctrines that appertain thereto." When one has such a

---

* The first born in 1377, the second in 1386, and the third in 1387.

lively sentiment of classical perfection he is not far
from attaining to it. Toward 1400, at the age of
twenty-three, after a competition from which Brunelleschi withdraws in his favor, he secures the commission
for the execution of the two doors; under his hands
we see a revival of pure Greek beauty, and not merely
a vigorous imitation of the actual body as Donatello
comprehended it, but an appreciation of ideal and perfect form. In his bas-reliefs there are numerous female
figures which in the nobleness of their shape and of
their head and in the calm simplicity and development of their attitude, seem to be Athenian masterpieces. They are not too elongated, as with Michael
Angelo's successors, or too vigorous as with the three
Graces of Raphael. His Eve, just born, bending forward and raising her large calm eyes to the Creator, is
a primitive nymph, naïve and pure, in whom appear
balanced instincts in repose and in activity at the same
moment. The same dignity and harmony regulates
the groupings and arranges the scenes. Processions
defile and turn as around a vase; individuals and
crowds are mutually opposed and related as in an antique chorus; the symmetrical forms of ancient architecture dispose around colonnades the grave, manly
figures, the falling draperies, the varied, appropriate
and moderate attitudes of the beautiful tragedy
enacted beneath its porticoes. One of the youthful
soldiers seems to be an Alcibiades; before him marches
a Roman consul; blooming young women of incomparable freshness and vigor turn half-round, gazing
and extending an arm, one of them like a Juno and another an amazon, all arrested at one of those rare moments when the nobleness of physical life attains to its
plenitude and perfection without an effort and without
reflection. When passion excites the muscles and disturbs countenances it is without deforming or dis-
torting them; the Florentine sculptor as formerly the

Grecian poet, does not allow it to pursue its course
to the end ; he subjects it to the law of proportion and
subordinates expression to beauty. , He does not wish
the spectator to be disturbed by a display of crude
violence, nor borne away by the thrilling vivacity of
impetuous action suddenly arrested. For him art is a
harmony which purifies emotion in order to render
the spirit healthy. No man, save Raphael, has more
happily found that unique moment of natural, choice
inventiveness, the precious moment when a work of art
unintentionally becomes a moral work. The "School
of Athens" and the *Loggia* of the Vatican seem to be of
the same school as the doors of the Baptistery, and, to
complete the resemblance, Ghiberti handles bronze as
if he were a painter; in abundance of figures, in the
interest of the scenes, in the grandeur of the landscapes, in the use of perspective, and in the variety and
relationship of the several planes which recede and
sink down, his sculptures are almost pictures.—But the
north wind blows amongst the masses of stones as
through a mountain defile, and when one has wielded
an opera-glass for half an hour in it he turns away,
even from Ghiberti himself, for a cup of poor coffee in
a miserable auberge.

BOOK III.

THE FLORENTINE SCHOOL OF ART.

CHAPTER I.

THE EARLY PAINTERS.— THE BYZANTINES.—CIMABUE.— GIOTTO.— FIRST EVIDENCES OF THE LAIC, ITALIAN AND PAGAN SPIRIT.— THE SUCCESSORS OF GIOTTO.—ART AT THIS EPOCH REPRE- SENTED IDEAS AND NOT OBJECTS.

April 12.—Here are five or six days passed in the Academy of the Fine Arts, at the Uffizj, in the convent of St. Mark, at Santa Croce, Santa Maria Novella and in the church of the Carmine, Vasari in hand. One may here note every step of Painting; and it is impor- tant to note them for, otherwise, in this semi-barbarous age, it has little interest.

From what low depths has it not arisen! At the Academy a St. Mary Magdalen, painted by some By- zantine artist, has shapeless feet, wooden hands, pro- jecting ears, and the figure and the pose of a mummy; her tresses, which fall to her feet, form a hairy robe, appearing at the first glance like that of a bear. The most ancient picture in the Uffizj is a Madonna by Rico of Candia, a figure apparently of gingerbread. These are sign-painters, copyists by the yard, and their sim- plicity is grotesque.

The distance between the mechanic and the artist is infinite, like that between night and day; but between night and day comes the paleness of dawn, and how- ever dim the dawn it is nevertheless daylight. Thus is it with Cimabue, who already belongs to the new order of things, for he invents and expresses; his

Madonna at the Academy, as yet somewhat lifeless, is not deficient in a certain grave benignity ; two angels below her stand in an attitude of mournful grace and meekness. Of the four old men at the bottom of the picture, two have no necks ; but you recognize in them a certain aspect of seriousness and of grandeur, one of them appearing to be attentive and surprised. An expression, even when a feeble one, is it not a miraculous thing, like the first confused stammerings of a mute on suddenly recovering his speech? We can understand how the Madonna of Santa Maria Novella, whose hands are so meagre and who seems so doleful to us, excited "the wonder of all to such a degree that they brought the King of Anjou to the studio, and all the men and women of Florence gathered there in grand festivity with a great concourse of people, and the picture was transported from Cimabue's house to the church with great pomp, and with trumpets and in solemn procession." On whatever side we study his works we find that he anticipates all subsequent innovations. He executed, says Vasari, a St. Francis after nature which was a new thing, and opposed to the system of the Greeks his masters,* who only painted according to tradition. To return to the living figure, to discover that in order to imitate the human form it is necessary to contemplate the human form, what could be simpler? And yet therein lies the gist of all art. This is perceptible in the Uffizj gallery, in a small picture representing St. Catherine in her cauldron. The muscles of the torso are indicated and the bosom is quite made out; the three women in long green robes are nobly posed. You remember the grave Madonna in the Louvre, and the grandeur, and spirited action of the angels that surround her. "Cimabue,"

---

* This refers to Byzantine painters who were the conventional artists of the day.

says a commentator on Dante, "was more noble than can be told, and, withal, so proud and disdainful, that if any one detected, or he discovered, a defect in any of his works, he immediately abandoned it however great its value." We find some traces of this proud spirit in the haughty and calm attitudes of some of his figures. A soul with a life of its own, a distinct and characteristic personality disclosing itself even in a vague mist, what a novelty! All art, its principle, its dignity, its recompense, is therein manifested—to reveal and to perpetuate a personality, that of the artist, and of this personality whatever is essential. In every degree, and in every domain, his business is to say to men, "Behold that which is in me and what I am; it is for you to contemplate, to appreciate and to appropriate whatever seems to you good!"

The second step, that taken by Giotto, is much greater, and, with due proportion, equal to that which separates Raphael from Perugino, or da Vinci from Verocchio. Alongside of him, Margheritone, maintaining traditionary practices, designedly executed ugly and sometimes hideous figures; Giotto attained to the beautiful through the lively, spontaneous invention of a complete, happy and even gay genius of the Italian order. Although born in a mystic century he is not himself mystic; and if he was the friend of Dante he did not resemble him. His, above all, was a varied, fertile, facile and richly creative nature; at Florence, Assisi, Padua, Rome, Ferrara, Rimini and Avignon are entire chapels and churches, painted by his hand. "He labored at so many works that if one were to recount them all no person would credit it." These fecund and facile genuises are inclined to joyousness and are disposed to take life easily. "He was very ingenious," says Vasari, "and very agreeable in conversation and highly skilled in sayings of wit, the meaning of which is still preserved in this city."

Those reported of him are coarse and obscene, wit, in
those days conforming to the manners and customs
which were those of peasants. Some are even tolerably religious; on explaining why, in pictures, St.
Joseph has a melancholy air, he might be taken for a
contemporary of Pulci. We discover in him the
laic spirit, sententious and even positive, satiric and
inimical to asceticism and hypocrisy. He who painted
"The Marriage of St. Francis with Poverty" ridicules
and openly rebukes the vaingloriousness and rapacity
of the monks. "For the poverty which seems deliberate and chosen," says he in his little poem, " experience plainly shows that it is practised or not according to what is in the pocket. And if it is practised
it is not to render it laudable, for there is no discern-
ment of the mind in it, nor knowledge, nor courtesy,
nor virtue. Certainly it seems to me a great shame, to
call that virtue which suppresses good; and it is evil-
doing to prefer a beastly thing to the virtues, which
bring salvation to all wise understandings, and which
are such that the more they are prized the more de-
lectable they are." Here is laic virtue, moral dignity,
and the superior culture of the intellect openly preferred to monkish rigors and christian mortifications.
Giotto, indeed, is already a thinker among other
thinkers, side by side with Guido Cavalcanti and his
father, who are reported as epicureans and fortified
with arguments against the existence of God, and
Cecco d'Ascoli and many others. "Giotto," said his
friends, " is a great master in the art of painting; he
is something more—he is master of seven liberal arts."
Accordingly we have only to look at the figures of this
Campanile to see that he is thoroughly imbued with
philosophy; that he formed for himself an idea of
universal human civilization; that, in his view, christianity was only a part of it; that Chaldea, Greece and
Rome could claim the half of it; that inventors of

useful and beautiful arts hold the first rank in it; that he considers the life, progress and happiness of man in the broad and liberal spirit of the Renaissance and of modern times; and that a free, ample and complete expansion of the natural faculties is the end to which the rest must be subordinated. As he thought so did he act. "He was very studious," says Vasari, "and always wandered about contemplating new objects and inquiring of nature, so that he merited to be called the disciple of nature and of no other. . . . . He painted divers landscapes full of trees and rocks, which was a novelty in his day." He did much more than this, and although his principal works are at Padua and at Assisi, it is easy to estimate here, by the small pictures in the Uffizj, in the Academy and in Santa Croce, the magnitude of the revolution he effected in his art. He seems to have discovered all, the ideal and nature, the nobleness of figures and the lively expression of sentiments. In his "Nativity," at the Academy, he has caught from the life the action of the kneeling shepherd, who, moved by profound respect, dares not approach nearer. In the picture of "Christ and St. Thomas" Jesus raises his arm with the most affectionate and mournful air. In the "Last Supper" Judas, who is departing abashed, is a poor dwarfed specimen of a miserly Jew; while elsewhere, amongst the hands and heads and in the attitudes, the draperies show a refinement, order and beauty approaching the breadth and dignity of the antique. "Jesus disputing with the Doctors" seems an adolescent Greek. In the "Visitation" the Virgin has a beauty, purity and meditative sentiment, which Raphael may express better but not feel more truly. The countenance of a magi king, in the softness of the eye and of the contours, is almost that of a woman. One might cite twenty others; he reveals an entire world to his contemporaries, the actual world and the superior one, and it is easy to

comprehend their astonishment, admiration and delight. For the first time they saw what man is and
what he ought to be. They were not repelled, as we
are, by the imperfections and lack of power which the
contrast of more complete works signalizes to us and
had not signalized to them. They did not notice anatomical deficiencies, the stiff legs and arms and violent
attitudes badly expressed; the apostles awkwardly
bending backward in the "Transfiguration," and the
thick necks of the "Doctors of the Temple;" that
absence of relief and incompleteness of being which
sets before the eyes not a body but the semblance of a
body. We realize the defects of imagery only in contact with painting; Raphael in the time of Giotto
would have been, like Giotto, simply an image-maker.

We went to Santa Croce, and then to Santa Maria
Novella, to see the development of this art. Santa
Croce is a church of the thirteenth century modernized
in the sixteenth, half-gothic and half-classic, austere at
first and afterward decorated, which incongruities
prevent it from being either beautiful or striking. It
is filled with tombs: Galileo, Dante, Michael Angelo,
Filicaja, Battista Alberti, Machiavelli, almost all the
great Italians, have monuments here, most of them
being modern, ostentatious and cold. That of Alfieri
by Canova shows the hand of a sculptor of the Empire,
akin to David and Girodet. The only one that makes
any impression on the mind is that of the Countess
Zamoiska, a sweet, pale, emaciated face, and a portrait
in which the sculptor has dared to be simple and sincere. There is no allegory; truth in itself is sufficiently
impressive. Life is just departed; we see her on her
couch in her invalid's costume of a cap and a long
robe gathered at the neck; a sheet covers the rest,
leaving the forms of the feet to be divined. Such is
the slumber of the peaceful dead, extended after the
last agony.

This is the church in which some small frescoes by Giotto were lately discovered beneath the plaster, the stories of John the Baptist, St. John the Evangelist and St. Francis. Are they really by him, and has the restorer been faithful? In any event they belong to the fourteenth century, and are curious. They do not lack diversity; you see a number of personages kneeling, reclining, standing, seated, bent over and in action, in short in all attitudes. The devout simplicity of the middle ages is well expressed and the rendering of sentiments is spirited. Around St. Francis, who has just expired, stand several monks with a cross and sacred banners; one of them, near his face, holds a prayer-book, while others, in order to absorb sanctity, touch the stigmata of his feet and hand, another at the same time, in his monk's zeal, pressing his hand into the wound on his flank. The latter, and the most affecting, with hands clasped and contracted visage is still speaking to him. It is an actual scene in a feudal monastery. Small figures like these, however, are not far removed from missal paintings, displaying but little more than a contour and a few shadows; everything is reduced to a general grayish tint; the figure is less a man than an indeterminate phantom of a man. If we pass on to the following generation a fresco by Taddeo Gaddi, his most celebrated pupil, is no better; the long, neckless heads of the old men are disproportioned. On coming down to the second generation the paintings by Giottino, on the gothic tomb of Bettino dei Bardi, show that art does not advance. His Christ in a red mantle appearing among angels before the armed cavalier who issues kneeling from his tomb, is, for the believer, a striking image, but an image only. Painting, indeed, seems to decline. A " Coronation of the Virgin" by Giotto, this one authentic and intact, displays on a golden background, between delicate ogives, four beautiful ideal angels at the feet of a noble and beneficent

Madonna. This search for ample and beautiful form,
this remote souvenir of healthy antique beauty is peculiar to him as to Nicholas of Pisa. His successors
have preserved his defects—feet unable to turn round,
dislocated arms and bodies scarcely corporeal—without
reproducing the images of force, happiness and serenity
first descried by him and which he alone had fixed.

On entering into the spirit of his contemporaries
we find, on the whole, a desire to see the representation
not of *beings* but of *ideas.** Cloistral mysticism and
scholastic philosophy had filled their heads with abstract formulas and exalted sentiments: if sacred and
sublime truth was indicated to them, that sufficed ;
physical form only partially interests them ; they do not
pursue it curiously and passionately for the love of it ;
they demand of it only a symbol and a suggestion.
Little does it concern them whether a wrist is fractured
or a neck badly set on its shoulders ; they are contemporary with Dante, and contemplate on their knees
this coronation of the Virgin, black like a silhouette
against the mystic radiance of aureoles and golden
backgrounds ; they feel in it the rendition of a celestial
vision, the visible embodiment of an intense reverie like
those with which the poet filled his Paradise.   Their
desire is to see, not a gladiator's breast, or the living
anatomy of an athlete, but the Church, with its trials,
hopes and triumphs ; truth in its group of sciences and
the concourse of its discoveries ; scholastic and encyclo-
pedic history ; the grand and symmetrical structure of
doctrines and experiences which St. Thomas had just
provided as a shelter for all active souls and all reflec-
tive intellects.   Understandings sublimated by theology
and reverie can neither desire nor produce other work.

---

* The analogy between this state of mind and that of modern
Germans accounts for the admiration of these pictures by the
German critics.

In painting as in poetry they are impelled to it; they are restricted to it in painting as in poesy, it being only necessary to see the cloister of Santa Maria Novella to realize the limitations and the exigencies of such preoccupations and such necessity. Taddeo Gaddi here represents philosophy, fourteen women, the seven profane sciences and the seven sacred sciences, all ranged in a straight line, each seated on a richly ornamented gothic chair, and each with the great man at her feet who acts as her interpreter; above them, in a still more delicate and elaborate chair, is St. Thomas the king of all sciences, trampling under foot the three great heretics Arius, Sabellius and Averröes, whilst on either side sit the prophets of the old and the apostles of the new Law gravely presiding with their insignia, and to whom, in the circular space around their heads, are angels, symmetrically posed, bringing books, flowers and flames. Subject, composition, architecture and characters, the entire fresco resembles the sculptured portal of a cathedral.—Quite like this and still more symbolical, is the fresco by Simone Memmi, which, opposite to it, represents the Church. The object here is to figure the entire christian establishment, and allegory is pushed even to the ludicrous. On the flank of Santa Maria di Fiore, which is the Church, the Pope, surrounded by cardinals and dignitaries, regards a community of believers at his feet in the shape of a flock of lambs reposing under the protection of a faithful dominican police. Some, the dogs of the Lord (*Domini canes*) are strangling heretical wolves. Others, preachers, are exhorting and making converts. The procession turns, and the eye following it upward, beholds the vain joys of the world, frivolous dances, and, after this, repentance and penitence; farther on the celestial gates guarded by St. Peter into which pass redeemed souls that have become young and innocent like babes; after these the thronging choir of the Blessed who continue on into heaven in the shape of angels, while the Virgin and the Lamb are surrounded by four symbolic animals, with the Father on the summit of the beam rallying and drawing to him the triumphant militant crowd ranged in successive stories from earth to Paradise.—The two pictures face each other and form a sort of abridgment of dominican theology. But this is all, and theology is not painting any more than an emblem is a bodily entity.

CHAPTER II.

April 12.—The number of painters and the talent of
this school is surprising; more than a hundred have
been enumerated,—Angiolo Gaddi, Giovanni da Milano,
Jacopo di Casentino, Buffalmaco, Pietro Laurati, and
all those I saw at Sienna; the Uffizj and the Academy
have specimens of it;—no positive shadows, no gradation of tints, no relief, imperfect perspective and
anatomy are phases common to all of them. From
1300 to 1400 there is no perceptible progress; even
according to Sacchetti the story-teller, Taddeo Gaddi,
one of the best among these painters, regarded art as
having degenerated, and as steadily degenerating every
day. At all events the noble pursuit of ideal forms
declined in order to make room for an interesting imitation of actual life, and from Giotto to Orcagna, as
from Dante to Boccaccio, the spirit fell from heaven to
earth. And therefore, thanks to this fall, another art
was springing up. "Considering," says Sacchetti,
"the present time and the conditions of human existence, so frequently visited with pestilences and sudden
deaths, and seeing what great destruction and what
vast civil and foreign wars are acclimatized here, and
meditating over the many individuals and families that
have thus sunk into poverty and misery, and with what
painful effort they endure the evils thus inflicted upon
them, and again representing to myself how many peo-

ple there are curious in novel things, and principally of
that description of reading which is easy to comprehend, and particularly where they derive comfort
therefrom, so that a little laughter may mingle with
their sorrows. . . . . . I, Franco Sacchetti, a Florentine, have proposed to myself to write these tales."
Such, substantially, is the vast change then effected in
the public mind; terrible municipal enmities had produced so much evil as to relax ancient republican
energy. After so much destruction repose was necessary. To antique sobriety and gravity succeed love of
pleasure and the quest of luxury. The belligerent
class of great nobles were expelled and the energetic
class of artisans crushed. Bourgeois rulers were to
rule, and to rule tranquilly. Like the Medicis, their
chiefs, they manufacture, trade, bank and make fortunes
in order to expend them in intellectual fashion. War
no longer fastens its cares upon them, as formerly, with
a bitter and tragic grasp ; they manage it through the
paid bands of *condottieri*, and these, as cunning traf-
fickers, reduce it to cavalcades; when they slaughter
each other it is by mistake ; historians cite battles in
which three, and sometimes only one soldier remains on
the field. Diplomacy takes the place of force, and the
mind expands as character weakens. Through this
mitigation of war and through the establishment of
principalities or of local tyrannies, it seems that Italy,
like the great European monarchies, had just attained
to its equilibrium. Peace is partially established and
the useful arts germinate in all directions upon an
improved social soil like a good harvest on a cleared
and well-ploughed field. The peasant is no longer a
serf of the glebe, but a *metayer ;* he nominates his own
municipal magistrates, possesses arms and a communal treasury; he lives in enclosed bourgs, the houses of
which, built of stone and cement, are large, convenient,
and often elegant. Near Florence he erects walls, and

near Lucca he constructs turf terraces in order to favor cultivation. Lombardy has its irrigations and rotation of crops; entire districts, now so many deserts around Lombardy and Rome, are still inhabited and richly productive. In the upper class the bourgeois and the noble labor since the chiefs of Florence are hereditary bankers and commercial interests are not endangered. Marble quarries are worked at Carrara, and foundry fires are lighted in the Maremmes. We find in the cities manufactories of silk, glass, paper, books, flax, wool and hemp; Italy alone produces as much as all Europe and furnishes to it all its luxuries. Thus diffused commerce and industry are not servile occupations tending to narrow or debase the mind. A great merchant is a pacific general, whose mind expands in contact with men and things. Like a military chieftain he organizes expeditions and enterprises and makes discoveries; in 1421 twelve young men of the first families set out for Alexandria in order to negotiate with the Sultan and found foreign agencies. Like the head of a state he conducts negotiations, enters into diplomacy, speculates on the strength of governments and on the interests of peoples; the Medicis possess sixteen banking-houses in Europe; they bind together through their business Russia and Spain, Scotland and Syria; they possess mines of alum throughout Italy, paying to the Pope for one of them a hundred thousand florins per annum; they entertain at their court representatives of all the powers of Europe and become the councillors and moderators of all Italy. In a small state like Florence, and in a country without a national army like Italy, such an influence becomes ascendant in and through itself; a control over private fortunes leads to a management of the public funds, and without striking a blow or using violence, a private . individual finds himself director of the state.

How is he to use his power? As a Rothschild of

to-day would use it; and here does the precocious conformity of this fifteenth-century civilization with our
own strikingly appear. Consider nowadays the pros-
perous and intelligent classes of Europe. How do they
regard life and order things? Not according to the military and heroic standard of ancient cities, or of the Germanic tribes; not according to the mystic and melancholy standard of the early christians, of believers in the
middle ages, or of protestants in the renaissance; not
according to the brutal, dissolute, torpid standard of
half-savage races or of the great oriental empires. We
are not anxious to become heroes or ascetics, to be oppressed or degraded. We regard ourselves as humane
and cultivated, somewhat epicurean and dilletant.
We hold the supreme end of all effort and of human
progress to be a state in which foreign or civil wars
may become rarer and rarer; in which order may be
maintained without disruption or constraint; wherein
steadily increasing comforts may be widely extended
to each and to all; where man's intellectual forces
may be constantly applied to the amelioration of his
condition and to the increase of knowledge; where,
finally, in the midst of civil security, industrial development, lasting tranquillity and universal harmony,
he may see flourish, as in a mild and equable atmosphere, the broadest spirit of investigation, the inventions of a comprehensive and tolerant mind, the delicate and superior appreciation of all human and
natural objects, philosophy, genius, and research in
literature, science and the arts. Such is the idea which
these Florentines, reared like ourselves in contact with
pacific and cosmopolitan industrial interests, begin like
ourselves to form of happiness and human culture.
For they are not simple voluptuaries or vulgar pagans; it is the whole man that they develop in man,
the intellect as well as the senses, and the intellect
above the senses. Cosmo founded an academy of

philosophy, and Lorenzo revived the platonic banquets. Landino, his friend, composes dialogues* the characters of which retiring to the convent of the Camaldoli to enjoy the cool atmosphere, discuss many days in order to decide which of the two, an active or a contemplative life, is superior. Pierro, the son of Lorenzo, institutes a discussion on true friendship in Santa Maria del Fiore, and offers a silver crown as a prize to the victor. We find in the narratives of Politian and Pic de la Mirandola that the princes of commerce and of the state in those days enjoyed speculations of a refined and superior order, lofty and broad ideas, high flights of the intellect soaring in freedom and joyousness toward elevated and distant summits. Is there a greater pleasure than conversing thus in an apartment adorned with rare busts, before the recovered manuscripts of ancient wisdom, in choice and rich language, without the restrictions of etiquette or of rank, prompted by a conciliating and generous spirit of investigation? It is the fête of the intellect; it is perfect in Lorenzo's palace, and no preconceptions of social reform, or asperities of religious polemics interfere as they do later in the eighteenth century, to disturb its poetic harmony. Instead of attacking christianity they interpret it; their tolerance is that of the contemporaries of Goethe; Marsile Ficin seems to be a Schleiermacher. Educated by Cosmo he explains to Lorenzo "that between philosophy and religion the closest relationship prevails, that, the heart and the understanding being, according to Plato, the two wings by which man ascends to his celestial home, the priest approaches him through the former, and the philosopher through the latter; that every religion contains something good; that those alone honor God truly who render him incessant homage through their actions,

---

* *Disputationes Camaldulenses*, 1468.

their goodness, their veracity, their charity, and in
efforts to attain to a luminous intelligence." Similarly to this he asserts with Plato that "the celestial
spheres are moved by spirits that turn perpetually,
ever seeking each other," and he develops a pagan
astronomy beneath a christian sky. Finally, he resolves the origin of the Word into that universal law
by which "each existence generates the seed of its
own being within itself before making itself outwardly
manifest" and, combining together philosophy, faith
and the sciences, he constructs out of these a harmonious edifice in which lay wisdom and revealed dogma
complete and purify each other, not only to furnish a
retreat and images for the ignorant many, but again to
open an aerial pathway and a boundless horizon to the
élite of the thoughtful.

Out of this leading trait others follow. What they
are in quest of is not simply pleasure, but beauty and
happiness, that is to say the expansion of noble as
well as of natural instincts. These banking magistrates
are liberal as well as capable. In thirty-seven years
the ancestors of Lorenzo expend six hundred and sixty
thousand florins in works of charity and of public
utility. Lorenzo himself is a citizen of the antique
stamp, almost a Pericles capable of rushing into the
arms of his enemy the king of Naples in order to
avert, through personal seductions and eloquence, a war
which menaces the safety of his country. His private
fortune is a sort of public treasury, and his palace a
second hotel-de-ville. He entertains the learned, aids
them with his purse, makes friends of them, corresponds with them, defrays the expenses of editions of
their works, purchases manuscripts, statues and medals,
patronizes promising young artists, opens to them his
gardens, his collections, his house and his table, and
with that cordial familiarity and that openness, sincerity
and simplicity of heart which place the protected on

a footing of equality with the protector as man to man and not as an inferior in relation to a superior. This is the representative man whom his contemporaries all accept as the accomplished man of the century, no longer a Farinata or an Alighieri of ancient Florence, a spirit rigid, exalted and militant to its utmost capacity, but a balanced, moderate and cultivated genius, one who, through the genial sway of his serene and beneficent intellect, binds up into one sheaf all talents and all beauties. It is a pleasure to see them expanding around him. On the one hand writers are restoring and, on the other, constructing. From the time of Petrarch greek and latin manuscripts are sought for, and now they are to be exhumed in the convents of Italy, Switzerland, Germany and France. They are deciphered and restored with the aid of the savants of Constantinople. A decade of Livy or a treatise by Cicero, is a precious gift solicited by princes; some learned man passes ten years of travel in ransacking distant libraries in order to find a lost book of Tacitus, while the sixteen authors rescued from oblivion by the Poggios are counted as so many titles to immortal fame. A king of Naples and a Duke of Milan select Humanists for their chief councillors, and wherever in contact with this reconquered antiquity the scholastic rust vanishes. A fine latin style again flourishes almost as pure as in the times of Augustus. On passing from the painful hexameters and heavy pretentious epistles of Petrarch to the elegant distich of Politian or, to the eloquent prose of Valla, one feels himself stirred as if by an almost sensuous delight. The mouldy and abortive fruits of the middle ages, soured by feudal frosts, or rotted by the close atmosphere of cloisters, suddenly become ripe and of delicious flavor. The fingers and the ear involuntary scan the easy march of poetic dactyls and the ample flow of oratorical periods. Style again becomes noble and at the same time clear, and the health, joy and serenity diffused through antique life re-enters the human mind with the harmonious proportions of language and the measured graces of diction. From refined language they pass to vulgar language, and the Italian is born by the side of the latin.

In this renewed spring Lorenzo di Medici is the first poet, and in him first appears not only the new style, but the new spirit. If he imitates Petrarch in his sonnets, and perpetuates the sighs of ancient chivalric love, he portrays in his pastorals, satires and verses for private circulation, a refined philosophic life, the graceful charms of classic landscape, the delicate enjoyments of eye and intellect, ·whatever he loves and those around him love, his poetry, through an easy rich and simple development, testifying to a sure hand, an adult century and a complete art.

Out of this rich harmony rises a joyous strain, that of the epoch, and which indicates the fatal declivity to which they are tending. Lorenzo himself amuses the crowd and composes for it the plan and triumphs of the carnival. "How beautiful is youth!" say the singers in his "Triumph of Bacchus and Ariadne." "But youth flies; let him who seeks happiness be happy to-day, for there is no certainty in the morrow." Here, in the restored paganism, shines out epicurean gaiety, a determination to enjoy at any and all hours, and that instinct for pleasure which a grave philosophy and political sobriety had thus far tempered and restrained. With Pulci, Berni, Bibiena, Ariosto, Bandelli, Aretino, and so many others, we soon see the advent of voluptuous debauchery and open skepticism, and later a cynical unbounded licentiousness. These joyous and refined civilizations based on a worship of pleasure and intellectuality—Greece of the fourth century, Provence of the twelfth, and Italy of the sixteenth—were not enduring. Man in these lacks some checks. After

sudden outbursts of genius and creativeness he wanders away in the direction of license and egotism ; the
degenerate artist and thinker makes room for the sophist
and the dilletant. But in this transient brilliancy his
beauty was charming, and following ages, less brilliant
externally although firmer on their foundations, cannot
refrain from sympathetically gazing on the harmonious
edifice whose elegance no effort of theirs can revive and
whose finesse condemned it to fragility.

It is in this world, again become pagan, that painting
revives, and the new tastes she is to gratify show beforehand the road she is to follow ; henceforth she is to
decorate the houses of rich merchants who love antiquity and who desire to live daintily. With the direction the point of departure is already traced ; the goldsmith's art furnishes it ; through the small dimensions
of his works the goldsmith is the natural ministrant to
private luxury ; he chases arms, plate, bedposts, chim-
ney-piers and the ornamentation of buffets. All
jewelry and gems issue from his hand, and, like bronze
and silver, he works in wood, marble, stucco and precious
stones ; there is nothing appertaining to the embellishment of domestic life that does not stimulate his talent
or develop his art. This art moreover, through its precocious maturity, outran all the others. Nicholas of
Pisa, in the middle of the thirteenth century already
sculptures small figures which, in their gravity, beauty,
noble expression and solid structure, recall a virile antiquity and announce a virile renaissance. Through a
unique privilege sculpture, at its very first step, found
complete models in the relics of Greece and Rome, and
at the same time complete instruments in the founder's
furnace and the mason's mallet ; whilst painting, poorly
guided and poorly provided, had to wait until the slow
progress of centuries could free perfect corporeal forms
from the disturbed visions of the middle ages, until a
revival of geometrical studies could teach perspective,

and until the educated eye and professional experiments could introduce the use of oil and gradations of color. Hence it is, in the new race about to be run, that the elder sister surpassed and instructed the younger. Toward 1400 Ghiberti, Donatello and Jacopo della Quercia are adults, and the works they produce during the twenty following years are either so full of life, so pure, so expressive or so grand that art is not to go beyond it. All are goldsmiths and all issue from a workshop; Brunelleschi himself, their master, began there; it is in this shop that is formed the new generation of painters. Paolo Uccello worked in it under Ghiberti; Mazzolino acquired in it the reputation of a skilful polisher and excellent in modelling the folds of drapery. Pollaiolo, the pupil of Ghiberti's father-in-law and then of Ghiberti himself executed a quail on the doors of the Baptistery which "only had to fly." Dello, Verocchio, Ghirlandaio, Botticelli, Francia, and later Andrea del Sarto, with all the sculptors who make their debut in the goldsmith's art, Lucca della Robbia, Cellini, Bandinelli and—how many more might I name! Those who did not file bronze felt, nevertheless the ascendancy of the workers in bronze; Masaccio, the friend of Donatello, studied under Brunelleschi; Leonardo da Vinci in the studio of Verocchio, modelled clay statuettes and then draped them with wet linen in order to draw them afterward and imitate their relief. Through such practices and such an education, the hands thus manipulating forms imbibed the sentiment of solid substance and carried this sentiment into painting. Henceforth the painter feels that a flat image is not a body. It is essential that a figure should have something within it as well as without it, that behind external appearance and superficial color the spectator should feel depth, fulness, flesh, bones, middle distances, backgrounds, firmness of posture, actual spaces and exact proportions. He traces his lines, studies his perspective, undrapes bodies, marks the muscles, feels their joints, lifts them up and dissects them, and at length, master of every process by which superficial color affords the eye the sensation of living substance, he places art on its enduring foundation, the exact and complete imitation of nature as the artist sees nature and as nature is.

Nature, indeed, as he sees her and as she is, is henceforth to interest men. Liberated from the celestial world and brought back to the natural world, they are no longer to contemplate ideas or symbols but persons and existences. For them actual objects are no longer a simple sign through which flashes mystic thought; they have a beauty and value of their own, and the age that fixes itself on them no longer leaves them in order to gaze beyond. Thus exalted and ennobled they merit representation without suppression; their proportions and forms, the minutest details of aspect and situation assume importance, and the picturesque infidelity of the artist would now be as offensive as would have been formerly the theological infidelity of the christian. In this imitation of sensible appearances the first point is a knowledge of the dimensions of objects as affected by remoteness; their size varies to the eye according to distance, and the truth of the whole is the indispensable foundation on which is to be placed the truth of detail. Paolo Uccello, instructed by the mathematician Manetti, promulgates the laws of perspective and passes his life fanatically developing the results of his invention. Everybody is astonished and delighted at comprehending for the first time through him the veritable outward phases of objects, to see a vanishing ditch, avenue or the furrows of a ploughed field, to measure the distance separating two figures, to feel the foreshortening of a man's body reclining feet foremost, to detect the innumerable and rigorously defined changes which the slightest variation of distance imparts to the forms and dimensions of a figure. But

he goes further and peoples this nature of which he
has re-established the proportions. He conceives an
affection for all sorts of living creatures, and through
him we see entering within the circle of human sympathy, dogs, cats, bulls, serpents, lions, "ready to bite and
full of haughtiness," deer and fawns "expressing velocity and fear," birds with their plumage, fish with their
scales, all with their own forms and peculiarities, formerly overlooked or despised, but now discovered and
reanimated; they are still distinguishable in his faded
frescoes of Santa Maria Novella and public taste follows
him in the path he marked out. He paints in the
houses of the Medicis stories of animals, in those of the
Peruzzi the figures of the four elements, each with an
appropriate animal, a mole, a fish, a salamander and
a chameleon. Henceforth everybody desires to contemplate in his house the living images of the human
and of the natural world. The cornices of apartments,
the wood-work of bedsteads, huge chests for keeping
clothing are all painted with "fables from the works of
Ovid and other poets or with stories narrated by the
greek and latin historians; and similarly, jousts, hunting parties and tales of love . . . . fêtes, spectacles of
the day and other like subjects according to each man's
taste." They were to be found in the dwelling of Lorenzo di Medici and also in the noblest mansions of
Florence. "Dello thus painted for Giovanni di Medici
the entire garniture of a chamber, and Donatello modelled for him the gilded stucco of the surrounding frames.
The anatomists are coming to spread through the
houses, side by side with antique nudities, the excited
and muscular nudities of the new art, all those bold and
sensual effigies that are so obnoxious to the rigorism
of Savonarola. What a distance between this social
condition and that of the contemporaries of Dante, and
how plainly does worldly paganism in life begin with
picturesque paganism in art!

CHAPTER III.

WHAT conception of man is now to be developed, and what corporeal type is it which everywhere repeated is going to cover the walls? One there is which is to reign more than half a century and, until the advent of Leonardo da Vinci, Raphael and Michael Angelo, bind together into one sheaf the most diverse talents. This is the actual personage, the contemporary Florentine figure, a body undraped as it is presented in the living model, man exactly reproduced through literal imitation and not transformed through ideal conceptions. When actual life is for the first time recognized, and penetrating into its structure, the admirable mechanism of its parts is understood, this contemplation suffices and nothing more is desired. There are so many things in a body and in a head! Each irregularity, an elongation of the neck, a contraction of the nose, a peculiar curl of the lip, forms a part of the individual; to improve these would be to mutilate him: he would no longer be the same but another; the relationship which exists between this irregularity and the rest is so strong that it could not be dissolved without marring the whole. The personage is a unit and it can only be expressed by a *portrait.* Hence the portraits which the frescoes of the time display in lines and in groupings in the churches, and not merely portraits of the face but again portraits of the body. The anatomist-goldsmith Pollaiolo or Verocchio places

a nude subject on a table, removes the skin and notes
in his memory the projections of the bones, the expansion of the muscles and the interlacing of the tendons,
and then with lights and darks, he transfers the model
to canvas as he would have transfixed it in bronze
by reliefs and depressions. If you were to say to him
that this clavicle was too prominent, that that section of
the skin ridged with muscles resembled a coil of rope,
that these gladiators' and centaurs' masks had the repulsive ugliness of vulgar features convulsed and distorted by orgie and scuffle he would not comprehend
you. He would point to some workman, to a passing
figure, in the first place to his subject, especially the
flayed one, and he would reply, or feel, that to embellish life was to falsify life. It is just these folds of
the features, these dry angles of raised and intersecting muscles which interest him; his modeller's or
chaser's thumb buries itself into them and he imagines the contact; they harbor the active, accumulated
force which is about to concentrate and expend itself
in blows; they cannot be too boldly shown; in his eyes
they constitute the entire man. Luca Signorelli,
having lost a beloved son, has the body stripped and
minutely draws every muscle in order the better to
preserve him in his memory. Nanni Grosso, dying in
a hospital, refused a crucifix offered to him demanding
to have one by Donatello brought to him, declaring
that, otherwise, "he would die unredeemed, so dis-
pleasing to him were the badly executed works of his
art." Anatomical form is so impressed on their minds
that the human being in whom they do not feel it
seems to them empty and unsubstantial. An omo-
plate, a muscle gives them transports of pleasure.
"Know," says Cellini later, "that the five false ribs form
around the navel, as the torso bends backward or forward, a multitude of reliefs and depressions which are
among the principal beauties of the human body . . . . .

Thou wilt delight in drawing the vertebræ, for they are magnificent . . . . Thou wilt then draw the bone placed between the two hips; it is very fine and is called the crupper or sacrum . . . . . The important point in the art of drawing is to draw well a naked man or a naked woman." This is readily apparent in their works. In the "St. Sebastian" of Pollaiolo the interest of the subject no longer centres on the martyr but on the executioners. With the artist as with them the main thing is to properly transfix the patient. To this end six men leaning forward or bending back, all only two paces off so as not to miss the mark, string or draw their arbaletes, with half-open mouths through excess of attention, their brows frowning as the shot is made, and their legs extended and widened in order to steady their hands; the painter thought of nothing but of displaying bodies and attitudes. His brother Piero, in a similiar way at San Giminiano has put into a "Coronation of the Virgin" four tawny emaciated saints for no other purpose than to display their veins, muscles and tendons. Similarly, again, Verocchio in his "Baptism of Christ" at the Academy, displays an old dry wrinkled figure of Christ, an angular St. John and a gruff, melancholy angel in striking contrast to the handsome youth, half inclining, which his young pupil Leonardo da Vinci has placed in one corner as if the sign and dawn of a perfect art. Not only the anatomist, the amateur of the real, the plaster modeller of the naked figure, but again the goldsmith, the chaser of bronze and the cutter of marble are visible in all these figures. As soon as one imagines them cast in metal they appear beautiful. The draperies, in rigid and broken folds, would be suitable in an ornamental statuette. The action too stiff, and the attitude too forced, would be proper in a statue. A small "Hercules" by Pollaiolo in the Uffizj, with its muscles strained and swollen from foot to head in order to overpower

Antæus whom he clasps and is crushing, would be a
masterpiece if it were only in bronze. The sharp
elbows and knees would not be noticed, or the hardness of its outlines and its monotonous color; one
would be sensible of nothing but the torsion of the
frame and the furious energy of the effort. In this
limited field, and under its mistress, sculpture, painting progresses, still rigid and fettered, and is seen to
take the lead but once.

It is in the hands of Masaccio, a young man born
with the century who died at the age of twenty-six,
that she takes this great step; people at the present day
still go to the Brancacci chapel to contemplate this
isolated creator whose precocious example no one followed. Not only did he die too young, but again he
was indifferently appreciated during his life, "to such
an extent," says Vasari, "that no inscription was placed
on his tomb." In order to become the head of a school
and direct public taste, it is essential to be not merely
a great artist but again a skilful politician and a man
of the world. Masaccio was so poorly qualified for
self-advancement that he received no commission from
the Medicis. "He always lived self-concentrated,"
says Vasari, "neglecting everything else, as one who,
having fixed his whole mind and will on things of art,
thought little of himself and still less of others . . . . .
never disposed in any respect to dwell on the cares and
objects of this world, not even on his own clothing . . . . .
demanding money of his debtors only when pressed by
urgent necessities." Living in this way one may get
to have talent but not authority, and produce masterpieces without securing preachers to extol them.
Among the first he studied nudity and foreshortening,
scrupulously observing perspective and familiarizing his
hand with difficulties, thoroughly imbued with the sentiment of the real, "regarding painting as no other
than a reproduction from life of nature's objects by

means of color and drawing, and continually laboring to
make figures as living as possible in the imitation of
truth." Besides these gifts, which he held in common
with his contemporaries, he had another peculiar to himself, and which carried him higher. There is a picture
by him in the Uffizj gallery of an old man in a cap
and gray robe, with a wrinkled face and a somewhat
mocking expression; it is a portrait but not an ordinary
portrait; he copies the real, but it is copied *grandly*.
Such is the idea, or rather a faint idea of him, which
one bears with him into this Brancacci chapel, covered
by him with paintings. All, however, are not by his
hand; Masolino began and Filippino completed some
of them: but the portions painted by Masaccio can be
distinguished without much trouble; whether the three
artists are linked together by secret conformity of feeling, or the latter has adhered to the cartoons of the
second, the work in its different dates only indicates
the different courses of the same spirit.

What first strikes one is that they all set out from
the real, that is to say, from the living individual as
the eyes behold him. The baptized young man whom
Masaccio shows naked, shivering as he comes out of
the water, is a contemporary bather who has taken a
dip in the Arno on too cold a day. And likewise his
Adam and Eve driven from Paradise are Florentines
whom he has undraped, the man with slim thighs and
blacksmith's shoulders, the woman with a short neck
and clumsy form, and both with ugly-shaped legs: they
are artisans or ordinary people who have not led, like
the Greeks, a naked existence, and whose bodies have
not been fashioned by gymnastics. Similarly again
the resuscitated child by Lippi, kneeling before the
apostle, has the meagre boniness and spindling limbs
of a modern infant. And, finally, almost all the heads
are portraits; two cowled friars on the left of St. Peter
are monks leaving their convent. We know the names

of the contemporaries who loaned him their heads:
Bartolo di Angiolino Angioli, Granacci, Soderini, Pulci,
Pollaiolo, Botticelli, Lippi, himself; so that this art
seems to have owed its being to surrounding life, as
plaster applied to the face repeats the modelling of the
forms it is subjected to.

How is it then that these personages live with a superior
life? How does it happen that an exact imitation of
the real is not a servile imitation of it? And how did
Masaccio abstract noble personages from ordinary personages? Because in a multitude of observable details
he eliminated some of more importance than others, and
subordinated the rest to these. Because he distinguished, in the elements of the body and the head, different
values, and effaced or diminished the least in order to
augment and render prominent the greatest. Because,
having before him a nude man and woman when painting this Eve and this Adam, this baptized young man and
the rest, he did not adhere to the innumerable and infinite distinctions of color and form throughout. Because
this or that flabby stomach, or foot spoiled by its shoe,
or minute protuberance of a cartilage or bone did not
seem to him the essential of man. And, indeed, the
essential is elsewhere; it is in the solidity of the bony
structure, in the setting of the muscles and tendons, in
the present and possible action of balanced members,
in the universal quivering of the skin over contracting
flesh, in the impulse and general dilation of animal activity. The nude or the flayed model only served him
as an indication; he laid up details in his memory not
to repeat them as from a manual but to comprehend
their attachments and dependencies, and make their
functions and vitality realized. It is the same in this
respect with the face as with the body. That which
marks distinctions between contemporary heads, that
which distinguishes merchant from merchant, or monk
from monk, that which is accidental in each, the special

deformity or grimace stamped by habits of late hours
or of big dinners;—what heed can I give to these?
What concerns me and is of consequence is the grand
dominant passion, the proclivity and leading intellectual
character, and especially whatever is energetic, decided, peculiar to action or to thought, to calculation or
to resistance. What I desire to see is the grand lines
of physical structure as of moral structure. The rest is
secondary in life as in painting, and hence it is
that this painting although based upon the real
attains to the ideal. It copies individuals but only
that which is general in them; it leaves to heads
their originality and to bodies their imperfections,
but it makes character prominent in the heads and
life in the bodies. It abandons the flat and scrupulous style in order to enter upon the broad and simple style. Sometimes, indeed, carried away by
its impetus, it fully attains to it. Several figures,
through their severe grandeur, through the gravity of
their countenances, through their vigorous chins seem
to be antique consular characters. St. Peter heal-
ing the sick with his shadow walks with royal
energy like a Roman accustomed to lead multitudes;
Jesus paying tribute is as noble and calm as one of
Raphael's heads, and nothing is more beautiful than
these grand compositions of forty personages, all simply
draped, all grave and severe, all in different attitudes,
all ranged around the nude infant and St. Paul who
raises it up, between two masses of architecture and
before a decorated wall, a silent assembly framed upon
both flanks by two distinct groups, one of accidental
gazers, the other of kneeling men, corresponding to
each other and through their graduated harmony adding a richer fulness to this ample symphony.

Unfortunately they did not maintain themselves on
the heights they reached. Artists are still too absorbed
by the new discovery and the minute observation of

the real to lift their eyes upward. Their hands are not
free. In every art it is necessary to linger long over
the true in order to attain to the beautiful. The eye
fixing itself on an object, begins by noting details with
an excess of precision and fulness; it is only later, when
the inventory is complete, that the mind, master of its
wealth, rises higher in order to take or neglect what
suits it. The leading master of this epoch is Fra Filippo
Lippi, a curious, exact imitator of actual life; pushing
the finish of his works so far that, according to a contemporary, an ordinary painter might labor five years
day and night without succeeding in reproducing one of
his pictures; selecting for his figures short and round
heads, personages somewhat gross, virgins who are good,
simple lasses quite remote from the sublime, and angels
resembling stout and chubby school or choir boys,
somewhat vulgar and obstinate. At the same time,
however, he aims at relief, defines contour, makes the
petty details of a vestment wall or halo advance and
recede with that vigorous and accurate drawing which
conveys to the eye the sensation of a corporeal object
definitely placed and perfect. Otherwise, he is adapted in morals as well as in talent, to the spirit of the
time,—highly popular, greatly admired, impetuous,
jovial, a favorite of the Medicis and protected by them
in his freaks; he elopes with a nun although a monk;
he jumps from a window in order to find his mistress;
he is " extraordinarily lavish in love matters devoting
himself to them unceasingly, never stopping even up to
his death," at which his protectors " laugh," declaring
that rare geniuses must be pardoned, " because they are
celestial essences and not beasts of burden."

Although this imitation in which the Florentine
painters delight is too literal, it has, on the whole, a
special grace. It is necessary to visit the church of
Santa Maria Novella in order to appreciate its charm.
There, Ghirlandaijo, the master of Michael Angelo, has

covered the choir with his frescoes. They are poorly
lighted and awkwardly piled up on top of each other;
but toward midday they can be seen. They represent
the story of St. John the Baptist and the Virgin, the
figures being half the size of life. Through education
as well as instinct this painter, like his contemporaries,
is a copyist. He sketched people while passing his
goldsmith's shop and the resemblance of his figures
excited admiration. He regarded "painting as wholly
consisting of drawing." Man, to the artists of this
epoch, is still only a form; but he had so just a sentiment of this form, and of all forms, that on copying
the Roman amphitheatres and triumphal arches, he
drew them as accurately with the eye as if with a com-
pass. Thus prepared one can readily see what speaking, striking portraits he put into his frescoes; there
are twenty-one of these, representing persons whose
names are known, Christoforo Landini, Ficin, Politian,
the bishop of Arezzo, others of women—that of the
beautiful Ginevra de' Benci, all belonging to families
controlling the patronage of the chapel. The figures
are a little commonplace; several of them are hard and
have sharp noses, and are too literal; they lack grandeur, the painter keeping near the ground, or only cau-
tiously flying above the surface; it is not the bold
flight of Masaccio. Nevertheless he composes groups
and architecture, he arranges figures in circular sanctuaries, he drapes them in a half-Florentine half-Grecian
costume which unites or opposes in happy contrasts and
graceful harmonies, the antique and the modern; above
all this he is simple and sincere. An attractive moment this, a delicate aurora consisting of that youthfulness of spirit in which man first recognizes the poesy
of reality. At such a time he traces no line that does
not express a personal sentiment; whatever he relates
he has experienced; as yet there is no accepted type
which bodies forth in conventional beauty the budding

aspirations of his breast; the greater his timidity the more vivacious he is, and the forms somewhat dry on which he leans are the discreet confessions of a new spirit which dares neither to escape from nor reserve itself. One might pass hours here in contemplating the figures of the women; they are the flower of the city in the fifteenth century; we see them as they lived, each with her original expression and the charming irregularity of real life; all with those half-modern half-feudal Florentine features so animated and so intelligent. In the "Nativity of the Virgin" the young girl in a silk skirt, who comes in on a visit, is the plain demure young lady of good condition; in the "Nativity of St. John" another, standing, is a medieval duchess; near her the servant bringing in fruits, in statuesque drapery, has the impulse, vivacity and force of an antique nymph, the two ages and the two orders of beauty thus meeting and uniting in the simplicity of the same true sentiment. A fresh smile rests on their lips; underneath their semi-immobility, under these remains of rigidity which imperfect painting still leaves, one can divine the latent passion of an intact spirit and a healthy body. The curiosity and refinement of ulterior ages have not reached them. Thought, with them, slumbers; they walk or look straight before them with the coolness and placidity of virginal purity; in vain will education with all its animated elegancies rival the divine uncouthness of their gravity.

This is why I so highly prize the paintings of this age; none in Florence have I studied more. They are often deficient in skill and are always dull; they lack both action and color. It is the renaissance in its dawn, a dawn gray and somewhat cool, as in the spring when the rosy hue of the clouds begins to tinge a pale crystal sky, and when, like a flaming dart the first ray of sunshine glides over the crests of the furrows.

It lasts even after great genius has arisen above the
horizon.   Amidst the illuminated campagna one distinguishes a sort of valley in which the inanimate forms
of the ancient style are still perpetuated. Roselli,
Piero di Cosimo, Credi and Botticelli do not desire to
leave it; they retain dry outlines, feeble color, and
irregular, ungracious figures—the scrupulous imitation
of the real; their development is on another side, Botticelli especially, through the expression of deep and
fervid sentiment, through tenderness and humility,
through the intense morbid reverie of his pensive virgins, through frail emaciated forms, through the quivering delicacy of his nude Venuses, through the suffering and writhing beauty of his precocious and nervous creatures, all soul and all spirit, who portend the
infinite but are not sure of living. There is similar
merit in all the masters of this period, Mantegna, Pinturicchio, Francia, Signorelli, and Perugino; each one
invents for himself; each marks out his own path and
follows his own inspiration.   Let his path be a narrow
one and let him stumble occasionally, it is of little consequence; his steps are his own, his inspiration comes
from himself and not from another. Later, painters
are to do better, but they will be less original; they
will advance faster, but in a troop ; they will go farther,
but in the hands of the great masters. To my eyes
disciplined thought is not the equivalent of free
thought; what I penetrate to in a work of art, as in
every other work, is the state of the soul that produced
it. In setting up a standard, even without reaching
it, one lives more nobly and more manfully than in ac-
quiring one he has not himself created. Henceforward
all talent is to be mastered by genius, and artists are
to become less as art becomes greater.

CHAPTER IV.

April 13.—What commotion and what travail in this fifteenth century! In the midst of this pagan tumultuous hive there stands a tranquil convent wherein sweetly and piously dreams a mystic of ancient days, Fra Angelico da Fiesole.

This convent remains almost intact; two square courts in it expose their files of small columns surmounted by arcades, with their little old tile roofs. In one of the rooms is a sort of memorial or genealogical tree, bearing the names of the principal monks who have died in the odor of sanctity. Among these is that of Savonarola, and mention is made of his having perished through false accusation. Two cells are still shown which he inhabited. Fra Angelico lived in the convent before him, and paintings by his hand decorate the chapter-hall, the corridors and the gray walls of the cells.

He had dwelt a stranger in the world, and maintained amidst fresh sensations and curiosities the innocent, ravished life in God which the "Fioretti" describe. He lived in a state of primitive simplicity and obedience; it is said of him that "one morning being invited to breakfast by Pope Nicholas V. his conscience forbade him to eat meat without the permission of his prior, never reflecting that the Pope's authority was superior." He refused the dignities of his order, and concerned himself only with prayer and penitence. "When any work was required of him he would answer with singular goodness of heart that they must go and ask the prior, and if the prior wished it he would not fail them." He never desired to paint any but the saints, and it is narrated of him that "he never took up his brushes without kneeling in prayer, and never painted a Christ on the cross without his eyes being filled with tears." It was his custom not to retouch or recast any of his pictures, but to let them remain as they first left his hand, "believing that they were as they were through the will of God." We can well understand why such a man did not study anatomy or contemporary models. His art is primitive like his life. He began with missals and so continued on the walls; gold, vermilion, bright scarlet, brilliant greens, the illuminations of the middle ages display themselves on his canvases the same as on old parchments. He even sometimes applies them to the roofs; an infantile piety is eager to decorate its saint or idol and render it radiant to excess. When he abandons small figures and composes on a grand scale a scene of twenty personages, he falters;* his figures are bodiless. Their affecting devotional expression is inadequate to animate them; they remain hieratic and stiff; all he comprehended was their spirit. That which he paints understandingly, and which he has everywhere repeated, are visions and the visions of blessed and innocent spirits. "Grant, O most sweet and loving Jesus, that I may rest in Thee above all living creatures, above all health and beauty, all glory and honor......all gifts and presents that Thou canst bestow and diffuse, all joy and gladness that the soul can feel and can cherish.......In my God do I find all things........What do I desire more, and what greater happiness? God is my all. This sufficeth for him that understandeth; and to repeat it often is sweet to him that loveth.........When

---

* A Christ and seventeen saints in the convent of San Marco.

Thou art present all things yield delight; but when Thou art absent all is pain. Thou givest a tranquil heart, then bringest perfect peace and joy."*

Such adoration as this is never unaccompanied by inward images; with closed eyes they are persistently followed, and without effort, as in a dream. Like a mother who, on finding herself alone, sees floating in memory the features of a beloved son, like a chaste poet who, in midnight silence, imagines and again sees the downcast eyes of his beloved, so does the heart involuntarily summon up and contemplate the concourse of divine figures. No object disturbs him in this peaceable contemplation. Around him all actions are prescribed and all objects are colorless; day after day uniform hours bring before him the same white walls, the same dark lustre of the wainscoting, the same straight folds of cowls and frocks, the same rustling of steps passing to and fro between refectory and chapel. Delicate, indeterminate sensations vaguely arise in this monotony, while tender reverie, like a rose sheltered from life's rude blasts, blooms afar from the great highway clattering with human footsteps. There is displayed to the eye the magnificence of eternal day, and henceforth every effort of the painter centres on expressing it. Glittering staircases of jasper and amethyst rise above each other up to the throne on which sit celestial beings. Golden aureoles gleam around their brows; red, azure and green robes, fringed, bordered and striped with gold, flash like glories. Gold runs in threads over baldachins, accumulates in embroideries on copes, radiates like stars on tunics and gleams from tiaras, while topazes, rubies and diamonds sparkle in flaming constellations on jewelled diadems.† All is light; it is the out-

---

* From the "Imitation of Jesus Christ."

† See "The Coronation of the Virgin" in the Louvre, and the twelve angels around the infant Jesus in the Uffizj.

burst of mystic illumination. Through this prodigality of gold and azure one tint prevails, that of the sun and of paradise. This is not common daylight; it is too brilliant; it effaces the brightest hues, it envelops forms on all sides; it weakens and reduces them to mere shadows. In fact the soul is everything; ponderable matter becomes transfigured; its relief is no longer perceptible, its substance having evaporated; nothing remains but an ethereal form which swims in azure and in splendor. At other times the blessed approach paradise over luxuriant meadows strewn with red and white flowers, and under beautiful blooming trees; angels conduct them, and, hand in hand, they form fraternally a circle; the burden of the flesh no longer oppresses them; their heads starred with rays they glide through the air up to the flaming gate from which issues a golden illumination; Christ, aloft, within a triple row of angels pressed together like flowers, smiles upon them beneath his aureole. Such are the delights and the radiance that Dante has portrayed.

His personages are worthy of their situation. Although beautiful and ideal his Christ, even in celestial triumph, is pale, pensive and slightly emaciated; he is the eternal friend, the somewhat melancholy consoler of the "Imitation," the poetic merciful Lord as the saddened heart imagines him; he is not the over-healthy figure of the renaissance painters. His long curling tresses and blonde beard sweetly surround his features; sometimes he smiles faintly, while his gravity is never dissociated with affectionate benignity. At the day of judgment he does not curse; only on the side of the damned his hand falls, while on the right, toward the blessed, toward those whom he loves, his full regards are turned. Near him the Virgin, kneeling with downcast eyes, seems to be a young maiden that has just communed. Occasionally her head is too large as is

common with the inspired; her shoulders are narrow
and her hands too small; the spiritual, inward life, too
highly developed, has reduced the other; the long blue
mantle wrought in gold in which she is wholly enveloped, scarcely allows it to be supposed that she has a
body.   No one can imagine before having seen it such
immaculate modesty, such virginal candor; by her side
Raphael's virgins are merely simple vigorous peasant
girls.   And the other figures are of the same order.
Every expression is based on two sentiments, the innocence of the calm spirit preserved in the cloister,
and the rapture of the blessed spirit that sees God.
The saints are portraits, but refined and beatified; celestial transfiguration eliminates from the body as
from the soul the ideal portion concealed and
transformed by the grossness of terrestrial being.
No wrinkles appear on the countenances of the aged;
they bloom afresh under the touch of eternal youth.
No traces of physical austerity are visible; they have
entered into the realm of pure felicity.   The features
of the blessed are in repose, we feel that they rest passive suspended in ecstasy; to move, to disturb a fold of
their drapery would endanger some part of the vision;
they turn their eyes to the heights above without bending their bodies; they are wrapt in meditation in order the
better to enjoy their beatitude; they speak like the disciples of the Evangelist, "Lord, it is good for us to be
here; if thou wilt, let us make here three tabernacles;
one for thee, and one for Moses, and one for Elias."   A
few, the disciples, seem to be juvenile choristers, monastic novices imbued with a spirit of veneration, and
timid.   On seeing the infant Jesus they give way to a
movement of infantile sprightliness and then, fearful of
having done something wrong, hesitate and draw back.
There are no violent or eager emotions in this world; all is
partially veiled or arrested midway by the tranquillity

or the obedience of the cloister. But the most charming figures are those of the angels. We see them kneel down in silent rows around thrones or press together in garlands in the azure. The youngest are amiable, candid children, with minds unruffled by a suspicion of evil; they do not think much; each head, in its golden circle, smiles and is happy; it will smile forever, and this is its entire life. Others with flamboyant wings, like birds of paradise, play on instruments or sing, and their countenances are radiant. One of them, raising his trumpet to put it to his lips, stops as if surprised by a resplendent vision. This one with a violincello to his shoulder seems to muse over the exquisite tones of his own instrument. Two others with joined hands seem to be contemplating and adoring. One, quite youthful, with the full figure of a young girl, bends forward, as if to listen before striking her cymbal. To the harmony of tones must be added the harmony of colors. Tints do not increase or decrease in strength and intermingle as in ordinary painting. Every vestment is of one color, a red alongside of blue, a bright green alongside of a pale purple, an embroidery of gold placed on a dark amaranth, like the simple, sustained strains of an angelic melody. The painter delights in this; he cannot find colors for his saints pure enough or ornaments for them of sufficient preciousness. He forgets that his figures are images; he bestows upon them the faithful care of a believer, of a worshipper; he embroiders their robes as if they were real; he covers their mantles with filagree as fine as the finest work of the goldsmith; he paints on their copes small and perfect pictures; he applies himself to delicately unfolding their beautiful light tresses, to arranging their curls, to the proper adjustment of the folds of their tunics, to an accurate delineation of the round monastic tonsure; he enters into heaven with them in order to love and to serve them. Fra Angelico is the last of the mystic flowers. The society that surrounded him and of which he knew nothing, ended in taking an opposite direction, and, after a short respite of enthusiasm, proceeded to burn his successor, a Dominican like himself and the last of the christians, Savonarola.

CHAPTER V.

THE UFFIZJ COLLECTION.—THE TRIBUNE.—ANTIQUES, AND RENAIS-
SANCE SCULPTURE.—DIFFERENCE BETWEEN GREEK ART AND
THE ART OF THE SIXTEENTH CENTURY.—MICHAEL ANGELO.—THE
MEDICI CHAPEL.

WHAT can be said of a gallery containing thirteen
hundred pictures? For my own part I abstain. Examine catalogues and collections of engravings, or rather
come here yourself. The impressions borne away from
these grand storehouses are too diverse and too numerous to be transmitted by the pen. Observe this, that
the Uffizj is a universal depot, a sort of Louvre containing paintings of all times and schools, bronzes,
statues, sculptures, antique and modern terra-cottas,
cabinets of gems, an Etruscan museum, artists' portraits painted by themselves, twenty-eight thousand
original drawings, four thousand cameos and ivories
and eighty thousand medals. One resorts to it as to a
library; it is an abridgment and a specimen of everything. Add to this that one goes also to other places,
to the Palazzo-Vecchio, to the Palazzo Corsini, to the
Palazzo Pitti. A mass of notes accumulate, but I can
extract nothing from them. It seems to me that I have
completed and corrected or modified some former ideas;
but completions, corrections and modifications are not
.to be transcribed.

The simplest thing, therefore, is to leave study there
and promenade for pleasure. We ascend the great
marble staircase, pass the famous antique boar and
enter the long horseshoe corridor filled with busts and
tapestried with paintings. Visitors, about ten o'clock
in the morning, are few; the mute custodians remain
in their corners; you seem to be really at home. It

all belongs to you, and what convenient possessions !
Keepers and majordomos are here to keep things in
order, well dusted and intact : it is not even necessary
to give orders; matters go on of themselves without
jar or confusion, nobody giving himself the slightest
concern; it is an ideal world such as it ought to be.
The light is excellent; bright gleams from the windows
fall on some distant white statues, on the rosy torso
of a woman which comes out living from the shadowy
obscurity. Beyond, as far as the eye can see, marble
gods and emperors extend away in files up to the windows through which flickers the light ripple of the
Arno with the silvery swell of its crests and eddies.
You enter into the freedom and sweet repose of abstract life; the will relaxes, the inner tumult subsides;
one feels himself becoming a monk, a modern monk.
Here, as formerly in the cloisters, the tender inward
spirit, chafed by the necessities of action, insensibly
revives in order to commune with beings emancipated
from life's obligations. It is so sweet no longer to be !
Not to be is so natural ! And how peaceful the realm
of human forms withdrawn from human conflict ! The
pure thought which follows them is conscious that its
illusion is transient : it participates in their incorporeal
serenity, and reverie, lingering in turn over their voluptuousness and violence, brings back to it plenitude
without satiety.

On the left of the corridors open the cabinets of
precious things,—the Niobe hall, that of portraits, that
of modern bronzes, each with its special group of treasures. You feel that you have a right to enter, that great
men are awaiting you. A selection is made amongst
them ; you re-enter the Tribune : five antique statues
form a circle here,—a slave sharpening his knife ; two
interlocked wrestlers whose muscles are strained and
expanded; a charming Apollo of sixteen years whose
compact form has all the suppleness of the freshest

adolescence ; an admirable Faun instinct with the animality of his species, unconsciously joyous and dancing with all his might; and, finally, the "Venus de
Medici," a slender young girl with a small delicate
head, not a goddess like her sister of Milo, but a perfect mortal and the work of some Praxiteles fond of
hetairæ, at ease in a nude state and free from that somewhat mawkish delicacy and bashful coquetry which its
copies, and the restored arms with their thin fingers by
Bernini, seem to impose on her. She is, perhaps, a
copy of that Venus of Cnidus of which Lucian relates
an interesting story ; you imagine while looking at her,
the youths' kisses pressed on the marble lips, and the
exclamations of Charicles who, on seeing it, declared
Mars to be the most fortunate of gods. Around the
statues, on the eight sides of the wall, hang the masterpieces of the leading painters.. There is the "Madonna of the Goldfinch" by Raphael, pure and candid,
like an angel whose soul is a bud not yet in bloom;
his "St. John," nude, a fine youthful form of fourteen,
healthy and vigorous, in which the purest paganism
lives over again ; and especially a superb head of a
crowned female, radiant as a summer noonday, with
fixed and earnest gaze, her complexion of that powerful southern carnation which the emotions do not
change, where the blood does not pulsate convulsively
and to which passion only adds a warmer glow, a sort
of Roman muse in whom will still prevails over intellect, and whose vivacious energy reveals itself in repose
as well as in action.* In one corner a tall cavalier by
Van Dyck, in black and with a broad frill, seems as
grandly and gloriously proud in character as in proportions, primarily through a well-fed body and next
through the undisputed possession of authority and

---

* This picture is called "the Fornarina." It is not however the
Fornarina, and it is not certain that Raphael painted it.

command. Three steps more and we come to the
"Flight into Egypt," by Correggio, the Virgin with a
charming spirited face wholly suffused with inward
light in which the purity, archness, gentleness and
wildness of a young girl combine to shed the tenderest
grace and impart the most fascinating allurements.
Alongside of this a "Sibyl" by Guercino, with her
carefully adjusted coiffure and drapery, is the most
spiritual and refined of sentimental poetesses.

I pass twenty others in order to reserve the last look
for Titian's two Venuses. One, facing the door, re-
clines on a red velvet mantle, an ample vigorous torso
as powerful as one of Rubens' Bacchantes, but firmer—
an energetic and vulgar figure, a simple, strong unintellectual courtezan. She lies extended on her back,
caressing a little cupid naked like herself, with the vacant seriousness and passivity of soul of an animal in
repose and expectant. The other, called "Venus with
the Dog," is a patrician's mistress, couched, adorned
and ready. We recognize a palace of the day, the
alcove fitted up and colors tastefully and magnificently
contrasted for the pleasure of the eye; in the background are servants arranging clothes; through a window a section of blue landscape is visible; the master
is about to arrive. Nowadays we devour pleasure
secretly like stolen fruit; then it was served up on gold-
en salvers and people sat down to it at a table. It is
because pleasure was not vile or bestial. This woman
holding a bouquet in her hand in this grand columnar
saloon has not the vapid smile or the wanton and mali-
cious air of an adventuress about to commit a bad
action. The calm of evening enters the palace through
noble architectural openings. Under the pale green of
the curtains lies the figure on a white sheet, slightly
flushed with the regular pulsation of life, and developing the harmony of her undulating forms. The head
is small and placid; the soul does not rise above the

corporeal instincts; hence she can resign herself to them without shame, while the poesy of art, luxury and security on all sides comes to decorate and embellish them. She is a courtezan, but also a lady; in those days the former did not efface the latter; one was as much a title as the other and, probably, in demeanor, affection and intellect one was as good as the other. The celebrated Imperia had her tomb in the church of San Gregorio, at Rome, with this inscription: "Imperia, a Roman courtezan worthy of so great a name, furnished an example to men of perfect beauty, lived twenty-six years and twelve days, and died in 1511, August 25." Two centuries after this President De Brosses, at Venice, on being directed to a certain address found a lady so noble in her manner, so dignified in her bearing and so refined in her language that he stammered out an apology; he was about to withdraw, aghast at his mistake, when she smiled and bade him be seated.

On passing from the Italian into the Flemish galleries one is completely turned around: here are paintings executed for merchants content to remain quietly at home eating good dinners and speculating over the profits of their business; moreover in rainy and muddy countries dress has to be cared for, and by the women more than the men. The mind feels itself contracted on entering the circle of this well-to-do domestic life; such is the impression of Corinne when from liberal Italy she passes to rigid and dreary Scotland. And yet there is a certain picture, a large landscape by Rembrandt, which equals and surpasses all; a dark sky bursting with showers amongst flocks of screaming crows; beneath, is an infinite stretch of country as desolate as a cemetery; on the right a mass of barren rocks of so mournful and lugubrious a tint as to attain to the sublime in effect. So is it with an andante of Beethoven after an Italian Opera.

April 14.—*The Uffizj.*—A visit to the antiques and sculptures of the renaissance. The relationship of the two ages is immediately recognized. Both are equally pagan, that is to say wholly occupied with the present and physical life. Notwithstanding this they are separated by two notable differences; the antique is more calm, and, on coming down to the best period of Greek sculpture this calmness is extraordinary; it is that of animal life, almost vegetative; man lives for the sake of living and desires nothing beyond. We find in him, indeed, at the first aspect, an apathetic air, or at least dull, approaching melancholy, in contrast with the constant feverishness and profound elaboration of modern heads.

The renaissance sculptor, on the other hand, imitates the real more subtly, and aims more at expression. Contemplate the statues of Verocchio, of Francavilla, of Bandinelli, of Cellini, and especially those of Donatello. His "St. John the Baptist," emaciated by fasting, is a skeleton. His "David," so elegant, so well posed, has angular elbows and arms of extreme meagreness; individual character, passionate emotion, particular situation, intense will and originality peer out strongly in their works as in a portrait. They appreciate animation more than harmony.

Hence it is, in sculpture at least, that the only masters who perfectly present the sentiment of beauty are the Greeks. After them all is deviation; no other art has been able to put the soul of the spectator in so just an equilibrium. This is apparent on strolling an hour through this long gallery. The mind is suddenly tranquillized; it seems to have recovered its firmness. The heads of empresses are rapidly passed, almost all spoiled by an overloaded and pretentious coiffure; a glance is bestowed on the busts of the emperors, interesting to a historian and each of which is the summary of a reign and a character; but one stops before the statues of athletes, of the "Discobulus," of the small "Bacchante," and especially of the gods, "Mercury," "Venus" and the two Apollos. Muscles are obliterated; the trunk is prolonged without depressions or projections into the arms and thighs; there is no effort. How strange this term in our world where one encounters nothing but effort! The reason is that, since the Greeks, man, in developing himself, has become *distorted*; he has become distorted all on one side through the predominance of cerebral activity. Nowadays he desires too much, he aims too high and has too much to do. In those days after a youth had exercised in the gymnasium, when he had learned a few hymns and could read Homer, when he had listened to orators in the agora and to philosophers in the portico, his education was finished; the man was accomplished and he began life complete. A rich young Englishman of to-day, of good family and calm in blood, who has rowed, boxed and raced a good deal, who possesses healthy and precise ideas, who deliberately lives in the country, is, in these days, the least imperfect imitation of the young Athenian; he often possesses the same unity of feature and the same tranquil regard. But this does not last long. He is forced to imbibe too much knowledge, and too positive knowledge: languages, geography, political economy, Greek verses at Eton, mathematics at Cambridge, newspaper statistics and documents, besides the Bible and ethics. Our civilization overwhelms us; man staggers under the pressure of his ever-increasing task; the burden of inventions and ideas which he easily bore in infancy is no longer proportioned to his strength. He is obliged to shut himself up in a little province and become special. One development excludes others; he must be either laborer or student, politician or philosopher, manufacturer or man of family and confine himself to one thing at the expense of all the rest; he would be inadequate were he not mutilated. Hence the loss in him of calmness, and the loss in art of harmony. The sculptor, however, no longer addresses himself to a religious civic community, but to a crowd of isolated amateurs ; he ceases to act in the capacity of priest and of citizen, and is only a man and an artist. He dwells on the anatomical details that are to arrest connoisseurs, and on' the exaggerated expression which is comprehended by the ignorant. He is a sort of expert goldsmith desirous of gaining and of retaining public attention. He executes simply a work of art and not a work of national art. The spectator pays him in praise and he pays the spectator by pleasing him. Compare the "Mercury" of John of Bologna with the young Greek athlete near him. The former, springing on his toe is a *tour de force* which is to do honor to the artist, and prove an attractive spectacle to fix the eyes of visitors. The young Athenian, on the contrary, who says nothing, who does nothing, who is contented to live, is an effigy of the city, a monument of its olympic victories, an example for all the youths of its gymnasia ; he is of service to education as the statue of a god is of service to religion. Neither the god nor the athlete need be interesting; it suffices for them to be perfect and tranquil ; they are not objects of luxury, but instruments of public welfare ; they are commemorative objects and not pieces of furniture. People respect and profit by them ; they do not use them for their diversion nor as material for criticism. Likewise, again, the marble "David" of Donatello, so proudly erect, draped in so original a manner, so haughtily grave, is not a hero or a legendary saint, but a pure creation of the imagination ; the artist fashions a pagan or a christian according to order and his sole concern is to please people of taste. Consider, at last, Michael Angelo himself, his "Dead Adonis" with head inclined upon his bent arm, and the "Bacchus" who raises his cup and half opens his mouth as if to drink a health—two admirable figures, so natural and almost antique. With him, however, as with his contemporaries, action and interest predominate ; he, no more than they, contents himself with representing a simple existence calm in its own repose. Through this great transformation of human life, thus disjointed and dissevered in its various organs, the ideal model, public sentiment and the artistic spirit have radically changed, and that which henceforth the new art typifies is individual personality, striking peculiarities, uncontrollable passion, diversities of action, instead of the abstract type, of the general form, of harmony and of repose.

We follow out this idea and leave the Uffizj to see other statues. We enter the Palazzo-Vecchio. Its court is supported by columns entirely covered with ornamentation and with small figures, the rich and brilliant invention of the renaissance. In the middle of the court stands a fountain the perfection of elegance, (this term always recurs to one in Florence,) and, erect on its top, Verocchio has placed a charming, animated statue of a child in bronze. You ascend to the great Council-chamber painted by Vasari with large, insipid frescoes ; and around it you see a range of marble statues, the "Adam" and "Eve" of Bandinelli, both of them meagre and real ; "Virtue triumphant over Vice," by John of Bologna, a grand, sensual imperious fellow, entirely nude, with a singularly distorted thigh ; a youthful victor standing over a prisoner, by Michael Angelo, with an elongated body and a very small head, two traits which his school is to copy literally, and finally exaggerate. The same character reappears everywhere, that of beauty centred in exact imitation or in modifications of expression ; it is, however, a new field on which a whole world may be built.

In order to comprehend this it is necessary to visit the church of San Lorenzo, filled with the works of

Donatello, Verocchio and Michael Angelo. The church
is by Brunelleschi and the chapel by Michael Angelo,
one being a sort of temple with a flat ceiling sustained
by corinthian columns, and the other a square structure
surmounted by a cupola, the former being too classic
and the latter too cold;—one hesitates before writing
these two words; and yet nothing must be kept back
even in the presence of such great names. The two
pulpits however, by Donatello, the bronze bas-reliefs
which cover the marble, so many natural and impassioned little figures, and especially the frieze of nude
cherubs playing and running along the cornice, and the
charming balcony above the organ so delicately wrought
that it seems to be of ivory, with its niches, shells, columns, animals and foliage—how graceful and what
taste! And what ornamentalists they were, these renaissance sculptors! Thereupon you enter the Medici
chapel and contemplate the colossal figures which
Michael Angelo has placed on their tombs. Nothing
in modern statuary is equal to them, and the noblest
antique figures are not superior; they are different,
which is all one can say. Phidias executed serene
gods and Michael Angelo suffering heroes; but suffering
heroes are equal to serene gods; it is the same
magnanimity, here exposed to the miseries of the
world, there emancipated from the miseries of the
world; the sea is as grand in tempest as in repose.

Every one has seen a drawing or a plaster cast of
these statues; but, unless on this spot, no one has
seen their soul. It is essential to have felt, almost
through contact with them, the colossal and superhuman massiveness of these grand elongated forms whose
muscles speak to you; the hopeless nudity of these
virgins of which we see only the spirit, the grief and the
race, without the mind of itself being capable of entertaining any other sentiment but fear and compassion.
Their blood is different from ours; a fallen Diana, cap-

tive in the hands of the barbarians of the Taurica, would possess this visage and this form.

One of them, half-reclining, awakes and seems to be shaking off a fearful dream. The head is bowed, the brow frowning, the eyes hollow, and the cheeks emaciated. How much misery had to be endured in order that such a form might feel the burden of life! Its indestructible beauty has not succumbed, and yet inward suffering begins to reveal its corroding imprint. The superb animal vitality, the vivacious energy of the trunk and limbs are intact, but the spirit falters; she lifts herself painfully on an arm, and beholds the light with regret. How sad to raise the eyelids, and to feel that once more must be borne the burden of a human day!

By her side a man, seated, turns half round with a sombre air like one overcome, irritable and expectant. What an effort, and what writhing when the mass of muscles furrowing this torso swells and strains in order to clutch an enemy! On the other tomb an unfinished captive, his head half disengaged from its stone matrix, the arms rigid, the body contorted, raises his shoulder with a formidable gesture. I see there all of Dante's figures, Ugolino gnawing the skull of his enemy, the damned half springing from their flaming sepulchres; but these are not the cursed; they are grand wounded spirits justly indignant at slavery.

A grand female form extended is sleeping; an owl in front of it is placed at its feet. This is the sleep of exhaustion, the dull lethargy of an overtaxed being who has sunk down and rests inert. It is called Night, and Michael Angelo has written on the pedestal, "Sleep is sweet, and yet more sweet is it to be of stone while misery and wrong endure. Not to see, not to feel, is my joy. So wake me not! Ah, speak in whispers!" These lines are not necessary to make the sentiment which guided his hand understood; his statues tell their own story. His own Florence had just been vanquished; in vain had he fortified and defended it; after a siege of a year Pope Clement had captured it. The last free government was destroyed. Mercenaries broke into the houses killing its best citizens. Four hundred and sixty *emigrés* were condemned to death as outlaws, or read proclamations throughout Italy fixing a price on their heads. They had ransacked Michael Angelo's dwelling in order to seize and carry him away; had not a friend concealed him he too would have perished. He had passed long days confined in this asylum, knowing that death was taking the noblest lives and hovering around his own. If the Pope afterward spared him it was only through family interest, and in order that he might finish the Medici chapel. He shut himself up in it; he devoted himself to it passionately; he tried to forget in it, in intellectual strife and in weariness of hand, the ruin of vanquished liberty, the agony of a down-trodden country, the defeat of outraged justice, the tumult of suppressed resentments, of his impotent despair and of his devouring humiliations, and it is this indomitable rebellion of his soul, sternly confronting oppression and servitude, which he has here put into his heroes and his virgins. Above them, the mute Lorenzo, silent and tragic beneath his warrior's casque, with his hand on his lip, is about to arise. A king sits in this attitude when, in the midst of his army, he orders the execution of some judicial act like the destruction of a city. Frederic Barbarossa must have appeared thus when he caused Milan to be ploughed up.

Near the door is an admirable Virgin, unfinished, supporting her child on her hip; her tall draped form is of wonderful nobleness; she leans over and her hollow flank makes a peculiar curve following the folds of her robe; her thin face wears an expression of benevolent sadness. Like her reclining sisters she is of a more suffering and more exalted race than the human race; all are beings disproportioned to things below, bruised and tempest-tossed in life's career, encountering at long intervals respites of calm and of sublime reverie.

Between his tranquil "Pieta" of St. Peter's at Rome and this grandiose Virgin with such a subtle and melancholy spirit, what a distance! Add to these the "Moses" and the ceiling of the Sistine chapel. How the man has grown and suffered! How he has formed and revealed his original conception of life! This is modern art, wholly personal and manifesting the individual, the artist himself, in opposition to antique art which is wholly impersonal and unfolding a general idea expressive of the city. One finds the same difference between Homer and Dante, between Sophocles and Shakespeare; Art becomes more and more a confession, that of an individual soul, expressing itself and revealing itself fully to a dispersed and indefinite assembly of other souls. Thus was Beethoven, the most modern and grandest of all musicians.—The consequence is that an artist must be a personality; if not, he has nothing to say. An Italian remarked to me at Sienna; "Formerly artists painted with the passions they had; now they paint those they think they have. This is why after having given us men they now give us phantoms of men."

CHAPTER VI

THE PITTI PALACE.—THE MEDICI MONARCHY.—MANNERS AND CUS-
TOMS OF THE COURT.—PROMENADES AMONG THE PAINTERS.—
ANDREA DEL SARTO AND FRA BARTOLOMEO.—THE SPIRIT AND
INFLUENCE OF FLORENCE IN ITALY.

I DOUBT if there is a palace in Europe more monumental than the Pitti Palace. I have not seen one that
leaves such a simple, grandiose impression. Placed
on an eminence its entire outline appears in profile
against the clear blue sky, its three distinct stories
superposed one above the other like three regular
blocks, the narrowest on the top of the broadest. Two
terraces project crosswise on the two flanks adding to
it another mass. But what is really unique and carries
to an extreme the grandiose serenity of the edifice is
the vastness of the material of which it is built. It is
not stone, but fragments of rock and almost sections
of mountains. Some blocks, especially those supporting the terraces, are as long as five men. Scarcely
hewn out, rugged and dark, they preserve their original
asperity, as would a mountain if torn from its foundations, broken into fragments and erected on a new site
by cyclopean hands.

There is no ornamentation on the façade; a long
balustrade simply runs along the top, intersecting the
motionless azure. Colossal round arcades support the
windows, and each of their vertebræ forms a projection
with its primitive irregularities, as if the skeleton of an
old giant.

Inside is a square court like that of the Farnese palace, surrounded by four architectural masses as austere
and as vast as the exterior. Here also ornament is

wanting, and designedly. The entire decoration consists of a lining of doric columns upon which are ionic
columns and, over these, corinthian columns. But
these piles of round blocks, rising one above another
or alternating with square blocks equal, in the force of
their massiveness and the sharpness of their angles,
the ruggedness and energy of the rest. Stone reigns
supreme here; the eye seeks for nothing beyond variety of reliefs and substantial position; it seems as if it
subsisted in and for itself, as if art and man's will had
not intervened and as if there were no room for fancy.
On the ground-floor, stout, resistant doric pillars bear
arcades forming a promenade; and each curve, bristling with its bosses, seems to be the joint of an antedi-
luvian spine. A brown tint like that of a crag corroded
by time, renders the huge edifice sombre from top to
bottom, extending even to the rude chequered flagging
of the court, enclosed within this accumulation of stones.
  A Florentine trader built this palace in the fifteenth
century and thereby ruined himself. Brunelleschi made
the plan, and, fortunately, his successors who completed
the structure, did not modify its character. If anything can give an idea of the grandeur, severity and
audacity of intellect which the middle ages bequeathed
to the free citizens of the renaissance it is the aspect
of such a dwelling built by a single individual for his
own use, and the contrast of its internal magnificence
with its external simplicity. The Medicis, become absolute princes, bought the palace in the sixteenth century and decorated it as princes. It contains five hundred pictures, all selected among the best, and several
are masterpieces. They do not form a musée according
to schools or centuries, as in our great modern collections, to serve the purposes of study or of history and
provide documents for a democracy which recognizes
science as its guide and instruction as its support; they
decorate the saloons of a royal palace, wherein the

prince receives his courtiers and displays his luxuriousness by festivities.   The age of creators is replaced by
the age of connoisseurs, and the pomp of golden vestments, the gravity of Spanish etiquette, the gallantry of
recent sigisbeism the diplomacy of official intercourse
and the license and refinements of monarchical habits
and tastes display themselves alongside of the noble
forms and living flesh of paintings, before golden arabesques on the walls and a sumptuous array of furniture
by which the prince manifests and maintains his rank
and figure.   Pietro di Cortona, Fedi and Marini, the last
of the painters of the decadence, cover the ceilings with
allegories in honor of this reigning family.   Here is
Minerva rescuing Cosmo I. from Venus and presenting
him to Hercules, the type of great works and heroic
exploits ; he in fact, put to death or proscribed the
leading citizens of Florence, and he it is who said of a
refractory city that he " would rather depopulate it
than lose it."   Elsewhere, Glory and Virtue are leading
him to Apollo, the patron of arts and letters ; he, in
fact, furnished magnificent apartments and pensioned
the writers of sonnets. · Farther on, Jupiter and the entire Olympian group are all astir to receive him ; he, in
fact, poisoned his daughter, caused his daughter's lover
to be killed and slew his son who had slain a brother ;
the second daughter was stabbed by her husband, and
the mother died on account of it ; these operations re-
commence in the following generation : assassinations
and poisonings are hereditary in this family.   But the
tables of malachite and of *pietra dura* are so beautiful !
The ivory cabinets, the mosaic furniture, the cups with
dragon handles are in such exquisite taste !   What
court better enjoys works of art and knows better how
to give fêtes ?   What is there more brilliant, what more
ingenious than the mythological representations in
honor of the marriage of Francis di Medici with the
famous Bianco Capello and of Cosmo di Medici with

Mary Magdalen of Austria?* What retreat could be better for academicians who purify language and compose dedications, for poets who turn compliments and point *concetti?* Obsequious politeness flourishes here with its magniloquence, literary purism with its scruples, contemptuous dilettantism with its refinements, sensuality in satisfied indifference, while "the most illustrious, most accomplished, most perfect gentleman," becomes the cicerone of Europe, explains with a complacent smile to *barbarians* from the North,† "the virtue" of his painters and "the bravery" of his sculptors.

There are too many of them,—I have to say the same as at the Uffizj, come and see them. Five or six pictures by Raphael stand out from the rest: one is that Madonna which the Grand Duke took with him on his travels; she is standing in a red robe and with a long green veil, the simplicity of the color heightening the simplicity of the attitude. A small diaphanous white veil covers the fine blonde hair up to the edge of the brow; the eyes are lowered and the complexion is of extreme purity; a delicate tint like that of the wild-rose tinges the cheeks and the small mouth is closed; she has the calmness and innocence of a German virgin. Raphael here is still of the school of Perugino.—Another picture, "The Madonna della Seggiola" forms a striking contrast to this. She is a beautiful Grecian or Circassian Sultana; her head is covered with a sort of turban while striped oriental stuffs of bright colors and embroidered with gold wind around her form; she bends over her child with the beautiful action of a wild animal and her clear eyes, without thought, look you full in the face. Raphael here has become the pagan and only thinks of the beauty of physical being and the embellishment of the human figure.—You recog-

---

* Nozze di Fiorenza, (with engravings.)
† Milton's Travels in Italy.

nize this in the "Vision of Ezekiel," a small canvas a foot high but of the grandest character. Jehovah, who appears in a whirlwind, is a Jupiter with nude breast, muscular arms and a royal bearing, and the angels around him have such chubby bodies as to be almost fat. None of the fury or delirium of the Hebrew seer subsists here; the angels are joyous, the grouping harmonious and the coloring healthy and beautiful; this vision which, with the prophet makes the teeth clatter and the flesh creep, with the painter only elevates and fortifies the soul. That which we find with him throughout is perfection in the proportionate.* All his personages, whether christian or pagan, are in equilibrium and at peace with themselves and with all the world. They appear to dwell in the azure as he himself lived in it, admired from the start, beloved by everybody, exempt from crosses, amorous without phrensy, laboring without restlessness and, in this constant serenity, occupied in obtaining a rounded arm and a doubling thigh for an infant, a small ear and curling tresses for a woman, searching, purifying, discovering and beaming as if only attentive to the music within his own breast. On this account he only feebly affects the spirits of those who know no repose.

Hence it is that subtle and impassioned painters, those that wield their art with some grand motive, according to a special and dominant instinct, please me more. Portraits, from this point of view, impress me more than all the rest, because they fully bring out peculiarities of individual character. One of these, attributed to Leonardo da Vinci, is called "The Nun." A white veil like a wimple, rests on the head; the breast, bare midway down the bosom, swells superbly passionless above a black velvet robe. The face is colorless, ex-

---

* The original is *la perfection dans la mesure.* The meaning I believe is, perfect parts in perfect relationship.—*Tr.*

cepting the powerful and strange red lips, and the whole
physiognomy is calm with a slight expression of disquietude.   This is not an abstract being, emanating
from the painter's brain, but an actual woman who has
lived, a sister of Mona Lisa, as complex, as full of
inward contrasts, and as inexplicable. Is she a nun,
a princess, or a courtezan? Perhaps all three at once,
like that Virginia de Leyva whose history has just
been exhumed. With the deadened pallor of the
cloister she has the splendid nudity of the outward
world, and the carnation of the lips on the impassible
pale face seems like a scarlet flower blooming on a
sepulchre. It is a soul, a dangerous, unfathomable
soul, slumbering or watchful, within that marble breast.

In this domain the Venetians are the greatest masters, and Titian is of the highest rank.   Raphael's portraits (of which there are five here) tell me less; he gives
the essential of the type, simply, soberly and broadly, but,
not like the former, the profound moral expression, the
mobile physiognomy, the personal originality utterly infinite, the entire inner nature of a man. Titian has
here eight or ten portraits,—Andrea Vesale the anatomist, Aretino, Luigi Cornaro, Cardinal Hippolyte di
Medici in the costume of a Hungarian magnate, all
of them full of life, with a look strange, disquieting
and uneasy but passive;—Philip II. of Spain standing
in an official costume, with slashed breeches and hose
reaching to the middle of the thigh, a wan, cool-blooded
being with projecting jaw, seeming to be abortive, disproportioned, incomplete, and steeped in birth and etiquette; but especially a Venetian patrician whose name
is not known, one of the greatest masterpieces I am
familiar with. He is about thirty-five years old, in
black, pale, and with an intense look. The face is
slightly emaciated, the eyes are pale blue, and a delicate moustache connects with a thin beard; he is of a
noble race, and of high rank, but his enjoyment of

life has been less than that of a common laborer; accusations, anxieties and the sentiment of danger have wasted and undermined him with secret and incessant usury. It is an energetic, worn, and meditative brain, used to sudden resolves at critical turns of life, and glows in its surroundings of sombre hues like a lamp gleaming in an atmosphere of death.

Sometimes truthfulness is so vivid that the painter, without knowing it, reaches the superlatively comic. Such is the portrait which Veronese has painted of his wife. She is forty-eight years old, double-chinned, has the air of a court dowager and the coiffure of a poodle-dog; with her black-velvet robe cut low and square on the neck in a framework of lace she looks pompous enough and proud of her charms; she is a well-preserved ample figure, well-displayed, majestic and good-natured, her ruddy flesh, perfect contentment and general roundness suggesting a fine turkey ready for the spit.

It is hard to leave these Venetians, the deep blue of their landscape, their luminous nudities in warm shadows, their rotund shoulders enveloped in palpable atmosphere, quivering flesh blooming like conservatory flowers, the changeable folds of lustrous stuffs, the proud bearing of venerable men in their simarres, the voluptuous elegance of female lineaments, the force of expression of structure and of embrace with which contorted or erect bodies display the opulence of their vigor and the vitality of their blood. A Giorgone portrays a nymph chased by a satyr,—how can words render the enjoyment of the eye and the power of tones? All is bathed in shadow, but the ardent motionless face, lovely shoulder, and bosom all issue forth like an apparition; one must see the living flesh emerging from the deep shadow, and the intense splendor of scarlet tones in deep and bright gradation from the blackness of night to the radiance of open day. Facing this, a Cleopatra by Guido, pearly gray on a light slaty background, is nothing but a dull phantom, the vanishing form of a sentimental young damsel.—Equally animated as the nymph of Giorgone is the woman entitled "Titian's mistress," in a blue robe embroidered with gold and slashed with violet velvet. Her auburn tresses of a clear blonde glow amidst light scattered curls; her lovely hands, of an exquisitely refined flesh tone, are in repose, because her toilet is complete, while her head, that of a gay young girl, happy in her splendid attire, is enlivened by a scarcely perceptible half-malicious smile. She resembles the "Venus with the Dog." If she is the same person, draped here and undraped there, one can comprehend how painter, patrician and poet lost themselves in such felicity; the heart and the senses are all absorbed; such a woman according to attitude and toilette, combined in herself fifty other women. No soul, indeed, was required; all that was requisite were joyousness, beauty and adornment. Read in Aretinos' letters the description of his own, and of other households in Venice.

But I must stop short. I have done wrong to let my own taste divert me; I ought to have confined myself to the Florentine painters. Of these there are two, Andrea del Sarto and Fra Bartolomeo, whom we scarcely know at home, and who have reached the summit of their art through their elevation of type, beauty of composition, simplicity of process, harmony of draperies and tranquillity of expression. Perhaps in these average, complete geniuses one obtains the most accurate and purest idea of the art and of the taste of Florence. There are sixteen large paintings by Andrea del Sarto in the Pitti Palace, others in the Corsini Palace and in the Uffizj gallery, and frescoes, still finer, in the portico of the Servites. There are five large works by Fra Bartolomeo in the Pitti Palace and especially a colossal "St. Mark," less spirited and impetuous but as grave and as grand as the Prophets of Michael Angelo ; others in the Uffizj and, finally, an admirable "St. Vincent" in the Academy. This monk is the most religious of the painters who have been complete masters of form ; none have so perfected the alliance between Christian purity and pagan beauty ; this same man designed his Madonnas nude before applying the color in order to secure a veritable and perfect body beneath the falling drapery ;* and he became a Dominican after the death of Savonarola in order to secure salvation ; a strange union of apparently contradictory actions, and which mark a unique moment in history ; that in which new paganism and old christianity, meeting without struggle and uniting without distinctiveness, permit art to worship sensuous beauty and to exalt physical life, with the single condition that it shall only prize nobleness and only portray the serious. With moderate, attenuated and always sober coloring, with a dominant taste for pure drawing, with exquisite proportion, balance and finesse of faculties and instincts, the Florentines have shown themselves better adapted than others to fulfil this task. Italian art centred in Florence as formerly Grecian art in Athens. As formerly in Greece other cities were inadequate or eccentric. As formerly in Greece other developments remained local or temporary, and like the Athens of former days, Florence directed or rallied them around herself. As formerly with Athens she maintained her supremacy until the decadence. Through Bronzino, Pontormo, the Allori, Cigoli, Dolci and Pietro da Cortona, through its language and academies, through Galileo and Filicaja, through its savants and poets and, at length, later through the tolerance of its masters and the spirit of its resurrection, she remained in Italy the capital of the mind.

---

* See the collection of original drawings in the Uffizj.

BOOK IV.

FROM FLORENCE TO VENICE.

CHAPTER I.

From Florence to Bologna, April 17.—A more beautiful or more fertile country could not be imagined. After leaving Pistoija the mountains commence; from hill to hill, then from crag to crag, the carriage slowly ascends for two hours over a zigzag road, and from the bottom to the top all is cultivated and inhabited. At each turn of the road, we see houses and gardens, terraces of olive-trees, fields sustained by walls, fruit-trees sheltered in the hollows, bits of green meadow and, everywhere, sparkling streams. Women on their knees are washing clothes at the mouths of bubbling fountains, or in the little wooden conduits that distribute freshness and moisture to the surrounding declivities. As far as the eye can reach, both valleys and elevations bear the marks of labor and of human prosperity. Everything is turned to account; chestnut-trees cover the sharp points and the steep portions of the soil. The mountain is like one enormous terrace of multiplied grades expressly arranged for diverse species of culture. Even on the summit, in the vicinity of snow, small terraces about six feet wide furnish grazing for the flocks. Signs of this industry and prosperity are as visible among the inhabitants as upon the soil; the peasantry wear shoes and the women, while tending their flocks or walking, are braiding straw. The houses are in good condition and the villages are numerous and provided with communal schools and, on the summit of the·Apennines, is a café bearing the name of the mountain range. This is truly the heart of Italy; in genius, power of invention, prosperity, beauty and salubrity, Florence surpasses Rome, and against foreign invasion this barrier of mountains would be a defence.

The other slope forms a second barrier; the Apennines with its bastions is as broad as it is high; on the descent the road winds among little wooded gorges trickling with water, all green beneath their ruddy vesture of woods framed in by the sober forms of bare rocks. Night comes on, and the railroad buries itself in the defiles of a new mountain: a fantastic, horrible, devastated landscape like those of Dante: mountains shattered, rocks broken, long subterranean passages wherein the roaring machine plunges as into a vortex, and dismantled valleys no longer anything but a skeleton; the torrent rushes almost under the wheels of the carriages and great slides of gravel suddenly appear, whitened in the bright moonlight. In this desert, amidst beds of boulders accumulated during the winter, and in the recesses of a sepulchral gorge is occasionally seen a thorny tree like a spectre in its crypt, and when the train stops, all that the ear catches is the roar of the icy water falling over naked stones.

Bologna, April 17.—Bologna is a city of arcades; they extend on both sides of the principal streets. It is quite pleasant to walk under them in summer in the shade, and, in winter, protected from the rain. Almost all of the Italian cities have thus some special contrivance or construction adding to the conveniences of life and of service to everybody. Only in Italy do people really and universally comprehend the agreeable; for the reason, perhaps, that everybody has need of it and aspires to it.

That which strikes one among the young men here, as in Florence and elsewhere, that which is noticeable in the faces at the theatre, on our promenades and in the streets is a certain amorous air, a gracious smile and tender and expansive ways; nothing is there of French hardness or irony. They utter the terms *bella, veggosa, vaga, leggiadra,* with a peculiar accent like that of Don Ottavio in Mozart or of the young tenors of the Italian Opera. On the stage in Florence the tenor kneeling to Marguerite was inconsistent but he perfectly expressed that state of mind. For the same reason people dress in light colors pleasing to the eye and wear rings and heavy gold chains; their hair is glossy and there is something blooming and brilliant throughout their persons.

As to the women, the bold and dark eye, their deep black hair audaciously knotted or massed in lustrous plaits, the vigorously defined forms of cheek and chin, the brow often square, the large and well-set visage below it and the solid boniness of the skull forestall any appearance of gentleness or delicacy and, generally, even any air of nobleness and purity. To make amends the structure and expression of their features denote energy, brilliancy, gay self-confidence, a positive and clear intellect, and talent and will to turn life to the best account. On looking in the windows of the bookstores at the figures provided by the makers of political caricatures for Italy and its provinces, we recognize this very character; although goddesses and allegorical goddesses, their heads are short and round, and grossly gay and sensual. Nothing can be more significant than these popular personages and these recognized types. By way of contrast look at the mild English female of " Punch," with long curls, and bran-new frocks; or the Frenchwoman of Marcelin, coquettish, sprightly, and extravagant, or the candid, honest, primitive German woman, somewhat stupid, of the "Kladderadatsch" and the minor journals of Berlin. I have just strolled through the streets of Bologna; it is nine o'clock in the morning; out of four women there are always three of them frizzled and nearly in full dress; their keen eye boldly fixes itself on the passers-by; they go bareheaded, some of them merely letting a black veil hang down over their shoulders; their hair swells out superbly on both sides of the head; they seem to be equipped for conquest; nobody could imagine a more naturally triumphant physiognomy, an air more like that of a prima-donna in the clouds. With a character like this, the spirit and the imagination of men, they must control.

What can be done at a table-d'hote if not to look about one? In this forced silence and society the brain and eyes are both busy. The lady facing me is the wife of a major on garrison duty in the Abruzzi, beautiful although mature, gay, prompt, self-confident, and what a tongue! Northern and Southern Europe, the latin and the germanic races are a thousand leagues apart in this facility of expression, in bold judgment and in promptitude of action. She argues and decides every-thing—the indolence of the Abruzzi peasantry, their *vendette*, the embarrassments of the government, her dog, her husband, the officers of the battalion, "our fine regiment, the 27th." She addresses me and then turns to her neighbor, an ecclesiastic, who, like the rest, has the same Italian air, that is to say he is gallant and obsequiously polite. Her sentences flow out with the velocity and sonorousness of an inexhaustible torrent. Day before yesterday, another, about forty-eight, in a black spencer puffed with ribbons, and with a red face, entirely absorbed the conversation and made the apart-ment ring with her tattle and exclamations. The other day a pretty little *bourgeoise* became indisposed in the

diligence *intérieure*, and her husband had her removed
up to the *impériale* by our side. She questioned us all,
and corrected my errors of pronunciation; after having
two or three times in succession misplaced an accent
or not having caught the precise tone, she became im-
patient and gave me a scolding. She informs us that
she is just married, that she and her husband hadn't a
cent with which to begin housekeeping, etc.; there are
three men alongside of her and she it is who takes and
keeps the lead. I have in my mind fifty others, all of
whom may be grouped around these three types. The
dominant trait is a vivacity and a clearness of conception boldly exploding the moment it is born. Their
ideas are all cut out at sharp angles; she is the
Frenchwoman, more vigorous and less fine; like the
latter, and more than the latter, she is self-willed; she
makes of herself a centre; she does not await direction
from another, she takes the initiative. There is nothing in her of the mild, the timid, the modest or the reserved, no capacity for burying herself in her household with her children and husband in germanic
fashion. I involuntarily compare her with the English women who are present. Some there are very
peculiar, puritanic at heart, rigid in morality, the fruit
of mechanical principles, one especially, in her straw-
hat like an extinguisher, a genuine spinster in embryo,
without toilet, grace, smile or sex, always silent or,
when she speaks, as keen as a knife-blade. She belongs,
without doubt, to that species of young lady who is
found ascending the White Nile alone with her mother,
or clambering up Mount Blanc at four in the morning
tied to two guides by a rope, her dress converted into
trowsers and striding along over the glaciers. In that
country artificial selection has produced sheep especially for meat, and natural selection, women especially
for action. But the same force has operated more
frequently in another sense; the despotic energy of

the man, and the necessity of a tranquil home to the overworked daily laborer have developed in the woman qualities belonging to the ancient germanic stock, namely a capacity for subordination and respect, timorous reserve, aptitudes for domestic life, and the sentiment of duty. She remains, accordingly, the young girl even into matrimony; on being spoken to she blushes; if, with all possible precaution and circumspection, one tries to draw her out of the silence in which she is immured she expresses her sentiments with extreme modesty and immediately relapses. She is immeasurably removed from any aspirations of command, of taking the initiative, of independence even. In all the English couples I have recently met the man is chief; in every Italian couple it is the woman.

And this is not very surprising. People here seem to be lovers naturally and organically. The drivers and conductors of the diligences talk about nothing else. Before a woman, as in the presence of every beautiful or brilliant object, they leap at a single bound to admiration and enthusiasm. *O quanto bella!* Twenty times a day I hear these earnest and emphatic expressions. They resemble actors and exaggerating mimics. *Bello, bello, bellissimo palazzo! La chiesa è magnifica, stupenda, tutti di marmo, tutti di mosaica!* Their eyes ensnare and their senses transport them. The more the diverse races are studied the more do aptitudes for enjoyment appear unequal. Some are scarcely moved to pleasure; others are transported and overcome by it. Enjoyment, with some, resembles the taste of a flavorless apple; with others the melting and delicious savor of clusters of golden grapes. With some the effect of external objects is an almost uniform series of moderate sensations; with others it is a tumultuous contrast of extreme emotions. Hence the ordinary current of life is changed; in every breast the charm is proportioned to the degree of enjoyment. I might give, in this connection, two or three stories, and especially one, worthy of Bandello and Pecorone: I was a confidant, and almost an eye-witness, in a small town;—but such stories are to be told and not written; the French language allows no expansion of simple nude instinct; that which is beautiful it pronounces crudity. Here they are more tolerant; they are addicted to espionage, it is true, as in our provincial towns, but society is content to laugh; it does not exclude lovers, and is not prudish.

Bologna, April 17.—The churches are ordinary, incomplete or modernized; but the sculptures are striking.

The most precious are in San Domenico, on the tomb of Saint Dominic decorated in 1231 by the restorer of art, Nicholas of Pisa. This is the first of the monuments displaying the renaissance of beauty in Italy. Bear in mind that at this period the ascetic spirit through the Dominicans and Franciscans, gained fresh energy; that gothic art ruled throughout Europe; that it crossed the Alps and built Assisi. Just at the height of this mystic fever, and on the marble tomb of the first inquisitor, a statuary revives the virile beauty of pagan forms. None of his figures are morbid, exalted or emaciated; on the contrary all are robust, healthy and oftentimes joyous. If they have any defect it is excess of vigor. Ordinarily their cheeks are too full, the head too massive and the body, overstout, is too heavy. The grand Virgin in the centre has the satisfied serenity of a good and happy mother of a family; her *bambino* is chubby and is growing finely. A mother, whose son has been killed by his horse and who is restored to life, shows the liveliest expression of joy. Several figures of young girls, and one in particular on the extreme left of the façade, seem to be vigorous, blooming Greek caryatides. The most ascetic personages are transformed in this artist's

hands; numbers of the big hooded monks' heads are
real and humorous; the dominant traits of all these
figures are placidity, solidity and good-humor. This
beautiful marble procession thus turns around the
panels of the tomb, and the statuettes decorating the
capitals, executed by Niccolo dell' Arca, two centuries
later, only repeat with a greater degree of skilfulness
the same firm and free conception; two youths especially, one in a coat of mail and the other booted like
the archangels of Perugino, have an admirable spirited
attitude. This shrine lacks nothing of the combination in a few square feet of the entire development of
sculpture. A kneeling angel on the left, noble and
serene, and a St. Petronius, grandiose and severe,
holding the city in his hand, were chiselled by Michael Angelo, and from the first to the last matter, all
the works are of the same family, pagan, energetic and
well proportioned.—If now we promenade through the
church we will see that in this great period of three
centuries the primitive idea did not falter. A tomb of
Taddeo Pepoli in 1337, substantial and beautiful, displays no gothic finery; on the two sides two standing
saints, tranquil and in large mantles, regard a kneeling
figure offering them a small chapel.—Farther on the
monument of Alexander Tartegno, in 1477, in an
arched niche decked with flowers, fruits, animals' heads
and small corinthian columns, shows, above the recumbent body, three Virtues with full and cheerful
countenances in richly carved drapery and in a studied
and expressive attitude. These are the complicated
groupings, the minglings of ideas through which, in the
fifteenth century, the renaissance commences; but,
among the various turns of thought, the sculptor has
preserved the same race of body imprinted on his
memory, and it is always the sentiment of the human
framework, the solid muscularity and the natural and
nude life which have guided him.

This great city is dull and miserable. Several quarters seem to be deserted; vagabonds are playing and wrangling in the open spaces. Numbers of stately mansions seem gloomy like the houses of our provincial towns. It was, in fact, a provincial city governed by a pope's legate; from an active republic it was converted into a city of the dead.—The best café is pointed out to us and we leave it as soon as possible; it is simply a grog-shop. We stop for a moment before two leaning towers, square and curious, built in the twelfth century, and which have none of the elegance of that of Pisa. We reach the principal church, San Petronio, an ogival basilica with a dome of the Italian gothic and of an inferior species: the mind dwells with regret on the fine monuments of Pisa, of Sienna, and of Florence; a republican government and a free creative energy did not last long enough here to allow the edifice to be completed. The building is cut in two, and is half-finished; the interior is whitewashed; three quarters of the windows have been closed up and the façade is incomplete. In the dim light which the too few windows allow to enter there are some good sculptures pèrceptible; "Adam and Eve" by Alfonso Lombardi, and an "Annunciation,"—but one has not the courage to look at them, as the eye is saddened. We go out, and from the dilapidated steps, gaze on a dirty square with its beggars, and a crowd of idle vagabonds. We retrace our steps in order to obtain relief and suddenly get interested. Over the central door is a cordon of superb figures, grand and vigorous nude bodies, pagan in action and in shape, an admirable new-born Eve, another Eve spinning while Adam ploughs, Adam reaching up to pluck the apple with a gesture of vigorous vitality. They are by Jacopo della Quercia, who executed them in 1425, at the same time that Ghiberti chased the gates of the Baptistery; but Ghiberti anticipated

Raphael, and Quercia seems to have been the pre-
cursor of Michael Angelo.

This is reviving, and we proceed to a fountain that
we discover on the left.   Here the renaissance and paganism reach their extreme point.   On the summit is
a superb Neptune, in bronze, by John of Bologna
(1568) and not an antique god, calm and worthy of
adoration, but a mythological god serving as an ornament, naked and displaying his muscles.   On the four
corners of the basin four children, joyous and well
posed, are seizing so many leaping dolphins; under the
feet of the god are four females with fishes' legs displaying the magnificent nudity of their bending forms,
the open sensuality of their bold heads and closely
clasping their swollen breasts to force out the jutting
water.

CHAPTER II.

HAVING once made a tour of the Musée, one immediately feels himself led, re-led to, and arrested before the principal picture, the "Saint Cecilia," by Raphael. She is standing, surrounded by four personages also standing, and overhead in the sky are angels singing from a music-book; this is all. The painter evidently does not aim at variety of attitude, nor at dramatic interest; there is no elaboration or effects of color; a reddish tone of admirable force and simplicity prevails throughout the painting. All the merit lies in the species and quality of the figures; color, drapery, action and the rest are there, like a grave sober accompaniment, which serves only to secure the solidity of the body and the nobleness of the type.

How define this type? The saint is neither angelic nor ecstatic; she is a vigorous, healthy, well-developed girl, of rich warm blood, and gilded by the Italian sunshine with glowing and beautiful color. On her left another young girl, less robust and more youthful, has more innocence, but her purity is yet only passivity. To my mind, however innocent and chaste they may be they are less so through temperament than through their youth; their placid minds are not yet disturbed, their tranquillity is that of ignorance. And, as with Raphael, we have to go in quest of our comparisons to the summit of the ideal, I will say for myself that but two types surpass his, one that of the Greek goddesses, and the other that of certain young girls of the north.

With the same perfection of organization and the same soul-serenity they yet possess something more, the former the sovereign pride of aristocratic races and the latter the sovereign purity of the spiritualistic temperament.

One readily sees here the exact moment in art which this painting represents. These five standing figures, no more than those of Perugino opposite to them, are not allied to each other, and impelled by a common impulse ; each figure exists for itself ; the composition is as simple as possible, almost primitive ; it is an ecclesiastical picture and not a parlor decoration ; it has been commissioned by some devout old lady and ministers to piety more than to pleasure. But again the personages are not as stiff as those of Perugino ; their immobility does not interdict action. They are robust, muscular and broadly draped ; beautiful, free, composed, like antique figures. The painter enjoys the unique advantage of standing between a christianity that is declining and a paganism that is becoming triumphant, between Perugino and Julio Romano. In every cycle of development there is one fortunate moment, and one alone ; Raphael benefited by one of these like Phidias, Plato and Sophocles.

What a distance between this St. Cecilia and the pictures of his master Perugino, and of his friend Francia whom he begged to correct his work! There are six of Francia's near it,—benevolent Madonnas copied from life ; a little less precise and dry than those of Perugino, but always instinct with literal art and the hard hand of the goldsmith. How expanded, noble and free everything becomes in the hands of the youthful painter! And how comprehensible are the admiring shouts of Italy!

He has a bad effect upon his successors, the Bolognese, who fill this gallery. On passing from a picture by Raphael to one of their works it seems like going

from a simple writer to a rhetorician. They aim at
effects, and are extravagant; they no longer know how
to use language correctly; they force or falsify the sense
of terms; they refine or exaggerate, their ambitious
style contrasting with their feeble conceptions and
their negligent diction. And yet they are zealous laborers, so many restorers of the language. Compared
with the Vasaris, Sabbatinis, Passerottis and Procacin-
nis, to their predecessors and rivals, to the degenerate
disciples of the great masters, they are painstaking
and moderate. They are not disposed to paint con-
ventionally, according to prescription like some of
their contemporaries, who, expeditious artists, gloried
in executing figures fifty feet high, in turning out half
a mile of painting per diem, painting even with both
hands, forgetful of nature and deriving everything
from their own genius, heaping together incredible muscles, extraordinary foreshortenings, theatrical attitudes
on a grand scale and treating all with the indifference
of a manufacturer and a charlatan. They stem this
tide; they study the old masters, remain poor and un-
employed a long time, and, finally, open a school. Here
they labor and neglect nothing in order to become
instructed in every department of their art. They
copy living heads and draw from the nude model; casts
from the antique, medals and original drawings by the
masters supply them with examples. They acquire a
knowledge of anatomy from corpses and of mythology
from books. They teach architecture and perspective; they discuss and compare the processes of ancient and modern masters; they observe the transformation of features through which a virile trait is converted into a feminine trait, an inanimate form into a
human form, a tragic attitude into a comic attitude.
They become learned, even erudite, eclectic and systematic. They fix principles and devise canons for painters
as the Alexandrians formerly did for orators and for

poets. They recommend "the drawing of the Roman school, the action and shadows of the Venetians, the beautiful color of Lombardy, the terrible style of Michael Angelo, the truth and naturalness of Titian, the pure and masterly taste of Correggio, the dignity and solidity of Pellegrini the creativeness of the wise Primaticcio and a little of the grace of Parmegiano."* They lay up stores and exercise themselves. Let us see what fruit this patient culture is going to produce.

There are thirteen large pictures here by Ludovico Caracci, and among them, a "Nativity of St. John the Baptist" and a "Transfiguration on Mount Tabor." Few personages can be imagined more declamatory than the three figures of the apostles, half thrown backward and especially the one with a naked shoulder; they are colossi, too rapidly executed and are without substance or solidity.—His nephew, Augustino, is a better painter, and his "Communion of St. Jerome" furnished the principal points for a similar picture by Domenichino; nevertheless, like his uncle he subordinates the essential to the accessory, truth to effect, forms and tones to action and expression.—The second nephew, Annibale Caracci, is the cleverest of all. Two of his pictures, representing the Virgin in her glory, conform to the sentimental piety of the age; his chiaroscuro and the multitude of tints fused into each other cater to the ambiguous emotions of effeminate devotion. His St. John designating the Virgin resembles an *amoroso*; near him a man kneeling, with a large black beard, expresses his emotion with a complacent tenderness not exempt from insipidity. The Virgin on her throne, the two saints male and female that accompany her, bend over with languishing grace. That beautiful saint herself in a pale violet robe, with parted fingers and plump hands, that Virgin with her

---

* From a sonnet by Augustino Caracci.

amiable dreamy air, are half-amorous and half-mystic
ladies. Seek for the sentiment which the art restored
by the Caracci serves to manifest, and there it is. In
Italy, toward the end of the sixteenth century the
character of man becomes transformed. The terrible
shocks and infinite ravages of foreign invasion, the ruin
of the free republics and the establishment of suspicious
tyrannies, the irremediable oppression of a rigorous
Spanish rule, the catholic restoration under the Jesuits,
the ascendency of bigoted popes and inquisitors, the
persecution of free thinkers and the organization of
clerical government snapped the spring of the human
will; society relaxes and grows enervated; people get
to be epicurean and hypocritical, and confess themselves
and make love. How great the distance between the
geniality, light careless fancy and naturally healthy
sensuality of Ariosto, and the forced phantasmagoria,
the morbid voluptuous derangement, the chivalry and
operatic piety found fifty years afterward in Tasso!
And poor Tasso is denounced as impious! He is compelled to recast his crusade, to prune his love scenes,
to exalt his characters, to transform them into allegories. Man has become effeminate and perverted; powerful and pure ideas no longer please him, but a
medley of refinements, conceits and graduated sentiments compounded of pleasure and asceticism, alternating betwixt the stage and the church, the crucifix
and the alcove. The same smile in this epoch rests
alike on the lips of saints and of goddesses; the nudity
of christian Madonnas is as attractively displayed as
that of pagan Venuses, the cavalier beholding his mistress decked, smiling and with open arms on the gild-
ing of his chapel as upon that of his own palace.
Love itself is transformed; it is no longer frank and
intense; Raphael's Fornarina to them would seem
simply a sound well-conditioned body; they would
prefer in her more affecting and more complex charms,

more delicate and more intoxicating seductions, a melancholy and mystic sweetness, the vague and winning grace of dreamy abandonment, moistened or ravished eyes interrogating space, soft forms melting away in the obscurity of shadows, draperies folded or displayed with studied ingenuity in the languor of artificial light or in the magic of chiaroscuro. They crave affectation and elaboration as their predecessors craved force and simplicity; on all sides, among the divergencies of the schools, with Baroche, Cigoli and Dolci, as with the Caracci, Domenichino, Guido, Guercino and Albano, we see a style of painting appear corresponding to the sugared beauties of the prevailing poesy to the new sigisbeism just introduced and to the opera about to commence.

When the soul has become enervated it demands powerful emotions; over-refinement leads to violence, and the nerves which, habituated to action have lost their stable balance, exact, after the tickling of delicate sensations, the uproar of extreme sentiments. Hence the extravagance of this sentimental art. The faithful have to be revived here by the pale face of a corpse, there by a butchery of martyrs, and there again by grossly coarse figures in contrast with those of an exquisitely celestial type; and always through the use of excessive gestures, imposing attitudes, a multitude of characters and dramatic effects. In this direction the Bolognese squander their talent and their art. A large work by Domenichino, "Our Lady of the Rosary," unites and masses together four or five tragic episodes aiming to show the efficacy of the sacred rosary: two females in mutual embrace and whom a cavalier tries to pierce with his lance, a soldier attempting to stab a shouting woman, a hermit dying on his straw pallet, a bishop in his cope supplicating Our Lady, all accumulated together in one frame; frightened or weeping figures, melodramatic executioners, pity, terror and

curiosity appealed to capriciously and without stint,
above all this, a shower of flowers and falling chaplets,
and the Madonna surrounded by frolicsome or tearful
angels bearing the crown of thorns with the cross,
Saint Veronica's handkerchief, and other insignia of
mechanical devotion; and, in the uppermost regions,
the little Jesus holding up, as if in triumph, a bouquet
of roses. Such is the piety of the day, as I have seen
it in Rome in the Jesuits' churches, a grand-orchestra
piety, aiming at conquering its public by dint of the
pleasing and by excitations.—His celebrated "Martyrdom of St. Agnes" is in the same taste. In the foreground lies a heap of corpses, the mouth of one opened
by his last cry, a horror-stricken woman thrown backward with a theatrical air and her infant concealing
itself in her robe. The saint meanwhile on her block,
pale, her eyes upturned to heaven, stretches out her
neck while a lamb, the symbol of her meekness, tries to
draw near and lick her feet. Behind her is the executioner with his skull illuminated and his face in shadow
all red and brown, the strength of the color and the
ferocity of his visage setting off the pallor and gentleness of his victim; he has a narrow hard head and is
an excellent executioner, studious to strike his blade
home. At the top appears a choir of noisy angels,
while Christ bends forward with an interested air to
take the crown and the palm-branch which an angel, a
genuine domestic, respectfully offers to him. And yet
it is full of talent; this work abounds with richness,
truth and expression. Domenichino is a true artist;
he felt, studied, dared and found. Although born in
a time when types were prescribed and classified he
was original; he reverted back to observation and discovered a hitherto unknown part of human nature. In
his "Peter of Verona" the fright of the saint, his
wrinkled and contracted brow, the crisped hands extended to ward off the blow, the terrified face of the

other monk who runs off raising his arms in despair
mingled with horror, every attitude and every physiognomy in the picture are new creations; here, for the
first time, is the full, hopeless expression of passion;
the terror, even, is so true that both the heads approach
the grotesque. Domenichino is never afraid of vulgarity. He sets out from the real, from the object
seen; the contrast between his classic education and
his native sincerity, between what he knows and what
he feels is certainly a strange one.

Almost all the painters of this school are here represented. There are three of the principal works of
Albano, all of a religious character, but equally as sentimental as his pagan pictures. For example, in his
"Baptism of Christ" the angels are gallant pages of
good birth; of all the masters he is perhaps the one
who best expresses the taste of this epoch, affected and
insipid, fond of sentimental nudities and gay mythological subjects.—Five or six pictures by Guercino with
cadaverous tones and powerful effects of shadows, are
striking but inferior to those I saw at Rome. Those
of Guido, on the contrary, are superior. I was only
familiar with his productions in his second manner,
almost all of them being gray, pale, formless and
without substance, produced quickly and according to
prescription, simple agreeable contours of easy, worldly
elegance but without embodying a substantial animated
figure, He possessed however, a fine genius, and if his
character had equalled his talent he would have been
qualified to attain to the first rank in his art. Here,
in the freshness and vigor of early inspiration he is
tragic and grand. He has not yet fallen into a faded,
bleached style of coloring; he feels the dramatic power
of tones, and all that strong contrasts and the lugubrious mournfulness of mingled dark tints speak to the
heart of man. Around his Christ on the cross and the
weeping saints about him the sky is nebulous, almost

black and overcast with storm-clouds, the personages
standing in these vast floating draperies—St. John in
his enormous red mantle, his hands clasped in despair,
the Magdalen at the foot of the cross streaming with
hair and falling drapery, the Virgin in her mournful
blue robe enveloped in an ashy mantle,—all this suffering choir, forming, through its color and masses, a sort
of grandiose, clamorous declamation which ascends upward to heaven.   Still more grandiose is the tragedy
entitled "Our Lady of Pity," and which covers an entire panel of the wall.   Five colossal figures, the protecting saints of Bologna, in large damascene copes,
earthy-hued monks' frocks and warriors' coats, appear
together, and behind them, in the distance, you can distinguish the obscure forms of bastions and the towers
of the city over which their protection extends.   Above
them, as if in an upper story of the celestial world, a
dead Christ between two weeping angels, displays his
livid pallor; still higher, at the summit of the mystic
region, a grand mournful Virgin enveloped in blue drapery, finds in her own grief more profound compassion
for human miseries.   This is a chapel background;
purer and more christian subjects were executed in the
times of perfect and primitive piety; but for the excited piety of subsequent eras, for a catholic and an epicurean city suddenly swept by pestilence and bowed
down by great anguish there is no painting more appropriate or more affecting.

CHAPTER III.

April 18.—This country seems to be made for the delight of a northern man, for eyes which satiated with too distinct forms and wearied with too bright light, gladly repose on a hazy indefinite horizon covered with a vapory atmosphere. It has rained; heavy dark clouds sleep quietly overhead, and, near the horizon, almost drag along the ground. Sometimes, the white back of a cloud exposes its satin lustre in the midst of the pale mist; an invisible sun warms the banks of vapor, while, here and there, scattered rays peer out like a diamond brooch from soft gray gauze. Toward the east extends an infinite flat plain. Its myriads of trees form in the distance at the edge of the sky a prodigious spider's web of innumerable thin and mingled threads. Their tops still brown are wedded to the young spring verdure, to willows, budding poplars, and the bright green grain. The earth has imbibed largely; the water glistens in the furrows, ditches and lagunes, and league after league, both right and left, the eye always falls on the tilled fields, and interminable rows of elms between which, travelling from trunk to trunk, are interlaced the tortuous stems of the vines.

I enter into conversation with an ecclesiastic of the country, and formerly a director in a college. The clergy here support the Pope on principle ; but all the *bourgeoisie,* every partially educated person, the larger portion of the nobility, even at Ravenna where aristocratic pride runs so high, are for the new order of things.

My ecclesiastical friend is liberal, strongly commends the schools and army which are the two latest great institutions. According to him "character in this country is naturally very violent; people resort to the stiletto *instanter;* (Lord Byron in his letters calls them superb two-legged tigers.) On receiving an insult they conceal themselves at night and kill the offender. Nothing can be more serviceable to such people than schools; instruction, reflection and reason are the sole counterpoises to instinct and temperament. As to the army, not only is it a school of obedience and honor but again an ulcerous issue; nothing could be more pertinent here than the proverb, *oziosi, viziosi;* excessive ferocity must be utilized against enemies instead of being criminally expended on neighbors; many energetic men who would have been private malefactors are thus converted into public protectors. The refractory, however, are not numerous; their numbers diminish annually. In the beginning the unknown, and transplantation frightened them; since that time the narratives of their comrades have reassured them, and a brilliant uniform begins to entice them. Another wholesome influence is the severity of the tribunals; assassinations are less frequent since convicts have ceased to be pardoned at the end of six months. The important thing in this country is to bridle the passions which are quite savage and the new regime labors in this direction."

It is now clear to me that the promoters and supporters of revolution throughout Italy are the enlightened and intelligent among the middle and *bourgeois* class; and that the difficulty lies in winning over and civilizing or italianizing the people. Lord Byron in 1820, at Ravenna, already states that the instructed alone are liberal, and that, in the projected insurrection, the peasantry would not rise.

The train stops, and, at a quarter of a league from

the city a round low dome appears between the green tops of the poplars; this is the Tomb of Theodoric. Its columns plunge down into a morass; its doors are falling, rotted by dampness; the stones of the rotunda seem to have been knocked away by blows from a hammer. The enormous cupola, one single mass thirty-four feet in diameter, has been riven by lightning. There is nothing in the interior save one altar and the names of witless travellers and stupid inscriptions written in lead-pencil on the dripping walls. The sarcophagus in which the body reposed has been removed; the old king was driven out of his sepulchre at the same time as his Gothic subjects from their domain, and only croaking frogs are heard in the stagnant pool filling the empty crypt.

On returning to Ravenna the spectacle is still more melancholy. One cannot imagine a more deserted, more miserably provincial, more fallen city. The streets are deserts; a few sharp stones serve as a pavement; a foul gutter runs midway through them; there are no palaces or shops. Two façades of public edifices, well scraped, the Academy and the theatre, are all that stand out in bold relief against this desolation through their cleanliness and commonplace character. You perceive old, rusty and dilapidated towers, the remains of ancient structures adapted to new uses, small white columns inserted in one of Theodoric's walls and plenty of nooks and corners for the populace. What could poor Byron accomplish here, even with his Countess Guiccioli? Sombre dramas, conspiracies, Byronism. The city has been dead for I know not how many centuries. The sea has receded; it is the last station· of the Roman empire, a sort of stranded waif which, when Byzantium withdrew, she abandoned on the strand. This city, on this rarely-visited, unhealthy coast could not revive in the middle ages like those of Tuscany. Even to-day it is still Byzantine, and more

desolate than a ruin because corruption is worse than
extinction. A canal leads to the sea, and on its sleepy
waters a few boats are seen and four or five sailing-craft.
The only beautiful object about the city is a forest of
pines which has taken root between it and the brackish
waves, and whose distant tops like so many dark circles
form a bar on the line of the horizon.

Ravenna.—Travellers who have visited the Orient
say that Ravenna is more Byzantine than Constantinople itself. A city like this is unique; what can be
more strange than this Byzantine world? We are not
sufficiently familiar with it; we have a collection of
dull chroniclers and Gibbon, who gives of it a very fair
idea; but the distance is infinite between mere ideas
and a complete, colored image. What a spectacle,
that of a world in which antique civilization drags
along for a thousand years and ends under a perverted
christianity and among oriental importations! Nothing
like it can be found in history; it is a unique moment
of the human soul and culture. We have a good
knowledge of the origins, growth and perfection of various peoples, and even of partial declines like those of
Italy and Spain; but a degeneracy so long and complicated, a gigantic mouldering away of a thousand years
in a closed retort, aggravated by the fermentations of
so many and such opposite species, is without example.
There are two civilizations, both of them resembling
the immense ulcers, swellings and deformities of humanity, which I would like to see narrated, not by an
antiquary but by an artist, those of Alexandria and
Byzantium. Add to these India and China, when the
archæological soil shall have been well ploughed up by
the erudites.

The first church you encounter, San Apollinare, is a
large gable-shaped façade, furnished with a portico
that supports arcades resting on columns. The nave
still retains the form of the latin basilica with a flat

ceiling, and twenty veined marble columns brought from
Constantinople profile their corinthian capitals, already
perverted, up to the round apsis. The edifice is of the
sixth century, but the unchangeable mosaics which on
both sides cover the frieze of the nave show as clearly
as at the first day what Greek art had got to be in the
monastic hands of theological disputants and of the
rouged Cæsars of the Lower Empire.

It is still Greek art. Ten centuries after their death
the sculptors of the Parthenon keep their hold on the
human mind, and the babbling idiots who now usurp
the world's stage ever detect with their blinking eyes,
as through a mist, the grand forms and noble drapery
which once ranged themselves on the pediments of pagan temples. Two processions extend above the capitals, one of twenty-two saints ending with the Virgin,
and the other of twenty-two saints ending with Christ,
and in neither of them do the extreme ugliness, the
close imitation of vulgar reality as seen in the middle
ages, yet appear. On the contrary the figures of the
women, regular, rather tall, calm although sad, have
an almost antique dignity; their hair falls in tresses
and is gathered at the top of the brow as in the coiffure of nymphs: their stoles depend in long, grave
folds. Equally grave, a file of grand virile figures develops itself, and near Christ and the Virgin are angels
praying in large white vestments their foreheads encircled with white bandlets. But here all reminiscences
end: the artists know traditionally that a form must be
draped, that a certain adjustment of the hair is preferable and a certain form of the face; they no longer
know what virile form and what young and healthy
soul lived beneath these externals. They have un-
learned observation of the living model, the Fathers
having interdicted it; they copy authorized types;
their mechanical hands servilely repeat, copy after
copy, the contours which their minds no longer compre-

hend, and which unskilful imitation is to falsify. From artists they have become mechanics, and in this fall, deeper and deeper every day, they have forgotten the half of their art. They no longer recognize human diversity; they repeat twenty times in succession, the same costume and action; their virgins can do no more than wear crowns and advance with an air of immobility, all in great white stoles, one, especially, in a striped or mottled gold cloth like a Chinese frock, with a large white veil attached to the head and with orange-colored shoes, in short the costume of ancient Greece lengthened in monastic fashion and embroidered with oriental spangles. They possess no physiognomy; the features, frequently, are as barbarous as those of a child's drawing. The neck is rigid, the hands woodeny and the folds of the drapery mechanical. The personages are rather indications of men than men themselves; and when the man is got at through the indication the spectacle revealed is still more melancholy, which is the debasement of the model beyond the ineptitude of the mosaicist and the decadence of man beyond the decadence of art.

There is not, indeed, one of these figures that is not that of a vacant, flattened, sickly idiot. Words are wanting to express their physiognomy, that air of a well-built man and with ancestors of a fine race, now half destroyed, as if dissolved by a system of long fasting and paternosters. They have that dull aspect, that species of lax debility and resignation in which the living creature, vainly struck, returns no sound.* They no longer possess action, will, thought, or spirit; they are no longer capable of standing up although erect. One would imagine secret vices, so evident is the exhaustion of blood and human vitality. The angels are great simpletons with staring eyes, hollow

---

* See, in particular, the seventh figure alongside of Christ.

cheeks and that prim and chilled air common to peasants who, taken from the fields and transported amid
the bickerings, formalities and restraints of theology
and the seminary, become bleached and yellow, stupid
and abashed. Above the angels several of the saints
seem to be emerging from a long fit of nausea or a
tedious fever: nobody would believe, before having
seen them, that an animated being could become so
inert and flabby and lose to such a degree, his physical and moral substance. But that which most inten-
sifies the impression is the figure of Christ and of the
Virgin. Christ in a brown mantle, with the beard and
hair of the ancient gods, is nothing but an impoverished, belittled god; his brow, the seat of intelligence, is contracted and almost effaced; his lips are
thin, the face attenuated, and his big eyes cavernous.
This degradation is unequalled except by that of the
Virgin. The *panagia* has sunk away to an extraordinary degree; nothing is left to her but her eyes; the
nose and mouth are almost gone, while her emaciated
hands and fleshless face are those of a dying consumptive; she has the action of a manikin, or of a skeleton
whose bones and tendons just move, her large violet
mantle letting no sign appear of the contracted body
beneath it.

CHAPTER IV.

CHARACTER OF THE CIVILIZATION OF CONSTANTINOPLE.—CHANGE
AND ABASEMENT OF THE SOCIAL AND ARTISTIC SPIRIT.—SAN
VITALE, ITS ARCHITECTURE AND MOSAICS.—JUSTINIAN AND
THEODORA.—THE TOMB OF PLACIDIA.

WHAT kind of machinery is it which, catching the
human sprout in its cogs insensibly expresses all its
sap and succulence in order to leave of it simply an
empty form and an inert detritus? First comes the
brutal Roman republic, then the onerous imposts of the
Roman Cæsars, then the still more onerous imposts of
the Byzantine Cæsars, and a despotism in which all
forces capable of depressing man are found combined.
—The emperor is a pacha, who may deprive any of his
subjects, even a bishop, of life without trial; he may
confiscate whatever private property he covets or declare himself heir to any fortune he likes ; all dignities,
all estates, all lives in this society anxiously hang upon
the caprices of his arbitrary will.—The emperor is an
inquisitor. Under Justinian twenty thousand Jews are
massacred and twenty thousand sold. The Montan-
ists are burned along with their churches. The patrician Photius, forced to abjure Hellenism stabs himself
with a poniard, and in other reigns, we see heretics
exiled, despoiled, mutilated or burnt alive.—The emperor is the head of a faction or sect, at one time
orthodox, and at another heretic, now persecuting the
"Blues" and now the "Greens," allowing his own
party to commit robberies, assassinations and other outrages on the public highways.—The emperor is a pre-
fect over morals and manners. Under Justinian vo-

luptuousness is punished the same as assassination, and parricides, and debauchees are paraded bleeding through the streets of Constantinople.—The emperor is a bureaucrat. His systematic administration, extending downward through all provinces, everywhere stifles human enterprise in order to leave on the soil nothing but functionaries and tributaries.—The emperor is a professor of etiquette. A complicated ceremonial prescribes under him a hierarchy of officials who are machines only, and whose actions, like his own, are subordinated to empty forms, the significance of which is often quite unknown to them.* Every mechanical contrivance which can suppress in man his power of will and activity work together continuously and for centuries, the violent ones that crush, and the enfeebling ones that undermine, terror as in oriental monarchies, denunciations as in Imperial Rome, orthodox persecutions as in Spain, legal rigorism as in Geneva, the *camorra* as in Naples, and official routine and bureaucratic enrollment as in China. Like an axe that fells, like a file that wears, like an acid that corrodes, like a rust that defaces, the various elements of despotism in turn, hack, break, decompose or soften the solid and trenchant steel subjected to their action. This is readily apparent in the language of their writers ; they no longer know how to praise or to blame. Trebonius, associated with Justinian, says that he fears that he will see him disappear, borne off by angels because he is too celestial. Procopius thinks that Justinian and Theodora are not human beings but demons and vampires sent to desolate the earth ; after eight books of adulation he at last lets loose his hatred and heaps up furious detractions with the blind awkwardness and mechanical rage of a desperado who, having escaped torture, stammers, repeats

---

* Codinus Curopalates.

himself and remains dumb.* Others are courtiers, cav-
illers, and scribes, and the nation is the same as its
writers. The characters which such a regime multiplies
or brings forward consists first of palace domestics, embroidered chamberlains, flaunting mercenaries, the
eunuchs,† the intriguers, the extortioners and after
these the scribblers, the casuists, the bigots, the
pedants and the rhetoricians, and, by their side on
the broad stage of society, horse-drivers, buffoons,
actresses, lorettes and *gandins.*

Such, indeed, are the conspicuous characters in the
play. Old Roman iniquity subsists under the monkish
crust which Christianity has formed over it; the condemned are still given up to lions in the arena; the entire city takes sides in the chariot-races, and the
"Greens" like the "Blues" bear the colors of their drivers as badges, and conceal daggers in baskets of fruit
in order to assassinate each other at their leisure. As
formerly in the Floral Games, women appear naked on
the stage; if new regulations impose a girdle on them,
Theodora, the bear-keeper's daughter, and the future
empress, takes advantage of the prohibition to invent
lascivious refinements under the spectators' eyes. And
these are the same people that surrender themselves
furiously to theological passions. "Ask a man," says
Gregory of Nazianza, " to change a coin for you and he
will inform you how the Son differs from the Father.
Demand of another the price of bread and he will reply
that the Son is inferior to the Father. Try to ascertain
if your bath is ready, and you will be told that the Son
is created without substance." They massacre each
other on account of these doctrines, and the only point
of interest likely to excite a revolt at Constantinople is

---

* Compare in Procopius and in Tacitus a dunce's hatred with that
of a man.

† A wealthy widow bequeathed to the Emperor Theophilus three
hundred of these characters.

the question of azymite wafers or the twofold nature of Jesus Christ. The *trisagion*, simple or complete, is sung simultaneously in the cathedral by two inimical choirs, and the adversaries fall to belaboring each other with stones and clubs. Justinian passes entire nights with graybeards examining ecclesiastical documents while the monks who swarm in the Archipelago equip a fleet in order to defend images against Leo the Isaurian. These circus amateurs and the young beaux who dress like Huns through a fashionable caprice, these courtezans worn out with vices, these languid voluptuaries who people the summer palaces of the Bosphorus, all fast, form processions, recite religious symbols and demand persecutions of newly installed emperors.* "Long live the Emperor! Long live the Empress! Unearth the bones of the Manichæans! He who will not curse Severus is a Manichæan! Cast Severus out! Cast out the new Judas! Put down the enemies of the Trinity! Unearth the bones of the Eutychians! Cast the Manichæans out of the Church! Cast out the two Stephens!" Incompetent to fight, to rule; to labor or to think they still know how to wrangle and to enjoy themselves. The sophist and the epicurean live on the remnants of human dissolution; the play of formulas in vacant minds, and the cravings of the senses in degenerate bodies are the last springs of activity, and the two works to which this civilization tends, both marked with the same imprint, both artificial, vast and void, both formed without taste or reason by the routine of logical or industrial processes are, first, the complicated minute scaffolding of the symbolry and distinctions of theology, and, second, the glittering composite scaffolding of accumulated wealth and extravagant luxury.

---

* Codinus, notes to page 281. Compare the acclamations of the Senate on the death of Commodus, set forth in the history of Augustus.

Whoever could have visited Constantinople before its
pillage by the Crusaders would have witnessed a
strange spectacle.* After passing the enclosure of
high crenelated walls and the towers which defended
the city like a mediæval fortress, he would have found
an image of ancient Imperial Rome consisting of ranges
of two-story porticoes traversing the city in every sense
and from one extremity to another, domes whose gilded
metal glittered in the sunlight, gigantic pillars supporting colossal equestrian statues, eleven forums, twenty-
four baths, so many monuments, palaces, columns and
statues that antique civilization, eradicated elsewhere
in the world, seems to have collected in this last asylum
all its masterpieces and all its treasures. Effigies of
victorious athletes brought from Olympus, statues of
ancient gods wrested from sanctuaries and figures of
emperors multiplied by public adulation, covered the
squares and filled the baths and amphitheatres. A
bronze Justinian arose on a pillar of seventy cubits
high, its base vomiting forth water. A sculptured column within which ran a spiral staircase, bore on its top
the equestrian statue of Theodosius in gilded silver.
Figures of tortoises, crocodiles and sphinxes placed
upon other pillars lifted in the air the emblems of
conquered nations. The sombre bronze of colossi, the
pallid whiteness of statues gleamed between shafts of
porphyry under the variegated marbles of the porticoes,
amidst the luminous rotundities of the cupolas, among
the long silken robes, embroidered simarres, and the
gilded and motley costumes of an innumerable populace. In a marble circus chariots raced around an
Egyptian obelisk. Outside, a brazen column around
which wound enormous serpents, and farther on, fantastic figures of Scylla and Charybdis, the antique boar

---

* Du Cange, "Description of Constantinople." All authorities
are here combined.

of Calydon and various marble and bronze monsters,
indicated the fêtes where lions, bears, panthers and
wild asses let into the arena, amused the people with
their yells and combats.   There on a throne supported
by twenty-four columns the Emperor, on Christmas-day,
gave the signal, and men of all nations delighted the
eyes of the crowd with the novelty of their costumes
in form and in color.   Farther on an amphitheatre
afforded the spectacle of criminals abandoned to wild
beasts.   Toward the east St. Sophia displayed its
glittering domes, its hundred columns of jasper and
porphyry, its precious marbles veined with rose, striped
with green and starred with purple whose saffron,
snowy and metallic tints commingled as in Asiatic
flowers among balustrades and capitals of gilded
bronze before a silver sanctuary facing a tabernacle
of massive gold, near golden vases incrusted with
gems and beneath innumerable mosaics decking its
walls with lustrous stones and spangles of gold.   The
dominant characteristics of this church, as throughout
the city, were disorderly accumulation and unintelligent
wealth.   Magnificence was regarded as art and people
sought not beauty but bewilderment.   Precious materials were accumulated and fashioned into barbarous
capitals.   Greek models whose simplicity they could
not comprehend were abandoned for oriental prodigality the display of which could be imitated.   The emperor Theophilus had the palace of the Caliphs of
Bagdad copied, and the luxury of his new dwelling, in
its oddities and extravagance, announced the puerilities
and dotage of a perverted intellect reverting back in
old age to the toys of its infancy.   In the throne-room
a tree of gold sheltered with its branches and leaves a
flock of golden birds whose diverse voices imitated the
warbling of living birds.   At the foot of the platform
stood two golden lions of natural size which roared
when foreign envoys were presented.   The high digni-

taries of the palace formed rows each with its special
costume, its right of precedence, its attitude and other
details prescribed in a book written by the hand of an
emperor.   Ambassadors bowed their foreheads to the
ground three times and while in this prostrate attitude
a theatrical machine elevated the prince and his throne
to the ceiling in order that he might descend again in a
more sumptuous apparel.   His bootees were of purple
and his robe was starred with jewels ; on his head
glittered a high Persian tiara strewn with diamonds,
attached to the cheeks by two strings of pearls and surmounted by a globe and a cross ; the most skilful
coiffeurs had arranged false hair in tiers above his
head and his face was painted.   Thus bedizened he
remained mute and impassible with fixed eyes in the
attitude of a god revealing himself to mortal eyes ; he
was worshipped as an idol and paraded himself like a
manikin.*

Some idea of this luxuriousness, and of this worship
and society, can be had in the church of San Vitale in
Ravenna.   It was built in the reign of Justinian and
to-day, although defaced on the exterior, miserably
repainted within, ruined in many places, or plastered
with discordant additions, is still the most byzantine of
western churches.   It is a singular structure, and in it
we find a new type of architecture as remote from Grecian as it is from Gothic conceptions.   The edifice consists of a round dome surmounted by a cupola through
which the light descends.   On the cornice turns a two-
story circular gallery composed of seven smaller half-
domes, the eighth, largely expanded, forming an apse
and containing the altar, in such a way that the central
rotundity is enveloped in an enclosure of smaller ones,
the globular form prevailing throughout like the pointed

---

* These proceedings and this attitude are already encountered with
Constantine and Constance.

form in mediæval cathedrals and the square form in antique temples.

In order to support the cupola eight heavy polygonal pillars, connected by round arcades, form a circle, while smaller columns, two and two, bind together the intermediate spaces. The effect is peculiar; the eye accustomed to following columns in rows is here surprised with curious intersections, an odd diversity of profiles, with upright forms cut off by round arches and other changing aspects at every turn presented by its discordant features. This edifice is the organism of another kingdom, arranged according to unknown symmetries and for other conditions of being, like a lustrous spiral shell for one of the articulata or vertebrata, pompous and strange if you please, but of a less simple type and of a less healthy construction. Degeneracy is visible at once in the capitals of the pillars and columns. They are covered with clumsy flowers and by a coarse network; others, still more changed, present a cypher; the elegant corinthian capital is so deformed in the hands of these masons and embroiderers as to be nothing but a jumble of barbaric designs. The impression is stamped at once on contemplating the mosaics. You see the empress Theodora, the ancient stage-tumbler and circus prostitute, bearing offerings along with her female attendants: the face is pallid and almost gone like that of a consumptive lorette; there are only enormous eyes, eyebrows joined together and a mouth; the rest of the visage is reduced and thin; the brow and chin are too small, and the head and body are lost under their ornamentation. There is nothing left of her but her ardent gaze and the feverish energy of a meagre and satiated courtezan, now enveloped in and overburdened with the monstrous luxury of an empress; a glittering diadem displays on her head stories of ruby and emerald stars; pearls and diamonds are scattered in embroideries upon her robe, and her purple mantle and shoes are embroidered with gold. The women around her sparkle like herself, striped with gold and strewn with pearls: the same fulness of eye absorbing the entire face, the same contraction of brow invaded by the hair, the same pallor of the blanched and plastered countenance. It matters little whether the mosaicist is a mechanic copying a recognized type or a painter executing a portrait; we have here an idea of the woman such as he beheld her or as she represented herself to him, an exhausted lorette bedizened with gold.

On the other side appears Justinian, with his warriors on his right and his clergy on the left, a sort of solemn simpleton in a grand brown mantle and purple bootees, decked and gilded like a shrine. He is an inert wooden figure; his two ministers on the right are about to fall; and his warriors, with their large oriental bucklers are marionettes. The artist is fallen as low as his model.

Back of the apse and on both flanks of the chapel run files of sacred personages: Christ between two angels and two saints holding a book; near by diverse episodes from the Bible; Abel sacrificing, Abraham entertaining his celestial visitants, and, on the vault above, peacocks, urns and animals. The art of grouping figures is not yet extinct,—at least they know how to arrange a symmetrical composition. One can occasionally detect in a head of St. Peter or of St. Paul the remains of an antique type; but the figures are stiff and jointless, closely resembling those of feudal tapestries. Ever the same large hollow eyes, the same cornea, the same brown, livid, deathly visage: Christ seems like a corpse resuscitated from the tomb, the vision of a diseased intellect.

I visited two or three other churches, Santa Agatha and the Baptistery. The latter is of the fifth century, somewhat like that of Florence, upheld by two stories of arcades, the columns and capitals of which seem, through their incongruities, to have been taken from pagan temples; already in the time of Constantine impotent architects despoil pagan edifices of their marbles and sculptures. Clumsy arabesques cover the walls, and on the vault appears the baptism of Jesus Christ around which the twelve apostles are ranged in a circle, so many figures of gigantic proportions in white tunics and gilded mantles. Their heads are small and of extraordinary length; their shoulders are narrow and their eyes are buried in their great arched concavities. Nevertheless the ascetic regime has not yet narrowed them down to the same extent as their descendants of the succeeding century at San Vitale; St. Thomas still preserves a trace of energy; St. John the Baptist, half-naked, is still half-alive; his thigh, shoulder and head are sound. You see in the water the entire nudity of Jesus; excepting his arm the muscles still contract. Perhaps the christian artist had some pagan painting before him and his eyes, obscured by the tyranny of mystic ideas, followed contours which his dull trembling hand could not or dared not more than partially trace.

Three or four other monuments fully demonstrate this decadence. That Placidia, an imperial princess to whom the Goth Ataulf her husband made a wedding present of fifty slaves; each bearing a basin filled with gold and another with precious stones, has her monument near San Vitale. It is a small low temple in the shape of a cross into which one descends by several steps into a sort of sombre reddish subterranean chamber decked with mosaics. Rosaces, leaves, fantastic birds, fawns at the foot of the cross, evangelists, a rude figure of the good shepherd surrounded by his lambs, the entire work is savage and of barbaric, extravagant luxuriousness. Several tombs find shelter in the humid shadows; one of them represents the divine lamb, with a fleece of shells, and under the cross of Placidia's sepulchre you perceive a flock—of what—sheep, horses or asses? Another cave contains a tomb of the Exarch Isaac who died in the middle of the seventh century. You see bas-reliefs here which a modern mason would repudiate; the three magi dressed as barbarians with the pantaloons, cloaks and caps of German shepherds, a Daniel, and a Lazarus whose head forms a quarter of his body, and peacocks that can scarcely be recognized. All this art is feebleness and decomposition, like a decayed building tottering and going to pieces. Ravenna, at this period, in passing into Lombard hands, only falls from one barbaric stage to another; whether Byzantine or Gothic the two arts are equivalent. Along with man the soil becomes perverted; the fevers of summer kill the inhabitants, the marshes spread out and the city sinks in the earth. They have been obliged to raise the pavement of San Vitale in order to protect it from water. On visiting San Apollinare in Classe, half a league from the city, you see on your way a marble column; this is the remnant of an entire city, the last fragment of a ruined basilica. The church itself seems to be abandoned; it subsists alone in a desert, formerly one of the three quarters of Ravenna; the crypt is often invaded by the tide, while near it a forest of pines, mute and the sojourn of vipers, has replaced, on the side of the sea, the cultivation and habitations of man.

CHAPTER V.

FROM BOLOGNA TO PADUA.—ASPECT OF THE COUNTRY.—PADUA.—
STATE OF SOCIETY IN THE FOURTEENTH CENTURY AND OF ART
IN THE FIFTEENTH CENTURY.—SANTA MARIA DELL' ARENE AND
THE WORKS OF GIOTTO.

IT seems as if this country was entirely alluvial. It
is an Italian Flanders. On both sides of the railway
extends an immense plain, entirely green, filled with
cattle and horses pasturing. The vernal sun everywhere diffuses its joyous beams; nothing impedes them
except, on the horizon, a belt of slender trees like a
delicate silken fringe; the broad cupola of the sky is
of the tenderest azure.

The soil is thoroughly soaked with water and, soon, the
canals commence. After leaving Ferrara the road
forms an elevated causeway protected from inunda-
tions; ditches abound everywhere, and pools of water
filled with rushes; on the right is the silvery surface
of the Po, so placid that it seems to be motionless;
thus does it glide along amply expanded amidst the
universal freshness among polished sands and islands
covered with wood. You travel along a straight road
compact and clean as in Flanders, between poplars of
a charming green. The trees are all budding; spring
as far as the eye can see is diffusing itself over all
things.

Often, at the end of a long white ribbon of road rises
a bell-tower, and then a cluster of houses appears on a
flat piece of ground; this is a village; the houses, plastered white and the ruddy bricks of the campanile
relieve sharply on the sky. Excepting the light it
might be called a Dutch landscape. Calm and spark-

ling water is everywhere visible and, as evening approaches, the frogs croak.

Meanwhile, on the left, rises a lofty blue barrier, a drapery of mountains fringed with snow and relieving with exquisite delicacy; the sky arches clear and pale and the young verdure overspreads the plain with an almost equally delicate tint.

Padua, April 20.—Here I am in an Austrian country. One would scarcely believe it on seeing the books and engravings displayed in the shops of the booksellers, the most prominent being "le Maudit," the "Vie de Jesus" by Renan and by Strauss, (the latter translated by Littré,) Victor Hugo, Hegel, etc. One engraving represents Garibaldi asleep, and Alexander Dumas contemplating him; Garibaldi lies on a floor and near him is a pitcher of water and a crust of bread, the epigraph, by Alexander Dumas, comparing him to Cincinnatus.—The bookseller tells me, with a smile, that "le Maudit" is prohibited in Italian, but is not yet forbidden in French; portraits of Garibaldi are interdicted but not lithographs that contain a number of figures. Under this systematic administration the law is executed to the letter, and before making any innovations instructions are awaited from Vienna.

Proceeding onward we find a city in good order, provincial in aspect, provided with arcades and a green grassy *prato*. Its tranquillity, its respectable appearance and its gray-coated sentinels remind the traveller that here, as in every well-governed city, the people must eat well, sleep better, take ice-creams at cafés, amuse themselves without disturbances and attend lectures at a university which create no excitement; the only matter of serious import to the inhabitants is the payment of their taxes on the day prescribed. Thereupon he ponders over what it was in the middle-ages; on its *podestat* Ezzelin the terror of children; on the sufferings of its nobles who day and night screeched with tortures; on those condemned young seigneurs who escaped from their guards, stabbed their judge and ripped up the face of their persecutor with their teeth; on its sanguinary struggle and the romantic adventures of the Carrari. And here, as at Bologna, Florence, Sienna, Perugia, and Pisa, he cannot avoid contrasting the terrible, hazardous and energetic life of feudal cities and principalities with the orderly precision and tameness of modern monarchies.

Here all that remains of the picturesque and the grand proceeds from the reaction of this great epoch. In every country a rich invention in the field of art is preceded by indomitable energy in the field of action. A father has fought, founded and suffered, heroically and tragically; the son gathers from the lips of the old heroic and tragic traditions, and, protected by the efforts of a previous generation, less menaced by danger, installed on paternal foundations, he imagines, expresses, narrates, sculptures or paints the mighty deeds of which his heart, still throbbing, feels the last vibration. * This is why works of art are so numerous in Italy; each town has its own; there are so many that the visitor is overwhelmed by them; one would be obliged to rewrite his descriptions constantly. I am quite content not to go to Modena, Brescia or Mantua; all I regret is Parma. I shall leave Italy with but a partial idea of Correggio; but I shall compensate myself with the Venetian masters.

Even at Padua, which is a second-class city, it is necessary to make a choice. We go accordingly to the

---

* Take, for example, the generation between 1820 and 1830 after the Revolution and the wars of the Empire; Dutch art after the struggle of the Netherlands with Spain; Gothic architecture and mediæval poesy after the consolidation of feudal society; the literature of the XVII century in France after the establishment of a regular monarchy; Greek tragedy, architecture and sculpture after the defeat of the Persians, etc.

church of Santa Maria dell' Arena, situated at the end
of the city in a quiet corner. It is a private chapel,
and stands in a large *bourgeois* garden, enclosed by
walls, somewhat neglected, where vines on a green
grass-plot are climbing up the fruit-trees. A servant
pushes back a bolt, and the visitor is introduced into a
nave which Giotto (1304) has covered with paintings.
He was twenty-eight years old, and he has here portrayed in thirty-seven great frescoes, the entire story of
Christ and the Virgin. No monument better represents the dawn of the Italian Renaissance. Several
traces of barbarism still remain; for example, he does
not know how to render all actions; in his "Christ at
the Sepulchre," the attendants expressing their grief
open their mouths with a grimace, and his "Hell," like
that of Bernardo Orcagna, is filled with the grotesque.
The big hairy Satan is a scarecrow like those of our
ancient mysteries, and inferior demons are consuming
or sawing up small naked bodies with meagre legs
heaped together as in a salting-tub. Near by the resuscitated leaving their tombs, have spare and twisted
claws, and, what is still more repulsive, the huge disproportioned heads of tadpoles; the quaint and impotent fancy of the middle ages peers out and flourishes
here as on the doors of the cathedrals. Jacomino of
Verona, a minor friar of this epoch, described these
torments of the damned with still greater triviality.
Satan, according to him, commands "the wicked to be
roasted like a pig on an iron turnspit;" then, when the
charred figure is brought to him, he replies: "Begone,
tell that miserable cook that the morsel is not well
done; put it back on the fire and let it stay there."
Dante alone could free himself from this popular buffoonery and endow his condemned ones with souls as
proud as his own. He was here in Padua the same
time as Giotto and, it is said, stayed at his house, both
being friends. But the domain of painting is not the

same as that of poesy, and what one accomplished
with words the other could not accomplish with colors.
People were not yet familiar enough with the muscles
and energies of the human organism to combine, like
Michael Angelo, in a few colossal and contorted figures
the tragic elements which Dante displayed in his numerous visions and in his lugubrious scenery. Moreover, the talent and humor of the painter were not
those of the poet; Giotto was as gay as Dante was
sad; his fine genius, facile invention, his love of nobleness and pathos, led him toward ideal personages and
affecting expressions, and it is in this field, peculiar to
him, that here, for the first time, with extraordinary
richness and success, he innovated and created.

Here, for the first time in a fresco,.we find almost
antique heads; it is the same stroke of genius as that
of Nicholas of Pisa: after a lapse of fifty years painting and sculpture unite, and healthy, regular beauty
reappears on the walls of churches as on the tombs of
the saints. Around Christ on the Cross and in the
Last Judgment, the noble heads of the saints have the
solidity of structure and the firm chins of the Greek
statues: nothing can be graver and simpler than the
draperies, and nothing more beautiful than the figures
of the ten seraphims crowned with glories. Extending
along the entire nave, at the base of the wall, is a range
of ideal women representing, in gray, the different virtues, all robust and calm, ample and finely draped; two
especially, Charity and Hope, seem to be Roman empresses; another, Justice, possesses a face of the
sweetest and purest type. You feel that the painter
lovingly seeks after and discovers perfection of form;
his Christs are not portraits; their features are too regular and too serene; one of them in the "Marriage
Feast at Cana," in a wine-colored mantle reminds one
of that which Raphael has placed in his "Transfiguration." The artist, evidently, does not paint from the

model before him but, like Raphael, " according to a certain conception of his own." This inventiveness is observable on all sides, in his landscapes, in his architecture, in the careful composition of his groups, and, above all, in the expressions. Some there are which come direct from the heart, so spontaneous, so true that none more genuine can be found. At the foot of the cross the Virgin in a blue hood, her brow wrinkled and pale, swoons and yet, through a supreme effort, remains erect.* The Magdalen extends her arms to the resuscitated Christ, with stupor and tenderness, as if desirous of advancing and yet remaining fixed to the ground. Lazarus, enveloped in his bandages, and rigid like a mummy in its coffer, but erect and with animated eyes, is an overpowering apparition.—This man possessed genius, ideas, feeling everything, save science which is the fruit of time, and finish in his execution; his drawings were generalizations, consisting simply of outlines and folds of drapery; in address, and in the art of the hand he was deficient. In a neighboring church, that of the Eremitani, are some frescoes by Mantegna, quite perfect, admirable in relief and of studied correctness; this is what a century and a half would have taught Giotto; what a painter he would have been had he mastered such processes! Perhaps the world would have seen a second Raphael.

---

* This reminds us of one of Corneille's lines describing his Roman heroine suddenly falling like a statue:

"Non, je ne pleure pas, madame, mais je meurs."

CHAPTER VI.

PADUA, CONTINUED.—SAN GIUSTINA.—SAN ANTONIO.—THE SCULP-
TORS AND DECORATORS OF THE FIFTEENTH AND SIXTEENTH
CENTURIES.—THE MUNICIPAL SYSTEM COMPARED WITH THE
EXTENDED GOVERNMENTS OF MODERN TIMES.—THE ADVANTA-
GES AND DRAWBACKS OF CONTEMPORARY CIVILIZATION.

WE return to the Prato, which is green and radiant
with Spring. A canal crosses it and statues are ranged
among the trunks of the trees. Around it rise high
walls of red brick ; blue domes profile themselves in
powerful masses against the pure blue sky, and, on the
cornices of the churches, birds are carolling in the midst
of the solitude and the silence.

In front, is San Giustina and its eight domes. Although built in the sixteenth century the byzantine
form, with its rotundities, prevails. Spherical projections form a circle around the cupolas ; within, between
round arcades, the roof hollows out into concave bucklers, its ample vault expanding like an interior firmament filled with light. One comprehends immediately
here the expressive force of lines. According as the
ruling form differs so does the general sentiment differ.
The acute angle and upspringing ogive excite mystic
emotion ; the right angle and the solid square pose of
the Greek construction suggest an idea of calm serenity ;
the byzantine imperial or modern curve of the round
arch gives a decorative aspect. Such is the impression
made by this church ; with its portal of black, red and
white marbles, its square pilasters, its projecting entab-
latures, its Roman capitals, its grand proportions and
its fine light it imposes on you not without a certain
degree of quaintness and pomposity. Behind the

choir, and by the hand of Veronese, a deluge of little angels, amidst strong contrasts of light and shadow, is precipitating itself on the spot where the saint, in a splendid robe of yellow silk, surrenders himself to the executioner about to sever his throat. The rest of the edifice is filled with theatrical sculptures, gesticulating martyrs, rumpled draperies and writhing flesh-forms in the style of Bernini, only still more insipid. The grandiose of the sixteenth century thus terminates with the affectation of the eighteenth.

But the principal monument, the most celebrated for its sanctity and the richest in works of art, is the church of San Antonio. On the solitary square surrounding it stands the bronze equestrian statue of the condottiero Guattemalata, executed by Donatello, and the first that was cast in Italy (1453). In his cuirass, with his head bare and his baton of command in his hand, he sits firmly on a stout-limbed charger, a vigorous animal for use and for war, and not for show ; his bust is full and square ; his great two-handed sword hangs below his horse's belly ; his long spurs with big rowels can bury themselves deep in the flesh when a perilous leap is to be made over a fosse, or to surmount a palisade ; he is a rude warrior ; and as he sits there in his harness you see that, like Sforza his adversary, he has passed his life in the saddle. Here, as at Florence, Donatello dares to risk the entire truth, the crude details that seem ungracious to the vulgar, the faithful imitation of the actual person with his own features and professional traits ; the result of which is, here as in Florence, a fragment of living humanity, snatched breathing out of his century, and prolonging, through its originality and energy, the life of that century down to our own.

As to the church it is very peculiar, it being an Italian-Gothic structure complicated with Byzantine cupolas ; round domes, pointed spires, little columns surmounted with ogive arcades, a façade borrowed from the Roman

basilica, a balcony modelled after Venetian palaces
fuse together in one composite medley the ideas of
three or four centuries, and of three or four countries.
The great saint of the city, St. Anthony, lies here, one
of the leading characters of the twelfth century, a
mystic preacher who addressed himself to fishes as St.
Francis did to birds, the fishes flocking to him in shoals
and signifying to him that they comprehended him.
The sanctuary contains his tongue and chin; at the
most flourishing period of Jesuitic devotion, in 1690, it
was decorated by Parodi with an incredible expenditure
of magnificence and affectation. The windows are embossed with silver, and a profusion of gay and animated
marble figures with arch expressions and suffused eyes
cover the walls with their sentimental graces. Back of
the chapel a legion of angels bear away the saint in
glory. There are perhaps sixty of them crowded and
piled together like a swarm of cupids on a boudoir
ceiling, with trim legs, smooth little bodies, pouting
visages, demure, and with plump dimpled cheeks;
some, leaning on the cross have the lively and tender
smile of a grisette asleep and dreaming. The whole
chapel seems to be an enormous console of ornamental
marble, and, to complete the impression, here and
there throughout the church, are gallant virgins coquet-
tishly lowering their coifs and playing with their fat
bambinos. The vapid devotion of the decadence evidently usurped for its own use the sanctuary of simple
old piety and overspread the popular faith with its own
veneering and varnish.

Other chapels show another age of the same sentiment; one, on the left, dedicated to the saint, was built
and decorated by ten sculptors of the sixteenth century,
Riccio, Sansovino, Falconetto, Aspetti, Giovanni di
Milano, Tullio Lombardo and others. Richness of
imagination, the superb sentiment of a pagan, natural
life, the entire spirit of the renaissance here shows itself

in striking characteristics. The façade of white marble, sewn with caissons of colored marble framed by black marble, resembles an antique triumphal arch. Marble columns covered with bas-reliefs and surmounted by round arcades give to it a monumental entrance. Shell niches, friezes of foliage, bucklers, horses, naked men, swans, fishes and cupids expose in the background the full diversity and breadth of heroic or animated nature. A multitude of petty sculptured figures embroider the walls and pillars; here the naked Fates among grapes and flowers, with a somewhat lank and literal imitation of the human figure for the first time comprehended; there a resurrection in which a studied aim at picturesque form mingles with the poetic sentiment of ideal form. And, as if to testify to the ardent faith which ever endures the same through all artistic transformations, you find amidst this imposing sensual decoration hundreds of *ex-votos*, in the shape of crutches, little ten-sous pictures and a quantity of charity boxes appealing for contributions.

Nothing is wanting here for the assemblage on one spot of the entire series of human sentiments. Facing this monument built by the pagan renaissance, is a chapel of the fourteenth century, that of St. Felix, ogival, painted and gilded, whose niches, similar to trefoils or bishops' bonnets, place gothic art before the eye brightened with oriental reflections through its proximity to Venice. It is red and sombre; its azure vaults deflect into small arches; arabesques run over the entire archway; sculptured stalls with gilded canopies divide into finials; ancient paintings by Altichierri and Jacopo Avanzi, figures draped and armed as in the middle ages, crowd together stiff, as yet, and awkward, among gothic castles covered with Saracenic ornamentation. Venice, at this time, had a foothold in the Orient, and at Cyprus she alone carried on the christian crusade.

But what makes this church a really unique monument,

a memorial of all ages, are the tombs it contains. In the
church of the Erematani I had just seen those of the
Carrari. No work is better fitted to make us comprehend the tastes and ideas of a century; the architect's
hand has labored at it as well as the sculptor's, and
whatever diversity there may be in the monuments all
symbolize the same idea, one of simple and prime significance, that of death, in such a way that the spectator follows in their differences the different modes in
which man regarded the most formidable moment of
life, the most poignant, the most universal and the most
intelligible of his interests. The series here is complete. A lady deceased in 1427 sleeps, reclining in an
alcove; underneath her three small figures in a shell
niche gravely meditate, and their heavy heads, their
attitudes and their drapery are as simple as the funereal
chamber in which her dead body reposes. Near this are
tombs of the sixteenth century, that of Cardinal Bembo, a grand figure somewhat bald with a superb beard
and the spirited air of a portrait by Titian; the other,
as grandiose and pompous as a triumph, that of the
Venetian general Contarini. A frieze of vessels, cuirasses, arms and bucklers winds around the courses of
marble. Shouting tritons and caryatides of chained
captives display the emblems and insignia of maritime
victory. A series of nude bodies, and heads having a
simple air rise upward, possessing the vigor and frank-
ness of expression characteristic of a healthy art in its
bloom and vitality. On the sides are displayed two figures of women, one young and spirited in a close-fitting
tunic, the breasts salient, and the other aged and weeping but not less robust and muscular. On the top of
the pyramid a beautiful Virtue with downcast eyes, but
with leg and breast exposed, seems like one of the
youthful and glorious divinities of Veronese. You continue on, and suddenly, at the end of the seventeenth
century, the change in taste appears; art becomes de-

votional, worldly, pretentious and vapid. A tomb of 1684 combines figures half naked or cuirassed in pagan panoply, but bending over, affected, and in a flutter of curtains, garlands and skulls. Another of 1690, is a scaffolding of men, angels, busts and pennons, beginning with a desiccated skull and crossbones and ending with, at the top, a winged skeleton blowing a blast on a trumpet. After the plain memorial representing actual death comes the pagan memorial overspreading death with heroic pomp; then the devotional memorial which puts into the same parade the horrors of the sepulchre and all mundane elegancies.

How gladly one reverts back to the works of the Renaissance! How noble, how vigorous, how grand man seems between gothic insufficiency and modern artificiality! The rest of the day I passed in the choir. Large bronze statuettes stand on a bronze balustrade near bronze gates. Bronze carpets the enclosure, covers the altar, bristles in bas-reliefs, rises on the pillars, and mounts upward in candelabras. Crowds of energetic figures display themselves everywhere in multiplied bosses on the sombre and lustrous tints of the gleaming metal. Here the apostles of Aspetti (1593) through their proud stature and disordered drapery, seem the grandchildren of Michael Angelo; there a candelabra by Riccio (1488) twice a man's height, with a base three feet square, rears itself upward in tier upon tier of figures; we cannot imagine greater richness of invention, so many and such diverse scenes, such luxury of ornamentation, such a complete world both christian and pagan magnificently combined in a single mass and yet distributed with so much art that every tier enhances the value of the others, its swarm of details producing groupings and its multitudes a unity. On the square sides are displayed stories of the New Testament, the interment of Jesus amidst the despairing cries and gestures of a weeping crowd, and, again, Jesus in limbo, amongst the stout bodies and fine naked limbs of redeemed sinners. On the cornices, and, here and there, on the angles and mouldings are pagan forms framing in the christian tragedy. Renaissance fancy has full play in a profusion of tritons, horses, twining serpents and torsos of women and children. Centaurs bear naked cupids on their cruppers brandishing torches; other cupids sport with masks or hold musical instruments; fawns and satyrs bound amidst the foliage; invention overflows, all this triumph of natural life, these panathenaic poesies of an unfettered creative human imagination displaying their action and exubérance in order to deck the candelabra which bears the pascal taper.

What the worker in bronze did in those days is incomparable. This art, that of the goldsmith, anticipates painting a century, and attains to its perfection while the other is just beginning. Master of all its processes it encroaches on those of its rivals. Knowledge of types, familiarity with the nude, the movement of draperies, study of expression, of composition, of perspective,—nothing is lacking. The modeller's thumb dispatches a picture complete,—thirty or forty figures grouped on different planes, active and excited multitudes, the entire human tragedy spread out on the public square between porticoes and temples.* Two by Donatello on the altar panels,† and twelve by Velano and Andrea Briosco on the panels of the choir, for fecundity of genius, boldness of conception, the management and arrangement of crowds, surpass anything I have ever encountered. Judith and the entire army of Holofernes are massacred and put to flight; Samson is wrenching away the columns of the temple

---

* See the "Martyrdom of St. Lawrence" by Baccio Bandinelli in the well-known engraving.
† 1446-1449.

crumbling under its crowded galleries; Solomon is seen under three stories of architecture surrounded by the assembled people; the ten tribes of Israelites crowd around the brazen serpent their bodies writhing and swollen with the bite of reptiles, suppliant women handing forward their infants to be cured, wounded men in heaps and in contortions, all in a vast landscape of rocks, palm-trees and flocks which diffuses the grandeur of a tranquil nature around the agitations of suffering humanity. All these souls and bodies live, and their energy reacts and communicates itself to the spectator. One feels exalted after a contemplation of them. Hence the nobleness of this art. Let the portraits and history of the men of this day be contemplated and we find that they fought the battle of life well, and that among artists, this exalts them to the highest rank. Let man strive and suffer, be wounded and downstricken, it matters not; it is his lot and he is made for trial and struggle. The great thing is to struggle bravely, to will, to work, and to create; the great source of action in him must not be wasted in a stagnant pool or in an administrative canal; it must flow on and steadily expand, not like a capricious torrent but like a broad river; the current once free should flow always, disturbed and tempestuous if necessary, but fertilizing, inexhaustible, and, from time to time, bright beneath celestial splendor and joy. At the last hour he may disappear in the sea; his career is over. At each turn of the century death swallows up and disperses the living generation; but it has no hold on its past. The dead may rest tranquilly; their work is done and their posterity in its turn, clearing its own pathway, must be content, when, after similar labor it lies down in similar repose.

On contemplating the great works which fill all Italy, on pondering over the decadence which followed their production, on remarking how greatly the generation

which produced them surpassed ours in active vigor
and in spontaneous invention, on reflecting that, thus
far, all civilizations have flourished only to wither
and to turn to dust, one asks himself whether that in
which we live will not meet with the same fate and
whether the great monument which protects us will not
in its turn provide fragments for some unknown construction in which a renewed humanity will secure protection of a superior order. Sentiment, in this connection, must not be listened to ; our response must come
from history and from analysis. Here are the foundations of our edifice, and, at first view, they seem to
guarantee its solidity.

The States of modern times are not simple cities
provided with a territory and which extermination or
conquest may destroy, like Sienna, Florence, Carthage,
Crotona or Athens. They embrace thirty or forty millions of men forming distinct races and nations, and,
so regarded, may resist invasions. Napoleon could not
make a subject of Spain, so weak, nor put down Germany, so divided. When in 1815 William Humboldt
proposed to partition France, too strong as he thought,
the allies drew back, aware that at the end of twenty-
five years the pieces would of themselves again unite.
Look at the difficulties of Russia in these days in respect to a third of Poland. A garrison of five hundred
thousand men, the half of a nation, is necessary to restrain the other half, and the profit is not worth the
expense.

In the second place, the European states are formed
of diverse races and nations ; hence one may replace
or restore its neighbor if its neighbor falls. When
Portugal, Spain and Italy fell in the seventeenth century, England, France and Holland resumed and continued in their own way and for their own account the
work they began. If in the course of a hundred years
France should become a common administrative camp,

the protestant nations of England, Germany, the United States and Australia would individually develop and their civilization flow back on France at the end of two or three centuries, as that of France, after two or three centuries, now flows back on Italy and Spain. A monarchy, on the contrary, like that of China, a theocracy like that of India, a group of cities like Greece, a grand unique organization like the Roman Empire, wholly perish for the lack of equal and independent neighbors to subsist after them and renew their existence.

Three-quarters of the labor of humanity is now done by machinery, and the number of machines like the perfectibility of processes, is constantly increasing. Manual labor diminishes in the same ratio, and, consequently, the number of thinking beings increases. We are accordingly exempt from the scourge which destroyed the Greek and Roman world, that is to say the reduction of nine-tenths of the human race to the condition of beasts of burden, overtasked, and perishing, their destruction or gradual debasement allowing only a small number of the *élite* in each state to subsist. Almost all of the republics of Greece and of ancient and modern Italy* have perished for want of citizens. At the present day the machinery now substituted for subjects and slaves prepares multitudes of intelligent beings.

In addition to this, again, the experimental and progressive sciences are now recognized as the sole legitimate mistresses of the human intellect, and the only safe guides for human activity. This is unique in the world. Among the Islamites, under the Ptolemies, and

---

* Sparta perished δί ολιγανθρωπιαν, says Aristotle. At Florence, there were but 2,500 voting citizens in the time of Savonarola. See Venice also. At the commencement of the sixteenth century the number of citizens enjoying political rights of all kinds in Italy was estimated at 18,000.

in Italy in the sixteenth century, the sciences were confined to a small circle of the curious who might at any time have been extinguished by a proscription. Now they have obtained control, and as they have visibly ameliorated practical life public assent and all private interests rally around them. Moreover, as their methods are fixed, and their discoveries constantly augmenting, it may be demonstrated that they will go on indefinitely renewing and completing the human understanding. Other developments of the mind, art, poetry, and religion may fail, diverge or languish; but this one cannot fail to endure, to diffuse itself, and to suggest to man forever concrete views with which to regulate his faiths and govern his actions.

These very sciences, having finally embraced in their domain moral and political affairs, and daily penetrating into education, transform the idea entertained by man of society and of life : from a militant brute who regards others as prey and their prosperity as a danger, they transform him into a pacific being who considers others as auxiliaries and their prosperity as an advantage. Every blade of wheat produced, and every yard of cloth manufactured in England diminishes so much the more the price I pay for my wheat and for my cloth. It is for my interest therefore not only not to kill the Englishman who produces the wheat, or manufactures the cloth, but to encourage him to produce and manufacture twice as much more.

Never has human civilization encountered similar conditions. For this reason it is to be hoped that the civilization now existing, more solidly based than others, will not decay and melt away like the others; at least there is reason to believe that amidst partial convulsions and failures, as in Poland and in Turkey, it will subsist and perfect itself on the principal areas whereon its constructions are now seen rising.

But, on the other hand, the magnitude of states, the development of industry, the organization of the sciences, in consolidating the edifice, prove detrimental to the individuals who live in it, every man finding himself belittled through the enormous extension of the system in which he is comprised.

Societies, in the first place, in order to become more stable have become too large, and most of them in order the better to resist foreign attack havǫ too greatly subordinated themselves to their governments. Among the men who compose them nine out of ten, and commonly ninety-nine out of a hundred, do not concern themselves about public affairs; they are indifferent to general passions, and enter into the community like beams in a building, or at least vegetate, discontented and inert, in petty pleasures and in petty ideas after the fashion of parasite mosses on an old roof. Compare this life to that of the Athenians in the fifth century, and to that of the Florentines in the fourteenth.

Moreover, in order to become efficacious, industry has become too subdivided and man, transformed into a drudge, becomes a revolving wheel. Fourier used to say that man, in the ideal partnership of the globe, on finding that little pies had not yet arisen to a level with civilization, would collect two caravans of a hundred thousand culinary artists on a suitable spot, say on the banks of the Euphrates, and there compete under grand combinations of genius and of experiences; the victor on receiving a centime per head for every person, would become very rich and, moreover, receive a medal. This is the grotesque image of our industrialism. Consider, in a universal exposition, the enormous effort directed to the perfecting of wash-bowls, boots and elastic cushions, along with their proportionate recompenses. It is sad to see a hundred thousand families employing their arms and thirty

superior men expending their genius in efforts to increase the lustre of a piece of muslin!

In the last place, science, in order to become experimental and sure, being subdivided into provinces growing smaller and smaller, the truly thoughtful, who are
the inventors, are obliged to restrict themselves each to
a special compartment, and there live confined to a
chemical or philological recess like a cook in his kitchen.
In the mean time, facts having accumulated to a vast
extent the human head becomes overcharged; there is
no longer an Aristotle : those who desire to attain to
an approximative idea of the whole are forced to
abandon the life of the body and overburden their
brain ; the contagion spreading through the rest of
society, a too highly developed cerebral life undermines
the health both physical and moral. Compare the
German doctors, the men of letters, even our pale and
polished men of the world, all our amateurs, all our
learned specialists, to Greek citizens,—philosophers,
artists, warriors and gymnasts,—to those Italians of
the sixteenth century who each possessed, besides a
military education, five or six arts or talents, and, many
of them, a perfect encyclopædia.

The work of man, in brief, has become stable because
it has expanded ; but it has expanded only because
man has become *special*, and a specialty *narrows*. Hence
it is that we now see the great works declining which
demand the natural comprehension and lively sentiment of a complete whole, that is to say, art, religion
and poetry. The way the Greeks and the Italians
of the Renaissance regarded life was at once better
and worse ; it produced a civilization less enduring,
less comfortable, and less humane, but more complete
souls and more men of genius.

For these evils there are palliatives, perhaps, but no
remedies, for they are produced and maintained
through the very structure of the society, of the indus-

try and of the science upon which we live. The same sap produces, on the one hand, the fruit, and on the other the poison; whoever desires to taste one must drink the other. In this, as in every other constitutional complaint, the physician dresses the ulcer, recommends soothing applications, opposes the disease symptom by symptom, warns his patient to avoid excesses and, above all, enjoins patience. Nothing more can be done, for he is incurable and to cure him would be equivalent to recasting him. In writing this, what do I show myself but an exemplification of the evil? To travel as a critic with eyes fixed on history, to analyze, reason and define instead of living gaily and creating with imaginative power, what is it but the mania of a man of letters and the routine of an anatomist?

BOOK V.

VENICE.

CHAPTER I.

April 20, 1864.—The railroad enters on the lagunes,
and suddenly the landscape assumes a peculiar color
and aspect. There is no grass or trees; all is sea and
sand; as far as the eye can see banks emerge, low and
flat, some of them half-washed by the waves. A light
breeze wrinkles the glittering pools, and gentle undulations die away at intervals on the uniform strand. The
setting sun throws over it purple tints, which the swell
of a wave now darkens, and now makes changeable.
In this continuous motion all tones are transformed and
melt away. Dark and brick-hued depths become blue
or green, according to the sea which covers them; according to the aspects of the sky the water itself changes,
all mingling together amid bright coruscations and
golden stars bespangling the light waves, under silvery
threads fringing the falling crests, under broad illuminations and sudden flashes reflected from the side of a
billow. The domain and the habits of the eye are transformed and renewed. The sense of vision encounters
another world. Instead of the strong, clean and dry
tints of solid earth, it is a flickering, a softening, an incessant glow of dissolving tints—a second sky as lumin-

ous as the other but more diversified, more changeable,
more rich and more intense, formed of superposed tones,
the combination of which is a harmony. Hours might
be ' passed in contemplating these gradations, these
delicate shades, this splendor. Is it to a spectacle like
this contemplated daily, is it to this nature involuntarily accepted as mistress, is it to the imagination forcibly charged by these fluctuating and voluptuous appearances of things that the Venetian coloring is due?

April 21.—A day in a gondola. It is necessary to
wander about and see the whole.

Venice is the pearl of Italy. I have seen nothing
equal to it. I know of but one city that approaches it,
—very remotely, and only on account of its architecture—and that is, Oxford. None can be compared to
it throughout the peninsula. On recurring to the dirty
streets of Rome and Naples ; on thinking of the dry and
narrow streets of Florence and of Sienna, and then on
contemplating these marble palaces, these marble
bridges, these marble churches, this superb embroidery
of columns, balconies and windows, these gothic, moor-
ish, and byzantine cornices, and the universal presence
of the moving and glittering water, one wonders why
he did not come here first ; why he lost two months in
other cities, and why he did not devote all his time to
Venice. One begins to think of making it his home,
and vows, at least, that he will return here. For the
first time one admires not only with the brain, but also
with the heart, the senses and the entire being. One
feels fully disposed to be happy ; one confesses that
life is beautiful and good. All that is essential is to
open the eyes, there being no need of effort ; the gondola glides along insensibly, and, reclining in it, one
wholly abandons himself physically and mentally. A
bland and gentle breeze caresses the cheeks. The broad
surface of the canal undulates with the rosy and white
forms of the palaces asleep in the freshness and silence

of dawn; everything is forgotten, profession, projects, self; one gazes, becomes absorbed, and revels as if suddenly released from life and soaring aerially above all things in light and in azure.

The curve of the Grand Canal sweeps between two ranges of palaces, which, built each apart and for itself, involuntarily combine their diversities for its embellishment. Most of them are of the middle ages, with ogive windows capped with trefoils, and balconies trellised with foliage and rosaces, all this rich gothic fancy blooming forth in the midst of its marble lacework, without ever subsiding into the dull or the ugly; others, of the renaissance, display their three superposed ranges of antique columns. Porphyry and serpentine incrust the upper sections of the doors with their polished and precious material. Several façades are rosy, or mottled with delicate hues, their arabesques resembling the foam of waves delineated on the finest sand. Time has clothed these forms with gray, melting livery, and the morning light sports in gladness over the broad expanse at their feet.

The canal turns, and you see rising from the water, like a rich marine vegetation, or some strange and magnificent piece of white coral, Santa Maria della Salute, with its domes, its clusters of sculpture and its pediment loaded with statues, and beyond, on another island, San Giorgio Maggiore, rotund and bristling like a pompous mother-of-pearl conch. You carry your eye to the left, and there is St. Marks, the Campanile, the Piazza, and the Ducal Palace. Probably no gem in the world equals it.

It is not to be described; you must go to engravings —but what are engravings without color? There are too many forms, too vast an accumulation of masterpieces, too great prodigality of invention; all one can do is to abstract from it some dry, general impression like a broken branch picked up and preserved in order to convey some idea of a blooming tree. Supreme over all is a rich exuberant fancy, parts that glide into a whole, a diversity and contrasts that terminate in harmony. Imagine eight or ten jewels encircling the neck or the arms of a woman, and all in harmony through their own magnificence or through her beauty.

The admirable piazza, bordered with porticoes and palaces, extends rectangularly its forests of columns, its corinthian capitals, its statues, its noble and varied arrangement of classic forms. At its extremity, half gothic, half byzantine, rises the Basilica, under bulbous domes and tapering belfries, its arcades festooned with figures, its porches laced with light columns, its arches wainscoted with mosaics, its pavements incrusted with colored marbles, and its cupolas scintillating with gold; a strange mysterious sanctuary, a sort of christian mosque in which cascades of light vacillate in ruddy shadows like the wings of genii within the purple, metallic walls of subterranean abodes. All this teems with sparks and radiance. A few paces off, bare and erect like a ship's mast, the gigantic Campanile towers in the air and announces to distant mariners the time-honored royalty of Venice. At its base, closely pressed to it, the delicate *loggetta* of Sansovino seems like a flower, so many statues, bas-reliefs, bronzes and marbles, whatever is rich and imaginative of living and elegant art, crowd around it to adorn it. Famous fragments, scattered about, form in the open air a museum and a memorial: quadrangular columns brought from St. Jean d'Acre, four bronze horses taken from Constantinople, bronze pillars to which the city standards were attached, two granite shafts bearing on their tops the dragon and winged lion of the Republic, and, in front, a wide marble quay and steps to which the black flotilla of gondolas lies moored. The eye turns to the sea and you no longer desire to contemplate anything else; it may be seen in the pictures of Canaletti, but

only through a veil. Painted light is not actual light.
Around the architecture, the water, expanded into a
lake, entwines its magical frame with its green and
blue tones and its flickering sea-green crystal. Myriads
of little waves sport and gleam in the breeze, and their
crests palpitate with scintillations. On the horizon toward the east, at the end of the Slaves' quay appear
masts of vessels, tops of churches and the pointed verdure of an extensive garden. All this issues from the
water; on every side the flood fills the canals, sweeping along the quays, losing itself on the horizon, rushing between the houses, and skirting the sides of the
churches. The lustrous, luminous, enveloping sea pen-
etrates into and encircles Venice as if with a halo.

Like a magnificent diamond in a brilliant setting
the Ducal Palace effaces the rest. I can describe
nothing to-day—all I care to do is to enjoy myself.
Never has the like architecture been seen; all, here, is
novel; you feel yourself drawn out of the *conventional ;*
you realize that outside of classic or gothic forms,
which we repeat and impose on ourselves, there is an
entire world; that human invention is illimitable; that,
like nature, it may break all the rules and produce a
perfect work after a model opposed to that to which we
are told to conform. Every habit of the eye is reversed,
and we see here with surprise and delight, oriental fancy
grafting the full on the empty instead of the empty on
the full. A colonnade of robust shafts bears a second
and a lighter one decorated with ogives and with trefoils,
while above this support, so frail, expands a massive
wall of red and white marble whose courses interlace
each other in designs and reflect the light. Above, a
cornice of open pyramids, pinnacles, spiracles and festoons intersects the sky with its border, forming a
marble vegetation bristling and blooming above the
vermilion and pearly tones of the façade, reminding
one of the luxuriant Asiatic or African cactus which on

its native soil mingles its leafy poniards and purple petals.

You enter and immediately the eyes are filled with forms. Around two cisterns covered with sculptured bronze, four façades develop their statues and architectural details glowing with the freshness of the early Renaissance. There is nothing bare or cold; everything is decked with reliefs and figures, the pedantry of erudites and critics not having yet intervened, under the pretext of purity and correctness, to restrain a lively imagination and the craving for visual enjoyment. People are not austere in Venice; they do not restrict themselves to the prescriptions of books; they do not make up their minds to go and yawn admiringly at a façade sanctioned by Vitruvius; they want an architectural work to absorb and to delight the whole sentient being; they deck it with ornaments, columns and statues, they render it luxurious and joyous. They place colossal pagans like Mars and Neptune on it, and biblical figures like Adam and Eve; the sculptors of the fifteenth century enliven it with their somewhat realistic and lank bodies, and those of the sixteenth, with their animated and muscular forms. Rizzo and Sansovino here rear the precious marbles of their stairways, the delicate stuccoes and elegant caprices of their arabesques: armor and boughs, griffins and fawns, fantastic flowers and capering goats, a profusion of poetic plants and joyous, bounding animals. You mount these princely steps with a sort of timidity and respect, ashamed of the dull black coat you wear, reminding one by contrast of the embroidered silk gowns, the sweeping pompous dalmatics, the byzantine tiaras and brodekins, all that seigneurial magnificence for which these marble staircases were designed; and, at the top, is Tintoretto's "St. Mark" to greet you, launched in the air like an old Saturn, also two superb women, "Power" and "Justice," and a doge who is receiving from them the sword of command and of battle. At the top of the staircase open the two halls, the government and state saloons, and both are lined with paintings; here Tintoretto, Veronese, Pordenone, Palma the younger, Titian, Bonifazio and twenty others have covered with masterpieces the walls of which Palladio, Aspetti, Scamozzi and Sansovino made the designs and ornaments. All the genius of the city at its brightest period assembled here to glorify the country in the erection of a memorial of its victories and an apotheosis of its grandeur. There is no similar trophy in the world : naval combats, ships with curved prows like swans' necks, galleys with crowded banks of oars, battlements discharging showers of arrows, floating standards amidst masts, a tumultuous strife of struggling and engulphed combatants, crowds of Illyrians, Saracens and Greeks, naked bodies bronzed by the sun and deformed by contests, stuffs of gold, damascene armor, silks starred with pearls, all the strange medley of that heroic, luxurious display which transpires in its history from Zara to Damietta and from Padua to the Dardanelles ; here and there, grand nudities of allegorical goddesses ; in the triangles the "Virtues" of Pordenone, a species of colossal virago with herculean, sanguine and choleric body ; throughout, a display of virile strength, active energy, sensual gaiety, and, preparing the way for this bewildering procession, the grandest of modern paintings, a "Paradise" by Tintoretto, eighty feet in length by twenty feet wide, with six hundred figures whirling about in a ruddy illumination as if the glowing volumes of a conflagration.

The intellect seems to reel—blinded as it were ;—the senses stagger. You stop and close your eyes, and then, after a few moments, make your selection. I have to-day seen but one picture well, the "Triumph of Venice" by Paul Veronese. This work is not merely food for the eye but a feast. Amidst grand architectural forms of balconies and spiral columns sits Venice, the blonde, on a throne, radiant with beauty, with that fresh and rosy carnation peculiar to the daughters of humid climates, her silken skirt spreading out beneath a silken mantle. Around her a circle of young women bend over with a voluptuous and yet haughty smile, possessing that Venetian charm peculiar to a goddess who has a courtezan's blood in her veins, but who rests on her cloud and attracts men to her instead of descending to them. Relieving on their pale violet draperies and on mantles of azure and of gold, their living flesh, their backs and shoulders, are impregnated with light or swim in the penumbra, the soft roundness of their nudity harmonizing with the tranquil gaiety of their attitudes and features. Venice, in their midst, ostentatious and yet gentle, seems like a queen whose rank merely gives her the right to be happy, and whose only desire is to render happy those who contemplate her. On her serene head two angels, thrown backward, place a crown.

What a miserable instrumentality is words! A tone of satiny flesh, a luminous shadow on a nude shoulder, a flickering light on floating silk, attract, retain and recall the eye for a quarter of an hour and yet there is only a vague phrase to express it. With what can one convey the harmony of blue relieving on yellow drapery, or of an arm one half of which is in shadow and the rest in sunshine? And yet almost all the power of painting lies there; in the effect of one tone on another as in music that of one note on another, the eye enjoying corporeally like the ear, a piece of writing which reaches the intellect having no effect upon the nerves.

Beneath this ideal sky and behind a balustrade are Venetian ladies in the costume of the time, in low-neck dresses cut square and closely fitting the body. It is actual society, and it is as seductive as the other.

They are gazing, leaning over and smiling, the light
which illuminates portions of their clothes and faces
falling on or diffusing itself in such exquisite contrasts that one feels himself moved with transports of
delight. At one time a brow, at another a delicate ear,
or a necklace, or a pearl, issues from the warm shadow.
One, in the flower of youth, has the archest of looks.
Another, about forty and amply developed, glances upward and smiles in the best possible humor. This
one, a superb creature, with red sleeves striped with
gold, stops and her swelling breasts expand the chemise
of her bodice. A little blonde and curly-headed girl
in the arms of an old woman raises her charming little
hand with the most mutinous air and her fresh little
visage is a rose. There is not one of them who is not
happy in living, and who is not, I do not say merely
cheerful, but joyous. And how well these rumpled
changeable silks, these white and diaphanous pearls accord with these transparent tints as delicate as the petals of flowers!

Away below, finally, is the restless activity of the
sturdy and noisy crowd: warriors, prancing horses,
grand flowing togas, a soldier sounding a trumpet bedizened with drapery, a man's naked back near a cuirass, and in the intervals, a dense throng of vigorous
and animated heads; in one corner a young mother
and her infant, all being disposed and diversified with
the facility and opulence of genius, and all illuminated
like the sea in summer with superabundant sunshine.
This is what one would have to bear away with him in
order to retain an idea of Venice. . . . . . .

I got some one to show me the way to the public
garden; after such a picture one can only contemplate
natural objects. This is an embankment at the end of
the city, and facing the Lido. Green shrubbery forms
hedges; red and yellow flowers are already blooming
on the parterres; smooth plateaus and knotty oaks,

with their budding tops, reflect themselves in the luminous water. To the east is a terrace commanding a view of the horizon, and of the remoter islands. From this one contemplates the sea at his feet, rolling up in long thin waves on the ruddy sand ; exquisite melting silken tints, veined roses and pale violets, like the draperies of Veronese, golden orange, yellows, vinous and intense, like Titian's simarres, tender greens drowned in dark blue, sea-green shades striped with silver or flashing with sparks, undulate, conflict, and lose themselves under the innumerable flaming darts descending from above at every discharge of the sun's rays. A vast sky of tender azure forms an arch of which one end rests on the Lido, while three or four motionless clouds seem to be banks of pearl.

I strolled on farther, and finished my day on the sea. Toward night the wind arose and it became dark. Wan hues of a yellowish gray and of a purple green overspread the water ; this sends forth an infinite, indistinct murmur, its blackening surge exciting a prolonged sentiment of disquietude. The wind moans and roars, and heavy clouds whirl across the sky ; all remains of the conflagration reddening the west are gone. Occasionally the moon glimmers through the rents in the clouds, and thus drifts from opening to opening, extinguished almost as soon as lighted, and shedding for a moment only its flickering beams on the restless flood. The rotundity and enormity of the celestial cupola are however still discernible ; the land on the horizon is but a thin black band ; the agitated sea, the vague mist, and overhead opaque masses of moving clouds alone fill all space.

No words can define the tint of the water on such a night : brown and of dark jasper, at times ashy but audible through innumerable murmurings, one first hears it almost without seeing it, unable to distinguish objects in this vast desert of floating forms. Gradually the eyes become accustomed to it, and sensitive to the imperishable light ever emitted from it. Like icicles in a close and gloomy vault, or one of those magic mirrors of unfathomable depth which legends describe, it gleams obscurely, mysteriously, but it always gleams ; at one time the point of a wave emerges, at another the back of a broad billow, now the smooth side of a tranquil concavity, now the whirl of a flashing eddy, some distant reflection, or the sudden break and dash of foam. All these feeble glimmerings cross, override each other and commingle steadily, emitting from this great blackness a dubious luminousness like the lustre of metal seen in shadow, an infinite field of pallid brightness, the inextinguishable glow of living water vainly bedimmed by the deadened sky.

Two or three times the moon shines out clear, and its long vacillating train seems like that of a funereal lamp beaming among pendent draperies, before the black pall of some prodigious catafalque. On the horizon, like a procession of torches and of tombs in limitless perspective, appears Venice with its lamps and its buildings, a group of lights here and there crowding together like clusters of tapers around a bier.

The boat approaches. On the left, in extraordinary silence, the Orfano canal recedes motionless and deserted ; this calm of the dark and gleaming water, thrills the nerves with pleasure and likewise with horror. The mind involuntarily plunges into these cold depths. What a strange life, that of this mute nocturnal element!—Meanwhile the churches and palaces grow and swim on the water with the air of spectres. San Marco looms up, its architecture raying the gloomy deep with its multiplied domes and pinnacles. Like the phantasm of a magician, or the aerial splendor of an imaginary palace, the *piazza* with its columns and campanile bursts out between two ranges of light. Then the boat buries itself in suspicious lanes, where, at long intervals, a street

lamp casts on the water its flickering radiance : not a
figure, not a sound, save the warning of the gondolier
on turning the corners; every few moments the gondola
pierces the obscurity of a bridge, and slowly, like a
crawling worm, glides by the foundations of a palace,
invisible in the dense cavern-like shadow. Suddenly
it emerges, and an isolated lantern appears ahead lugu-
briously trembling in the darkness, kindling a reflection,
or casting a fugitive scintillation on the livid back of a
wave. At other times the water plashes against disjointed steps and crumbling masonry ; the eye discerns
a grated window, some leprous wall, and all around, a
labyrinth of intersecting canals and tortuous streams,
ceaselessly burying themselves in each other amidst
unintelligible forms.

Streets and Squares.—All is beauty; I suppose that
there are sympathies of temperament,—I find one of
these here; give me a grand forest on a river-bank, or
Venice.

Even to these watery lanes, even to the most insig-
nificant places, there is nothing here which does not
please. From the Loredan palace where I lodge, one
winds around, in order to reach St. Mark's, quaint and
charming *calle* tapestried with shops, drygoods, melons, vegetables and oranges, and thronged with gay
costumes, sensual insinuating faces and a noisy and
ever-changing crowd. These passages are so narrow, so
oddly contracted between their irregular walls that one
can scarcely see the ragged strip of blue sky above
them. You emerge on some *piazzetta*, some deserted
campo all white beneath a sky white with light. Flagging, walls, enclosures, pavement all is of stone : round
about are closed houses, and their rows form a triangle
or a bulging square through the necessities of enlarge-
ment or the chances of construction; a delicately
carved cistern forms the centre and sculptured lions,
and little nude figures sport around the margin. In

one corner is some odd church, San Mose—a Jesuit
façade—or San Apostoli, or San Luca, so many portals
covered with statues browned by the damp salt air and
by the prolonged action of the blazing sun;—a jet of
light falling obliquely on the edifice cuts it into two
portions, and one half of the figures seem to be moving
about on the pediments or issuing from the niches,
whilst others remain tranquil in the blue transparency
of the shadow. You advance and, in a long outlet
traversed by a bridge, gondolas are furrowing the marbled surface of the water with silver; quite at the end
of the perspective a golden flash marks the stream of
sunshine, which, from a roof-top, makes the striped
flank of the wave dance with lightning. An arch
springs over the canal and a grisette in a black man-
tilla raises her petticoat, exposing her white stocking,
trim ankle and heelless shoe. She has not the spirited
and hard air of her Roman sisters; she trips along
wavingly under her veil and exposes her snowy neck beneath the curls of her auburn tresses. Plump, smiling
and soft she has the air of a peacock, or rather of a
pigeon pluming his neck in the sunshine. I get lost—and
so much the better; without a *cicerone* I find my way
by the sun and the inclination of the shadows. Before
every church, at every spot within reach of a gondola,
are groups of picturesque rogues, true lazzaroni, whose
sole occupation consists in holding the boat close
against the steps, and in summoning the gondolier
when the passenger returns to it, or in loitering about
in the sun, or sleeping, or begging. They stretch forth
their palms, and we regard their dusty, dingy, mottled
rags through which their ruddy flesh projects; they are
of a fine, low, transparent tone and they harmonize
well with the sculptured recesses, or afar with the vacant quays. We reach the square of San Marco; the
sun has disappeared; but San Giorgio, the towers, and
the brick structures are as rosy as a peach blossom,

and, toward sunset, a purple vapor, a sort of luminous
dust, a furnace-glow inflames the horizon.   To the
west each dome and pinnacle emerges from the sea,
gleaming like cups and candelabra of agate and porphyry; all these points and all these crests intersect
the grand celestial conch with extraordinary clearness,
and quite low down on the sky we see a distant and
growing tinge of emerald.

Garlands of light begin to shine beneath the arcades
of the Procurates.   Taking a seat in the café Florian,
in a small cabinet wainscoted with mirrors and decked
with agreeable allegorical subjects, one muses with
half-closed eyes over the imagery of the day falling
into the order of and transformed as in a dream;
odorous sorbets melt on the tongue and are rewarmed
with exquisite coffee such as is found nowhere else in
Europe; one smokes tobacco of the Orient and beholds flower-girls approaching, graceful and hand-
somely attired in robes of silk, who silently place on the
table violets and the narcissus.   Meanwhile the square
fills up with people; a dark crowd buzzes and moves
about in the shadow rayed with light; strolling
musicians sing or give a concert of violins and harps.—
On getting up, behind the square thronged with moving
shadows, at the end of a double fringe of gay and
brilliant shops, appears San Marco with its strange
oriental vegetation, its bulbs, its thorns, its filigree of
statuary and the darkening recesses of its porches beneath the trembling glimmer of two or three lost
lamps.

CHAPTER II.

THAT which is peculiar and special to Venice, that
which makes her a unique city, is that she alone in
Europe, after the fall of the Roman empire, continued
a free city and maintained uninterruptedly the regime
and the social and intellectual characteristics of the
ancient republics. Imagine Cyrene, Utica, Corcyra or
any other Greek or Punic colony miraculously escaping invasion or universal regeneration, and prolonging
down to the French Revolution the ancient form of
humanity. The history of Venice is as wonderful as
Venice itself.

Venice, in fact, is a colony from Padua, which took
refuge from Alaric and Attila in an inaccessible spot,
as formerly Phocea transferred itself to Marseilles in
order to escape similar devastators in Cyrus and
Darius. Like the Greek colonies she at first maintains
the liens which bind her to the metropolis. In 421
Padua decrees the formation of a city at the Rialto,
sends consuls and constructs a church. The daughter
grows up under the protection of the mother and then
abandons her. From this time forth, and for thirteen
centuries, no barbarian, no German or Saracen monarch lays his hand on her. She is not included in the
great feudal organization; Charlemagne's son fails
before her lagunes; the German or Frank emperors

regard her as not depending on them but on Constantinople. And this dependence which is only nominal
soon disappears. Between the gilded Cæsars of
Byzantium and the cuirassed Cæsars of Aix-la-Chapelle,
against the ponderous vessels of the degenerate
Greek and the heavy Germanic cavalry, her marshes,
her bravery and her skill maintained her free and
latin. Her old historians begin their annals with the
boast of being Roman, much more Roman than the
Romans of Rome so many times vanquished and so
repeatedly stained with foreign blood. In fact she
withdrew in time from imperial corruption in order to
revive in the laborious and militant fashion of the ancient cities, in a safe retreat where the inundation of
feudal brutes could not reach her. Man, with her, did
not become enervated in the simarre of Byzantium
silk, or rigid in a German suit of mail. Instead of
becoming a scribe in the hands of palace eunuchs, or a
soldier obeying the baron of a fortified castle, he works,
navigates, constructs, deliberates and votes like an
Athenian or Corinthian of old with no other master
than himself among his fellow-citizens and his equals.
From the very beginning, for two centuries and a half,
each islet appoints a tribune, a sort of mayor renewa-
ble every year and responsible to a general assembly
of all the islands. Early chroniclers state that ali-
ments and habitations are everywhere alike. In the
sixth century Cassiodorus says that " the poor man is
the equal of the rich, that their houses are uniform,
that with them there are no quarrels and no jealousies." We see reappearing an image of the sober and
active Greek democracies. When in 697, they give
themselves a doge their liberty only becomes the
more tempestuous. There are conflicts between families and personal encounters in the assemblies. If the
doge becomes tyrannical and aims to perpetuate the
office in his family they banish him, force him to be-

come a monk, or put out his eyes, and sometimes
massacre him according to the custom of the cities
of antiquity. In 1172, out of fifty doges, nineteen
had been slain, banished, mutilated or deposed. The
city has its local god, a sort of Jupiter Capitolinus or
Athene Polias; at first St. Theodore with his crocodile,
then St. Mark with his winged lion, while the apostle's
body, craftily obtained from Alexandria, protects and
sanctifies the soil of the state as formerly Œdipus,
interred at Colonna, sanctified and protected the Athenian soil. Public spirit is as vigorous as in the times
of Miltiades and Cimon. Urseolo I. founded a hospital and rebuilt the palace and church of St. Mark at
his own expense. His son Urseolo II. leaves two
thirds of his property to the state, and the rest to his
family. Behold a second growth of the antique olive,
fresh and green in the midst of feudal frost! In the
form of his government and in the limitations of his
faith, in his usages and sentiments, in his perils and
enterprises, in the motives which stimulate and in the
conceptions which guide him man here finds himself
once more launched forth on a career which other
human societies have forever abandoned.

We no longer comprehend the force with which they
ran on this narrow field. We no longer behold the energies developed by limited societies. We are lost in
an over-large state. We cannot imagine the constant
provocations to bravery and to enterprise which com-
ports with a community reduced to a town. We can
no longer conjecture the inventive resources, the patriotic outbursts, the treasures of genius, the marvels of
devotion, the magnificent development of human powers and of generosity to which the individual attains
when moving in a sphere proportioned to his faculties
and adapted to his activity. What is rarer nowadays
than to feel, being a citizen, that one belongs to his
country! It is necessary for it to be in danger which

happens but once in a century.* Ordinarily we do not
see it; it is for us only an abstract entity; we interest
ourselves in it only through a rational process of the
brain. We appreciate it simply as a piece of complex
mechanism which incommodes us and is useful to us
but which, on the whole, lasts and does not go to
pieces. A wheel broken or an accident, however grave
it may be, merely depresses the funds and that is all.
Our own life and that of our neighbors is not affected
by it; we always find policemen in the streets to protect us; our business suffers but little and our pleasures
not at all. Since private life became divorced from
public life, the State, transferred to the hands of the
government, no longer seems to be an individual concern. On the contrary, at this epoch, a blow given to
the community deeply wounds the individual; national
matters are personal matters. When the Hungarians
arrive before Venice there is no need of stimulating the
Venetian to rush off to the Malamocco channel; his
house, his children, his wife are at stake, and he man-
ages his boat himself as we of to-day work fire-engines
on a fire breaking out a couple of yards from our own
door. One hundred and sixty years of war against
Dalmatian pirates is not a matter of government calculation, the plan of a cabinet, a system elaborated by
a dozen political craniums and embroidered uniforms,
like our African expeditions. Vessels intercepted,
brides torn from churches, captive citizens chained to
the oars, individual wounds on all sides bleed and
bleed afresh in order to transform private persons
into so many citizens. When the city, later, surrounds
the Mediterranean with its colonies, the same situation
maintains the same patriotic ardor. The Navagieri,
dukes of Lemnos, the Sanudo, princes of Naxos and

---

* France in 1594 under Henry IV., in 1712 under Louis XIV. and
during the Convention.

of Paros, the five hundred and thirty-seven families of cavaliers and foot-soldiers who have received a third of Crete in fief, know that their own security depends on that of the public. A defeat of Venice involves with them invasion, conflagrations, mutilations and impalement. When Greeks, Egyptians and Genoese launch their flotillas or when Germans, Turks or Dalmatians move their armies, the humblest inhabitant, whether trader, sailor or boat-calker, knows that his trade, his wages and his limbs are in danger. Through constant absorption of himself in the common weal he becomes accustomed to act with the entire body, to feel himself incorporated with the country, to be insulted and wounded in and through her, to admire her and disdain others, to become enamored of himself as the soldier of a noble, conquering and intelligent army led by St. Mark, the favorite of the Deity, as its general. A man, thus exalted, is very strong. Feeling great he does great things ; generosity doubles the power of the spring which personal interest had already tempered. Consider the life of a modern city like Rouen or Toulouse, a simple collection of individuals each of whom, under a passable police, vegetates alone, solicitous only about himself, languidly occupied in getting rich or with pleasures, and, more frequently, in self-compression and in self-extinction. Contemplate the enterprising life of a free city like ancient Athens or old Rome, or Genoa or Pisa in the middle ages, like this Venice a borough of fishmongers, planted on mud, without earth, without water, without stone, without wood, which conquers the coasts of its own gulf, Constantinople, the Archipelago, the Peloponnesus and Cyprus, which suppresses seven rebellions in Zara and sixteen rebellions in Crete, which defeats the Dalmatians, the Byzantines, the sultans of Cairo and the kings of Hungary, which launches on the Bosphorus flotillas of five hundred sail, which arms squadrons of two hundred galleys,

which keeps afloat at one time three thousand vessels,
which annually with four fleets of galleys unites Tre-
bizond, Alexandria, Tunis, Tangiers, Lisbon and London; which finally, creating manufactures, an architecture, a school of painting and an original society,
transforms itself into a magnificent jewel of art whilst
its vessels and its soldiers in Crete and in the Morea
defend Europe against the last of barbarian invasions.
We can comprehend by this contrast between its activity and our inertia what society can force out of man;
what man may dare and create when the State makes
him sovereign and a patriot; what the ancient municipal regime, which we have abandoned and which Venice revived, develops of courage and of genius in erecting and binding together in one single sheaf, the faculties which we allow to become insulated and wasted in
our overgrown states.

When a society thus develops itself through itself it
has its own taste and art; spontaneous life generates
original productions, and invention stimulates the
spring of the mind after invigorating that of action.
But one thing is necessary to man, and that is respect
for the source of inspiration within his own breast; let
each one guard his own, keep it from being impeded or
disturbed, and see that it is made to flow freely; the
rest, work, fame and power, will come afterward and
through increase. These Venetians betook themselves
to Constantinople and brought back for their church
the round forms, vaulted arcades and globular cupolas
in which Byzantine architecture delighted; but in repeating them on their own soil, they transformed them,
and the church of San Marco differs as much from St.
Sophia as a young and simple nation, creative and victorious, differs from a punctilious and grandiose old
empire. Architects murmur on contemplating it; rules
are violated at every step, and styles are commingled.
They were ignorant of the way or, perhaps, did not

dare to copy, on this shifting soil the vast dome of St.
Sophia; but its rotundities pleased them and, instead of
one single grand dome they erected five small ones,
expanding them on the outside in bulbous form with
pinnacles and singular curvatures. An exuberant fancy
indulged itself to the utmost. From the peristyle
throughout one is impressed with its overflowing richness. The antique arch of the porches is capped with
a vaulted casing setting off in gothic points its garland
of statues. Delicate spires are introduced on the buttresses. Five hundred porphyry, verd-antique and
serpentine columns bind together and support on the
façades their incoherent stories, their barbaric or classic
capitals and the magnificent medley of their polychro-
matic marbles. Saracenic gates glitter with small
horse-shoe trellises between quaint capitals where
birds, lions, foliage, grapes, thorns and crosses intermingle their gross and fantastic designs. On the arch
innumerable mosaics display stiff realistic bodies,
meagre Eves with pendent breasts, lank Adams, all so
many undressed laborers, numerous biblical subjects as
naïvely indecent and as childishly awkward as the illuminations of the most ancient missals. You recognize
the mediæval man who embroiders an original gothic
decoration on an imported classic background; who,
refined and disturbed by christianity, no longer loves
simplicity and unity but the complex and the multiple;
who has to cover the field of his vision with the
saliency and confusion of a prodigality of forms, with
the novelty, luxury and search for capricious ornamentation; who, becoming more imaginative as well as more
sensitive, can only satisfy his eye with an illimitable
swarm of populous surfaces and with the brusque
overflow of curious irregularity; who, finally, led by
his maritime destiny to Byzantine basilicas and Ma-
hometan mosques heaps up marbles, bronzes, purple
hues and golden gleams in order to express through

his christianity the composite and gorgeous poesy with which the spectacle of the Orient has imbued him.

To-day is St. Mark's fête day. Women and young girls in black veils, violet-colored shawls, and long loose petticoats, forming a gay crowd, throng the porches, and surge to and fro within the church. They kneel on the pavement, touch the feet of a bronze Christ with their fingers, and make the sign of the cross; others mumble prayers and drop pennies in a box carried around for alms "in behalf of the poor dead." A procession of prelates passes, and you see their white and gold mitres, and sparkling damask copes winding around amongst the pillars. A chant is heard, quaint, and beautiful, composed of extreme high and low voices, a sort of monotonous melopœia and which, perhaps, comes from Byzantium. The singers are invisible, nobody knowing from whence the music issues as it floats about ascending into the sombre, ruddy atmosphere like an incorporeal voice in a gleaming grot of fairies and genii.

Nothing can be compared to this spectacle for strangeness and magnificence. We had just seen the square of St. Mark so gay and beautiful, its elegant colonnades, the rich azure of the sky, and the broad luminous expanse of light. We descend one step and the eye plunges suddenly into the purple gloom of a small sanctuary of unknown form filled with smothered gleams and reflections, surcharged and confined, like the low vaulted chamber in which a Jew or a pacha conceals his treasures. Two colors, the most powerful of all, cover it from pavement to dome; one, that of the red-veined marble shimmering on the shafts of the columns, decks the walls and displays itself on the floor; the other, that of gold, tapestries the cupolas and overspreads the mosaics, reflecting the light with its myriads of square cubes. Red on gold in shadow,—nobody can imagine such a tone! Time has deepened and fused them together; over the marble pavement, cracked by depressions, the quivering domes flash with ruddy brightness; there is no daylight except that from the little rounded bays enclosed with stained glass. Innumerable forms, pillars seamed with sculptures, bronzes, candelabras, and with hundreds of mosaics, an asiatic luxuriousness of complicated decorations and barbarous figures, blend together in an atmosphere filled with spiral threads of incense, and floating with luminous atoms of sunny and nocturnal contrasts. Language cannot express the power of the light imprisoned in and scattered throughout this gloom. A chapel on the right is as sombre as a subterranean cavern; a gleam of light flickers on the curvature of the arches. Alone, three brass lamps emerge from the palpable obscurity; the eye dwells on their round forms, and follows the ascending chains scintillating overhead and losing themselves in unintelligible gloom; thus visible, pendent from a train of coruscations, they might be taken for the mysterious corolla of magical flowers. These architects of the tenth and twelfth centuries had a sentiment peculiarly their own. It matters little whether they imitated the Byzantine or the Arab; this St. Mark, whom they brought from Alexandria, this Syrian apostle whose country and sky they were familiar with, filled their imagination with a poesy unknown to the barbarians of the north. They do not seek to express a melancholy sentiment, or go in quest of the enormous; there is a groundwork of southern joyousness in their fancy, in the warm coloring which they infuse into their church, in that universal coating of lustrous mosaics, in that marble marquetry, in those sculptured galleries, in those pulpits, those balconies, and in those rich arab or gothic doors, each surrounded with its cordon of apostles. In this vision-like fête all discords harmonize and awkwardness is no longer felt. The four columns around the high altar supporting the baldachin disappear beneath a profusion of figures which from base to capital, each in its niche, cover the entire shaft. If we take them one by one they are barbarian; we are repelled by their lack of force and the evidences they furnish of fruitless groping. The hands are out of proportion and the heads oftentimes absorb a third or quarter of the whole body; almost all are commonplace, and frequently stupid and vulgar looking. The sculptor was some boorish monk who copied boorish people. His hand wanders and unconsciously lapses into caricature. One saint is a grotesque figure with a swollen cheek, a hectic dropsical subject; others are shapeless monsters that are not likely to live, and similar to the specimens preserved in an anatomical cabinet. And yet, a few paces off the general effect is admirable; you are struck by the superabundance of this indistinct dusky multitude tier upon tier under capitals of golden leaves, and dimly wavering in the tremor of the lamplight. The mediæval artist, unable to render the individual has a feeling for masses and *ensembles*. He does not comprehend, as did the ancient Greek, the perfection of the isolated figure, of the god, of the self-sufficing hero; he goes outside of that beautiful enclosure; what he perceives is the people, the multitude, the poor human species utterly humbled, like a vast throng in the presence of the Supreme Ruler. He leaves to it its ugliness, its deformities, its servility; he even frequently exaggerates these; but sublime, intense reverie, joy mingled with anguish, all that belongs to spiritual emotion and aspiration he understands and expresses; and, if we do not find in his work the vigorous and healthy body of the independent and complete man, we distinguish the profound emotion of crowds and the impassioned religion of the heart.

This is what gives life to the rigid mosaics with which all the walls, the arches and the smallest angles are covered. It is evident that they have imported

their workmen from Constantinople; the puerility of a
superannuated art and the insufficiencies of an infantile
art have on all sides multiplied manikins whose
enamel eyes no longer see. A virgin over the door at
the entrance has no body; she is simply a skeleton
under a mantle. A Christ over the altar in the chapel
of the baptismal fonts has no longer a human form;
we would say that he had been disemboweled and
emptied: there is nothing left of him but a wan skin
badly filled with an indescribable soft stuffing. A
Herodias in a red robe starred with gold displays at
the end of her ermine sleeves the dried-up joints of a
consumptive patient. The extraordinary feet of the
angels must be seen; also the large cavernous eyes of
the saints, and the absorbed, inert, sunken features of
the entire group. And yet, miserable as these figures
are, the young who are obliged to borrow them from
the old make of them a beautiful and harmonious
whole. Lifeless, hieratic work enters as a fragment
into work full of sincerity and inspiration. At this
distance and in such profusion one ceases to note
meagre and mechanical forms. They simply appear as
so many heads in a crowd. The eye feels that it is
surrounded by an assemblage of saints, an infinite history, an entire legendary paradise; it is insensible to
detail; it beholds a kingdom and does not dream of
enumerating or criticizing its inhabitants. Ancient,
pious and heroic Venice thus regarded them; and
hence it is that, for centuries, she lavished her treasures,
her labor and her conquests. It is the ideal world as
her faith conceived it, as animated for her, as populated as the real world; such are her patrons, her
patriarchs, her angels, her Madonna whom she contemplates through these figures vivified by the empurpled
light and the rustling gold of her cupolas.

11

CHAPTER III.

April 26.—The gondola buries itself in deserted
canals to the north. Reflections from the water flicker
in the arched concave of the bridge, like figured silk
drapery, rose, white and green. We go out of the city;
it is noon, and the sky is of a glowing pallor. Stranded
rafts stretch their washed and shining logs on the plain
of motionless water. Facing us is an island surrounded
with walls, a cemetery, which rays the flaming brightness with its crude whites; farther on two or three
sails glide along the channels; on the horizon the
vapory chain of mountains develops against the sky its
fringe of snow. The indented prow rises out of the
water like a strange fish swimming tail foremost, while
the dark form of the boat projects forward in the grand
silence amidst innumerable shimmering golden waves.

On an open space rises the equestrian statue of Col-
leoni, the second one cast in Italy,* and a genuine
portrait like that of Guattemalata at Padua; the actual
portrait of a *condottiere* on his stout war-horse, in a
cuirass, with widespread legs, the bust too short and the
physiognomy that of a weather beaten camp-soldier
who orders and shouts,—not beautified, but taken from
life and energetic. Facing it is San Giovanni e Paolo,
a gothic church,† but Italian-gothic and therefore gay;
the round pillars, the broad, expansive arches, the win-

---

* By Verocchio, 1475.   † 1236–1430.

dows almost all white, forestall in the mind any mystic
funereal ideas such as northern cathedrals suggest.
Like the Campo-Santa at Pisa, and Santa Croce at
Florence, this church is crowded with monuments ; add
to these those of the church of the Frari and we have
a complete mausoleum of the Republic. Most of these
tombs belong to the fifteenth or to the early years of
the sixteenth century, the brilliant era of the city,
when the great men and great actions about to pass
away were still of sufficiently recent date for the new-
born art to catch its image and express its sincerity ;
others show the dawn of this great light ; others again
show its decline, so that one may thus follow through
a range of sepulchres the history of human genius
from its outburst, along its virility, to its final decay.

In the monument of the doge Morosini, who died in
1382, the pure gothic form blossoms out with all its
elegancies. A flowered arcade festoons its lacework
above the dead. Two charming little turrets ascend
on each side upheld by small columns enlivened with
trefoils, embroidered with figures and with canopies
and pinnacles, a kind of delicate vegetation on which
the marble bristles and expands like a thorny plant
with its needles and flowers. The Doge sleeps with
his hands crossed upon his breast. These are genuine
funereal monuments : an alcove, sometimes with its
baldachin or bed-curtains,* a marble couch carved and
ornamented like the wooden estrade on which the aged
limbs of the living man were wont to repose at night,
and, within it, the man himself in his ordinary dress,
calm in his slumber, confiding and pious because he
had well discharged the duties of life, a veritable effigy
without affectation or anguish, and which leaves to his
survivors the grave and pacific image which their
memory ought to retain of him.

---

* See the tomb of the Doge Tomaso Mocenigo, 1423.

This is the gravity of the middle ages. Already, however, beneath this religious rigidness we see dawning the sentiment of living corporeal forms, which is to be the special discovery of the following age. In the mausoleum of the doge Marco Corner, between five ogive arcades indented with trefoils and surrounded with light canopies, the Virtues, joyous angels in long robes, regard you with spontaneous and striking expressions. In this dawn of discovery the artists naïvely risked physiognomies and airs of the head which ulterior masters rejected through a sense of dignity and in obedience to accepted rules. In this particular the Renaissance which reduced art to classic nobleness really weakened it, as the purists of our seventeenth century impoverished the rich language of the sixteenth.

As we advance we see some feature of the new art disclosing itself. In the tomb of the doge Antonio Vennier, deceased in 1400, Renaissance paganism crops out in a detail of ornamentation, the shell niche. All the rest is still angular, florid, delicately slender and gothic, the sculpture as well as the architecture. The heads also, are heavy, clumsy, too short and often set on wry necks. Artists copy the real; they have not yet made a definitive choice of proportions; they still remain ignorant of the canons of the Greek statuaries, still plunged in the observation and in the imitation of actual life; but their lack of skill is charming notwithstanding. That Madonna whose neck is bent too much clasps her child with such exquisite tenderness! There is such an expression of goodness and candor in the heads of those young girls a little too round! These five virgins in their shell niches are so radiant with youthful purity and sincerity! Nothing affects one so sensibly as these sculptures with which mediæval art closes.* All these works are *inventive*, national

* Compare the sculptures on the tomb of the last Duke of Brittany

and, if you please, commonplace, but they possess such incomparable vitality! The brilliant and overwhelming predominance of classic beauty had not yet arisen to discipline the inspirations of original genius; there were provincial schools of art accommodated to the climate, to the country, to the entire social condition of things and still free of academies and of capitals. Nothing in the world is compensation for originality, the earnest and complete sentiment, the entire soul stamped upon a work of art; the work then is as individualized, as rich in subtleties as that soul itself. One believes in it; the marble becomes a sort of diary in which are recorded all the confessions of a human experience.

On advancing a few paces, following the course of the century,* one feels that this simplicity, this *naïveté* in art gradually diminishes. The funereal monument is converted into one of heroic pomp. Over the dead are round arcades developing their noble span. Arabesques run gaily around their polished borders. Files of columns display their blooming acanthus capitals; sometimes they overtop each other and the four orders of architecture develop their variety to please the eye. The tomb thus becomes a colossal triumphal arch; a few have twenty statues of almost life-size. The idea of death disappears; the defunct is no longer couched awaiting the resurrection of the final day, but is seated and looking at you with open eyes; "he lives again," in the marble as an epitaph ambitiously states. In a similar manner the

---

at Nantes, of the tomb of the last Dukes of Burgundy and Flanders at Dijon and at Brou, of the tomb of the children of Charles VIII. at Tours.

* The tombs, for instance, of P. Mocenigo, deceased in 1476;—of Marcello, deceased in 1474;—of Bonzio, deceased in 1508;—of Loredan, deceased in 1509;—in the Frari, the tomb of Nicolas deceased in 1478 and of Pesaro in 1503.

statues that ornament the memorial become gradually
transformed. In the middle of the fifteenth century
they are still frequently rigid and restrained; the legs
of young warriors are a little lank, like those of
Perugino's arch-angels, and are covered with lion-
headed bootees and knee-pieces in which reminiscences of feudal armor mingle with admiration of
antique costume. Bodies and heads all trench on the
real; the merit of the figures consist in their involuntary earnestness, in their simple, intense expression, in
the force of their attitudes, in their fixed and profound regard. On approaching the sixteenth century
ease and activity appear. The folds of draperies are
displayed around robust forms in a grand manner.
Muscles expand and show themselves. A young
cavalier of the middle ages is, now, an athlete and an
ephebos. Virgins, passive and hooded in their rigid
mantles begin to smile and be animated. Their pendent, careless Greek robes leave visible the nude
breast and the delicate forms of their charming feet.
Inclining, half-thrown back, resting on one hip, or
haughtily erect and contemplative, they reveal beneath
their facile draperies the diversities of the living form,
the eye following the harmonious curves of a fine
human animal which, in repose, in action, in every attitude has only to be allowed to live in order to be
perfect and happy.

Nowhere are these figures more beautiful than on the
tomb of the doge Vendramini, deceased in 1470. Art
here is still simple and in its early bloom; ancient
gravity still subsists intact; but the poetic and picturesque taste now commencing to dawn casts over it its
richness and brilliancy. Under arcades of golden flowers, in the spaces of a corinthian colonnade, are warriors and females in antique costume, contemplative and
weeping. They do not exert themselves or seek to
attract attention; reserve only renders their expression

more powerful. The entire body speaks, the type and the structure, the vigorous neck, the magnificent hair and the unimpassioned countenance. One woman raises her eyes mournfully to heaven; another, half thrown back, utters an exclamation; one might call them figures by Giovanni Bellini. They are of that puissant, limited era in which the model like the artist, reduced to five or six energetic sentiments, enforces them through a still intact sensibility, concentrating into one effort complete faculties which at a later period are to be deadened by dissipation and wasted on details.

All the grand passions terminate with the sixteenth century. Sepulchres become great operatic contrivances. That of the doge Pesaro, in the Frari, who died in 1669 is simply a gigantic court-decoration rearing upward a massive pile of pompous extravagance. Four negroes clad in white and kneeling on cushions sustain the second story of the tomb, their tawny visages grimacing over their stout bodies, while, between them, in coarse contrast, parades a skeleton. As for the doge he throws himself back with the self-important air of a grand seigneur as if uttering a *fi, donc!* to clowns. Chimeras prance at his feet, a baldachin extends over his head and on its two sides are groups of statues in declamatory and sentimental demeanor.—Elsewhere, in the tomb of the doge Valier,* we see art abandoning turgidity for pettiness. The mortuary alcove is enveloped in a vast curtain of yellow marble wrought with flowers and upheld by a number of little nude angels as frolicsome as so many cupids. The doge displays the dignity of a magistrate, while his wife, frizzled, wrinkled and dressed in flowing drapery, turns up her left hand with the air of an old dowager. Lower down

---

* Deceased in 1656. The tomb, however, (at San Giovanni), is of the XVIII century.

an ordinary pier-glass Victory crowns the old gentleman who seems related to Belisarius, and all around
are bas-reliefs presenting groups of graceful sentimental women practising the airs of the drawing-
room.

All this is perverted art, but it is art nevertheless,—
that is to say the taste of the sculptor and his contemporaries was personal and true; they loved certain
things belonging to their own world and existence and
these they imitated and adorned; their preferences
were not due to academies, to education, to book-
pedantry, to conventionalism. There is nothing else in
our century. Canova's monument, so cold insipid and
farfetched, executed after his own designs, is ridiculous : a great pyramid of white marble fills the entire
field of vision; the door stands open and here the artist desires to rest like a Pharaoh in his sepulchre; a
procession of sentimental figures advances toward the
door, Atalas, Eudoras and Cymodoceas, while a nude
genii, extinguishing his torch, sleeps, and another, sobbing, bends his head tenderly downward like young
Joseph Bitaubé. A winged lion weeps in despair with
his nose resting on his paws, and his paws on a book.
It would require a twenty minutes' lecture by a professor of the Humanities to make this allegorical drama
intelligible.—Near this is a portico-like monument inflicted on poor Titian, rasped and polished like an old
empire clock, decked with four pretty pensive spiritualistic women, two poor expressive old men with sharp and
salient muscles, and two young barbers with wings
bearing crowns. It would seem as if these artists were
barren of all personal impressions, that they had nothing of their own to say, that the human form had no
voice for them, that they had to fall back to their port-
folios to find suggestions of its lines, that all their talent lay in composing a curious enigma according to the
latest æsthetic and symbolic manual. Death, neverthe-

less, is important, and it certainly seems that one might say something of one's own about it without a book; but I begin to think that we no longer have any idea of it any more than of any other matter of extreme interest. We drive it out of our minds as if it were a disagreeable and unsuitable guest. When we attend a funeral we do it from a sense of propriety, chatting all the time with our neighbor on business or on literature. We have emerged out of the tragical condition. If we apprehend any great misfortune on the horizon it is, at most, an affair of the pocket, simply involving transition from the first to the fourth story.* Our imagination seems to be absorbed by an infinite diversity of petty excitements and perplexities, visits, correspondence, gossip, disappointments and the rest. Smoothed off and frittered away as we are, through what portion of our being or experience could we comprehend the anxieties, the stupendous and prolonged terrors, the corporeal and phrenetic joyousness which once arose like mountains above the level of human life? Art lives on grand determinations as criticism lives on nice distinctions, and hence it is that we are no longer artists but critics.

The same idea recurs to one on contemplating the paintings. There are many admirable ones in the chapel of the church dedicated to the Sacred Chaplet. One of these by Titian is entitled "St. Peter Martyr."† Domenichino has repeated the same subject at Bologna, but his personages are disfigured by an ignoble fear. Those of Titian are grand, like combatants. That which impressed him was not the pain or grimaces of a convulsed face, but the powerful action of a murder, the display of an arm bestowing a blow, the agitated drapery of a man in flight, and the magnificent erect

---

* Meaning a change from superior to inferior apartments.—*Tr.*
† Lately destroyed by fire.—*Tr.*

trunks of trees extending their sombre branches above
a scéne of bloodshed. Still more vehement is a " Crucifixion" by Tintoretto. All is excitement and disorder.
The poesy of light and shadow fills the air with brilliant
and lugubrious contrasts. A jet of yellow light falls
across the nude figure of Christ, which seems to be a
glorified corpse. Above him float the heads of female
saints in a flood of glowing atmosphere while the body
of the perverse thief, contorted and savage, embosses
the sky with its ruddy muscular forms. In this tempest of intense, angry daylight, it seems as if the
crosses wavered, and that the sufferers were going to be
precipitated; to complete this grandiose confusion, this
poignant emotion, you perceive in the background under a luminous cloud a mass of resuscitated bodies.

The entire top of the wall is covered with paintings by the same hand. Christ is ascending into paradise, and around him are grand naked angels rushing
through space and furiously sounding their trumpets.
The Virgin is borne off by an impetuous crowd of
small angels in various complicated attitudes, whilst
beneath her are the apostles shouting and thrown
violently backward. Light vibrates on all sides and on
all the canvases. There is not an atom of the atmosphere that does not palpitate; life is so overflowing
as to breathe and bubble up from stones, trees, ground
and clouds, in every color and in every form that belong to the universal feverishness of inanimate nature.

CHAPTER IV.

PROMENADES.—SANTA-MARIA DELL' ORTO.—SAN GIOBBE.—LA GUI-
DECCA.—I GESUATI.—I GESUITI.—MANNERS, CUSTOMS AND CHAR-
ACTERS.—MISERY.—PUBLIC SPIRIT.—IDLENESS AND REVERIE AT
VENICE.

April 27.—I see pictures every day by Titian, Tintoretto and Paul Veronese, but I am not yet ready
to speak of them; they form a complete and too rich
a world. Tintoretto especially, is extraordinary; one
can have no idea of him without visiting Venice.

My walk to-day is to Santa-Maria dell' Orto to see
his great paintings of "The Worship of the Golden
Calf" and "The Last Judgment." I find the church
closed and the pictures rolled up and taken away
nobody knows where. The edifice seems to be abandoned. On one side is a dilapidated cloister broken
open and serving as a lumber-yard, with the grass
growing fresh and green along the arcades. This
is one of my greatest disappointments in Venice.

The gondolier makes the tour of the city away to
the north, and before this plain of light all vexations and disappointments are forgotten. One never
tires of the sea, of the infinite horizon, of the little
distant bands of earth emerging beneath a·dubious
verdure, of the strange close-packed streets, almost deserted, where the bricks of the houses totter, undermined by the water; where the piles below, incrusted
with shells, are so diminished as to render a crash
imminent. San Giobbe appears, a small church of the
Renaissance, white and bare outside, excepting an
elegant and delicately ornamented entrance. The interior overflows with ornament; a monument by
Claude Perrault, extravagant but not lifeless, displays

over a black marble sarcophagus a small sleeping angel, gross and vigorous, related one might say to the Flemish cherubs; lower down are crowned lions crouching with the grotesque solemnity of heraldic brutes. However decorated or perverted a church in Italy may be it always contains something beautiful and interesting. For example here is a fine picture by Paris Bordone, an old saint with a heavy beard bearing a cross between two companions, and, alongside of these, a pretty cloister bordered with columns uniting in arcades and whose cistern, decked with acanthus leaves, blooms luxuriantly above the pavement of the esplanade. These are the agreeable features of these promenades. One knows not what he is to encounter. He starts with two or three names of places in his head and that is all. He glides along noiselessly and is never jolted. No one speaks to him. He passes from a gilded temple crowded with figures to a solitary and dilapidated quarter. It seems as if he were liberated from his bodily tenement and that some benevolent genius delighted in feeding his mind with phantasmagoria and wondrous spectacles.

The gondola skirts Santa-Chiara and the side of the Champ de Mars. The spaces of water become broader and its mottled undulations swell gently under the breeze with an indescribable intermingling of melting tones and hues. This is not ordinary water. Enclosed within canals, and tinged by the exudations and infiltrations of the human colony it assumes an earthy ruddiness combined with pale, ochry tints and bluish miry darks, resembling the confused mixture of colors of a painter's palette. Under a northern sky it would be lugubrious; but here under the illuminating sun and in the silkiness of the tender azure overspreading the celestial canopy it fills the eye with almost physical delight. Veritably one swims in luminousness. It pours down from the sky, the water colors it and the

reflections multiply it a hundredfold; there is nothing,
even to the white and rosy houses, which does not reflect it while the poesy of forms ever adds to and completes the poesy of brightness.   Even in this miserable
and abandoned quarter we find palaces and façades
adorned with columns.   Poor and commonplace houses
have large balconies enclosed within balustrades and
windows indented with trefoils or capped with ogives,
and reliefs of intermingled foliage and thorns.   One
loses himself in reverie.   In vain does the Giudecca
canal, almost deserted await its flotillas in order to
people its noble port; one muses over nothing but
colors and lines.   Three lines and three colors form the
entire spectacle: the broad moving crystal, of a dark
sea-green which winds about with a hard lustrous hue;
above, detached in bold relief, the row of buildings following its curve; still higher in fine, the pure, infinite
and almost pallid sky.

The gondolier draws up to the quay and pretends
that it is necessary to see the church of the Gesuati.
We perceive a pompous façade of gigantic composite
columns, then a nave whose corinthian colonnade is
pretentiously joined to large pillars; on the flanks,
small chapels whose Greek pediments bear curved con-
soles; a coating of variegated marbles, an infinity of
statues and bas-reliefs, insipid and very appropriate;
on the ceiling a pretty piece of boudoir painting in the
shape of trim, rosy and bare legs;—in brief a work of
frigid luxury and costly magnificence.   The Italian
eighteenth century is still worse than ours.   Our works
always show some degree of moderation because they
preserve some degree of finesse; but theirs plant themselves triumphantly on the extravagant.   I saw yesterday a similar church, that of the Gesuiti.   Its walls
and pavement are incrusted with green and white
marbles, let into each other in order to form flowers
and branchings.   On the arches gold twists around in

the shape of vases, pompons and flourishes, all seeming like the velvet and gilt paper hangings of a drawing-room costly enough to attract the wealthy. The urns, lyres, flames, clusters of foliage and white garlands that emboss the domes could not be counted. Spiral columns of green marble flecked with white support the baldachin of the altar, and, on this, meagre and sentimental statues,—Christ with the cross, God the Father seated on a huge white marble globe,—parade themselves supported by angels, both being sheltered by a roof of marble shell-work so odd as to provoke laughter. Grotesque extravagance displays itself even in the grand architectural lines; not content with ordinary forms they have widened the arch of the nave, reducing its curve so low that it resembles the span of a bridge, and flanking this with cupolas that look like concave bucklers. You feel the effort of a barren and laboring imagination ending in rhetorical superlatives and in *concetti*, and which, in polished sonorous periods, furnishes a parlor worship for women and worldlings.

All these follies of the decadence vanish alongside of two pictures belonging to the great epoch. The first is an "Assumption" by Tintoretto. Around the Virgin's tomb grand old men bend forward and express their amazement with tragic gesture; they have those vigorous and lordly airs of the head which in the Venetian painters agree so well with the violent motion of draperies, and with powerful effects of light, shadow and color. The Virgin, aloft, whirls in the air, and the pallid, drowned changeable tints of her purple robe render still more striking her vigorous brown face, small brow, low hair and virile attitude. A woman of the people possessing the energy and magnificence of a queen, is the idea which arrests the eye; no painter had a greater admiration of the pomp and sincerity of force. Tintoretto encounters in the street a market or

a boat woman, and bears away with him her perfect
and rugged image; he surrounds her with the oriental
and patrician lustre of princely rank; he showers the
neighborhood with a deluge of small heads cravated
with wings, distributing them even over the drapery
held by the apostles.   He is quite indifferent to the resemblance of his bevy of angels to a dish of decapi-
tated heads; at one dash he translates the instantane-
ous apparition to his canvas and there leaves it, for his
work is finished.

The other picture, a St. Lawrence by Titian, seems a
fantasy of some Italian Rembrandt, a vision in gloom.
It is night; at first nothing is distinguishable but a
great blackness vaguely spotted with two or three
lights.   It consists of a wide street.   In a dusky tint
like that of a cavern illuminated by a dying flambeau
you perceive, through their more opaque darkness,
some architectural forms, a statue and a distant multitude.   A peculiar lantern, a sort of torch within iron
bars, glimmers at the end of a stick, while the brazier
casts its sinister beams along the pavement.   Near this
a superb executioner, a sort of tragic porter, leans
backward, the muscles of his breast swelling with
vinous tones in powerful relief on a herculean torso;
around him black reflections rest on cuirasses, or tremble on the blue steel of the lances.   Meanwhile a
luminous flame descends from the sky above, piercing
the shadows like a glory, a bright gleam falling on the
white figure of the martyr, and arousing on its passage
the yellow flickerings, indistinct palpitations and mysterious floating dust in the shadows.

April 27.—*Manners, customs and character.*—I go this
evening to the Benedetto theatre.   Toward midnight,
on returning, the dimly lighted and crooked streets,
lost between the high houses, seem like places of
ambush.

The audience is poor; the house is almost empty;

out of a large number of boxes there are only about twenty half filled. Many of the lower class of the *bourgeoisie* and even the common people are in the parterre. And yet the house is beautiful.

They play this evening, "Mary Stuart" translated from Schiller. To-morrow they are to give *un interessantissima comedia del Signore Dumas padre, Mademoiselle de Belle-Ile.* I have seen others by him at Florence. We furnish the whole of Europe with vaudevilles, comedy, agreeable romances, toilet objects, etc. I have seen abroad, on the tables of nobles, collections of free songs, and, in splendid libraries, Paul de Kock's novels, richly bound, on the lowest shelves. By our works we are judged: dancing-masters, hairdressers, vaudevillists, lorettes and milliners,—but few other titles are bestowed upon us, save, perhaps, that of soldiers.

The theatrical corps is as pitiful as possible. The faces of the musicians are subjects for pictures: one might pronounce them fatigued, haggard old tailors. The prompter prompts so loud that his voice sounds like a continuous bass. Mary Stuart in a black velvet robe, has the hands of a washerwoman; she must certainly cook her own dinner and sweep her own room; otherwise she has vigor, a sort of furious and brutal energy. Elizabeth, rouged by the square foot, attired in frills and mock jewelry, responds to her in a shrill and stifled voice; both of them are market-women showing their teeth. In order to get Mortimer to assassinate her rival she rants like a maniac. All overdo the matter horribly, which, perhaps, is requisite for an Italian parterre. Mary Stuart is called out three times after the scene when she upbraids Elizabeth.

This is only a second-class theatre. "La Fenice" and the other leading theatres are closed. The nation is so hostile to Austria that a noble, indifferent or politic, would not dare to go to them; it would be re-

garded as a sign of satisfaction and he would be
hooted at. With such a disposition before them theatres may well decline. Everything indeed is declining.
The " Guidecca," which is a capacious harbor has
scarcely any vessels in it; all commerce and business go
to Trieste. The city is cut off from the Milanese by
custom-houses. People do not work ; dejection undermines all effort as it undermines all pleasure ; the nobles live immured on their estates ; many of the palaces
have degenerated and some seem to be abandoned. Out
of a hundred and twenty thousand inhabitants there are
forty thousand poor, thirty thousand of which live on
alms and are inscribed on the charity registers. I have
seen the report of the podestat, Count Piero Luigi, for
the last four years. Out of 780,000 florins expended,
10,000 went for instruction, 129,000 for benevolent
purposes and 94,000 for public charity. I visited the
hospital for the insane and I have its statistics ; the
pellagre,* bad food and excessive poverty furnish the
greatest number of the demented. Taxes, it must be
said, are overwhelming. I am told of a house having
an income of 1,000 florins which pays a tax of 400.
A *podere*, that is to say a piece of ground with a habi-
tation on it, brings 1,130 francs and pays 500. Another
house, at Venice, is let at 238 florins and pays 64. In
general a piece of real estate pays the third of its
revenue. This big slice once devoured the fiscal teeth
operate on another taxable piece. Besides imposts on
successions, transmissions, food and others, besides
those on rent and for the privilege of trading, there is a
sort of income tax as in England. According to the
merchant who furnishes me with these particulars this
tax is a twentieth. A merchant pays the twentieth of
his estimated profits, an employé the twentieth of his
salary. It is the worse for him if at the end of

---

* A local cutaneous disease.—*Tr.*

the year his gain proves less than he anticipated. It is still worse if it be nothing, and worse yet if he should make a loss. He is obliged to make his declaration in advance under oath. If he is convicted of having concealed any portion of his profits he pays a heavy penalty and, moreover, he is amenable to the penalty imposed on perjurers. Spies selected for the purpose speculate on his condition; they calculate how much he expends per day,—so much for rent, so much for assistance and servants and so much for provisions; then, conjecturing what the profits may be according to the expenses, they control his declaration. This forms a sort of inquisition which discourages all industry. In this state of misery and inertia it is only the foreigners who have money, and all contend for them. Nowhere in Italy is living so cheap for the traveller; a boat for an entire day costs five francs; at the slightest nod the gondoliers rush forward; they strive to get ahead of each other and beg you to take them by the week at a discount; there is no city where a man of moderate means and an amateur of the beautiful could be better off in a pecuniary way and indulge his day-dreams; it is only necessary to neglect politics. The Venetians, it is true, do not neglect them. On asking a peasant woman if the Austrians were liked in the country, she replied "We like them, but outside (*fuori.*") My poor old gondolier, on telling me of his poverty, added by way of consolation, "Garibaldi will do something."—It seems that everybody here, even the Mayor, an official magistrate, is a patriot. It is well known that in 1848 the people, armed with pieces of broken pavement, drove away the Austrian soldiers and fought with courageous obstinacy after the defeat of the Piedmontese at Novara. On the French squadron coming in sight of the city during the late war the people became wild with excitement and, what is more, the excitement lasted. At the first shot from the fleet the revolt was to break out; the common people, the gondoliers, all were prepared. Several of them became insane on hearing of the armistice. Many emigrated and have since established themselves in Lombardy; they could not get accustomed to the idea that Venice, which for so many years in Italy had escaped a foreign yoke, should alone remain in the hands of strangers: imagine five or six sisters in a family having become ladies and the last one and the most beautiful, the charming Cinderella, remaining a domestic.

Whether domestic or lady she is to the traveller ever the most gracious and poetic of all; in contemplating her one has to make an effort in order to think of graver matters, on the interests of politics; Austrian or Italian she is a fairy. One would like to dwell here. What dreams six months would furnish! What delightful promenades through art and history! The library of San Marco contains a breviary which Hemling, the great painter of Bruges, has filled with his delicate figures. There are ephemerides by Sanudo in fifty-eight volumes, daily recorded and describing the manners and customs at the beginning of the sixteenth century, the brightest epoch of painting. What a happy life, that of any historian, amateur of pictures, who might come here to study, to meditate, to write! Glancing up from his page he would see on the ceiling of the library the "Adoration of the Magi" by Veronese, its figures framed between two grand pieces of architecture, the noble white head and splendid figured robe of the first king, of his retinue, of all the characters displayed, that white horse rearing in the hands of an amply draped attendant, the two angels overhead, the exquisite carnation of their nude limbs and the rare beauty of their rosy vestments seemingly dipped in magical light. One would readily appreciate the idea exhaling from all this pomp, that of a joyous,

expansive, unrestrained force, but ever noble, which
swims in full prosperity and in full contentment. One
would descend the marble staircases and leisurely
enjoy luxuries which no monarch in Europe possesses.
One would contemplate on a quay, in the shadow filled
with watery reflections, some of the figures which formerly supplied the great masters with their personages,
some blonde and ruddy girl with hair flying around her
brow and playing in careless flow; the tanned and
sombre visage and neck of some boatman under an
old straw hat; the great bulging nose, bright eyes and
ample gray beard of some old fellow serving as a model
for Titian's patriarchs; the white and somewhat fat
neck, rosy cheeks, fine beaming eyes and waving
tresses of some young girl tripping along and lifting
her dress. One would feel the fertility and freedom of
the geniuses who, from these slight, incomplete and
scattered motives, derived so rich and so majestic a
symphony. One would stray off to the Slaves' quay,
to a little bench I know well, and there, in the cool
shade, he would contemplate the marvellous expansion
of sunlight, the sea still more glowing than the sky,
the long smooth waves succeeding each other and
bearing on their backs innumerable and tranquil
sparkles, the light ripples, the quivering eddies beneath
their golden scales; and, farther on, the churches, the
ruddy houses rising upward from the midst of polished
glass, and that eternal, rustling, moving splendor which
seems like one beautiful smile. One would push on to
the public gardens to gaze on the remoter islands on the
vague banks of sand and the opening sea. All is a
plain here up to the horizon, a glittering plain, trembling with flashes, and blue-green like a sombre tur-
quoise. The eyes would always be virginal to this
sensation. They would never become satiated in
looking at these masses of piles strewing the azure
with their black specks, these flat islets forming a deli-

cate line below the sky on the verge of the sea, farther
on a belfry, the white spot of an illuminated house
which at this distance seems no larger than the hand,
and here and there the ruby sail of a fisherman's bark
returning homeward slowly impelled by the breeze.
One would finish the day on the Square of San-Marco,
between a sorbet and a bouquet of violets, listening
to Bellini's or Verdi's airs played by the wandering
musicians. The eyes meanwhile would fix themselves
on the firmament above the illuminated square seemingly a dome of black velvet incrusted with silver
nails; they would follow the outline of the Basilica,
white like a marble gem, displaying in the darkness its
rounded bouquets of columns and its fretwork of
statues. One would thus pass a year like an opium-
smoker, and to good account, for, the only true way to
endure life is to be insensible to it.

CHAPTER V.

IT is about in this fashion that the people in this country contrived to support their decadence. This beautiful city ended, pagan-like, like its sisters the Greek republics, through nonchalance and voluptuousness. We find, indeed, from time to time, a Francis Morosini who, like Aratus and Philopœmen, renews the heroism and victories of ancient days ; but, after the seventeenth century, its bright career is over. The city, municipal and circumscribed, is found to be weak, like Athens and Corinth, against powerful military neighbors who either neglect or tolerate it; the French and the Germans violate its neutrality with impunity ; it subsists and that is all, and it pretends to do no more. Its nobles care only to amuse themselves; war and politics with them recede in the background ; she becomes gallant and worldly. With Palma the younger and Padovinano high art falls ; contours soften and become round; inspiration and sentiment diminish, stiffness and conventionalism are about to rule. Artists no longer know how to portray simple and vigorous bodies; Tiepolo, the last of the ceiling decorators, is a mannerist seeking the melodramatic in his religious subjects and excitement and effect in his allegorical subjects, purposely upsetting columns, overthrowing pyramids, rending clouds and scattering his figures in a way that gives to his scenes the aspect of a volcano in eruption. With him, Canaletti, Guardi and Longhi, begins another art, that of *genre* and landscape.

The imagination declines; they copy the petty scenes
of actual life, and make pleasing views of surrounding
edifices; they imitate the dominos, the pretty faces and
the coquettish and provoking airs of contemporary
ladies. These are represented at their toilets, at their
music-lessons and getting out of bed; they paint charming, languishing, smiling, arch and disdainful belles,
genuine boudoir queens, whose small feet in satin shoes,
pliant forms and delicate arms shrouded in laces fix the
attention and secure the compliments of men. Taste
grows refined and fastidious the same time that it becomes insipid and circumscribed. But the evening of
this fallen city is as mellow and as brilliant as a Venetian sunset. With the absence of care gaiety prevails.
One encounters nothing but public and private fêtes in
the memoirs of their writers and in the pictures of their
painters. At one time it is a pompous banquet in a
superb saloon festooned with gold, with tall lustrous
windows and pale crimson curtains, the doge in his
simarre dining with the magistrates in purple robes, and
masked guests gliding over the floor; nothing is more
elegant than the exquisite aristocracy of their small
feet, their slender necks and their jaunty little three-
cornered hats among skirts flounced with yellow or
pearly gray silks. At another it is a regatta of gondolas and we see on the sea between San-Marco and San-
Giorgio, around the huge Bucentaur like a leviathan
cuirassed with scales of gold, flotillas of boats parting
the water with their steel becks. A crowd of pretty
dominos, male and female, flutter over the pavements;
the sea seems to be of polished slate under a tender
azure sky spotted with cloud-flocks while all around, as
in a precious frame, like a fantastic border carved and
embroidered, the Procuraties, the domes, the palaces
and the quays thronged with a joyous multitude, encircle the great maritime sheet. A company of seignors
who are at Pavia with Goldoni, in order to return to

Venice, send for a large pleasure-barge covered with an awning, decked with paintings and sculpture and furnished with books and musical instruments; there are ten masters and they travel only by day, leisurely and selecting good halting-places or, in default of these, lodging in the rich Benedictine monasteries. All play on some instrument, one on the violincello, three on the violin, two on the oboe, one on the hunting-horn and the other on the guitar. Goldoni, who alone is not a musician, versifies the little occurrences of the voyage and recites them after the coffee. Every evening they ascend on deck in order to give a concert, and the people on the two banks of the stream assemble in crowds waving their handkerchiefs and applauding. On reaching Cremona they are welcomed with transports of joy; the inhabitants honor them with a grand banquet; the concert recommences, the local musicians join them and the night is given up to dancing. At each new evening halt there is the same festivity.* One cannot imagine a readier or more universal disposition for refined amusements. Protestants like Misson, who chance to witness this kind of life, do not comprehend it and only make scandalous reports of it. The way of considering things there is as pagan as in the time of Polybius, for the reason that moral preoccupations and the germanic idea of duty could never take root there. In the days of the Reformation one writer already states that "there was never known to be one Venetian belonging to the party of Luther, Calvin and the rest; all follow the doctrines of Epicurus and of Cremonini his interpreter, the leading professor of philosophy at Padua, which affirm that the soul is engendered like that of the brute animal through the virtue of its own seed and accordingly that it is mortal. . . . And among the partisans of this doctrine are found the élite of the city, and in particular

---

* Memoirs of Goldoni, Part I. Chap. XII.

those who take part in the government."* In truth
they never concern themselves with religion except to
repress the Pope ; in theory and in practice, in ideas
and in instincts, they inherit the manners, customs and
spirit of antiquity, and their christianity is only a name.
Like the ancients, they were at first heroes and artists,
and then voluptuaries and diolettanti ; in one as in the
other case they, like the ancients, confined life to the
present. In the eighteenth century they might be compared to the Thebans of the decadence who, leagued
together to consume their property in common, bequeathed what remained of their fortunes on dying to
the survivors at their banquets. The carnival lasts six
months ; everybody, even the priests, the guardian of
the capucins, the nuncio, little children, all who frequent
the markets, wear masks. People pass by in processions disguised in the costumes of Frenchmen, lawyers,
gondoliers, Calabrians and Spanish soldiery, dancing
and with musical instruments ; the crowd follows jeering
or applauding them. There is entire liberty ; prince or
artisan, all are equal ; each may apostrophize a mask.
Pyramids of men form "pictures of strength" on the
public squares ; harlequins in the open air perform parades. Seven theatres are open. Improvisators declaim
and comedians improvise amusing scenes. "There is
no city where license has such sovereign rule."† President De Brosses counts here twice as many courtezans
as at Paris, all of charming sweetness and politeness
and some of the highest tone. "During·the carnival
there are under the Procuratie arcade as many women
reclining as there are standing. Lately five hundred
courtiers of love have been arrested." Judge of the

---

* Discorso Aristocratico, quoted by Daru, Vol. IV. p. 171.

† See the pictures of the Carnival by Tiepolo, the Memoirs of Gozzi,
Goldoni and Casanova, the travels of President De Brosses, and
especially the four German volumes of Maier, 1795 ;—in the seventeenth century, Amelot de la Houssaye, Saint-Didier, etc.

traffic.   Opinion favors it; a noble has his mistress come
for him in a gondola on leaving the church of San-Marco; a Procurator in a dressing-gown stands at his window and publicly interchanges amorous signals with a
well-known courtezan residing opposite to him.   "A
husband does not scruple to state in his own house that
he is going to dine with his mistress and his wife sends
there whatever he orders."   On the other hand wives
compensate themselves; whatever they do is tolerated.
"*E donna maritata*," excuses everything.   "It would be
a kind of dishonor for a wife not to be in public relationship with some man."   The husband never accompanies her—it would be ridiculous; he permits a sigisbe
to do so in his place.   Sometimes this substitute is designated in the marriage contract; he visits the lady in
the morning when she arises, takes chocolate with her,
assists at her toilet accompanies her everywhere and
is her servant; frequently, when very noble, she has
five or six, and the spectacle is curious to see her at the
churches giving her arm to one, her handkerchief to
another and her gloves or mantle to another.   The fashion prevails in the convents.   "Every charming young
nun has her attendant cavalier."   Most of these recluses
are immured by force and they insist on living like women of the world.   They are fascinating with "their
crisp, curly hair, white gauze kerchief projecting over
their brow, white camlet frock and flowers placed on
their open breast."   They receive any one they please
and send their friends sugar-plums and bouquets; during the carnival they disguise themselves as ladies and
even as men, and thus enter the parlor and invite masked
courtezans there.   They go out of doors and in the
work of that scapegrace Casanova we may see for what
purpose.   De Brosses states that on his arrival intrigues
between the convents were active in order to decide
"which should have the honor of giving a mistress to
the new nuncio."   In truth there is no longer any family

life. After the seventeenth century men say that " marriage is purely a civil ceremony which binds opinion and not conscience." Of several brothers one alone, ordinarily, marries; the embarrassment of perpetuating the family falls on him; the others often live under the same roof with him and are the sigisbes of his wife. Three or four combine together to support a mistress in common. The poor traffic with their daughters quite young. " Out of ten who are abandoned" Saint-Didier already states, " there are nine whose mothers and aunts themselves negotiate the bargain." Thereupon follow some details which one would suppose to be taken from the oriental bazaars. With the dissolution of the family comes the abandonment of the domestic hearth. There is no visiting; people meet each other at public or private casinos, of which some are for ladies and some for men. There are no home comforts; a palace is a museum, a family memorial, only a resting-place for the night. " The Foscarini palace contains two hundred rooms filled with wealth, but not one chamber or chair offering a seat on account of the delicate carvings." Domestic authority has disappeared. " Parents dress their children ostentatiously as soon as they can walk." Boys of five or six years of age are seen wearing black hooded sacques trimmed with lace and figured with silver and gold. They are spoiled to excess; the father dares not scold them. When they get to be seventeen or eighteen he gives them mistresses; a Procurator, grieving at the loss of the company of a son who passes his time with a courtezan goes and beseeches him to bring her home with him. This demoralization extends from manners to dress; people are seen attending mass or frequenting the public squares in slippers and in dressing-gowns under their black cloaks. Many of the indigent nobles live as parasites at the expense of the coffee-house keepers, of whom they are the pest. Others, half-ruined, pass most of the day in bed, their feet protruding through tattered sheets, and the abbé of the house, meanwhile, composing for them licentious stories. In this corruption, following upon the death of militant virtues, only one living trait subsists, the love of beauty. Delicate, *spirituelle* painting of landscape and of *genre* flourishes up to the last. Music is born and soon passes from the church to the theatre. Four hospitals of abandoned young girls furnish so many seminaries of musicians and of incomparable singers. Almost every evening, there is on the banks of the Grand Canal an "academy" with music, and "with an inconceivable gathering," of people who crowd to it in gondolas and along the quays in order to enjoy it. At the theatre the light capricious fancy of Gozzi throws over their misery a diaphanous tissue of golden reveries and diverting grotesques. Noble races are beautiful even in ruin; the poetic imagination which illuminated the vigorous years of their youth accompanies them even to the brink of the grave in order to warm and to color their last moments, and this privilege saves their decrepitude as well as their adult age from the only two unpardonable vices, bitterness and vulgarity.

The Lido.—One can do nothing here but dream. And yet dream is not the proper word since it simply denotes a wandering of the brain, a coming and going of vague ideas; if one dreams at Venice it is through sensations and not through ideas. For the hundredth time to-day I have remarked, looking west, the peculiar color of the water in the vicinity of the sand-banks, consisting of the dun tints of Florentine bronze crawling with sinuous gleams of light. The sunset glow is depicted on it and is there transformed into tones of reddish or greenish orange. Occasionally the tint becomes auroral like silk drapery inflated and tossed by a current of air. Beyond, the infinite and imperceptible motion of the great blue surface mingles, unites and extends between sky and sea a network of radiant whiteness; the boat swims in light; only around it is seen the mingled green and azure, always changing, always the same.

In an hour we reach the Lido, a long bank of sand protecting Venice from the open sea. In the middle is a church with a village and, around it, gardens palisaded with straw and filled with young fruit-trees, all in full bloom. On the left runs an avenue of older trees, revived, however, with the early spring; their round tops are already white like bridal bouquets. On advancing a hundred yards the broad sea appears, no longer motionless and converted into a lake as at Venice but wild and roaring with the eternal resonance of its flux and reflux and the dash of its foaming surge. No one is visible on this long sandy bar; the most one sees at intervals, on turning an angle, is the gray capote of a sentinel. No human sound. I walk along in silence and gradually find myself enveloped in the grand monotonous voice of nature; each step is imprinted on the wet sand; the shells crackle under the crushing feet; hundreds of little crabs run away obliquely and when caught by the wave seek refuge in the ground. Meanwhile night comes on, and in front to the east, all grows dark. In the deepening obscurity two or three white sails are still discernible; these disappear; the green tones of the water become darker and darker until drowned in the universal night; from time to time a single wave breaks its snowy crest and falls with a feeble tremor upon the beach. On all sides, like the dull clamor of distant hounds, rises a hoarse and infinite roar which in the absence of other sensations, menaces the soul with its threats, reviving the idea, lost at Venice, of the indomitable and malevolent power of the sea.

On returning, and toward sunset, the sky seems like a brasier, and the rampart of houses, towers and churches rays the ruddy glow with opaque blackness,

It is actually the image of a vast conflagration, like those occurring in the upheavals of the globe when eruptions of lava have buried the vegetation of ages. It seems to be a furnace let loose and flaming yonder out of sight, and yet throwing up volleys of sparks in sight with the sombre scarlet of still blazing trunks and of the smothered and deadened brands amassed by the crumbling and crash of mighty forests. Their funereal shadows lengthen out infinitely on the ruddy waves and vanish in the night already covering the heaving sea with its pall.

April 29.—I promised to write you something about Venetian painting, and yet day after day I defer it. There are too many great works, and the work is too original ; one experiences here too many emotions and lives too bountifully and too fast ; it is like living in a green and primitive forest; it is much easier to sit down and gaze than to seek for a path and embrace the whole ; you resign yourself and grow indolent, and are always repeating that this or that must be seen over and over again. You are at last wearied out body and soul and say to yourself, to-morrow. The next day a fresh idea comes—for example, this morning at daybreak I ascended the tower of San-Marco.

From the top of this tower you see Venice and the entire lagune ; at this height man's works never seem to be more than those of beavers ; nature reappears, just as she is, sole subsistent, vast, scarcely defaced or spotted here and there with our petty ephemeral life. All is sand and sea ; only one grand flat plane is visible barred to the north by a wall of snow-peaks, a sort of intermediary domain between the dry and the fluid element, an infecund territory varied by neutral sands and lustrous pools. Red islets, washed by the falling tide, send forth vague slaty reflections. All around are tortuous canals and motionless surfaces mingling the infinite confusion of their shapes and the metallic

niellos of their leaden waters.   It is a desert, a strange
dead desert.   There is no life save a flotilla of boats
returning to port and oscillating beneath their orange
sails. From time to time, beyond the Lido, a jet of sunshine piercing the clouds casts on the broad sea a brilliant ray like a flashing sword severing a sombre
mantle.   One may remain here for hours, indifferent to
all human interests, before the uniform dialogue of two
grand objects, the concave sky and the flat earth, occupying space and the field of being.   Between two troops
of blonde clouds rushes a breath of sea-air.   They pass
in turn before the thin crescent moon which indefat-
igably buries her blade in their mass like a scythe in a
field of ripened grain.

BOOK VI.

VENETIAN ART.

CHAPTER I.

CLIMATE.—TEMPERAMENT.—ART, AN ABSTRACT OF LIFE.—MAN IN
THE INTERVAL BETWEEN HEROIC AND DEGENERATE ERAS.

April 30, 1864.—I find it more difficult to speak of
Venetian painters than of any others. Before their
pictures one has no disposition to analyze and discuss;
if it is done it is an effort. The eyes enjoy and that
is all; they enjoy the same as those of the Venetians
of the sixteenth century; for Venice was not a literary
or critical city like Florence, painting there being simply
the complement of surrounding voluptuousness, the
decoration of a banquet-hall or of an architectural
alcove. In order to explain this to himself a man
must withdraw to a distance and close his eyes, and
wait until his sensations become subdued; the mind
then does its office. Here are three or four prelim-
inary ideas; on such a subject a man divines and
sketches but does not perfect.

Venice is not only a distinct city differing from other
cities in Italy, free from the beginning and for thirteen
hundred years, but again a distinct community differing
from all others, having a soil, a sky, a climate, and an
atmosphere of its own. Compared with Florence,
which is the other centre, it is an aquatic world by the
side of a terrestrial world. Man here has not the same
field of vision. Instead of clear contours, sober tones
and motionless planes the eye ever finds, in the first

place, a moving and brilliant surface, a varied and uniform reflection of light, an exquisite union of varied and melting tones prolonged without fixed limit into those in contact with them; and then a soft vapory haze due to an incessant evaporation from the water enveloping all forms, rendering distances blue and filling the sky with magnificent clouds; again the contrast which the hard, intense and lustrous color of the water everywhere opposes to the subdued and stony hue of the edifices it bathes. In a dry country the eye is impressed by the *line*, in a wet one by the *spot*. This is very evident in Holland and in Flanders. The eye there is not arrested by delicacies of contour half-blurred by the intermediate moist atmosphere; it fixes itself on harmonies of color enlivened by the universal freshness and graduated by the variable density of ambient vapor. In the same way at Venice, and, save the differences which separate this sea-green element and these empurpled sands from the dingy mire and sooty sky of Amsterdam or of Antwerp, the eye, as at Antwerp and Amsterdam, becomes colorist. Proof of this may be found in the early architecture of the Venetians, in these stripes of porphyry, serpentine and precious marbles incrusting their palaces; in the sombre purple starred with gold filling San-Marco; in their original and persistent taste for the lustrous tints and luminous embroideries of mosaic and in the vivacity and brilliancy of their oldest national paintings. Vivarini, Carpaccio and Crivelli, and later John Bellini, already announce the splendor of the coming masters. These almost always used oil, finding fresco too dull; and Vasari like a true Florentine, reproaches Titian for painting "immediately from nature and not making a preparatory design, imagining that the only and best way to obtain a good design is to use color at once without previously studying contours with a pencil on paper."

A second reason and a stronger one is that besides the surroundings of a man the climate modifies his temperament and his instincts. Physiologists have only glanced at this truth, but it is plain to all who travel.* The living body is a condensed, organized gas, plunged into the atmosphere and constantly wasting and renewing itself, in such a way that man forms a portion of his *milieu* incessantly renewed by his *milieu*. According to the greater or less difficulty or rapidity of the escape or absorption of the entire machine so is its tension and its activity different; cerebral operations, like the rest, depend on the ease and the rapidity of the current of which, like the rest, they form a wave. A northern man, for instance, absorbs and wastes two or three times as much as a southern man, and consequently his sensibility, that is to say the suddenness and vehemence of his emotions, are two or three times less great. Compare a peasant or a horse of Friesland in Holland with a peasant or a horse of Berri in France; a Lombard Italian with a Calabrian Italian and a Russian with an Arab.† We are as yet ignorant of the precise laws which apportion to the colder or moister atmosphere, alimentation, respiration, muscular force, capacity for emotion and generation of diverse orders of ideas; but it is plain that such laws exist. Everywhere, and powerfully, climate, physical temperament and moral structure interdepend like three successive links of a chain; whoever disturbs the first, disturbs the second and, consequently,

---

* Experiments have been made with a view to ascertain the effect of a carnivorous diet. French workmen performing half as much labor as English workmen were fed on meat; at the end of a year their capacity for labor, that is to say, their powers of attention and their muscular energy, had doubled.

† The Duke of Wellington says: "When a French army has the necessary, a Spanish army has too much and the English army is dying with hunger."

the third. Venice and the valley of the Po are the
Netherlands of Italy; hence it is that temperament
and character are here transformed as they are in the
Netherlands of the north. We find here, the same as in
Flanders, bright rosy carnations, blonde and red hair,
soft, pulpy and slightly flabby flesh in contrast with
the black hair, energetic spareness, noble sculptural
features and firm muscles of the Italians of central
Italy. We find here as in Flanders, a passionate
fondness for sensuous enjoyment, exquisite appreciation
of material resources, and an inferior literary or speculative spirit, forming a contrast to the subtle, argumen-
tative, delicate intellect tending to purism, running
through all the lives and writings of the Florentines.*
In the beginning, architecture so gay and so little classic, voluptuous tastes after the fifteenth century,†
later, a publicity of pleasure, the six months carnival
and registered and innumerable courtezans, music a
state institution, at all times magnificence of costumes
and of festivals, pompous, variegated dalmatics, embroidered silk robes, a prodigality of gold and diamonds, constant contact with oriental magnificence and
fancy, fixed toleration in religious matters and allow-
able indifference in political matters, exuberant prosperity, voluptuousness encouraged, supineness proscribed, all announce the same primitive and leading
disposition, that is to say an aptitude for imbuing
sensual life with poesy and a talent for combining
enjoyment with beauty. It is this national naturalness
which the painters represent in their types; this it is
which they flatter in their coloring; its effects and
surroundings are displayed by them in their silks,

---

* The Florentines called the Venetians *grossolani*.

† Antonella da Messina, says Vasari, went to reside in Venice, in
which city he introduced oil-painting. He preferred this city and
was much esteemed and caressed by the nobles, "being a person
much addicted to pleasure and licentiousness."

velvets and pearls, in their balustrades, their colonnades and their gildings. It is more clearly seen in
them than in itself. They have disengaged, defined
and incorporated it in a visible shape. Great artists,
everywhere, are the heralds and interpreters of their
community; Jordæns, Crayer, Rubens in Flanders and
Titian, Tintoretto and Veronese in Venice. Their instinct and their intuition make them naturalists, psy-
chologists, historians and philosophers; they ruminate
over the idea constituting their race and their epoch,
and the broad and involuntary sympathy forming their
genius brings together and organizes in their minds in
true proportions the infinite and commingled elements
of the society in which they are comprised. Their tact
goes farther than science, and the ideal being they
fetch to light is the most powerful summary, the liveliest concentrated image, the most complete and definite figure of the real beings amongst whom they have
dwelt. They again seize the mould in which nature
has cast her objects and which, charged with a refractory metal, has only furnished rude and defective
forms; they empty it and pour their metal into it, a
more supple metal, and they heat their own furnace,
and the statue that issues from the clay in their hands
represents for the first time the veritable contours of a
mould which preceding castings, crusted with scoria
and traversed with fissures, could not express.

Let us now consider the moment of their appearance.
In all times and in every land that which inspires
works of art is a certain complex and mixed condition
of things encountered in the soul when placed between
two orders of sentiments: it is in train to abandon the
love of the grand for the love of the agreeable; but in
passing from one to the other it combines both. It is
necessary still to possess the taste for the grand, that is
to say, for noble forms and vigorous passions, without
which works of art would be only pretty. It is neces-

sary to have already possessed a taste for the agreeable,
that is to say, a craving for pleasure and interest in
decoration, without which the mind would concern
itself only with actions and never delight in works of
art. Hence the transient and precious flower is only
seen to bloom at the confluence of two epochs, betwixt heroic and epicurean habits, at the moment
when man, terminating some long and painful war, or
foundation, or discovery, begins to take repose and look
about him, meditating over the pleasure of decorating
his great bare tenement whose foundations his own
hands have laid and whose walls they have erected.
Before this it would have been too soon ; absorbed with
labor he could not think of enjoyment ; a little time
after it would be too late, as, dreaming of enjoyment
only, he no longer conceives of an effort. Between the
two is found the unique moment, lasting longer or
shorter according as the transformation of the soul is
more or less prompt, and in which, men, still strong,
impetuous and capable of sublime emotion and of
bold enterprise, suffer the tension of their will to relax
in order to magnificently enliven the senses and the intellect.

Such is the change effected in Venice, as in the rest
of Italy, between the fifteenth and sixteenth centuries.
The Chiogga campaign is the last act of the old heroic
drama ; there, as in the best days of the ancient republics a besieged people is seen to save itself against all
hope, artisans equipping vessels, a Pisani conqueror
undergoing imprisonment and only released to renew
the victory, a Carlo Zeno* surviving forty wounds, and
a doge of seventy years of age ; a Contarini, who makes
a vow not to leave his vessel so long as the enemy's
fleet is uncaptured, thirty families, apothecaries, grocers,
vintners, tanners admitted among the nobles, a bravery,

---

* He died in 1418. He lived the life of one of Plutarch's characters

a public spirit like that of Athens under Themistocles
and of Rome under Fabius Cunctator. If, from this
time forth, the inward fire abates we still feel its warmth
for many long years, longer kept up than in the rest of
Italy, and sometimes demonstrating its power by sudden outbursts. Venice is always an independent city,
a cherished soil when Florence, Rome and Bologna are
nothing more than museums for the idle and for amateurs. A subjected people are still found to be citizens
on occasion; on Louis XII. and Maximilian becoming
masters of the Venetian possessions on the mainland
the peasants rebel in the name of St. Mark and the
volunteers, in spite of the doge, retake Padua. On
Pope Paul V. attempting to impose his will on Venice
the Venetian clergy remain patriotic and the people
hoot away the papalistic monks.* On the spreading of
the ecclesiastic inquisition over Italy the Venetian senate causes Paolo Sarpi to write against the Council of
Trent, tolerates on its soil protestants, Arminians, Ma-
hometans, Jews, and Greeks, leaves them in possession
of their temples and permits the interment of heretics
in the churches. The nobles, on their side, are always
ready to fight. During the whole of the sixteenth century, even up to the seventeenth and beyond, we see
them in Dalmatia, in the Morea, over the entire Mediterranean, defending the soil inch by inch against the
infidels. The garrison of Famagouste yields only to
famine† and its governor, Bragadino, burnt alive, is
a hero of ancient days. At the battle of Lepanto the
Venetians alone furnish one half of the christian fleet.
Thus on all sides, and notwithstanding their gradual
decline, peril, energy, love of country, all, in brief,
which constitutes or sustains the grand life of the soul
here subsists, whilst throughout the peninsula foreign
dominion, clerical oppression and voluptuous or aca-

---

* "Siamo Veneziani e poi cristiani." † 1571.

demical inertia reduces man to the system of the antechamber, the subtleties of dilettantism and the babble of sonnets.

But if the human spring is not broken at Venice, it is seen insensibly losing its elasticity. The government, changed into a suspicious despotism, elects a Mocenigo doge, a shameless speculator profiting on the public distress, instead of that Charles Zeno who had saved the country; it holds Zeno prisoner two years and intrusts the armies on the mainland to condottieri; it is tied up in the hands of three inquisitors, provokes accusations, practices secret executions and commands the people to confine themselves to the indulgences of pleasure. On the other hand luxury arises. About the year 1400 the houses "were quite small;" but a thousand nobles were enumerated in Venice possessing from four to seventy thousand ducats rental, while three thousand ducats were sufficient to purchase a palace. Henceforth this great wealth is no longer to be employed in enterprises and in self-devotion, but in pomp and magnificence. In 1495 Commines admires "the grand canal, the most beautiful street I think, in the world, and with the best houses; the houses are very grand, high and of excellent stone,—and these have been built within a century. All have fronts of white marble, which comes from Istria a hundred miles away, and yet many more great pieces of porphyry and of serpentine on them : inside they have, most of them, at least two chambers with gilded ceilings, rich screens of chimneys with carved marble, the bedsteads gilded and the *ostevents* painted and gilded and well furnished within." On his arrival twenty-five gentlemen attired in silk and scarlet come to meet him ; they conduct him to a boat decked with crimson silk; "it is the most triumphant city that I ever saw." Finally, whilst the necessity of pleasure grows the spirit of enterprise diminishes; the passage of the Cape in the beginning

of the sixteenth century places the commerce of Asia
in the hands of the Portuguese ; on the Mediterranean
and the Atlantic the financial measures of Charles V.
joined to bad usage by the Turks, render abortive the
great maritime caravans which the state dispatches
yearly between Alexandria and Bruges. In respect to
industrial matters, the hampered artisans, watched and
cloistered in their country, cease to perfect their arts
and allow foreign competitors to surpass them in processes and in furnishing supplies to the world. Thus,
on all sides, the capacity for activity becomes lessened
and the desire for enjoyment greater without one
entirely effacing the other, but in such a way that, both
commingling, they produce that ambiguous state of
mind similar to a mixed temperature which is neither
too mild nor too severe and in which the arts are
generated. Indeed, it is from 1454 to 1572, between
the institution of state inquisitors and the battle of
Lepanto, between the accomplishment of internal despotism and the last of the great outward victories, that
the brilliant productions of Venetian art appear.
John Bellini was born in 1426, Giorgone died in 1511,
Titian in 1576, Veronese in 1572 and Tintoretto in
1594. In this interval of one hundred and fifty years
this warrior city, this mistress of the Mediterranean,
this queen of commerce and of industry became a
casino for masqueraders and a den of courtezans.

CHAPTER II.

THE EARLY PAINTERS.—JOHN BELLINI.—CARPACCIO.—VENETIAN SO-
CIETY IN THE SIXTEENTH CENTURY.—UNRESTRAINED VOLUPTU-
OUSNESS.—DOMESTIC ESTABLISHMENT OF ARETINO.—SENTIMENT
OF ART.—COLOR INSTINCTS.

THE Academy of the Fine Arts contains a collection
of the works of the earliest painters. A large picture
in compartments, of 1380, quite barbarous, shows the
first steps taken : here, as elsewhere, the new art issued
from Byzantine traditions. It appears late, much
later than in precocious and intelligent Tuscany. We
encounter, indeed, in the fourteenth century, a Semit-
ecolo, a Guariento, weak disciples of the school which
Giotto founded at Padua ; but, in order to find the first
national painters, we must come down to the middle of
the following century. At this time there lived at
Murano a family of artists called the Vivarini. With
the oldest of these, Antonio, we already detect the
rudiments of Venetian taste, some venerable beards
and bald heads, fine draperies with rosy and green
tones, little angels almost plump and Madonnas with
full cheeks. After him his brother Bartolomeo, educated undoubtedly in the Paduan school, inclines painting for a time to dry and bony forms.* With him, however, as with all the rest, a feeling for rich colors is
already perceptible. On leaving this antechamber of
art the eyes keep a full and strong sensation which
other vestibules of art, at Sienna and at Florence, do
not give, and, on continuing, we find the same sensation, still richer, before the masters of this half-legible
era, John Bellini and Carpaccio.

---

* A Virgin of 1473, at Santa Maria Formosa.

I have just examined at the Frari a picture by John
Bellini which, like those of Perugino, seems to me a
masterpiece of genuine religious art. At the rear of a
chapel, over the altar, within a small piece of golden
architecture, sits the Virgin on a throne in a grand
blue mantle. She is good and simple like a simple, innocent peasant girl. At her feet two little angels in
short vests seem to be choir-boys and their plump
infantile thighs are of the finest and healthiest flesh-
color. On the two sides, in the compartments, are two
couples of saints, impassible figures in the garbs of
monk and bishop, erect for eternity in hieratic attitude,
actual forms reminding one of the sunburnt fisher-
men of the Adriatic. These personages have all lived ;
the believer kneeling before them recognized features
encountered by him in his boat and on the canals, the
ruddy brown tones of visages tanned by the sea-breezes,
the broad and pure carnation of young girls reared in
a moist atmosphere, the damask cope of the prelate
heading the processions, and the little naked legs of
the children fishing for crabs at sunset. He could not
avoid having faith in them ; truth so local and perfect
paved the way to illusion. But the apparition was one
of a superior and august world. These personages do
not move ; their faces are in repose and their eyes fixed
like those of figures seen in a dream. A painted niche,
decked with red and gold, recedes back of the Virgin
like the extension of an imaginary realm ; painted
architecture in this way imitates and completes actual
architecture, while the golden Host on the marble,
crowned with rays and a glory, displays the entrance
into the supernatural world disclosing itself behind her.

On regarding other pictures by John Bellini, and
those of his contemporaries in the Academy, it is evident that painting in Venice, while following a path of
its own, ran the same course as in the rest of Italy.
It issues here, as elsewhere, from missals and mosaics,

and corresponds at first wholly to christian emotions ;
then, by degrees, the sentiment of a beautiful corporeal
life introduces into the altar-frames vigorous and healthy
bodies borrowed from surrounding nature, and we wonder at seeing placid expressions and religious physiognomies on flourishing forms circulating with youthful blood
and sustained by an intact temperament. It is the confluence of two ages and of two spirits, one christian
and subsiding and the other pagan and about to become
ascendant.   At Venice, however, over these general
resemblances special traits are delineated.   The personages are more closely copied from life, less transformed by the classic or mystic sentiment, less pure
than at Perugia, less noble than at Florence ; they
appeal less to the intellect or to the heart and more to
the senses.   They are more quickly recognized as men,
and give greater pleasure to the eye.   Powerful, lively
tones color their muscles and faces ; living flesh is
already soft on the shoulders, and on children's thighs ;
open landscapes recede in order to enforce the dark
tints of the figures; the saints gather around the Virgin in various attitudes unknown to the monotonous
perceptions of other primitive schools.   At the height
of its fervor and faith the national spirit, fond of diversity
and the agreeable allows a smile to glimmer.   Nothing
is more striking in this respect than the eight figures
by Carpaccio relating to St. Ursula. *   Everything is
here ; and first the awkwardness of the feudal image-
fabricator. He ignores one half of the landscape, and
likewise the nude : his rocks bristling with trees, seem to
issue from a psalter ; frequently his trees are as if cut
out of polished sheet-iron ; his ten thousand crucified
martyrs on a mountain are grotesque like the figures of
an ancient mystery ; he did not, evidently, live in Florence, nor study natural objects with Paolo Uccello, nor

* Pictures of from 1490 to 1515.

human members and muscles with Pollaiolo. On the other hand we find in him the chastest of mediæval figures, and that extreme finish, that perfect truthfulness, that bloom of the christian conscience which the following age, more rude and sensual, is to trample on in its vehemences. The saint and her affianced, under their great drooping blonde tresses, are grave and tender, like the characters of a legend. We see her, at one time asleep and receiving from the angel the announcement of her martyrdom, now kneeling with her spouse under the benediction of the pope, now translated in glory above a field of crowded heads. In another picture she appears with St. Anne and two aged saints embracing each other; one cannot imagine figures more pious and more serene; she, pale and gentle, her head slightly bent, holds a banner in her beautiful hands and a green palm-branch; her silky hair flows down over the virginal blue of her long robe and a royal mantle envelops her form with its golden confusion; she is indeed a saint, the candor, humility and delicacy of the middle ages entirely permeating her attitude and expression. Such is the age, and such the country! These paintings provide scenes of social significance and rich decorations. The artist, as at a later period his great successors, displays architecture, fabrics, arcades, tapestried halls, vessels, processions of characters, grand bedizened and lustrous robes, all in petty proportions but in brilliancy and in diversity anticipating future productions as an illuminated manuscript anticipates a picture. And in order fully to show the transformation under way he himself once attains to perfect art; we see him emerging from his primitive dryness in order to enter on the new and definitive style. In the middle of the grand hall is a "Presentation of the boy Jesus" which one would not believe to be by him, were it not signed by his hand (1510). Under a marble portico incrusted with mosaics of gold

appear personages almost of the size of life, in admirable
relief, exquisitely finished, and perfect in composition
and amidst the most beautiful gradations of light and
shadow ; the Virgin, followed by two young females,
leads her child to the aged Simeon ; beneath, three
angels play on the viol and the lute. Save a little
rigidity in the heads of the men, and in some of the
folds of the drapery, the archaic manner has disappeared; nothing remains of it but the infinite charm
of moral refinement and benignity, while, for the first
time, the semi-nude bodies of little children show
the beauty of flesh traversed and impregnated with
light. With this picture we cross the threshold of
high art, and, around Carpaccio, his young contemporaries, Giorgone and Titian, have already surpassed
him.

The Masters.—When, in order to comprehend the
milieu in which an art has flourished, we strive, according to the documents at hand, to form some idea of the
life of a patrician at Venice during the first half of the
sixteenth century, we encounter in him first, and in the
foremost rank, a spirit of haughty security and grandeur. He regards himself as the successor of the
ancient Romans, and holds that, except in conquests,
he has surpassed, and does still surpass them.*
" Among all the provinces of the noble Roman empire
Italy is queen," and in the Italy overcome by the
Cæsars, and devastated by the barbarians, Venice is
the sole city that remained free. Abroad she has just
recovered the provinces on the mainland wrested from
her by Louis XII. Her lagunes and her alliances protect her against the emperor. The Turk fails in his
encroachments on her domain, and Candia, Cyprus, the
Cyclades, Corfu and the coasts of the Adriatic held by
her garrisons, extend her sovereignty to the extremities

---

* Donati Gianotti, *La Republica di Venezia* (dialogues).

of the sea. Within, " she has never been more perfect."
In no state in the world do we see " better laws, better
preservation of order, more complete concord," and in
this admirable system, which is unique in the universe, " she does not lack valorous and magnanimous
souls." With the dignified coolness of a grand seignor,
Marco Trifone Gabriello regards the prosperity of the
glorious city as due to its aristocratic government, and
" the suppression of the council developed it up to a
point of grandeur not previously reached." According
to him all citizens excluded from suffrage are only
inferior people, boatmen, subjects and domestics. If,
in the course of events, any of these become wealthy
and prominent it is due to the tolerance of the state
which gathers them under its wing; still, in this day
they are protected, they have no rights; clients and
plebeians they rejoice in the patronage awarded to
them. The sole legitimate rulers are "three thousand
gentlemen, seigneurs of the city and of the entire state
on land and on sea." The state belongs to them; " as
formerly with the Roman patricians they hold public
affairs in fee, and the wisdom of their rule confirms the
stability of their right." Thereupon the " magnifico"
describes with patriotic complacency the economy of
the constitution and the resources of the city, the order
of the functions and the election of magistrates, the
fifteen hundred thousand crowns of public revenue, the
new fortifications on land and the armament in the
arsenals. In gravity, proud spiritedness and nobleness
of discourse one might take him for a citizen of antiquity. In fact his friends compare him to Atticus; he,
however, courteously declines the title, declaring that
if, like Atticus, he has withdrawn from public affairs it
is for a different motive and wholly creditable to his
city, since the retirement of Atticus was excused by
the powerlessness of worthy citizens and the decline
of Rome, whereas his own is authorized by the su-

perabundance of capable men and the prosperity of
Venice. Thus does the dialogue proceed in terms of
noble courteousness, in fine periods and with substantial arguments; the apartment of Bembo at
Padua is the theatre for this, and the reader may imagine these lofty Renaissance halls, decorated with
busts, manuscripts and vases, in which the grandeurs
of paganism and of antique patriotism reappeared
with the eloquence, the purity and the urbanity of
Cicero.

How do our "magnifici" amuse themselves? Some
of them are serious I can readily believe, but the prevailing sentiment at Venice is not a rigid one. At
this time the most prominent personage is Aretino,
the son of a courtezan, born in a hospital, parasite by
profession, and a professor of black-mail, who, by
means of calumnies and sycophancies, of luxurious
sonnets and obscene dialogues, becomes the arbiter of
reputations, extorts seventy thousand crowns from
European magnates, calls himself "the scourge of
princes" and succeeds in passing off his inflated effeminate style as one of the marvels of the human intellect.
He has no property and lives like a seignor on the
money bestowed, or on the presents showered, on him.
At early morning, in his palace on the Grand Canal,
solicitors and flatterers fill his antechamber. "So
many seignors,"* he says, "importune me with their
visits that my stairs are worn with the friction of their
feet like the Capitol pavement with the wheels of
triumphant chariots. I doubt if Rome ever saw so
great a medley of nations and languages as that which
is visible under my roof. Turks, Jews, Indians,
Frenchmen, Spaniards and Germans, all resort to it.
As to the Italians imagine how many there must be!
I say nothing of the vulgar; it is impossible to find me

---

* Lettre, Vol. I. p. 206. He came to Venice in 1527.

free of monks and priests . . . . I am secretary for
everybody." Nobles, prelates and artists pay court to
him; they fetch him antique medals, gold collars,
velvet mantles, pictures, purses of five hundred crowns
and the diplomas of Academies. His bust of white
marble, his portrait by Titian, the medals of bronze,
silver and gold that represent him display to the gaze
of his visitors his brutal and impudent mask. We see
him on these crowned, clad in long imperial robes, sitting on an elevated throne and receiving the homage
and gifts of the surrounding people. He is popular
and sets the fashion. "I see," he says, "my effigy on
the façades of palaces; I encounter it again on comb-
boxes, on mirror ornaments, on majolica ware like that
of Alexander, Cæsar or Scipio. Moreover I assure
you that at Murano there is a certain kind of crystal
vase called an Aretino. A breed of horses is called
Aretino, in commemoration of one I received from
Pope Clement and which I gave to Duke Frederick.
The stream bathing one side of the house which I
occupy on the Grand Canal is baptized with the name
of Aretino. People refer to the style of Aretino,—how
the pedants burst with vexation! Three of my cham-
bermaids or housekeepers, having left my service to
set up for ladies, call themselves Aretines." Thus
protected and fed by public favor he enjoys himself,
not furtively and delicately, but openly and ostentatiously. "Let us eat, drink and be merry, and . . . . like
liberal men!" I am a liberal man, says he often,
which signifies that he does what he pleases and pam-
pers all his senses. At this epoch the nerves are still
rude and the muscles vigorous; only toward the end
of the seventeenth century does society incline to insipidity and roguery. At this time all desires are
gluttonous rather than dainty; in the Venuses which
the great masters undrape on their canvases the torso

is masculine and the eye audacious; voluptuousness,
rank and open, leaves no place for polish or for sentimentality. Aretino had been a vagabond and soldier,
and his pleasures smacked of the life he had led.
There was great carousing under his roof; he had
"twenty-two women in his house, and frequently with
infants at the breast." Revelling and disorder were
constant. He has the generosity of a robber, and if he
takes he lets others take. "Double my pension of five
hundred crowns—even if I had a thousand times as
much—I would always be straitened. Everybody
comes to me, as if I were custodian of the royal
treasury. Let a poor girl be confined and my house
pays the expenses. Let any one be put in prison and
the cost falls on me. Soldiers without an equipment,
unfortunate strangers, and quantities of stray cavaliers
come to my house to refit. It is not two months since
a young man wounded near my residence, was brought
into one of my apartments." He is plundered by his
domestics. All is confusion in this free tenement;
vases, busts, sketches, caps and mantles presented to
him, Cyprus wine, birds, hares and rabbits sent to him,
melons and grapes that he himself buys for the evening entertainment. He eats well, drinks better and
makes his marble halls ring with his jovial sallies.
Partridges arrive; "roasted, as soon as caught, I
stopped my hymn in honor of hares and began at once
to sing the praises of the winged! My good friend
Titian, bestowing a glance on these savory morsels, began to sing in duet with me the *Magnificat* I had already commenced." To this music of the jaws is added
another. The famous songstress Franceschina is one of
his guests; he kisses "her beautiful hands, two charming robbers which take not alone people's purses but
their hearts." "It is my wish," says he, "that where
my dishes prove unsavory there may the sweetness of

your voice appear." Courtezans are at home in his domicile. He has written books* for their use and taught them the accomplishments of their profession. He receives them, pets them, writes to them and recruits them. In the morning, after having got rid of his visitors, when he does not go to amuse himself in the studios of Titian and Sansovino, he visits grisettes, gives them "a few sous" and has them sew "handkerchiefs, sheets and shirts in order that they may earn their living." Thus occupied he collects and installs under his roof six young women who are called *Aretines*, a seraglio without walls where pranks, quarrels and imbroglios make the most remarkable uproar. He lives in this way thirty years, sometimes horsewhipped but always pensioned, familiar with the highest, receiving from a bishop blue morocco shoes for one of his mistresses, and a companion of Titian, of Tintoretto and of Sansovino. And better still, Aretino founds a school; he has imitators as parasitical and as obscene as himself, Doni, Dolce, Nicolo Franco his secretary and enemy, the author of the *Priapea* and who ended his career at Rome on the gibbet. Thus flourished at Venice a literature of buffoonery and of lewdness which, tempered by the gallantries of Parabosco, repels a superior one with the sonnets of Baffo. Judge of readers by the book and of guests by the mansion. With this glimpse we partially recognize the inner character of men of whom the painters have transmitted to us the outward image; here it is that we obtain the principal traits explanatory of contemporary art, the haughty grandeur suitable to the undisputed masters of such a republic, the brutal and teeming energy surviving the ages of virile activity, the magnificent and impudent sensuality which, developed by accumulated wealth and by unquestioned

---

* Ragionamenti.—Letters to Zufolina and Zafetta.

security, expands and revels in the full brightness of
sunshine.

One point remains, the sentiment itself for art. We
find it everywhere in Venice in those days, in private
houses, among bodies of great public functionaries,
among the patricians, among people of the ordinary
class, even in those coarse and practical natures who,
like Aretino, seem to be born to live jollily and to speculate on their associates. Whatever remains of inward
nobleness blooms in that direction. Their libertinage
and their assurance sympathize without effort with
the embellished image of license and force. They find
in muscular giants, in stout naked beauties, in the architectural and luxurious pomp of painting an aliment
suited to their energetic and unbridled instincts. Moral
baseness does not exclude sensuous refinements; on the
contrary it throws the field open, and the man whose
propensities are wholly on one side is only therefore the
better qualified to appreciate the nicest shades of pleasure. Aretino bows reverentially to Michael Angelo ; all
he asks of him is one of his sketches " in order to
enjoy it during life and to bear it with him to his
tomb." With Titian he is a true friend, natural and
simple ; his admiration and his taste are sincere. He
speaks of color with a precision and vivacity of impression worthy of Titian himself. " Signor," he
addresses him, "my dear companion, I have to-day,
against my usual practice, dined alone, or rather in
company with the annoyances of that quatran fever
which leaves me no relish for the savor of any dish.
I arose from table wearied with the depressing ennui
with which I sat down, and then leaning my arm on
the window-sill, and resting my breast and almost all
my person thereon, I fell into contemplation of the
admirable spectacle of the innumerable barks which,
filled with strangers and Venetians, delighted not alone
those in them but again the Grand Canal. . . . . All

at once two gondolas appear and, manned by some famous oarsmen, contend for speed, and furnish the public with pastime. I also took great pleasure in contemplating the multitude which, in order to witness this amusement, had stopped on the Rialto bridge, on the Camerlinghes bank, at the Pescarita, on the *traghetto* of St. Sophia and on that of Casa di Mosto. And whilst on both sides the crowd dispersed, each his own way with hilarious applause, I, as one irksome to himself, who knows not what to do with his mind or with his thoughts, turn my eyes up to the firmament. Never, since God created it, was the sky so adorned with the exquisite painting of lights and shades! The atmosphere was such as those who envy Titian would like to produce, because they are not able to be a Titian. . . . at first the buildings which, of genuine stone, seem nevertheless a material transfigured by artifice, then daylight, in certain spots pure and lively and in others disturbed and deadened. Consider yet again another marvel, dense and humid clouds which, on the principal plane, descend to the roofs of the edifices, and on a remoter one sink behind them even to the middle of their mass. The entire right consisted of a subdued color suspended under a dark gray-brown. I gazed in admiration on the varied tints which these clouds presented to the eye, the nearest brilliant with flames from the solar realm, the remotest with a ruddy and less ardent vermilion. Oh, the fine strokes of the pencil which from this side colored the air and made it recede behind the palaces as Titian practises it in his landscapes! In certain parts appeared a blue-green, in others an azure rendered green and truly commingled by the capricious invention of nature, the mistress of all masters. It is she who with clear or obscure tints retires or models forms according to her own conception. And I myself who know how your pencil is the soul of your soul, exclaimed three or four times: ' Titian,

where art thou ?'" One here recognizes the backgrounds
of the pictures of the Venetian artists ; behold the grand
white clouds of Veronese sleeping suspended beneath the
colonnades, the blue distances, the atmosphere palpitat-
ing with vague gleams, the ruddy, warm, brown shadows
of Titian.

CHAPTER III.

THE DUCAL PALACE.—CHARACTERS OF THE DAY.—THE ALLEGORICAL
PAINTINGS OF VERONESE AND TINTORETTO.—THE RAPE OF
EUROPA.

THERE are families of plants with species so near akin
that the resemblances are greater than the differences :
such are the Venetian painters, and not only the four
most celebrated, Giorgone, Titian, Tintoretto and Veronese, but others less illustrious, Palma-Vecchio, Bonifazio, Paris Bordone, Pordenone, and that crowd
enumerated by Ridolfi in his "Lives," contemporaries,
relatives and successors of the great men, Andrea Vi-
centino, Palma the younger, Zelotti, Bazzaco, Padovinano, Bassano, Schiavone, Moretti, and so many others.
What the eye clearly detects is the common and general
type; special and personal traits remain, at the first
glance, in the background. All have labored together
and in turn at the Ducal Palace ; but, through the involuntary unity of their talents, their paintings form a
complete whole.

At the first glance the eyes are disappointed; excepting three or four halls the apartments are low and of
small dimensions. The chamber of the Council of Ten
and those around it are gilded cabinets inadequate for
the figures which occupy them ; but after a few moments the cabinet is forgotten and nothing is seen but
the figures. Power and voluptuousness display themselves superbly and unrestrainedly. Naked men and
painted caryatides in the angles project in such relief
that at first sight one takes them for statues ; a colossal
breath inflates their breasts ; their thighs and shoulders
are writhing. On the ceiling a Mercury seen on the

belly, entirely nude, is almost a Rubens figure but with a more marked sensuality. A gigantic Neptune urges on his marine steeds who are dashing off on the waves; his foot rests on the edge of the chariot, and his enormous ruddy torso throws itself back; he raises his conch with the glee of a bestial divinity; the salt air whistles through his scarf, hair and beard; one cannot imagine, without seeing it, such furious inspiration, such overflowing animal vigor, such joyous pagan carnality, such a triumph of grand, free, licentious being revelling in air and in sunshine. What an injustice, that of reducing the Venetians to the depicting of happy repose and to the art of flattering the eye! They, too, have painted grandeur and heroism; the energetic and acting body has of itself affected them; like the Flemings they have their own colossi. Their drawing, even without color, is of itself capable of expressing the full solidity and vitality of the human structure. Take, for example, in this very hall, the four *grisailles* by Veronese, five or six veiled or half-naked women, all so vigorous and of such a frame that their thighs and arms might embrace and crush a combatant, and yet of a physiognomy so simple or so spirited that in spite of their gaiety they are virgin like the Venuses and the Psyches of Raphael.

The more the ideal figures of Venetian art are considered the more do we feel behind us the breath of an heroic age. The grand draped old men with bald brows are patrician kings of the Archipelago, barbaric sultans who, trailing their silken simarres, receive tribute and order executions. Superb women in long variegated and disordered robes are the imperial daughters of the republic, like that Catherine Cornaro of whom Venice received Cyprus. There are combatants' muscles within the bronzed breasts of sailors and captains; their bodies, tanned by sun and wind, have been contending with the athletic forms of janissaries

their turbans, pelisses and furs, and their sword-hafts
gleaming with jewels, the whole of Asiatic magnificence mingles on their persons with flowing antique
drapery and with the nudities of pagan tradition.
Their straightforward look is yet tranquil and savage,
and the spirit and tragic grandeur of their expression
tells of the proximity to a life in which man, concentrated in a few simple passions, thought of being master only because he would not be a slave, and of slaying
only because he would not be slain.   Such is the spirit of
a painting by Veronese which, in the hall of the Council
of Ten, represents an old warrior and a young woman;
it is an allegory—but the subject is of little consequence.   The man is seated and bending forward with
a grim air, his chin resting on his hand; his colossal
shoulders and arm, and his naked leg, bound with a
lion-headed cnemide, issue from his massive and disordered drapery; with his turban and white beard, a
meditative brow, and the features of a wearied lion
he looks like a pasha suffering with ennui.   She, with
downcast eyes, rests her hands on her soft breast; her
superb tresses are looped up with pearls; she seems to
be some captive awaiting her master's will; and her
neck and inclining face become of a deeper glow in
the shadow that bathes them.

Almost all the other halls are empty; the paintings
have been removed to an inner apartment.   We go in
quest of the keeper of the gallery, and tell him in bad
Italian that we are without letters of introduction and
have no claim or right whatever to be admitted to see
them, whereupon he condescends to lead us to the
closed apartment, to lift the curtains one after the other
and to lose a couple of hours in showing them to us.

I have enjoyed nothing more keenly in Italy; the
canvases are lower than our eyes; we can look at them
as closely as we please, at ease, and we are alone.
Here are bronzed giants by Tintoretto, the skin folded

by the play of muscles ; Saint Andrew and Saint Mark, veritable colossi like those of Rubens. There is a Saint Christopher by Titian, a sort of bronzed and stooping Atlas, his four limbs in action to sustain the burden of a world, and on his neck, in extraordinary contrast, a little soft smiling urchin whose infantile flesh has the delicacy and the grace of a flower. Above all, a dozen of mythological paintings and allegories by Tintoretto and Veronese of such brilliancy, of such entrancing seductiveness that a veil falls from the eyes, revealing an unknown world, a paradise of delights extending far beyond all that one could dream or imagine. When the Old Man of the Mountain transported his youths asleep into his harem in order to qualify them for extreme devotedness to him such, without doubt, was the spectacle he prepared for them.

On a strand, on the margin of the infinite sea, Ariadne in serious mood receives the ring from Bacchus, while Venus, with a golden crown, approaches in the air to honor their nuptials. She is the sublime beauty of nude flesh, as she appears on rising from the waves vivified by the sun and graduated by shadows. The goddess swims in liquid light, and her curved back, her thigh and her full forms palpitate half-enveloped in a white diaphanous veil. Where is the language with which to paint the beauty of an attitude, of a tone, of a contour ? What will portray healthy and rosy flesh under the amber transparency of gauze ? How represent the mellow fulness of a living form and the undulating limbs losing themselves in a flexible body ? She really swims in light as a fish swims in its lake and the atmosphere filled with vague reflections embraces and caresses her.

Alongside of this are two young women, "Peace" and "Plenty." Peace, with a tremulous delicacy, inclines toward her sister ; she has turned away and her head is seen only in shadow, but she possesses the

freshness of immortal youth. How luminous their
gathered tresses, blonde as the ripened wheat! Their
legs and bodies are slightly deflected; one seems to be
falling, and this moving curvature as it commences is
wonderful. No painter has to the same degree appreciated full, yielding forms or so vividly arrested the
flight of action. They are about to take a posture or
to walk; the eye and the mind involuntarily expand the
situation; we see in their present a future and a past;
the artist has fixed a fleeting moment but one big with
its environment. Nobody, save Rubens, has thus expressed the incessant flow and fluidity of life. Pallas,
meanwhile, repels Mars, and her manly cuirass with
dark reflections brings out with irresistible coquetry
the exquisite whiteness of the shoulder and knee.

More animated and more voluptuous still is the
coquetry of the group of Mercury and the Three
Graces. All three are deflected; with Tintoretto a
body is not a living one when its posture is passive;
the display of a deflected figure adds a mobile grace to
the universal attractiveness emanating from the rest of
its beauty. One of them, seated, extends her arms,
and the light that falls on her flank makes portions of
her face, neck and bosom glow against the vague purple of the shadow. Her sister, kneeling, with downcast
eyes, takes her hand; a long gauze, fine like those silvery webs of the fields brightened by the morning
dawn, clings around the waist and expands over the
bosom whose blush it allows to appear. In the other
hand she holds a blooming bunch of flowers, ascending
upward and resting their snowy purity on the ruddy
whiteness of the ample arms. The third, tortuous, displays herself in full, and from neck to heel, the eye
follows the embracing of the muscles covering the
superb framework of the spine and hips. Waving
tresses, small chin, rounded eyelids, nose slightly
turned up, dainty ears coiled like a mother-of-pearl

shell, the entire countenance expresses a joyous archness and malice similar to that of a hardy courtezan.

This is the trait recognizable in Tintoretto, ruder and
more decisive, also his more powerful color, more impetuous action and more virile nudities.   Veronese has
tones more silvery and more rosy, gentler figures, less
darkness of shadow and a richer and calmer decoration.
Near a half column an ample and noble woman, Industry,
seated before Innocence, weaves an aerial tissue; her
beaming eyes look up to the blue of the sky; her
waving blonde tresses are full of light, her half-open
mouth seems like a pomegranate ; a vague smile allows
her pearly teeth to appear and the transparency in
which she is steeped has the rosy tinge of a brilliant
aurora.   The other, alongside of a lamb, bends over
with perfect abandonment ; the silvery reflections of
her silk drapery glow around her ; her head is in shade
and an auroral flush lightly falls on her lips, ear and
cheek.

Figures like these are not to be described.   We cannot imagine beforehand what poesy there is in a vestment or in rich attire.   In another picture by Veronese,
" Venice Queen," she sits on a throne between Peace
and Justice; her white silk robe embroidered with
golden lilies undulates over a mantle of ermine and
scarlet ; her arm, delicate hand and bending dimpled
fingers rest their satiny purity and soft serpentine
contours on the lustrous material. The face is in shadow
—a half-shadow roseate with a cool, palpable atmosphere enlivening still more the carmine of the lips ;
the lips are cherries while all the shadow is intensified
by the lights on the hair, the soft gleams of pearls on
the neck and in the ears and the scintillations of the
diadem whose jewels seem to be magical eyes.   She
smiles with an air of royal and beaming benignity like
a flower happy in its expanded and blooming petals.
Near her, Peace, inclining abandons herself, almost

falling; her robe of yellow silk studded with red flowers gathers into folds under the richest of violet mantles; strings of pearls wind around under her white veil among her pale tresses, and how divine the small ear!

There is another picture still more celebrated, "The Rape of Europa." For brilliancy, fancifulness, extraordinary refinement and invention in color it has no equal. The reflection of the foliage overhead bathes the entire picture with an aqueous green tone; the white drapery of Europa is tinged with it; she, arch, subtle and languishing, seems almost like an eighteenth century figure. This is one of those works in which, through subtlety and combination of tones, a painter surpasses himself, forgets his public, loses himself in the unexplored regions of his art, and, discarding all known rules, finds, outside of the common world of sensible appearances, harmonies, contrasts and peculiar successes beyond all verisimilitude and all proportion. Rembrandt has produced a similar work in his "Night watch." One has to look at it and keep silent.

CHAPTER IV.

THE "Lives" of Ridolfi are very dry, and all that
Vasari adds to them is of little import. In attempting
to picture Titian to ourselves we imagine a happy man,
"the most fortunate and most healthy of his species,
heaven having awarded to him nothing but favors and
felicities," first among his rivals, visited at his house by
the kings of France and of Poland, favorite of the
Emperor, of Philip II. of the doges, of Pope Paul III,
of all the Italian princes; created a Knight and
count of the empire, overwhelmed with commissions,
liberally compensated, pensioned and worthily enjoying his good fortune. He lives in great state, dresses
splendidly and has at his table cardinals, seignors, the
greatest artists and the ablest writers of the day. "Although not very learned" he is in his place in this
high society; for he has "natural intelligence, while
familiarity with courts has taught him every proper
term of the Knight and of the man of the world,"
so well that we find him "very courteous, endowed
with rare politeness, and with the sweetest ways and
manners." There is nothing strained or repulsive in
his character. His letters to princes and to ministers
concerning his pictures and his pensions contain that
degree of humility which then denoted the *savoir-
vivr* of a subject. He takes men well and he takes
life well, that is to say he enjoys life like other men

without either excess or baseness. He is no rigorist; his correspondence with Aretino reveals a boon companion eating and drinking daintily and heartily, appreciative of music, of elegant luxury and the society of pleasure-seeking women. He is not violent, not tormented by immeasurable and dolorous conceptions; his painting is healthy, exempt from morbid questionings and from painful complications; he paints incessantly, without turmoil of the brain and without passion during his whole life. He commenced while still a child, and his hand was naturally obedient to his mind. He declares that "his talent is a special grace from heaven;" that it is necessary to be thus endowed in order to be a good painter, for, otherwise "one cannot give birth to any but imperfect works;" that in this art "genius must not be agitated." Around him beauty, taste, education, the talents of others, reflect back on him, as from a mirror, the brightness of his own genius. His brother, his son Orazio, his two cousins Cesare and Fabrizio, his relative Marco di Titiano, are all excellent painters. His daughter Lavinia, dressed as Flora with a basket of fruit on her head, furnishes him with a model in the freshness of her carnation, and in the amplitude of her admirable forms. His thought thus flows on like a broad river in a uniform channel; nothing disturbs its course, and its own increase satisfies him; he aims at nothing beyond his art, like Leonardo or Michael Angelo. "Daily he designs something in chalk or in charcoal;" a supper with Sansovino or Aretino makes the day complete. He is never in a hurry; he keeps his paintings a long time at home in order to study them carefully and render them still more perfect. His pictures do not scale off; he uses, like his master Giorgone, simple colors, "especially red and blue which never deform figures." For eighty years and over he thus paints, completing a century of existence, a pestilence, at last, being the cause of his death; the state sets aside its regulations in order to honor him with a public funeral. It would be necessary to revert to the brightest days of pagan antiquity in order to find a genius so well adapted to things around him, an expansion of faculties so natural and so harmonious, a similar concord of man with himself and with the world without.

We can see at the Academy the two extremes of his development, his last picture, a " Descent from the Cross" finished by Palma the younger, and one of his early pictures, a " Visitation," which he probably executed on quitting the school of John Bellini. In the latter work the contours are precise ; the figure of St. Joseph is almost dry, the sentiment of the color manifesting itself only through the intensity of the dark tint, an opposition of tones and the softness of a pale violet robe enlivening the full blue of a mantle. It is, again, an-altar-piece, the sober memorial of a revered legend. At the other extremity of his career he converts the legend into a grandiose and splendid decoration. That which he first displays in this " Descent from the Cross" is a broad white and gray architectural construction so arranged as to give relief to the brightest tones of the drapery and of the flesh-coloring, a portico bordered with monumental statues and with iron-headed pedestals, where living flowers twine around the subdued brilliancy of the marbles, forming those beautiful effects of light and shade which the sun defines on the rotundities of arches. Under these, the Magdalen, in a green robe, and the great red mantle of Nicodemus, unite their mingled hues with the pallid and peculiarly luminous tone of the corpse; the aged disciple on his knees clasps his master's hand for the last time and the Magdalen, extending her arms, gives utterance to her deep feeling. It might be called a pagan tragedy ; the artist has freed himself from the christian mood and is now simply an artist. . We have here the history in full of the

sixteenth century both at Venice and elsewhere ; with Titian, however, the transformation was not long delayed.
An immense painting of his youth, the " Presentation
of the Virgin," shows with what boldness and facility he
enters, from almost the first flight which his genius takes
on the career which he is to pursue to the end. Whilst
the Florentines, educated by the goldsmiths, concentrate
art on the imitation of individual form, the Venetians,
left to themselves expand it until they embrace entire
nature. It is not one man or one group which they see
but a full scene, five or six complete groups, architecture, distances, a sky, a landscape, in short, a complete
fragment of being; here are fifty personages, three palaces, the façade of a temple, a portico, an obelisk, hillsides,
trees, mountains and banks of clouds all superposed in
the air. At the top of a vast series of gray stone steps
stands a body of priests and the high pontiff. The
young girl, meanwhile, blue in a blonde aureole, ascends midway, lifting up her robe ; she has nothing of
the sublime about her ; she is copied from life and her
little cheeks are plump, she raises her hand toward the
high-priest as if to steady herself and to inquire of
him what he wishes of her ; she is a perfect child, her
mind, as yet, being free of all thought ; Titian found
those just like her at catechism exercises. We see that
nature delights him, that real life is sufficient for him,
that he does not seek beyond this, that the poesy of
actual objects appears to him sufficiently great. In
the foreground facing the spectator and at the foot of
the staircase he has placed on old crone in a blue dress
and a white hood, a true village character who has
brought her marketing to town and keeps her basket
of eggs and chickens alongside of her ; a Fleming would
not risk more. But quite near to her, under the vines
clinging to the stones, is the bust of an antique statue ;
a superb procession of men and women in long vestments
displays itself at the foot of the steps; rounded arcades,

corinthian columns, statues and cornices form a magnificent decoration for the façades of the palaces. One feels that he is in an actual city peopled with peasants and ordinary men and women, attending to business and practising their devotions, but decked with antiquities, grandiose in structure, beautified by the arts, illuminated by the sun and situated in the noblest and richest of landscapes. More meditative, more divorced from realities the Florentines create an ideal and abstract world above our own; more spontaneous, more placid, Titian loves our world, comprehends it, shuts himself up within it and reproduces it, ever embellishing it without either recasting or suppressing it.

In seeking for the principal trait which distinguishes him from his neighbors we find it to be simplicity; by not refining on color, action and types he obtains powerful effect with color, action and types. Such is the characteristic quality of his "Assumption," so celebrated. A reddish, purple, intense tint envelops the entire picture, the utmost vigor of color and a sort of healthy energy breathing from the painting throughout. Below are the apostles deflected and seated, nearly all of them with their heads raised to heaven and as bronzed as the sailors of the Adriatic; their hair and their beards are black; an intense shadow bathes their visages; scarcely does the sombre ferruginous tint indicate the flesh. One of them, in the centre, in a brown mantle almost disappears in the darks rendered still darker by the surrounding brightness. Two pieces of drapery, red as living arterial blood, project still more vividly in contrast with two large green mantles, the whole forming a colossal commotion of writhing arms, muscular shoulders, impassioned heads and confused draperies. Overhead, midway in the air, rises the Virgin in the midst of a halo glowing like the vapor of a furnace; she is of their race, healthy and vigorous, unecstatic and without the mystic smile, proudly intrenched in her red mantle which is enveloped by one of blue. The stuff takes countless folds in the movements of her superb form; her attitude is athletic, her expression grave, and the low tone of her features comes out in full relief against the flaming brilliancy of the aureole. At her feet, extending over the entire space, is displayed a glittering garland of youthful angels; their fresh, empurpled, rosy carnations traversed by shadows diffuse amidst these energetic tones and forms the brightest bloom of human vitality; two of these detaching themselves from the rest, come forward and sport in full light; their infantile forms revel with divine freedom in the air around them. Nothing is effeminate or languid; grace here maintains its sway. It is a beautiful pagan festival, that of earnest force and beaming youthfulness; Venetian art centres in this work and perhaps reaches its climax.

Titian's pictures are not numerous in Venice, Europe, in general, having got possession of them; enough of them still remain, however, to show his full power. He was endowed with that unique gift of producing Venuses who are real women and colossi who are real men, that is to say, a talent for imitating objects closely enough to win us with the illusion and of so profoundly transforming objects as to enkindle reverie. He has at once shown in the same nude beauty, a courtezan, a patrician's mistress, a listless and voluptuous fisherman's daughter and a powerful ideal figure, the masculine force of a sea-goddess and the undulating forms of a queen of the empyrean. He has at once made visible in the same draped figure a warrior patriarch of the crusades, a veteran hero of maritime strife, a muscular, athletic wrestler, a podestat's or a sultan's grim and grandiose air, a stern imperial or consular head, and with this, or by its side a rude old soldier with swollen veins, the vulgar mask of a spectacled judge, the bestial features of a bearded Sclave, the sunburnt back and savage look of a galley-rower, the flattened skull and vulture eye of

an embittered Jew, the ferocious glee of a fat executioner, every kindred wave by which animal nature
joins itself to human nature. Through this comprehension of actual objects the field of art is ten times expanded. The painter is no longer reduced, like the classic
masters, to an imperceptible variation of fifteen or
twenty accepted types. The infinite diversities of Nature
with all her inequalities are open to him ; the strongest
contrasts are within his range ; each of his works is as
rich as it is novel ; the spectator finds in him, as in
Rubens, a complete image of the world around him, a
physiology, a history, a psychology in an epitomized
form. Beneath the small and sublime Olympus, with
a few Greek forms sitting there eternally worshipped
by the kneeling orthodox, the artist takes possession of
the broad populous earth whereon the bloom of all
things is incessantly repeating itself. The accidental,
the irregular, everything, to him, is good ; they constitute a part of the forces which keep the human sap
in circulation ; quaintness, deformities and excesses have
their interest as well as efflorescence and splendor ; his
only need is to feel and to render the powerful impul-
sion of the inward vegetation upheaving brute matter
and converting it into living forms in the heat of sunshine. Hence the ideas that crowd on the mind on re-
examining his paintings in San-Rocco, in the Salute
and in San-Giovanni, on meditating over those in Rome
and in Florence and in Blenheim and at London. We
linger in this church of Santa Maria della Salute : we
smile at the pretty, plump and rosy communicants of
Luca Giordano. We leave to it its pretentious decoration
and affected statues which the artists of the seventeenth
century have displayed under its arches. We comprehend the value of a simple and robust genius satisfied
with imitating and fortifying nature. We contemplate the ceiling of the choir, then, in the sacristy, the
manly Roman figure of Habakkuk, the bronzed and tra-

gic mask of Elias almost black beneath the white mitre, a bald-headed St. Mark thrown backward of so spirited a face and colored with such a beautiful reflection of youth that we feel in it the vitality of great races invincible against the attacks of time. Above all we return to the paintings of the ceiling: Goliath slain by David, Abraham sacrificing Isaac, and Cain killing Abel. We recognize in the boldness and inspiration of these colossi, the vigorous hand which traced the celebrated imageries, the "Six Saints" and the formidable "Passage of the Red Sea." Save Michael Angelo, nobody has thus handled the human frame. Abraham is a giant and exterminator; after seeing his head and gray beard, his thigh and two nude arms impetuously issuing from his yellow drapery we feel the presence of a genuine patriarch, combatant and dominator of men; he lifts his arm and all his muscles are fully distended; the head of the boy Isaac is already bent down by his violent hand. The movement is so energetic that one single impulse runs through all three of the personages from the feet of the precipitating angel arresting the sword to the half-contorted body of the man turning around, and across him, even to the yielding neck of the prostrate child.—More furious still is the gesture of the fratricide: not that Titian renders him repulsive; on the contrary his impetuosity bears the spectator along with him; it is not an assassin but a Hercules slaying an enemy. Abel, overthrown on his side, reels, stretching out his limbs. The other, as gigantic and muscular as an athlete, one foot on the victim's breast falls back and with the full might of his torso and rigid arms is about to destroy him. A sombre vinous tone reddens with its threatening hues the intersections and ridges of the muscles and tendons and the swellings and depressions of the excited flesh, while the bestial visage of the murderer, obliquely illu-

minated on one temple, is lost in a black foreshortening.

The Academy and the Churches.—I have neither courage nor leisure to speak of other paintings. The
Academy contains seven hundred of them, to which add
those of the churches. It would require a volume;
moreover the effect oftenest consists of a tone of
luminous flesh near a sombre one, and in the gradations of tint of a red or of a green piece of drapery.
One may characterize it in gross with words, but when
it comes to delicacies words are inadequate. The only
proper thing to do is to come and enjoy for yourself.
We go repeatedly and again and again to the Academy.
We traverse the suspension bridge, the sole modern
and ungraceful work in Venice. We enter haphazard
one of these twenty halls and select some of the masters with whom we will pass the afternoon, Palma-
Vecchio for instance and Bonifazio, whose color is as
rich and intense as Titian's. They are plants of the
same family; but the public eye is fixed on the top-
most branch of the stem. One of the pictures by
Bonifazio, "The Wicked Rich Man's Banquet," is admirable. Under an open portico, between veined
columns, are seated large and magnificent women in
square low-necked dresses and black velvet skirts, with
sleeves of ruddy gold and in robes rudely figured with
red and yellow; superb forms of a stout build, with
fleshy muscles audaciously displayed in the barbarous
luxury of variegated stuffs descending in heavy folds
about their heels. A little negro, a small domestic
animal, holds a scroll of music before a female singer
and some players on instruments; the air resounds
with voices, and, to complete this noisy pomp, we perceive outside of the gardens, horses, falconers and all
the paraphernalia of seigneurial parade. Amidst this
display sits the master in a great mantle of red velvet,

sanguine and sombre like a Henry VIII. with the hard
and stern expression of a sensuality gorging itself
without satiety.* Pleasures of this description would
repel us; we have become too cultivated and too tame
to comprehend them; courtezans of that stamp would
frighten us; they are too unintellectual and too gross;
their arms would fell us to the ground and their eyes
give an expression of too great hardness. Only in the
sixteenth century did people love massive and violent
voluptuousness : then the fury of lusts and sensual
gluttony were copied from life; but, on the other hand,
it was only in the sixteenth century, that they knew
how to paint perfect beauty. We recross the iron
bridge, so formal and so ugly, and, plunging into a
labyrinth of petty streets, go to Santa Maria Formosa,
in order to see the "Saint Barbara" of Palma-Vecchio.
She is no saint, but a blooming young girl, the most
attractive and lovable that one can imagine. She stands
erect, proud in her bearing with a crown on her brow
and her robe, carelessly gathered around the waist, undulates in folds of orange purple against the bright
scarlet of her mantle. Two streams of magnificent
brown hair glide down on either side of her neck; her
delicate hands seem to be those of a goddess; one half
of her face is in shadow and half-lights play upon her
uplifted hand. Her beautiful eyes are beaming and
her fresh and delicate lips are about to smile; she displays the gay and noble spirit of Venetian women;
ample and not too full, *spirituelle* and benevolent, she
seems to be made to give happiness to herself and to
others.

Let us set the others aside. What a pity, however,
to quit the five or six Veroneses in the Academy, his
"Repast at the house of Levi," his "Apostles on the
Clouds," his "Annunciation," his virgins, his lustrous

---

* Compare this with the same scene treated by Teniers.

variegated marble columns, his golden niches rayed
with dark arabesques, his grand staircases, his balustrades profiled on the blue sky, his ruddy silks striped
with gold, his white horses rearing under their scarlet
housings, his guards and his negroes decked in red and
green, his stately robes starred with intricate branchings and lustrous designs, and especially the wonderful
diversity of heads and the tranquil harmony that radiates like music from his silvery color, his serene figures
and his rich decorations! If Titian is sovereign, and
the dominator of the school, Veronese is its regent and
viceroy. If the former has the simple force and grandeur of its founders, the latter possesses the calmness
and genial smile of an undisputed and legitimate monarch. That which he seeks and finds is not the
sublime or heroic, not violence or sanctity, not purity
or softness : all these conditions show only one of the
faces of nature, and indicate a purification, an effort,
enervation or intractability ; what he loves is expanded
beauty, the flower in full bloom but intact, just when
its rosy petals unfold themselves while none of them
are, as yet, withered. He has the air of addressing
himself to his contemporaries and of saying to them :
" We are noble beings, Venetians and grand seignors
of a privileged and superior race. Let us not reject
or repress anything about us ; mind, heart and senses,
everything we have merits gratification. Let us delight
our instincts and our soul, and let us make of life a
fête in which felicity shall confound itself with beauty."

But you may see several of his great works in the
Louvre and you will understand him much better
through a picture than through any reasoning of mine.
One man of genius, on the contrary, Tintoretto, has
almost all his works at Venice. One has no suspicion
of his value until one has come here. As a day is still
left to me let us devote it to him.

CHAPTER V.

A MORE vigorous and more fecund artistic temperament is not to be found in the world. In many particulars he resembles Michael Angelo. He approximates to him in savage originality and in energy of will. But a few days transpire when Titian, his master, on seeing his sketches, becomes jealous, gets alarmed and sends him away from his school. Child as he is he determines to learn, and to achieve success unaided. He procures plaster casts from the antique and from Michael Angelo's works, seeks out and copies Titian's paintings, draws from the nude, dissects, models in wax and in clay, drapes his models, suspends them in the air, studies foreshortenings and works desperately. Wherever a painting is being executed he is present " and learns his profession by looking on." His brain ferments and his conceptions so torment him that he is obliged to get rid of them ; he goes with the masons to the citadel and traces figures around the clock. Meanwhile he practises with Schiavone, and thenceforth feels himself a master ; "his thoughts boil ;" he suggests to the fathers of the Madonna del' Orto four grand subjects, . "The Worship of the Golden Calf," the "Last Judgment," hundreds of feet of canvas, thousands of figures, an overflow of imagination and genius ; he will execute them gratuitously, requiring no pay but his expenses ; he requires nothing but an issue and an outlet. On another occasion the brotherhood of San-Rocco having demanded of five celebrated artists cartoons for a painting which they wish to have executed he secretly

takes the measure of the place, completes the picture in a
few days, brings it to the spot designated and declares
that he presents it to San-Rocco. His competitors
stand aghast at this fury of invention and of dispatch :
and thus does he always labor ; it seems as if his mind
was a volcano always charged and in a state of eruption.
Canvases of twenty, forty and seventy feet, crowded
with figures as large as life—overthrown, massed together, launched through the air, foreshortened in the
most violent manner and with splendid effects of light
—scarcely suffice to contain the rapid, fiery, dazzling
jet of his brain. He covers entire churches with them,
and his life, like that of Michael Angelo, is there exhausted. His habits are those of all savage, violent
geniuses out of harmony with society, in whom the
inner growth of the sentiments is so strong that pleasure is distasteful and who find refuge, composure and
tranquillity only in their art. "He lived in his own
thoughts, afar from every joy," absorbed in his studies
and with his work. On ceasing to paint he retires to
the remotest corner of his dwelling, and shuts himself
up in a chamber where, in order to see clearly, a lamp
has to be lighted in the daytime. Here, for diversion,
he fashions his models ; nobody is permitted to enter
never does he paint before any one except his intimates.
"His sole ambition is fame," and especially the desire
to surpass himself, to attain to perfection. His words
are few and trenchant ; his grave and rude physiognomy is the exact image of his soul.* On uttering a
piquant remark his face remains fixed, he does not
laugh. Bravely and proudly does he lay out his own
course, singly and against the open jealousy and hostility of other painters, and maintains himself erect
before the public as before the rulers of opinion. Pis-
tol in hand he silences, with cool irony, the cynic

---

* See his portrait by himself.

Aretino. On his friends exhibiting a picture in public he counsels them to stay at home : "let them shoot their arrows, people must get accustomed to your conceptions." The more one studies his life and works the more one sees in him a colorist Michael Angelo, less concentrated than he, less self-mastering, less qualified to refine upon his ideas, wholly given up to his fancies, and whose impetuosity makes of him an improvisator.

Hence it is that when his conception is just or matured he rises to an extraordinary height. No painting, in my judgment, surpasses or perhaps equals his St. Mark in the Academy ; at all events no painting has made an equal impression on my mind. It is a vast picture twenty feet square containing fifty figures of the size of life, St. Mark sombre in the light, and a slave luminous amidst sombre personages. The saint descends from the uppermost sky head foremost, precipitated, suspended in the air in order to rescue a slave from punishment; his head is in shadow and his feet are in the light; his body, compressed by an extraordinary feat of foreshortening, plunges at one bound with the impetuosity of an eagle. No one, save Rubens, has so caught the instantaneousness of motion, the fury of flight; alongside of this vehemence and this truthfulness classic figures seem stiff, as if copied after Academy models whose arms are upheld by strings ; we are borne along with and follow him to the ground, as yet unreached. Here, the naked slave, thrown upon his back in front of the spectator and as miraculously foreshortened as the other, glows with the luminiousness of a Correggio. His superb, virile, muscular body palpitates; his ruddy cheeks, contrasted with his black curled beard, are empurpled with the brightest hues of life. The axes of iron and wood have been shattered to pieces without having touched his flesh, and all are gazing at them. The turbaned executioner with upraised hands

shows the judge the broken handle with an air of
amazement, which excites him throughout. The judge,
in a red Venetian pourpoint, springs half way off his
seat and from his marble steps. The assistants around
stretch themselves out and crowd up, some in sixteenth
century armor, others in cuirasses of Roman leather,
others in barbaric simarres and turbans, others in Venetian caps and dalmatics, some with legs and arms
naked, and one wholly so except a mantle over his
thighs and a handkerchief on his head, with splendid
contrasts of light and dark, with a variety, a brilliancy,
an indescribable seductiveness of light reflected in the
polished depths of the armor, diffused over lustrous
figurings of silks, imprisoned in the warm shadows of
the flesh and enlivened by the carnations, the greens
and the rayed yellows of the opulent materials. Not a
figure is there that does not act and act all over; not a
fold of drapery, not a tone of the body is there that does
not add to the universal dash and brilliancy. A woman
supported against a pedestal falls back in order to see
better; she is so animated that her whole body trembles,
her eyes flash and her mouth opens. Architectural
forms in the background and men on the terraces or
clinging to columns add the amplitude of space to the
scenic richness. We can breathe freely there, and the
breath we take is more inspiring than elsewhere; it is
the flame of life as it flashes forth in gleaming lucidity
from the adult and perfect brain of a man of genius;
here all quivers and palpitates in the joyousness of
light and of beauty. There is no example of such
luxuriousness and success of invention; one must see
for himself the boldness and ease of the jet, the natural
impulse of genius and temperament, the lively spontaneous creation, the necessity of expressing and the
satisfaction in rendering his idea instantly unconscious
of rules, the sure and sudden dash of an instinct
which culminates at once and without effort in perfect

action as the bird flies and the horse runs. Attitudes, types and costumes of every kind, with all their peculiarities and divergencies flooded their minds and fell into harmony in one sublime moment. The curved back of a woman, a cuirass gleaming with light, an indolent nude form in transparent shadow, rosy flesh with the pulsating amber skin, the deep scarlet of careless folds, the medley of heads, arms and legs, the reflection of tones brightened and transformed by mutual illumination, all disgorged in a mass like water spouting from a surcharged conduit. Sudden and complete concentrations are inspiration itself, and perhaps there is not in the world one fuller and more animated than this one.

I believe that before having seen this work one can have no idea of the human imagination. I set aside ten other pictures that are in the Academy, a "Saint Agnes," a "Resurrection of Christ," a "Death of Abel" and an "Eve," a superb and solid sensual form with rude contours, stoutly built, the legs undulating, the head animal and expressionless but blooming and full of life, so strong and so joyous in its tranquillity, so richly mottled with lights and shadows that here, even more than in Rubens, one feels the full poesy of nudity and of flesh. It is in the churches and in the public monuments that he is to be understood; there is scarcely one of these that does not contain vast pictures by him,—an "Assumption" in the Jesuits', a "Crucifixion" and I know not how many other canvases in San Giovanni e Paolo, the "Marriage of Cana" at Santa Maria della Salute, four colossal paintings at Santa Maria dell' Orto, the "Forty Martyrs," the "Shower of Manna," the "Last Supper," the "Martyrdom of St. Stephen" at San Giorgio, twenty pictures and ceilings, a "Paradise" twenty-three feet high and seventy-seven feet long in the Ducal Palace, and finally, at the Church of San-Rocco and at the Scuola

of San-Rocco, which seem like his own galleries, forty
pictures, a few of them gigantic and capable together
of covering the walls of two square saloons in the
Louvre. Veritably we do not know him in Europe.
The European galleries contain scarcely anything by
him, the few examples they have acquired being small
or of minor importance. Save three or four scenes in
the Ducal Palace he has been poorly engraved; except a "Crucifixion" by Augustino Carrache his great
works have not been engraved. He is disproportionate
in everything, in dimensions as well as in his conceptions. Academic minds at the end of the sixteenth
century decried him as extravagant and negligent: the
prodigious and the superhuman in his genius prove
distasteful to minds of a common stamp or fond of repose. But the truth is no man like him is or has been
seen; he is unique in his way like Michael Angelo,
Rubens and Titian. Let him be called extravagant,
impetuous and improvisator; let people complain of
the blackness of his coloring, of his figures topsy-
turvy, of the confusion of his groups, of his hasty
brush, of the exhaustion and the *mannerism* which
sometimes lead him to introduce old metal into his new
casting; let all the defects of his qualities be adduced
against him, I am willing;—but a furnace like this, so
ardent, so overflowing, with such outbursts and flaming
coruscations, with such an immense jet of sparks, with
such luminous flashes so sudden and multiplied, with
such a surprising and constant volume of smoke and
flame has never been encountered here below.

I know not, indeed, how to speak of him; I cannot
describe his paintings, so vast are they and so numerous. It is the inward condition of his mind that must
be enlarged upon. It seems to me that, in him, we discover a unique state of things, the lightning-burst of
inspiration. The term is strong, but it corresponds to
ascertained facts of which examples may be cited. In

certain extreme moments, when confronting great danger, in any sudden crisis, man sees distinctly, in a flash,
with terrible intensity, whole years of his life, complete incidents and scenes and often a fragment of, the
imaginary world : the recollections of the asphyxiated
and the accounts of persons escaping from drowning,
the revelations of suicides and of opium-eaters,* and
of the Indian *Puranas* all confirm this. The activity of
the brain suddenly increased ten · or a hundredfold
causes the mind to live more in this brief foreshortening of time than in all the rest of life put together. It
is true that it commonly issues from this sublime state
of hallucination exhausted and morbid; but when the
temperament is sufficiently vigorous to support the
electric shock without flagging, men like Luther, St.
Ignatius, St. Paul and all the great visionaries accomplish works transcending the powers of humanity.
Such are the transports of creative imagination in the
breasts of great artists; with less of a counterpoise
they were as strong with Tintoretto as with the greatest.
If a proper idea be formed of this involuntary and extraordinary state in a tragic temperament like his, and
of the colorist senses such as he possessed, we can see
how everything else follows.

He never selects; his vision imposes itself on him;
an imaginative scene to him is a reality; with one dash,
he copies it instantaneously, along with whatever in it
is odd, surprising, vast and multitudinous; he ex-
tracts a portion from nature and transfers it bodily to
his canvas, with all the force and abruptness of a spontaneous creation knowing neither combination nor
hesitancy. It is not two or three personages he paints
but a scene, a fragment of life, an entire landscape and
a populous architecture. His " Marriage of Cana" is
a complete, gigantic dining-hall, with ceilings, windows,

---

* " Confessions of an Opium Eater," by De Quincey.

doors, floors, domestics, an exit into side-rooms, the
guests in two files around the receding table, the men
on one side and the women on the other, the two rows
of heads appearing like the two lines of trees of an avenue, and, at the far end, Christ, small and effaced, on
account of the multitude and the distance. His " Pis-
cinè probatique" at the Scuola San-Rocco is a hospital; half-naked women stretched on a sheet which people are lifting, others on couches with bare legs and
breasts, one in a tub entirely stripped and Christ in the
midst of them among fevers and ulcers. His " Shower
of Manna" is an encampment of people with all the
petty details of life, every diversity of landscape and all
the grandeur of illimitable distances : here is a camel
and his driver, there a man near a table with a pestle,
in another place two women washing, another young
woman listening and stooping to mend a basket, others
seated near a tree, others turning a reel with sheets attached to it to collect the manna and a grand draped
old man in consultation with Moses. In his exuberance
as in his genius he surpasses his own age and approximates to ours. His pictures seem to be " illustrations; "
only he produces in a length of forty feet, with figures as
large as life, what we try to do in the space of a foot
with figures no bigger than one's finger. Life in
general interests him more than the particular life of
one being ; he discards picturesque and plastic rules,
subordinating the personage to the whole and parts to
the effect. He is impelled to render, not this or that
man standing or lying, but a moment in nature or in
history. He is invaded as if from without ; he is over-
powered by an image which takes possession of him,
torments him and in which he has faith.

Hence his unprecedented originality. Compared
with him all painters are self-copyists ; you are always
astonished before his pictures ; you ask yourself where
he went for that, into what unknown and fantastic but

nevertheless real world. In the "Last Supper" the
central figure is a large kneeling servant, her head in
shadow and her shoulder luminous; she holds a platter
of beans and is bringing in dishes; a cat attempts to
climb up her basket. Round about are buffets, domestics, ewers and disciples in a perpendicular file bordering a long table. It is a supper, a veritable evening repast, which is for him the essential idea. Above the
table glimmers a lamp while a blue light from the moon
falls on their heads; but the supernatural enters on all
sides: in the background by an opening in the sky and
a choir of radiant angels; on the right by a swarm of
pale angels whirling about in the nocturnal obscurity.
With extraordinary boldness and force of verisimilitude
the two worlds divine and human, merge into each
other and form but one. When this man reads in the
Evangelists the technical term it is the corporeal object with all its details which forcibly impresses him
and which he forcibly renders. St. Joseph was a carpenter; instantly, in order to depict the Annunciation,
he represents the actual house of a carpenter,—on the
outside a shed in order to work in the open air, the
disorder of a workshop, bits of wood and carpentry
tumbled about, piled up, adjusted, leaning against the
walls, saws, planes, cords, a workman busy; within, a
large bed with red curtains, a bottomless chair, a
child's willow cradle, the wife in a red petticoat, a
vigorous, amazed and frightened plebeian. A Fleming
could not have more accurately imitated the confusion
and vulgarity of common life. But passion always
accompanies these intense and circumstantial visions.
Gabriel and a flock of tumultuous whirling angels dart
athwart the door and window; the unfinished domicile
seems to be shattered by the shock; it is the fury of
an invasion; the pigeons betake themselves in full
flight to their own tenement; they pitch all together
upon the Virgin. You may judge by this frenzied and

disproportionate activity the irresistible irruption with which tumultuous ideas are unloosed in his mind. No painter has thus loved, felt and rendered action. All his figures dart and re-dart forward and backward. There is a "Resurrection" by him in which no figure is in a state of equilibrium; angels descend head foremost from above; Christ and the saints swim in the air; the atmosphere is a resistant and palpable fluid which sustains bodies and allows them every attitude as water does the fishes. When he chances to paint a violent scene like the "Bronze Serpent" or a "Massacre of the Innocents" it is a delirium. The women freely seize the swords of the executioners, roll down precipitated from the heights of a terrace, strain their infants to their breasts with an animal gripe and fall upon them covering them with their bodies. Five or six bodies, one on top of the other, women and children, wounded, dying and living, form a mound. The space is covered with a mass of heads and limbs, and torsos falling, running, struggling and staggering as if a hurly-burly of inebriates; it is the infuriate bacchanalianism of despair. Near this, on a mountain cliff dog-headed serpents forage amongst a monstrous heap of prostrated men. One, already black, having died howling, lies on his back his limbs swollen with the venom, his muscles contorted with convulsions, the breast strained and projecting and the head cast backward; others, in the last agony, bleed and writhe, some on the flank, others erect and stiff, with bowed head, and others with their thighs drawn up and their arms contorted, all under livid lights contending with deathly shadows, rolling, heaving and pitching like a human avalanche down the side of a precipice. The artist is on his own domain; he wanders about grandly in the realm of the impossible. He sees too much at once, forty, sixty and eighty personages and their surroundings, aroused, commingled and crowded beneath a tragedy of lights and darks. Let his second *Piscine probatique* in the church of San-Rocco be contemplated: no sky, no background ; save the roof and four shafts of Ionic columns, all consists of bodies and heaps of bodies, naked backs and breasts, heads, beards, mantles and drapery, a monstrous accumulation of overthrown humanity, male and female, supporting each other and extending their arms to the Saviour Christ. A woman stretched on her back turns her eyes toward him to demand succor. An enormous torso in the agony of death reaches out and falls upon a pile of drapery in a last attempt to draw near the source of cure. Here and there are beautiful faces of suppliant spouses emerging into light, bald skulls of old soldiers, muscular breasts and grand beards like those of the river-gods. In the foreground a colossal attendant, a sort of athlete and porter, contracts his thighs and bows himself up on his loins to carry off a bundle of linen. Another, an old giant, almost naked, sits against a column, his legs hang down and he appears resigned like an old inmate of a hospital; his reddened and flabby skin wrinkles at every anfractuosity of the muscles; he has waited years and can wait still longer : he muses with an upturned face sensitive to the sunshine which rewarms his old blood.—Through this taste for the actual and the colossal, through these violent contrasts of light and dark, through this passion which bears him on to the end of his conception, through this audacity which leads him to thoroughly display his idea he is the most dramatic of painters. Delacroix should have come here ; he would have recognized one of his ancestors, sensitive like himself to crude reality, to unrestrained energy, to aggregate effects, to the moral force of color, but healthier, more sure of his hand and nurtured by a more picturesque age and in a broader sentiment of physical grandeur. None of Delacroix's pictures leave a more poignant impression than " St.

Roch among the Prisoners." They are in a vast sombre dungeon, a sort of antique *ergastulum*, where iron bars, stocks and straining chains rack and dislocate limbs through slow and prolonged turning. The saint appears; a miserable creature fastened by the neck raises toward him his twisted head; another, from the bottom of a grated fosse, fixes his face against the bars; spines reddened and rigid with muscles, breasts of the color of rust, heads brown like lions' manes, white, luminous beards appear in the midst of sepulchral obscurity; but higher up, in the duskiness of the shadow, float exquisite figures, silvery silken robes, tunics of pale violet and blonde radiant hair, the visitation of an angelic choir.

After having passed through the church and the two stories of the Scuola there still remains a grand hall to visit, the Albergo; the walls and ceilings here are also tapestried with paintings by Tintoretto. It is in vain to say to yourself that you are weary, and to accuse the painter of exuberance and excess, to feel that these forty immense pictures were executed too rapidly and rather indicated than perfected, that he presumes on his own and the spectator's powers. You enter, and you find strength left, because he imparts it to you in spite of yourself. Virgins and women thrown backward swim on the panels of the ceiling, their ample beauty, the magnificent rotundity of their flesh bathed in shadow, being displayed with inexpressible richness of tone. A " Christ bearing the Cross" develops itself on the winding escarpment of a mountain; Christ, with a rope around his neck, is dragged on in front, while the savage procession scales the rocks with the sorrowful and furious dash of a " Passion" by Rubens.* On the other side the meek Christ stands before Pilate, and the long white shroud wholly enveloping him contrasts its

---

* The same scene in the Brussels Musée, by Rubens.

funereal color with the black shadows of the architecture and with the blood-red vestments of the assistants. Over the door a ruddy corpse lies stiffened between the soldiers and the scarlet robes of the judges; but these are merely accompaniments. An entire section of the hall, a wall forty feet long and high in proportion, disappears beneath a " Crucifixion," ten scenes in one, and so balanced as to constitute a single composition; eighty figures grouped and spaced, a plateau strewn with rocks at the base of a mountain, trees, towers, a bridge, cavaliers, stony crests, and in the distance, a vast brownish horizon. Never did eye embrace such *ensembles*, or combine the like effects. In the centre Christ is nailed to the upraised cross, and his drooping head is obscure in the dim radiance of his nimbus. A ladder rises behind the cross, and executioners are climbing up and passing to each other the sponge. At the foot of the cross the disciples and women standing extend their arms, and those kneeling sob and weep; the Virgin swoons, and all these forms of bending, tottering, falling women under grand red and blue draperies of every hue, with a flash of sunlight on a cheek or a chin, produce a funereal pomp of the most imposing character. Like a grandiose harmony sustaining a rich and penetrating voice, surrounding crowds and incidents accompany the principal scene with their tragic variety and splendor. On the left, one of the two thieves is already bound to his cross and is being raised up; the upper part of his body glows in the light, and the rest is in shadow. Five or six executioners strain at the ropes and support those who are climbing up, pulling and pushing with all the might and force of the rigid muscular machinery. The light falls across their rosy and rayed cassocks, on the brown tendons of their necks and on the swollen veins of their foreheads. Their implements are there, axes, picks, wedges, a massive ladder, and, at the head of the cross, in a beautiful luminous shadow, an indifferent spectator leaning over his horse's neck and looking on.—On the other side, with equal splendor and diversity, is displayed the third execution, like one chorus corresponding to another chorus. The cross lies on the ground, and the victim is being attached to it; one executioner brings ropes, another, a superb, athletic fellow, expanding his twisted shoulder, turns an auger in one of its arms; at the foot of the plateau sits an old amateur of such spectacles; it interests him; he bends forward half reclining in his red mantle, and near him, on an iron-gray horse, a sort of ruffian in a cap, a tall, red scamp, fully illuminated, leans over in order to make a serviceable suggestion.— Beyond these three scenes, there rolls in tiers on five or six planes, with an innumerable variety of tints and forms, the broad and pompous harmony of the multitude, assistants of every kind, petty accessory incidents, diggers excavating the graves of the criminals, crossbowmen in a hollow drawing lots for the tunics, priests in grand robes, men-at-arms in cuirasses, cavaliers boldly draped and posed, simarres of Jews and armor of gentlemen, spirited horses in neutral and auroral trappings, women's orange and green skirts, contrasts of delicate and intense tones, popular visages and chivalric brows, easy and complicated attitudes, all in such amplitude of light, with such a triumphant expansion of genius and such perfect representation that one goes away half stunned, as from a too rich and powerful concert, all sense of the proportion of things gone and wondering if one ought to have faith in his own sensations.

May 1st.—I have just purchased the engraving of Augustino Carrache; it only gives the skeleton of the picture and even falsifies it. I returned to-day to see the picture again. He is a little less impressive on the second inspection; the effect of the whole, that of the first sight, is too essential in the eyes of Tintoretto; he subordinates the rest to these, his hand is too

prompt, he too readily follows out his first conception.
In this respect he is superior to the masters; he has
only done two complete things, his mythological subjects
in the Ducal Palace and his " Miracle of St. Mark."

May 2d.—When, after quitting Venetian art, one tries
to gather up his impressions into a complete whole, he
is sensible only of one emotion, and that is like the
sweet sonorous echo of perfect enjoyment. Part of a
naked foot issuing from silk mottled with gold, a
pearl whose milky brightness quivers on touching a
snowy neck, the ruddy warmth of life peering out beneath transparent shadow, the gradations and alter-
nations of clear and sombre surfaces following the
muscular undulations of the body, the opposition and
agreement of two flesh-tones lost in each other and
transformed by interchanging reflections, a vacillating
light fringing a piece of dark metal, a purple spot
enlivened by a green tone, in brief, a rich harmony
due to colors manipulated, opposed and composed as a
concert proceeds from various instruments, and which
fills the eye as the concert fills the ear,—this is the one
peculiar endowment. By this inventiveness forms are
vivified; alongside of these others seem abstract. Elsewhere the body has been separated from its surroundings, it has been simplified and reduced; it has been
forgotten that the contour is only the limit of a color,
that for the eye color is the object itself. For, so soon
as the eye is sensitive it feels in the object, not alone a
diminution of brilliancy proportioned to its receding
planes, but again a multitude and a mingling of tones,
a general blueness augmenting with distance, an infinity
of reflections which other bright objects intersect and
overlie with diverse colors and intensities, a constant
vibration of the interposing atmosphere where float
imperceptible irridescences, where there are growing
striæ quivering and speckled with innumerable atoms,
and in which fugitive appearances are incessantly dis-

solving and vanishing. The exterior as well as the
interior of beings is only movement, change and transformation, and their complicated agitation is life.
Starting from this the Venetians vivify and harmonize
the infinite tones uniting to compose a tint; they make
perceptible the mutual contagion by which bodies com-
municate their reflections; they augment the power by
which an object receives, returns, colors, tempers and
harmonizes the innumerable luminous rays striking on
it, like a man who straining soft cords enhances their
vibrating qualities in order to convey sounds to the ear
which our coarser ears had not yet detected. They
develop and thus exalt the visible existence of things;
out of the real they fashion the ideal: hence a newborn
poesy. Let there be added to this that of form, and
that genius through which they invent a complete
spontaneous, original, intermediary type between that
of the Florentines and that of the Flemings, exquisite
in softness and voluptuousness, sublime in force and in
inspiration, capable of furnishing giants, athletes,
kings, empresses, porters, courtezans, the most real
and the most ideal figures, in such a way as to unite
extremes and assemble in one personage the most exquisite charm of sensibility and the most grandiose
majesty, a grace almost as seductive as that of Correggio, but with richer health and more vigorous amplitude, a flow of life as fresh and almost as broad as that
of Rubens, but with more beautiful forms and a better
regulated rhythm, an energy almost as colossal as that
of Michael Angelo, but without painful severity or re-
volting despair:—then may one judge of the place
which the Venetians occupy among painters and I do
not know if I yield to personal inclination in preferring
them to any.

BOOK VII.

LOMBARDY.

CHAPTER I.

ON leaving Venice the train seems to pass over the
surface of the water; the sea glows on the right and
on the left and ripples up within two paces of the
wheels; the sandbanks are multiplied amidst the
shining pools. The lagunes diminish; great ditches
absorb whatever remains of the water and drain the
soil. The immense plain becomes green and is covered
with vegetation; the crops are sprouting young and
fresh, and the vines are budding on the trees while, on
the sloping declivities, pretty country-houses warm
themselves in the mid-day sunshine. Meanwhile, to
the north, between the great verdant expanse and the
grand blue dome overhead, the Alpine wall bristles up
dark with its rocks, towers and bastions, shattered
like the ruins of an enclosure demolished by artillery,
the pale clouds of smoke issuing from their anfractu-
osities and their crests indented with snow.

An hour more and we enter Verona, a melancholy
provincial town paved with cobble-stones and neglected.
Many of the streets are deserted; alongside of the
bridges are piles of ordure descending into the stream.
Remains of old sculptures and of tarnished arabesques

run here and there along the façades ; the once pros-
perous air of the city is evident but it is now fallen.

Beneath a parasite crust of sheds and shops an old
Roman amphitheatre, the largest and best preserved
after those of Nismes and Rome, uplifts its vigorous
curves. Lately it contained fifty thousand spectators.
When it possessed its wooden galleries I suppose it
might have held seventy thousand ; there was room
enough for the entire population of the place. In
structure and in use the amphitheatre is the peculiar
sign of Roman genius. Its enormous stones, here six
feet long and three feet wide, its gigantic round arches,
its stories of arcades one supporting the other, are
capable, if left to themselves, of enduring to the day of
judgment. Architecture, thus understood, possesses
the solidity of a natural production. This edifice, seen
from above, looks like an extinct crater. If one desires
to build for eternity it must be in this fashion. On the
other hand, however, this monument of grandiose common sense is an institution of permanent murder. We
know that it steadily afforded wounds and death as a
spectacle to the citizens ; that, on the election of a
duumvir or an ædile, this bloody sport formed the principal interest and the prime occupation of a municipal
city ; that the candidates and the magistrates multiplied them at their own cost to win popular favor ; that
benefactors of the city bequeathed vast sums to the
curia to perpetuate it ; that, in a paltry town like Pompeii, a grateful duumvir caused thirty-five pairs of
gladiators to contend at one representation ; that a
polished, learned and humane man attended these
massacres as we of to-day attend a play ; that this diversion was regular, universal, authorized and fashionable and that people resorted to the amphitheatre as
we now resort to the playhouse, the club or the café.
A species of being is there encountered with which we
are no longer familiar, that of the pagan reared in the

gymnasium and on the battle-field, that is to say, accustomed to cultivating his body and to conquering
men, pushing to extremes his admirable physical and
militant institutions and, traversing the activity of the
palestrum and of civic heroism, ending in the indolence
of the baths and in the ferocities of the circus. Every
civilization has its own degeneracy as well as its own
vitalizing forces. For us christians, spiritualists, who
preach peace and cultivate our understanding, we have
the miseries of a cerebral and bourgeois existence, the
enervation of the muscles, the excitement of the brain,
small rooms on the fourth story, our sedentary and artificial habits, our saloons and our theatres.

This amphitheatre is simply a relic : traces of Rome
are scant in the north of Italy ; the originality and the
interest of the place consist of its mediæval monuments. The impression it makes on the mind is an
odd one, because the Italian mediæval epoch is mixed
and ambiguous. Most of the churches, Santa-Anasta-
sia, San Fermo-Maggiore, the Duomo, San Zenone, are
of a peculiar style called *Lombard*, intermediary between
the Italian and the Gothic styles, as if the Latin and
the German artist had met in order to oppose and harmonize their ideas in the same edifice. But the work
is genuine; in every monument of a primitive era we
realize the lively invention of a budding spirit. Among
these diverse churches the Duomo may be taken as the
type ; this edifice, like the old basilicas, is a house surmounted by a smaller one and both presenting a gable
frontage. We recognize the antique temple raised for
the purpose of supporting another on the top of it.
Straight lines ascend in pairs, parallel as in later architecture, in order to be capped with angles. These
lines, however, are more extended, and the angles are
sharper than in the latin architecture ; five superposed
belfries render them still more attenuated. The new
spirit evidently appreciates less a solid posture than a

bold flight; the old forms are reduced by it and converted to new uses. The ranges of columns and the
two borderings of arcades let into the façade are simply small ornaments, the vestiges of an abandoned art,
like the rudimentary bones of the arm in the whale, or
in the dolphin. On all sides we detect the ambiguous
spirit of the twelfth century, the remains of Roman
tradition, the bloom of a new invention, the elegance
of an architecture still preserved and the gropings of
the new-born sculpture. A projecting porch repeats
the simple lines of the general arrangement and its
small columns, supported by griffins, rise above and
are joined into each other like sections of cordage.
This porch is original and charming; but its crouching
figures and its groups around the Virgin are hydro-
cephalous monkeys.

Gothic forms prevail in the interior, not yet complete,
but indicated and already christian. I cannot get rid
of the idea that ogives, arcades and foliations are alone
capable of imparting mystic sublimity to a church; if
they are lacking the church is not christian; it becomes
so as soon as they appear. This one is already mournfully grave like the first act of a tragedy. Clusters of
small columns combine in reddish pillars, ascend into
capitals bound with a triple crown of flowers, spread
out into arcades embroidered with twining wreaths and
finally end in the wall of the flank in a sort of terminal
tuft. On the flank the ogive of the chapel is enveloped
in a covering of leaves and complicated ornaments
joined together at the top in a spire and surmounted
by a statuette. Most of the figures have the grave
candor and the sincere and too marked expression of
the fifteenth century. A choir in the background, built
by San-Micheli, protrudes its belt of ionic columns
even into the nave. The various ages of the church
are thus shown in its various ornaments; its structure,
however, and its grand forms still secure to the whole

the sober simplicity and bright originality of primitive invention, and there is pleasure in contemplating a healthy architectural creation belonging to a distinct species and found nowhere else.

On trying to define the ruling type in other churches resembling this one we find the two superposed gables of Pisa and Sienna and the pointed canopies which Pisa and Sienna lack. This combination is unique : these canopies, over full walls and elegant lines, almost black and covered with rusty scales, bristle against the blue sky with their ferruginous points as if they were the remains of so many fossil carcasses. Sometimes a bevy of canopies crowd around the central cone or are perched on all sides on the crests and on the angles of the roofs, the ruddy tone of the bricks of which the edifice is built adding to the singularity of their rough and deadened forms. It is a unique growth like that of a pineapple slowly elongated and incrusted with smoky ochre. It is one that is peculiar to the country. Between the Roman arcade, now disappearing, and the Gothic ogive just indicating itself, it gathered around it the sympathies of men for two or three centuries. They discovered it at the first step they made out of savage life and many are the traits which render visible the barbarity from which they issued. The portal of Santa Anastasia displays heads one half as large as the body ; others are without necks or have them dislocated ; almost all are grotesque ; a Christ on the cross has the broken and bent-back paws of a frog.—Centuries, however, in their progress, dragged art out of its swaddling-clothes and, in later chapels, the sculpture becomes adult. Santa Anastasia is filled with figures of the fifteenth century, occasionally a little clumsy, stiff and too real, but so expressive that the perfection of the masters appears languid alongside of their animated deformity. In the choir a bush of thorns and large expanded flowers, twenty-five feet high, envelop a tomb in which stand rude figures of men-at-arms. In the Miniscalco chapel, amidst interlacings of elegant arabesques, you see four standing statuettes placed in couples above each other between the red columns supporting an entablature : they are those of a young man, a somewhat meagre, candid young girl, and two bald-headed doctors roughly chiselled the whole similar to the figures of Perugino. The chapel Pellegrini, wainscoted entirely with terra-cotta, is a large sculptured picture in compartments, where evangelical subjects unite and separate with admirable richness and originality of imagination ; two files of single figures, each under an ornamented ogive canopy, divide the various scenes, each of which is enclosed in a frame of spiral columns with acanthus capitals. In this graceful and overflowing decoration, among these fancies half gothic half greek, we find, along with the beautiful groupings of the new art, the sincerest and simplest expressions, virgins of infantile innocence and beaming beauty, saintly women weeping with the touching abandonment of genuine grief, noble, erect young forms displaying the sentiment of human vitality with the sincerity of the recent invention and a cuirassed St. Michael as spirited and simple as an ancient ephebos.—Never was sculpture more fecund, more spontaneous and, in my opinion, more beautiful than in the fifteenth century.

We take a cab and drive to the end of the town, to San Zenone, the most curious of these churches, begun by a son of Charlemagne, restored by the German emperor Otho I., but belonging almost entirely to the twelfth century.* Some portions, as, for instance, the sculptures of a door, belong to the more ancient times ; except at Pisa I have seen none so barbarous. The Christ at the pillar looks like a bear mounting a tree; the judges, the executioners and the personages belong-

---

* The spire is of the year 1045.

ing to other biblical stories resemble the gross caricatures of clumsy Germans in their overcoats. In another place Christ on his throne has no skull, the entire
face being absorbed by the chin ; the wondering, projecting eyes are those of a frog, while around him the
angels with their wings are bats with human heads.
The heads throughout are enormous, disproportionate
and pitiful; below badly jointed limbs toss about floating bellies. These figures all swim through the air on
different planes in the most insensate manner, as if the
sculptor or founder aimed to excite a laugh. To this
low level did art fall during the Carlovingian decadence
and the Hungarian invasions.—In the interior of the
church you follow the strange and whimsical gropings
of an experimental mind, catching glimpses of daylight
now and then from its obscure depths. The crypt,
belonging to the ninth century, low and lugubrious, is
a forest of columns crowned with shapeless figures;
sculptures still more shapeless cover an altar. To this
damp cavern people resorted to pray at the saint's tomb
for the expulsion of devastators and of-the yelling cavalry which, wherever it passed, left a desert behind it.
Higher up in the church, a curious altar is supported
by crouched brutes resembling lions ; from their bodies
of red marble spring four small columns of the same
material which, half way up, twine and interlace around
each other like serpents, and then, once knotted, resume
their rectilinear projection up to the corinthian capital.
Farther on Christ and his apostles in colored marble,
frescoes of the fourteenth century, a St. George with
his heraldic buckler, a Magdalen in drapery of her own
hair, range themselves along the wall, some lank and
grotesque like wooden dolls, others grave, enveloped in
the grand folds of their robes and with hieratic elevation and austerity. How slow progress is, and how
many centuries are necessary for man to comprehend
the human figure !

The architecture, more simple, is more precocious. It is satisfied with a few straight or curved lines, a few symmetrical and clearly defined planes; it does not exact, like sculpture, knowledge of receding rotundities and a study of the complications and reliefs of the oval. Uncultivated natures confined to a few powerful sentiments can be affected by and reveal themselves through it; it is perhaps their proper medium of expression. In half-barbarous ages indeed, in the times of Philippe Augustus and Herodotus, it obtained its original forms, while complete civilization, instead of sustaining it and developing it like other arts has rather impoverished or corrupted it. Within as without, San Zenone is grand in character, austere and simple : we here realize the Roman basilica making itself Christian. The central nave rests on round columns whose barbarous capitals, enveloped with foliage, lions, dogs and serpents, sustain a line of circular arcades ; on these arcades rises a grand naked wall bearing the arch. Thus far the structure is Latin ; but the nave, through its extreme height, fills the soul with a religious emotion. Its curious ceiling consists of a triple roof trellised with dark wood and inlaid with little squares starred with white and gold, its superposed hollows extending along with a wild and unexpected fancy. Beneath it, the pavement, lower down, connects the portal and the choir by high steps' provided with balustrades, while the differences of level break up and complicate all the lines. The capricious imagination of the middle-ages begins to introduce itself into the regularity of ancient architecture in order to disturb planes, multiply forms and transpose effects.

The same imagination reigns, but this time sovereign and complete, within an iron railing situated near Santa Maria l'Antica, and which is the most curious monument in Verona. Here are the tombs of the an-

cient sovereigns of the city, the Scaligers, who, either
by turns or always, tyrants and warriors, politicians
and sages, assassins and exiles, great men and fratri-
cides, furnished, like the princes of Ferrara, Milan and
Padua, examples of that powerful and immoral genius
peculiar to Italy and which Machiavelli has described
in his " Prince" or displayed in his Life of Castruccio.
The first five tombs display the simplicity and heaviness of heroic times. It seems that man after having
combated, slain and founded demands only of the sepulchre a spot for repose ; the hollow stone that receives
his bones is as solid and worn as the iron armor which
protected his flesh. It consists of an enormous and
massive tub formed out of a naked rock, a single red
block, and placed on three short supports of marble.
A single slab, thick and without ornaments, forms the
cover, as Hamlet says "the ponderous jaws" of the
tomb. This is a true funereal monument, a monstrous
rude coffer, built for eternity.

Out of this savage world, in which the ferocities of
Ecclin and his destroyers were let loose, an art appears.
Dante and Petrarch were welcomed at this court, now
learned and magnificent; the Gothic style, which from
the mountain-tops descends on Milan, and on all sides
impregnates Italian architecture, displays itself here
pure and complete in the monuments of its latest lords.
Two of these sepulchres, especially that of Cane Signorio (1375) are as precious in their way as the cathedrals
of Milan and Assisi. The rich and delicate commingling of twining, excavated and sharp forms, the transformation of dull matter into a filagree of lace, into the
multiple and the complex, is the aspiration of this new
taste. At the foot of the memorial small columns with
curious capitals connect through a sort of armorial turban
in order to bear on a platform the storied tomb and
the sleeping statue of the dead. From this basis springs
a circle of other small columns whose arcades laced

with trefoils, join in a dome crowned with foliated lanterns and with canopies tapering upward and clustering together like the vegetation of thorns. On the summit, Cane Signorio, seated on his horse, seems the terminal statue of a rich specimen of the jeweller's art. Processions of small sculptured figures deck the tomb. Six statuettes in armor, with bare heads, cover the edges of the platform, and each of the niches of the second story contains its figure of an angel. This crowd of figures and this efflorescence rise pyramidically like a bouquet in a vase while the sky shines through the infinite interstices of the scaffolding. In order to complete the impression each tomb by itself, as well as the entire enclosure, is shut in by one of those railings, so original and so intricate, in which mediæval art delighted, a sort of thread of arabesques wrought with four-leafed trefoils, united with halberd irons and crowned with triple-pointed thorn-leaves. It is to this side, toward the prodigality and interlacing of light capricious forms, that the imagination wholly turned. Figures, in fact, although well-proportioned, display nothing of the ideal. Cane is simply a laboriously exercised warrior. The statuettes in armor have that air of a grave sacristan so frequent in mediæval sculptures. The Virgin, sculptured in relief on the tomb, is a simple, gross, stolid peasant-woman and the infant Christ has the big head, lank limbs and protuberant belly of actual bantlings that do nothing else but suck, sleep and cry. The artist knows only how to copy the human form servilely and dolefully; his invention expends itself in other directions. I was thinking by contrast of a double Renaissance tomb which I had just seen in the sacristy of San-Fermo-Maggiore, that of Jerome Turriano, so simple, so elegant, so richly and so healthily imaginative; where small fluted columns form a medium space between medium masses, where the whiteness of marble is enhanced by the dim-

mer tints of bronze, where sphinxes, fawns and nymphs
in bas-relief caper amidst the flowers. One cannot
fail to realize that mediæval art so creative and so vigorous, has something of the strained and divergent.
The truth is it is a morbid art : a cheerful and healthy
mind could not accommodate itself to such a minute,
intricate and fragile ornamentation which seems so incapable of self-endurance and which demands a sheath to
protect it. We require monuments to be solidly based
and to have a consistency of their own. The imagination tires at being always kept suspended in the air,
diverted in its flight, caught by sharp angles and perched
on the points of needles. We retrace our steps to see
the Piazza dei Signori, where there is a charming
little Renaissance palace, resting on a portico of arcades
and corinthian columns. We enjoy the finesse of its
small columns and the elegant rotundities of its balustrades. The eyes wander over the sculptures twining
around the coins and cornices of the windows; branches
loaded with leaves, stately flowers springing out of
an amphora, Roman cuirasses, cornucopias, medallions,
every form and every emblem an artist would like to
surround himself with in order to make of his life a
fête. We contemplate the two statues in the shell
niches, a Virgin like the Madonna of the " Last Judgment," gathering herself up and turning her shoulder
with all the charm of Florentine finesse. I suppose that this constitutes the pleasure of travelling;
one's ideas are reconsidered and confirmed and developed and constantly corrected according as new
cities present to the mind new aspects of the same
objects.

Still one becomes weary. I saw too many pictures
at Venice to dwell on those in this place. There is, however, a Pinacotheca at the Palazzo Pompeii filled with
the works of the Veronese masters. A number of the

early painters, Falconetto, Turodi, Crivelli, are ranged in the order of their epoch. One of them, Paolo Morando, who died in 1522, fills an entire room with his works, somewhat stiff, realistic and finished to excess, in which, among the figures copied from life, are beautiful angels crowned with laurels and announcing the advent of ideal form, whilst a glow of color and skilful gradations of tints indicate Venetian taste. All these painters should be studied; they are the beginnings of a local flora;—but there are days when every effort to fix the attention is disagreeable, when one is only capable of enjoying himself. One turns away from the precursors for two or three of the pictures by the masters. There is one by Bonifazio, representing the rendition of Verona to the Doge, brilliant and decorative, in which the freest imitation of actual life is enlivened and embellished with every magnificence of color. Seignors in the costumes of the time of Francis I., in lustrous white silk and decked with flowers, appear on one side of the Doge, whilst on the other sit the councillors in the waving pomp of their grand red robes. Costume, in those days, is so fine that it alone affords material for pictures; in every epoch it is the most spontaneous and most significant of the works of art; for it indicates the way in which man comprehends the beautiful and how he desires to adorn his life; rely upon it that if it is not picturesque, picturesque tastes are wanting. When people truly love pictures they begin to depict their own persons; this is why the age of dress-coats and black trowsers is poorly qualified for the arts of design. Compare our vestments of a respectable undertaker or of a practical engineer to the superb portrait of Pasio Guariento by Paul Veronese (1556). He stands in steel armor rayed with black lines and damasked with gold. His casque, gauntlets and lance are by his side. He is a man of action, valiant and gay, although quite old; his beard is gray, but his cheeks possess the somewhat vinous 'ints of jovial habits. His military pomp and his simple expression harmonize; everything about the man holds together, within and without; he fashions his own costume, furniture and architecture, his entire outside decoration according to his inward necessities; but in the long-run the decoration reacts on him. I am satisfied that an armor like this would convert any man into a heroic ox. To fight well, to drink well and dine well and to display himself superbly on horseback was all he cared to do. A cavalier's life and picturesque sensations absorbed him entirely; he did not, like us closet-folks, require a learned subtle psychology; it would have set him yawning; he was himself too slightly complicated to incline to our analyses. On account of this the central art of the century is not literature but painting.—In this art Veronese, like Van Dyck, reaches that final moment when primitive impulse and energy begin to be tempered by the breath of worldly ease and dignity. People still sometimes wear the great sword but use the rapier; they don at need the solid battle-armor but more willingly deck themselves with the rich pourpoint and the laces of the court; a gentlemanly elegance comes to transform and brighten the ancient energy of the soldier. The Venetian like the Fleming paints that noble and poetic society which, placed on the confines of the feudal and the modern ages, preserves the seigneurial spirit without maintaining gothic rudeness and attains to the urbanity of the palace without falling into the insipidity of drawing-room politeness. By the side of Titian, Giorgione and Tintoretto, Veronese seems a delicate cavalier amongst robust plebeians. Here, in a fresco representing Music, the heads of the women possess charming sweetness; his voluptuousness is aristocratic, and often refined; the diversion of fêtes, the variety and the brilliancy of a smiling seducing beauty more readily respond to his mind than the force and simplicity of bodies and of athletic actions. He himself saluted Titian with respect " as the father of art," while Titian, on the square of San-Marco, affectionately embraced him, recognizing in him the head of a new generation.

CHAPTER II.

NEAR Desenzano we come in sight of the Lago di
Garda. It is quite blue, of that strange blue peculiar
to rocky depths; rugged mountains, marbled with glittering snow, enclose it within their curves and advance
their promontories into the middle of the lake. With
all their asperities they look genial; an azure veil, as
aerial and delicate as the finest gauze, envelops their
nudity and tempers their rudeness. After leaving Verona they are visible only through this veil. This soft
azure occupies the half of space; the rest is a tender
and charming green prairie, rendered still softer by the
faint yellow tinge overspreading the spring growth with
the freshness of new being.

At Desenzano the train stops on the very margin of
the lake. Its lustrous slaty surface buries itself between
two long rocky shores seeming to be the embossed and
jagged sides of a fantastic river. It forms, indeed, the
marble ewer into which, before they decline, the Alps
collects and retains its springs. On the projections of
this shore we see villages, churches and ancient fortresses extending down into the water, and, in the
background, a loftier wall lifting into the sky its snowy
fringe silvered with sunlight. Nothing can be gayer
and nobler. From the lake to the firmament all these
azure tints melt into each other graduated by diversities of distance and reminding one of the blue rocky
landscapes which Leonardo gives in the backgrounds
of his pictures.

The rest of the country as far as Milan is a vast orchard replete with crops, artificial fields and fruit-trees, where the mulberry, already quite green, rounds its tops amidst the vines and where petty canals bear life to the vegetation, so blooming and so prolific as to suggest an idea of superabundant prosperity; but in order to relieve this fertility of any vulgar or monotonous aspect, the Alps rise on the right in the evening glow, like a file of vast stationary clouds.

Milan, May 4.—One realizes that he is in a rich and gay land. The city is grand and even luxurious with its monumental gates and broad streets lined with palaces, full of vehicles and lively without being feverish like Paris or London. It is situated on a plain; the lakes, canals and river easily supply it with provisions from the well-cultivated and generously productive country. Its buildings are as pleasing as its environs. You enter the waiting-rooms of a railroad station; you see between the mouldings and their ornaments an azure ceiling full of floating clouds. The cafés are well patronized; ices and coffee cost four or five sous; an omnibus fare is two sous. Admission to both of the operas is but one or two francs; common people and the women are quite numerous in the parterre. Many of the women are beautiful, and almost all gay and good-humored; they walk well, having a spruce and attractive air; with their lively physiognomy, fine, cleanly chiselled head, and vibrating sonorous accent they stand out instantaneously in bold relief. Nothing can be prettier than the black veil serving as a coiffure; a circle of silver bodkins placed around the chignon forms a crown. Stendhal, who lived here a long time, says that this city is the land of good-nature and pleasure : to regard labor and serious preoccupations as a load to be reduced as much as possible, to enjoy themselves, to laugh, to go on country pic-nics, to get in love and not in sighing fashion, such is the way in which they regard life. I have had two or three interesting conversations, in this connection, with my travelling companions; all of them terminated in the same creed. One of these, half-bourgeois, another a lawyer, each remarked to me: "*Ho la sventura d'essere ammogliato,*—it is true I married my wife for love and that she is pretty and prudent, but I have lost my liberty." •

A transient visitor like myself can have no opinion on social matters; he can only talk about monuments. There are three conspicuous ones at Milan—the cathedral and two picture galleries.

The cathedral, at the first sight, is bewildering. Gothic art, transported entire into Italy at the close of the middle ages,* attains at once its triumph and its extravagance. Never had it been seen so pointed, so highly embroidered, so complex, so overcharged, so strongly resembling a piece of jewelry; and as, instead of coarse and lifeless stone, it here takes for its material the beautiful lustrous Italian marble, it becomes a pure chased gem as precious through its substance as through the labor bestowed on it. The whole church seems to be a colossal and magnificent crystallization, so splendidly do its forest of spires, its intersections of mouldings, its population of statues, its fringes of fretted, hollowed, embroidered and open marblework, ascend in multiple and interminable bright forms against the pure blue sky. Truly is it the mystic candelabra of visions and legends, with a hundred thousand branches bristling and overflowing with sorrowing thorns and ecstatic roses, with angels, virgins, and martyrs upon every flower and on every thorn, with infinite myriads of the triumphant Church springing from the ground pyramidically even into the azure, with its millions of blended and vibrating voices mounting upward in a

---

* Begun in 1886. Its architects were Germans and Frenchmen.

single shout, hosannah! Moved by such sentiments we quickly comprehend why architecture violated the ordinary conditions of matter and of its endurance. It no longer has an end of its own; little does it care whether it be a solid or a fragile construction; it is not a shelter but an expression; it does not concern itself with present fragility nor with the restorations of the future; it is born of a sublime frenzy and constitutes a sublime frenzy; so much the worse for the stone that disintegrates and for generations that are to commence the work anew. The object is to manifest an intense reverie and a unique transport; a certain moment in life is worth all the rest of life put together. The mystic philosophers of the early centuries sacrificed everything to the hope of once or twice transcending in the course of so many long years the limits of human existence and of being translated for an instant up to the ineffable One, the source of the universe.

We enter, and the impression deepens. What a difference between the religious power of such a church and that of St. Peter's at Rome! One exclaims to himself, this is the true christian temple! Four rows of enormous eight-sided pillars, close together, seem like a serried hedge of gigantic oaks. Their strange capitals, bristling with a fantastic vegetation of pinnacles, canopies, foliated niches and statues, are like venerable trunks crowned with delicate and pendent mosses. They spread out in great branches meeting in the vault overhead, the intervals of the arches being filled with an inextricable network of foliage, thorny sprigs and light branches, twining and intertwining, and figuring the aerial dome of a mighty forest. As in a great wood, the lateral aisles are almost equal in height to that of the centre, and, on all sides, at equal distances apart, one sees ascending around him the secular colonnades. Here truly is the ancient germanic forest, as if a reminiscence of the religious groves of Irmensul. Light

15*

pours in transformed by green, yellow and purple
panes, as if through the red and orange tints of
autumnal leaves. This, certainly, is a complete architecture like that of Greece, having, like that of Greece,
its root in vegetable forms. The Greek takes the trunk
of the tree, dressed, for his type; the German the entire tree with all its leaves and branches. True architecture, perhaps, always springs out of vegetal nature,
and each zone may have its own edifices as well as
plants; in this way oriental architectures might be
comprehended,—the vague idea of the slender palm
and of its bouquet of leaves with the Arabs, and the
vague idea of the colossal, prolific, dilated and bristling vegetation of India. In any event I have never
seen a church in which the aspect of northern forests
was more striking, or where one more involuntarily
imagines long alleys of trunks terminating in glimpses
of daylight, curved branches meeting in acute angles,
domes of irregular and commingling foliage, universal
shade scattered with lights through colored and diaphanous leaves. Sometimes a section of yellow panes,
through which the sun darts, launches into the obscurity its shower of rays and a portion of the nave glows
like a luminous glade. A vast rosace behind the choir,
a window with tortuous branchings above the entrance,
shimmer with the tints of amethyst, ruby, emerald and
topaz like leafy labyrinths in which lights from above
break in and diffuse themselves in shifting radiance.
Near the sacristy a small door-top, fastened against the
wall, exposes an infinity of intersecting mouldings similar to the delicate meshes of some marvellous twining
and climbing plant. A day might be passed here as in
a forest, the mind as calm and as occupied in the
presence of grandeurs as solemn as those of nature,
before caprices as fascinating, amidst the same intermingling of sublime monotony and inexhaustible
fecundity, before contrasts and metamorphoses of light

as rich and as unexpected. A mystic reverie, combined with a fresh sentiment of northern nature, such is the source of gothic architecture.

At the second look one feels the exaggerations and the incongruities. The gothic is of the late epoch and is inferior to that of Assisi; outside, especially, the grand lines disappear under the ornamentation. You see nothing but pinnacles and statues. Many of these statues are of the seventeenth century, sentimental and gesticulating, in the taste of Bernini; the main windows of the façade bear the imprint of the Renaissance and constitute a blemish. In the interior St. Charles Borromeo and his successors have in several places plastered it with the affectations of the decadence. A monument like this transcends man's forces; five hundred years of labor has been bestowed on it, and it is not finished yet. When a work requires so long a time for its completion the inevitable revolutions of the mental state leave on it their discordant traces: here appears that true characteristic of the middle ages, the disproportion between desire and power. Criticism, however, before such a work is out of place. One drives it from his mind like an intruder; it remains on the threshold and does not soon attempt to re-enter. The eyes of their own accord discard ugly features; in order to prolong their pleasure they fix themselves on some of the tombs of the great century, that of Cardinal Carraciulo (1538) and especially, before the Chapel of the Presentation, that of the sculptor Bambaja, an unknown man of the time of Michael Angelo. The diminutive Virgin is ascending a flight of steps amongst superb, erect forms of men and women; one meagre old man is looking at her, and his bony head, in its enormous frizzled beard, has a spirited and wild aspect; a woman on the left, between the columns, has the animated beauty of the most blooming youth. Farther on, another Virgin between two female saints is a mas-

terpiece of simplicity and force. We do not know and
cannot fully estimate the genius of the Renaissance;
Italy has only exported, or allowed to be taken, fragments of its work; books have popularized a few
names; but, for the sake of abridgment, others have
been omitted. Below, and by the side of great known
names, is a multitude of others equal to them.

Another celebrated church is cited, that of San-
Ambrogio, founded in the fourth century by St. Ambrose
and completed or restored later in the Roman style,
supplied with gothic arches toward the year 1300 and
strewn with divers bits—doors, pulpit and altar decorations—during the intermediary ages. An oblong court
precedes it through a double portico. A large square
tower flanks it with its sombre and reddened mass.
Remnants of sculpture plastered on the wall render the
porticoes a sort of defaced and incoherent memorial.
The old edifice itself raises its fretted gable upon a
double story of arcades. The portal is peculiar, being
striped and mottled with fine stone ornaments, consisting of networks of thread, rosaces, and of small
squares filled with foliage; on the columns we see
crosses, heads and bodies of animals, a decoration of
an unknown species.* These works of the darkest centuries of the middle ages always, after the first repulsion,
leave a powerful impression. We feel in them, as in the
saints' legends accumulated from the seventh to the tenth
centuries, the bewilderment of an appalled understanding, the awkwardness of clumsy hands, the alteration and
discordance of decrepit faculties, the gropings of a child-
ish and senile intellect which has forgotten everything
and as yet learned nothing new, its dolorous and semi-
idiotic uneasiness before vaguely conceived forms, its
impotent effort to stammer forth an anxious thought,

---

* Compare the cloister of St. Trophime at Arles, one of the most
curious and most perfect of mediæval monuments.

its first tottering steps in a profound cave where all is confusion and vacillation in the pallid rays of daylight. In the interior heavy pillars, composed of a mass of columns, support on their barbaric capitals a file of round arcades and low arches, and, at the far end, in the apsis, are meagre byzantine figures gleaming on gold. Under the pulpit a tomb, supposed to be that of Stilicon, is sculptured with coarse hunting-scenes where beasts of uncertain species, it may be dogs or crocodiles, are pursuing and biting each other; the decline of art is not greater than in the monument of Placidia at Ravenna. We look up and we see in the sculptures of the pulpit the first dawn of the Renaissance. It is a work of the twelfth century, a sort of long box resting on columns like the pulpits of Nicholas of Pisa. The figures sculptured on it represent the Last Supper; eleven personages seen in front view and with their two arms before them, all repeat the same posture; the heads are real, and even carefully studied, but quite bourgeois and vulgar. Between this early gleam of life and the formless chaos of the lower sepulchre, six centuries, perhaps, elapse;—behold the time requisite for incubation! No document exposes better than works of art the formations and metamorphoses of human civilization.

CHAPTER III.

THE LAST SUPPER OF LEONARDO DA VINCI.—CHARACTER OF HIS PERSONAGES.—CHARACTERISTICS OF HIS GENIUS.—HIS SCHOOL.— LUINI.—THE BRERA MUSÉE.—THE AMBROSIAN LIBRARY.

ONE church more is all that remains in my mind, that of Santa-Maria delle Grazie, a large round tower girdled by two galleries of small columns and resting on a square mass ; it is not the church however which one goes to see, but Leonardo da Vinci's "Last Supper," painted on a wall of the refectory, and which, to tell the truth, you do not see. Fifty years after its completion it became a ruin. In the last century it was entirely repainted, and, as it still scaled off, it was restored ten years ago. What is there now of Leonardo in this painting ? Less, perhaps, than in a master's cartoon transferred to canvas by his mediocre pupils. In one face, that of the Apostle Andrew,* the wry mouth is evidently spoilt. Only the general idea of the master can be seized ; its delicacies have disappeared. Still, among other traits, one can see without much trouble that the celebrated engraving by Morghen represents Christ as more melancholy and more spiritual.† The Christ of Leonardo has a sweet countenance but large, ample and divine ; his aim was not to portray a sad and tender dreamer but a type of humanity. In like manner the apostles with their strongly-marked features and speaking expressions are vigorous Italians whose excitable passions lead to pantomime. The picture of Leonardo, like those of Raphael in the Vatican,

---

* The third figure, beginning at the left.

† Compare contemporary copies, those of Marco d'Oggione at the Brera, and that in the Louvre.

depicted, probably, beautiful physical life as understood in the Renaissance. But he added to it a peculiarity of his own, the expression of different temperaments patiently studied and sudden emotions arrested in their flight. On this account he must have devoted a couple of hours daily to the low class of the Borgo in order to give to his Judas the head of a sufficiently vile and vigorous rogue.

Here, at Milan, he thought and lived the longest. His principal works should be here, but they have either been carried away or have perished. His great equestrian model in bronze, intended to commemorate the Duke Sforza, was cut to pieces by some gascon cross-bowmen. Nothing of his now remains but some manuscripts and a few sketches and studies. And yet, reduced as his work is, there is no other that is more striking. In the leading traits of his genius he is modern. There is in the Brera gallery by him a female head in red chalk which in depth and delicacy of expression surpasses the most perfect of pictures. It is not beauty alone he seeks, but rather individual originality; there is a moral personality and a delicacy of soul in his figures, the powerful emotion of the inner life slightly hollowing the cheeks and depressing the eyes. Two other studies in the Ambrosian library (Nos. 177, 178), especially that of a young female with drooping eyelids, are incomparable masterpieces. The nose and lips are not perfectly regular; form alone does not occupy him; the interior seems much more important to him than the exterior. Under this exterior lives a real, but superior, soul endowed with faculties and passions still slumbering, whose unlimited power glows in repose by the force of the maiden gaze, by the divine form of the brow and by the fulness and amplitude of the head superbly crowned with hair such as one never beholds. On examining his book of drawings in the Louvre, and calling to mind favorite figures in

his authentic pictures, on reading the details of his life
and character one perceives therein the same inward
strife. The world, perhaps, contains no example of a
genius so universal, so creative, so incapable of self-
contentment, so athirst for the infinite, so naturally
refined, so far in advance of his own and of subsequent
ages. His countenances express incredible sensibility
and mental power; they overflow with unexpressed
ideas and emotions. Michael Angelo's personages
alongside of his are simply heroic athletes; Raphael's
virgins are only placid children whose sleeping souls
have not yet lived. His personages feel and think
through every line and trait of their physiognomy;
some time is necessary in order to enter into communion with them: not that their sentiment is too
slightly marked, on the contrary, it emerges from its
whole investiture, but it is too subtle, too complicated,
too far above and beyond the ordinary, too unfathomable and inexplicable. Their immobility and silence
lead one to divine two or three latent thoughts, and still
others concealed behind the most remote; we have a
confused glimpse of their inner and secret world like an
unknown delicate vegetation at the bottom of transparent waters. Their mysterious smile moves and
disturbs one vaguely; skeptical, epicurean, licentious,
exquisitely tender, ardent or sad, what aspirations,
what curiosities, how many disappointments still remain to be discovered! Occasionally among spirited
young athletes, like Grecian gods, we find some ambiguous adolescent with a feminine body, slender and twining with voluptuous coquetry like the hermaphrodites
of the imperial epoch, and who seem, like them, to
announce a more advanced, less healthy, almost morbid
art, so eager for perfection and insatiable of happiness
that, not content with endowing man with strength and
woman with delicacy, it singularly confounds together
and multiplies the beauty of both sexes, losing itself in

the reveries and in the researches of ages of decadence and immorality. One goes far in pushing to extremes the craving for exquisite and deep emotions. Many men of this epoch, and notably this one, after repeated excursions through all the sciences, arts and pleasures, bring back from their sojourn in the midst of all objects I know not what of surfeit, of resignation and of sorrow. They appear to us under these various aspects without wishing to be wholly abandoned. They halt before us with a semi-ironical and benevolent smile somewhat veiled. However expressive the painting may be it reveals nothing of their interior but a complacent grace and superior genius; it is only later, and through reflection, that we distinguish in the sunken orbits, in the drooping eyelids, in the faintly furrowed cheeks the infinite exigencies and mute anguish of an over-refined, nervous and prolific nature, the languor of exhausted felicities and the lassitude of insatiate desire.

No artist has maintained so long and so complete an ascendancy over contemporary artists. Melzi, Salaino, Salario, Marco d'Oggione, Cesare da Cesto, Guadenzio Ferrari, Beltraffio, Luini,* all proportionately to and in view of their faculties, remained true to the venerated and beloved master whose voice they had heard or whose traditions they had gathered ; and we find here in their works the developments of the thought which his too rare productions have not wholly brought to light. They repeat his figures; in the Ambrosian library some of Luini's personages,—a female head, a small St. John kneeling with the infant Jesus against the Virgin, especially a Holy Family—seem to be designed or dictated by the master. They are much more delicate souls, much more capable of refined and powerful emotions than the simply ideal figures of the " School

---

* Rio, *Histoire de l'Art chrétien*, Vol. III., Ch. XVI. It is not certain that Luini was directly a pupil of Leonardo.

of Athens;" * no converse could be maintained with
Raphael's personages; they would at most utter two
or three words in a grave and melodious voice; one
would admire but not become enamored of them; the
sovereign and penetrating charm emanating from those
of Leonardo and his pupil would not be realized. There
is little flesh, for flesh denotes carnal life and indicates
excessive nourishment; the whole physiognomy lies in
the features; these are strongly marked, although delicate, so that through all its lineaments the countenance
feels and thinks; the chin is hollowed and often pointed; depressions and projections break the sculptural
uniformity and exclude the idea of luxuriant health.
The strange and indefinable smile of Monna Lisa
gleams on her motionless lips. A floating penumbra,
an intense and deep yellow hue, envelops the figures
with its shadowiness and mystery; at times the grace
of vanishing contours and the luminous softness of infantile flesh seem to indicate the hand of Correggio.†
The fulness of open daylight here would be discordant;
tender and dying tones, mellowness of light and shade,
the soothing caress of a wandering and refreshing
breeze are essential in order not to disturb such delicate bodies and such sensitive natures. Luini, in this
particular, goes even beyond Leonardo. If he impairs,
he softens him, if he has not, like him, the elevation
and superiority "of another Hermes or of another
Prometheus"‡ he attains to a still more feminine and
more affecting finish. Even this is not enough; he
seeks elsewhere and strives to add to the spirit of his
first the style of more modern masters. As to his frescoes one would suppose that he had studied in Florence.
In one of the lower halls of the Ambrosian library his

---

* The cartoon of this picture is placed opposite.

† No. 105, without the name of any artist. Luini was contemporary with and almost a townsman of Correggio.

‡ Lomazzo.

Christ crowned with thorns is scourged by the executioners; a large curtain and four columns encircle the
scene of suffering; on each side, in symmetrical order,
are two angels and three executioners; in the distance
is seen one of the disciples with the two Marys; on the
two flanks of the picture, a file of pious, kneeling alms-
receivers in black robes, cause, through their realistic
figures, the rhythmic attitudes and ideal forms of this
evangelical event to be still better felt. In like manner,
at the entrance of the Brera gallery, the twenty frescoes
which, for the most part, represent the various stories
of the Virgin, have the faintness of color, the simple
expression and the serene nobleness of the figures of
the Vatican. At one time it is a large Virgin accompanied by an aged man in a green mantle and by a young
woman in a golden-yellow robe, and, at their feet, on
the steps, a little angel who, with legs stretched apart,
tunes his cithern with the motionless pose and the
harmonious lines of the "Parnassus," or of the "Dispute of the Holy Sacrament." At another time, in the
"Nativity of the Virgin," it is a couple of nimble young
girls fetching water, and two aged women, so beautiful
and so grave, that one imagines in looking at them,
the corresponding scenes painted by Andrea del Sarto
in the portico of Santa-Annunziata. Luini here seems
to have adopted the precepts of the pure and learned
school in which Raphael was formed, the perfection and
moderation of which are best represented by the Frate
and Andrea del Sarto; the school which, founded by
the goldsmiths, always subordinated expression and
color to drawing; which placed beauty in the disposition of lines, and which, in the sobriety, elevation and
judiciousness of its mind was the Athens of Italy. But
here and there the form of a head, a delicate chin, large
eyes still more enlarged by the arch of the eyebrow,
some adorable infantile form, an air of intelligence, a
more subtle charm, recalls Leonardo. The three great

Italian artists matured at Florence have all added
something to paganism and to the Florentine Atticism,
—the pious ingeniousness of Raphael brought by him
from religious Umbria; the tragic energy which Michael
Angelo found in his own wrestling soul; the exquisite
and pensive superiority the example of which Leonardo
bequeathed to his Lombard pupils.

Two galleries more contain together six or seven
hundred pictures, and the only prudent course for a
man to pursue is to keep silent about them. I have
only noted five or six of them, and first, the "Marriage
of the Virgin" by Raphael. He was twenty-one years
old and copied, with a few alterations, a picture by
Perugino which is in the *Musée* at Caen. It is an auroral ray, the early dawn of his invention. The color
is almost hard, and cut out in clean spots by dry contours. The moral type of the virile figures is still but
indicated; two youths and several young girls have the
same round head, the same small eyes, the same lamb-
like expression characteristic of choir-children or of
communicants. He scarcely dares to venture; his
thought moves only in the twilight. But its virginal
poesy is perfect. A broad open space extends behind
the personages. In the background a rotund temple,
furnished with porticoes, profiles its regular lines on
the pure sky. The azure expands amply on all sides,
as in the country around Assisi and Perugia; the distant
landscape, at first green, then blue, encircles the ceremony with its serenity. With a simplicity which recalls
hieratic compositions, the personages all stand in a row
in the foreground of the picture; their two groups correspond to each other on each side of the two spouses,
and the high-priest forms the centre. Amidst this general repose of figures, of attitudes and of lines, the
Virgin, modestly inclining, and with her eyes downcast,
half-hesitatingly advances her hand on which the priest
is about to place the marriage ring. She does not

know what to do with the other hand, and, with adorable artlessness, she presses it close against her mantle.
A light, diaphanous veil scarcely touches her exquisite
blonde hair; an angel could not have placed it on her
with more becoming care and respect. She is, however, large, healthy and beautiful like a rural maiden,
and near her a superb young woman in light red,
draped in a green mantle, turns around with the pride
of a goddess. Pagan beauty, the animated sentiment
of an active and agile body, the spirit and taste of the
Renaissance, already peer out through monastic piety
and placidity.

The contrast is very great on contemplating the last
of the great painters of the Renaissance, Correggio and
his "Repose of the Virgin." The picture is signed Anto-
nius Lætus,* and, although there is doubt that it is by
him, I venture to find it charming. Two young women,
the Virgin and the infant Jesus, are under a tree
almost black, in a sort of sombre relief which greatly
enhances the extraordinary brilliancy of the heads.
The straight and symmetrical lines have become waving and curved. Figures, tranquil and slumbering,
have abandoned sculptural regularity and noble simplicity. Now their disturbed look bewilders and
excites; their animation, their pride, their innocence
remind one of the nervous vivacity of birds. Still
more winning and seductive than the Virgin is the
young woman in a yellow robe who is kneeling by her,
with a phial in her hand, among lights and half-lights
of marvellous delicacy and splendor; a kind of infantile
sullenness imperceptibly swells her lip. After the
virile figures expressing the energy of intact passions it
remained to art, becoming exaggerated before declining,
and to souls becoming over-refined before becoming
relaxed, the cult of feminine grace, at one time sport-

* Lætus the latin form of Allegri.

ive and pretty, at another genial and penetrating,
infinite in subtle and complex charms, alone capable of
absorbing hearts to which action was interdicted, appearing in Correggio like the softened glow of a flower
blooming too early and then fading, or like the extreme
maturity of a melting peach impregnated with evening
sunshine.

After him, the restoration of the Caracci does not
stay the decadence. These artists, so learned, so
ingenious, so painstaking, are either academic painters
or painters by system. If they still create it is outside of the proper field of painting, in moral expression.
They produce interesting or affecting dramas or melo-
dramas. Among twenty pictures of this school there
is a celebrated one by Guercino of " Abraham expelling
Hagar." Hagar is weeping with despair and indigna-
tion; but she masters herself and her feminine pride
renders her rigid; she will no longer allow Sarah her
fortunate rival to feed on her grief. The latter displays
the haughtiness of the legitimate wife who has driven
away a mistress; she affects dignity and yet glances
out of one corner of her eye with malignant satisfaction. Abraham is a noble patriarch who is good at
self-display, but empty-headed; it was difficult to find
any other part for him. All this is of a *spirituel* stamp
and would provide a Diderot with numerous pages;
but psychology here assumes precedence of painting.

How intact the Venetians maintain themselves and
how faithful they alone are to the true point of view!
There are five or six Titians in the Ambrosian gallery,
and as many Veroneses at the Brera, which, with folds
of stuffs, a curved body, a background of blue sky rayed
with ruddy foliage, suffice for every craving of the eyes.
A "Nativity" by Titian shows the Virgin under a species
of rustic shed of dark wood toward which advance the
three magi kings; one of them almost an Ethiopian
negro, comes forward in a green silken jacket wearing

on his head a sort of barbarous cap surmounted with
an enormous red feather;—imagine the effect, under this
relief, of a sooty tint illuminated by three small lights,
one on the eye, the other on the white teeth, and the
other on the lobe of the ear. The second one, a big,
bald well-fed potentate displays himself in a vast robe
of yellow silk figured with gold. The third, an old
warrior all in red, his sword by his side and standing,
scarcely dares let his rude gray beard touch the end of
the feet of the little infant. All these painters evidently
copied with sincere pleasure surrounding pomps and
festivals; pedantry does not intrude itself to bridle
them; their pictures come to them through the impetus
of a free instinct and not through the combinations of
academic precepts. In this respect a "Moses in the
Bulrushes," by Bonifazio would be amusing if it were
not splendid. Fortunately no one here thinks of
Moses; the scene is simply a pleasure-party near Padua
or Verona for beautiful ladies and grand seigneurs.
We see people in the gay costume of the day under
spreading trees in a broad, mountainous country. The
princess desires to take a promenade, accompanied by
her full retinue of dogs, horses, monkeys, musicians,
squires and ladies of honor. The rest of the cavalcade
arrives in the distance. Those who have dismounted are
enjoying the shade of the foliage and are indulging in a
concert; the seignors lie at the ladies' feet and are
singing with their caps on their heads and their swords
by their sides; the ladies, smiling, are chatting while
listening. Their robes of silk and of velvet, at one
time red and striped with gold, at another sea-green or
deep-blue, their sleeves puffed and slashed, form groups
of magnificent tones against the depths of the foliage.
They are at leisure and are enjoying life. Some of
them are looking at the dwarf giving fruit to the mon-
key, or at the little negro in a blue jacket holding the
hounds in a leash. In their midst, and still more

gorgeous, like the leading jewel in a brooch, is the princess standing erect; a rich surtout of blue velvet, open and fastened with diamond buttons, leaves visible her robe of autumnal hue : the chemise spangled with golden seeds enlivens with its whiteness the satiny flesh of the neck and chin, and pearls wind their soft light through the curls of her auburn tresses.

All this dwindles before a sketch by Velasquez, broadly executed with a few formless dashes of color. It is the bust of a dead monk, as large as life, of a sublime and fearful reality. He is not long dead, and the face is not yet earthy; but the lips are pale and the eyes heavily closed; the stiffness of the neck breaks the brown drapery. There is here nothing of the ideal; naked tragedy suffices and more too ; a ray of sunshine falls on the vulgar shaved mask, of one color, enveloped in the sombre folds of the cowl ; under that outward brilliancy the flight of the inner life becomes more tragic ; the man is now empty, and the livid, inert remains are only a shell. In vain the contracted brow bears the marks of an agonizing sweat ; the agony is just over and we now feel how heavy is the formidable hand of death. Under this hand the body has suddenly become a foul lump of clay, a pile of dust which, of itself, is about to disintegrate and retain only through a passing usurpation the imprint of the vanished spirit.

CHAPTER IV.

AFTER three months passed in the society of pictures
and statues a man gets to be like one who for three
months has been invited out daily to dine ;—give me
bread now and no more sweetmeats.

We take the railway with a light heart, knowing at
the terminus we shall find water, trees and veritable
mountains, and that the landscape will no longer be
merely three feet long and shut up within four margins
of gold. There is relief in looking at a beautiful,
fertile undulating country, where the white roads form
ribbons amidst the green cultures. We reach Monza,
an old and famous little town of the middle ages, and
take good care not to go to see the iron-crown and the
jewels of the Lombard queen Theodoline. Veritable
antiquities and historic *bric a brac* are let alone. There
is far greater pleasure in strolling through the pretty
streets ; the most one contemplates, in passing, is the
façade of the cathedral, of a gay Italian gothic, almost
plain, where the elegant pulpit, half-ogive half-classic,
decked with shell niches and spiral columns, frames
amongst its trefoils and ogives, the serious figures of
apostles and saints. These graceful or beautiful forms
leave in the mind a sort of poetic melody which lingers
there whilst the feet stray about the streets. This little
town, agreeable like those of our Touraine, does not seem
bourgeoise like these. We resume our carriage ; the
eyes wander over the slopes covered with trees succeeding each other along the road leading to the ancient
gates of Como. The hotels stand upon the shore, and

we see from the windows the great blue expanse losing
itself afar in the golden evening atmosphere. A stock-
ade protects the vessels, and the growing duskiness
spreads its mistiness over the glittering waves. Night
has come. In the universal darkness the mountains
form a darker circle around the lake; a lantern and
some distant lights vacillate here and there like surviving stars; the coolness from the water comes in
brought by a gentle breeze; the port and the square
are empty, and one feels himself protected and tranquillized by the all-pervading silence.

In the morning we take a steamboat in order to
make a tour of the lake, and for the entire day, without
fatigue or thought, we swim in a cup of light. The
shores are strewn with white villages, reaching down to
dip their feet in the water; the mountains descend
gradually, their pyramids being populated half-way up;
pale olive and round-topped mulberry trees stretch
away in rows along the eminences, and summer-houses,
framed in under a beautiful shade, extend their ranges of
terraces down to the beach. Toward Bellagio myrtle and
lemon trees and parterres of flowers form either white
or purple bouquets between the two azure branches of
the lake. But, as it retreats toward the north, the
country becomes grand and severe; the mountains rise
high and become shattered; rigid seams of primitive
rocks, indented crests white with snow, long ravines in
which lie ancient strata of frost, emboss or furrow with
their entanglements the uniform dome of the sky. Several lofty crags seem to be bastions ranged in a circle;
the lake was once a glacier, and the friction of its sides
has slowly eaten away and rounded off the declivities.
Within these inhospitable gorges there is no verdure or
trace of life; man ceases to regard himself as on the
habitable globe; he stands in the mineral world an-
terior to man, on a bare planet where his sole enter-
tainers are stone, the atmosphere and water, a vast

pool the child of eternal snows; around it is an assembly of grave mountains which dip their feet in its azure; behind them is a second range of whitened peaks, still wilder and more primitive, like an upper circle of giant gods, all motionless and yet all different, as expressive and as varied as human physiognomies, but bathed in a warm velvety tint through distance and the vapory air and tranquil in the enjoyment of their magnificent eternity. The breeze having subsided the great luminary of heaven, above the contracted horizon, flamed down with all its force. The blue of the lake became more profound; around the boat undulations of velvet rose and fell unintermittingly, and in the hollows, between the azured bands, the sun projected other moving bands like yellow silk spangled with sparks.

Como and the Cathedral.—It is in vain to have resolved to see no more works of art. They exist everywhere in Italy, and this little town has such a beautiful cathedral!

Nowhere have we found a happier union of the Italian and the Gothic,* a more beautiful simplicity relieved here and there with the pleasing and the fanciful. The façade consists of the ordinary gable composed of two houses joined together, the one upper and the other lower, clearly defined by four perpendicular cordons· of statues. You recognize the type and the bony framework of the national architecture such as Pisa, Sienna and Verona created it in refashioning the basilicas. Although christian it is gay. Although the solid parts dominate there is no lack of finesse and variety. You feel the substance of the wall but it is embroidered, and embroidered harmoniously. Statues stand in shell niches, but each file of niches terminates in a highly foliated and elegant little canopy. The nudity of the façade is diversified by a large rosace and

---

* Begun in 1396, the façade having been finished in 1526.

four high windows, and four files of niches and statues.
In order to entirely break the monotony the artist has
placed on the two flanks two grand projecting niches
and in these stand an angel on one side and the Virgin
on the other between pretty spiral columns capped
with pointed pinnacles. Over the rose-window run
two niches, one narrow and gothic containing a Christ,
and the other wide, in which ogive and renaissance
forms commingle, and where a second Christ, between
the angel and his mother, seems to be bestowing a
benediction on the entire structure. Still higher up,
on the extreme and central peak, above this elegant,
up-springing pyramid, you see arising like the crown of
a candelabra, an exquisitely charming little openwork
turret, four delicate stories of sculptured pilasters and
Greek columns, elevated and tapered by a capping of
gothic foliage and indentations. Nowhere have we
seen a latin façade in which the rich invention of the
Renaissance and the bewildering finish of ogival taste
harmonize in more exquisite sobriety and with a livelier
inspiration.

But the renaissance spirit predominates. This is
evident in the abundance and beauty of the statues.
The pleasure of contemplating and ennobling the
human form is the distinctive mark of this age in which
man, freed from ancient superstition and misery, begins
to feel his own power, to admire his own genius and to
assume for himself the position of the gods under which
he had humbled himself. Not only do cordons of
statues bind together the four lines of the edifice and
overlie each other above the rose-window, but the windows are bordered with them, the central door flanked
and crowned and the curves of the three portals peopled with them. They are of the best epoch, and
belong to the dawn of the renaissance.* Their sim-

---

* Two statues on the sides of the great door are dated 1496.

plicity, their gravity, their originality, their vigor of expression testify to a healthy and youthful art. Several
figures of young people in pourpoints and tight hose
are chivalrous pages with legs somewhat slender, such
as Perugino painted. Naïve and semi-awkward airs, a
too literal imitation of actual forms, undoubtedly indi-
·cate that the spirit has not yet attained to its full flight.
Again some exaggerated attitudes and superabundant
masses of hair like those of Leonardo da Vinci, still
announce the early excess and irregular pulsation of
invention;—but the sculptor so fully appreciates life!
You realize that he discovers it, that he is enamored
with it, that his soul is full of it, that a proud young
man, or virginal and passive Madonna, suffice to wholly
absorb him; that varieties of head and of human attitude, the movement of muscles and of drapery, all the
grandeur and all the action of the body are stamped
on his mind through direct contact with it, through
spontaneous comprehension and without academic tradition. From Ghiberti to Michael Angelo Italian sculpture multiplied its masterpieces; its statuettes, its bas-
reliefs, its jewelry form a complete world. If, in the
larger and isolated statues it remains inferior to Grecian
sculpture it equals it in subordinate statues and in
general ornamentation. The statue thus regarded
enters as a portion into a whole. The tops of the three
doors of the façade are pictures like the bas-reliefs of
Ghiberti; a "Nativity," a "Circumcision," "the Adoration of the Magi," and, on the northern façade, a
"Visitation" are displayed in complete scenes through
a multitude of grouped figures and sometimes with a
joyous profusion of arabesques the personages of which
are themselves only a fragment. The northernmost
door consists of an arc supported by two columns and
two pilasters, as crowded and as blooming as the fron-
tispieces of the books of the period. Naked children
cling to the cornices, play with dolphins and bestride

the goats, and others are blowing on bagpipes. Small
marine cupids are shaking their serpentine tails among
jumping frogs. Birds with outspread wings come to
peck at the cornucopias. On the neighboring windows
runs a frieze of large, expanded flowers, infantile bodies
and grave medallions. All the kingdoms of nature, all
the graceful and luxurious confusion of the fantastic
and of the actual world wind and move about in stone
like a pagan carnival in the gardens of Alcinous under
the capricious and facile inventiveness of Ariosto.
The architecture adapts itself to this elegant festival; it forms bijous to frame it in. The baptistery
is a charming little marble pavilion whose small columns
form a circle in order to support a round roof, protecting the sculptured vase containing the lustral water.
The niches flanking the great entrance are trim little
porticoes filled with delicate serpentine arabesques.
One ought perhaps to state that the centre of art in
the Renaissance is decorative art. Commissions in
Greece came principally from the city which desired to
have a memorial of its heroes and of its gods. Commissions in Florence came especially from wealthy individuals who craved ewers, ivory and ebony cabinets,
plate, painted walls and ceilings and sculptured stucco
in order to decorate their apartments.* Art, in the
former, was rather a public matter and therefore graver,
simpler and better calculated to express calm grandeur.
Here art is rather a private concern and therefore more
flexible, less solemn, and more inclined to seek the
agreeable, to excite pleasure and to proportion its
dimensions and its inventions to the luxury of which it
is the ministrant.

---

* See the lives of Paolo Uccello, Dello, Verocchio, Pollaiolo, Donatello in Vasari. Painting and sculpture in the fifteenth century issue
from the goldsmith's art.

CHAPTER V.

THE country is beautiful, green and fertile and strewn
with villages and country-houses; poplar avenues extend down to the road and terminate in a circle of stone
benches under a shade. The crops follow one after
another under lines of mulberry-trees; between these
runs the slender stem of a vine, expanding its young
leaves and traversed by sunlight. Wheat, wine and
silk compose everywhere a triple harvest on the same
field.

It is a fête day. The people are out of doors in their
Sunday clothes. They do not look indigent; their
dwellings are in good condition; the women wear
shawls striped with white and red, black skirts falling
in plaits, ear-rings, and a crown of silver pins which
fasten their veils and hair. Summing up things in
gross there is about the same degree of comfort as in
Touraine. Most of the children, however, go barefoot;
the diligence horses are lean nags as in Provence, and
a good many signs indicate the same neglect, ignorance
and love of pleasure and the same superstition as in
the south of France. Numerous Madonnas are seen,
and alongside of them a notice to the wayfarer to repeat an *Ave*. Sometimes the walls represent the
damned in the midst of flames, and bear an inscription
advising the living to take heed. At Milan, in the
cathedral, Jesus on a cross is surrounded by three or
four small silver hearts; repentant believers who have

confessed and who are willing to say a *Pater noster* or an *Ave* at the choir, obtain a hundred years' indulgence; if they are old or impotent they have only to send some one to do it in their place and thus derive no less benefit. One of my Venetian friends regards the state of mind in his province as about the same; the peasantry are devotees to the Holy Father; however poor they may be they give their money for masses, their lively imagination offering a firm hold for the religion of rites.

Hence it is that they are only very moderately patriotic. In the late campaign our officers found them better disposed toward the Austrians than to the Piedmontese. The German administration had been orderly, lenient enough and even paternal for the peasantry; these, unable to read and indifferent to politics entertained no bad feeling against Austria. When national pride and sentiment are wanting little does it matter if the master be a foreigner; if he allows dancing, drinking, love-making and pays well for services, that suffices. A boatman, a shrewd fellow, as they almost all are, said to me, "The Austrians are clever folks; they made a good deal of work, and there was more trade in their day. They were only ill-natured to the *signori* because the *signori* were always against them. Now the *signori* are satisfied;—they have everything and their sons are officers. It is only the poor who are miserable; none of the peasants have property; the land all belongs to the rich. A day-laborer earns thirty cents a day, a kilogramme of meat costs eighty-five centimes and we pay as many taxes as before."— This intelligent and sensuous race see but one object in life, that of pleasure and idleness. A country bourgeois tells me: "They would like to enjoy themselves and do nothing;" they esteem a government the more according as they happen to enjoy under it more amusements and more leisure.

To make amends the middle-class and the nobles, all who possess a cloth coat and read the newspapers, are enthusiastic for Italy. In 1848 Milan fought for three days and drove off the Austrians with its own forces. When the French, after the battle of Magenta, entered the city, their joy, gratitude and enthusiasm amounted to delirium. One soldier, at first, appeared, alone by himself; the throng of people rushing forward to welcome and embrace him was so great that he could not keep his feet; his head went bobbing about and he staggered with exhaustion. Soon after this the advanced battalions appeared. Young girls with their mothers ran through the streets embracing the soldiers and even the Turcos. These battalions remained a fortnight; cafés, restaurants, all was given up to them; they were not allowed to pay a cent. It was impossible for a resident to have a glass of ice-cream brought to him—everything being for the French; it was impossible for a sick Milanese to procure a physician, as they were all attending on the wounded French. After the battle of Solferino the ladies visited them in the hospitals; the private houses were all filled with them; people even disputed their possession; many of the captains on recovering wedded rich heiresses. It is not that the Austrians were brutal or insolent; on the contrary they were gentle, well brought up, refined and patient in the extreme. Through orders from their superiors the officers avoided duels; they were jostled at the theatres and people trod on their toes; but they kept silent; otherwise they would have been compelled to fight every day. The national sentiment was intractable toward them and it is so yet. Lately a Milanese lady, who had remitted money to the Pope, was recognized in her box in the theatre and hooted and whistled at until she was obliged to leave the house by a back-door. I peruse two or three newspapers every day, and I do not see one, except the "Unita," which is not patriotic. The caricatures of the Pope are brutal; you see Death, holding a ball, bowling at him between the legs of the Emperor Napoleon; Death again is a gambler making an unexpected cast and delivering Italy. Garibaldi is admired, exalted, adored even in the meanest inn; the conductor of the diligence shows me, at Varese, the house in which he married his second wife, "the wicked one," and the wall of which he made his barricade. Nobody can give an idea of his popularity in Italy; Joan of Arc enjoyed less in France. At Levano, I see on the wall of the café an inscription stating that the son of the proprietor died for his country in combating in Sicily by the side of the national hero. Every evening and afternoon, in the cafés, on the public squares, all the semi-bourgeois, the shopkeepers, the clerks, read their journal and discuss the plans of the ministers. To tell the truth they even discuss too much, and gratify themselves with words. These latin and southerly races seem to be composed of amateurs who, having a prompt conception and a facile tongue, soar and circulate above action without taking any part in it. They delight in argument for its own sake; discussion provides them with an outlet for their oratorical humor; political conversation forms a sort of *opera seria* the effect of which is enervating because it is complete and all-sufficing. They do not investigate; their political journals are as much below ours as ours are below the English journals: they contain the superficial ebullitions of impulsive faculties but not the true reflections of solid science. They divert rather than exercise their minds; but at this moment Italy has more need of works than of words. Financial matters are its stumbling-block. In order to become an independent people and a military power it is necessary to pay more and therefore to labor and produce more. A person who establishes a manufactory, a land-owner who drains his grounds, an artisan who lengthens

his day by an hour are at this moment its best citizens.
The object is not to read newspapers and to declaim,
but to dig, to manufacture, to calculate, to learn, to
invent every wearisome, positive and confining occupation which the people would so gladly leave to
northern blockheads. It is a sore trial to pass from
an epicurean and speculative life to an industrial and
militant life : the dilettant and the patrician seem to
become serfs and wheels of a machine ; but the choice
must be made. In aspiring to form a great nation it is
necessary, in order to subsist alongside of others, to accept the obligations others impose on themselves, that
is to say faithful and regular labor, self-constraint, a
discipline of the mind methodically devoted to fixed
purposes, an enrolment of persons confined to one
sphere and stimulated by competition, a loss of indifference, a diminution of gaiety, a mutilation and a con-
centration of faculties, constant and stern effort, everything, in short, that separates an Italian of the last
three centuries from a modern Englishman or American.

Lago-Maggiore, April 10th. If I had my choice of a
country-house I would take one here. From above
Varese where the road begins to descend, one sees at
his feet a broad plain over which is spread out a series
of low hills. The whole expanse is clothed with verdure and with trees, with fields and crops spotted with
white and yellow flowers like a velvet Venetian robe,
with mulberry-trees and vines, and, farther on, with
bouquets of oaks and poplars, and scattered among the
hills, with beautiful placid lakes, united and spreading
out broadly and glittering like mirrors of steel. It is
the freshness of an English landscape among the noble
lines of a picture by Claude. The mountains and the
sky impart majesty and the superabundant water imparts moisture and grace. The two natures, that of the
north and that of the south, here unite in a happy and

friendly embrace in order to combine the softness of a grassy park with the grandeurs of an amphitheatre of crags. The lake itself is much more varied than that of Como : it is not encased from one end to the other by naked and abrupt hills; it has rugged mountains but also gentle slopes, the drapery of the forests and a perspective of plains. From Laveno you see its broad, placid surface, scattered with rays and damasked like a cuirass under innumerable scales in a blaze of sunshine traversing the dome of clouds; scarcely does the light breeze impel a dying undulation against its gravelly shore. Toward the east a path winds half way up the bank among green hedges, blooming fig-trees, spring flowers, and every description of delightful perfume. The great lake opens out tranquil in full view; the swelling sail of a small vessel is seen, also two white hamlets which at this distance seem to be the work of beavers. Mountains bristling with trees descend at long intervals to the water's edge, expanding their pyramids, their misty peaks half lost in the cloudy grayness.

We take a boat at sunrise and traverse the lake in the transparent vapor of the dawn. It is broad like an arm of the sea, and its light waves of a leadeny blue shine feebly. The thin mist envelops both sky and water with its gray hue. By degrees it grows thinner and rises, and through its decreasing meshes penetrate the beautiful light and delightful warmth. Thus do we glide for a couple of hours in the soft and monotonous suavity of the half-transparent atmosphere stirred by the breeze as if by the gentle motion of waving plumes; then it becomes quite clear and nothing is visible around us but azure and light; the surrounding water seems to be a surface of wrinkled velvet, and the pure sky above a conch of glowing sapphire. Meanwhile a white spot appears, increases in size and becomes detached : this is Isola-Madre enwrapped in its terraces, the waves beating against its great blue stones and sprinkling its lustrous leaves with moisture. The boat draws near and we land. Aloes with their massive leaves and the Indian fig on the sides of the ledge are waving their tropical growths in the sunshine; avenues of lemon-trees wind along the walls while their green or ripe fruit clings close to the panels of the rock. Four series of foundations thus arise in stories under their decorations of. precious plants. On the summit the isle consists of a tuft of verdure expanding its masses of leaves above the water, laurels, evergreens, platanes, pomegranates, exotic shrubbery, flowering glycines and blooming clusters of azalia. One walks along surrounded by coolness and perfume; there is no one here but a custodian; the island is deserted, seemingly awaiting some youthful prince and his fairy bride to screen their nuptials; thus carpeted with tender grass and flowery shrubs it is simply a lovely morning rose, a white and violet bouquet around which hover the bees; its immaculate prairies are starred with the primrose and the anemone; peacocks and pheasants quietly parade their golden robes starred with eyes or coated with purple, the undisputed sovereigns among a population of twittering and frolicsome birds.

I was no longer capable of appreciating formal architectural works, and especially the perverted forms and artificial decoration of Isola Bella; its grottoes of rock-work and mosaic, its apartments wainscoted with pictures and filled with curiosities, its water-basins, its fountains appeared to me unsightly and made no impression. I gazed on the western and opposite shore, craggy and wholly green and which seems truly formed to please the eye. The lofty and tranquil mountains rise up in all their grandeur, and one longs to go and recline on their turfy beds. Sloping fields of an incomparable freshness clothe the near declivities. The narcissus, euphorbia and purple flowerets abound in the hollows; clusters of the myosotis open their little azure eyes and their tops tremble in the ooze of the springs. We see myriads of rills descending the hill-sides, tumbling about and intersecting each other; diminutive cascades strew the grass with their pearly showers while rivulets of diamonds, collecting these scattered waters, flow on and discharge themselves into the lake. Here and there over this blooming freshness and these soft murmurings spreading oaks extend the lustre of their early verdure, mounting upward tier upon tier until, finally, their height disappearing, the sky, at the summit, is barred by their limitless layers and the indefinite colonnade of the forest.

We take the diligence at two o'clock in the morning. This is the last day of the journey; nowhere is Italy more beautiful. Toward four o'clock an exquisite indistinct dawn peers out from the night like the paleness of a chaste statue; a remote opaline reflection rests on the heights and growing half-lights venture their pearly grays beneath the nocturnal blue. The stars glimmer but, otherwise, the atmosphere is dusky, while shadows similar to cloud-flocks creep along the ground. Our vehicle stops, and we cross a river in a ferry-boat. In this silence and in this total effacement of objects the water is the only living thing, moving and stirring imperceptibly, its flowing surface rayed and glittering with small eddies intermingling between its dark banks. The trees, meanwhile, peer out through the haze, and the buds on their tops become visible enveloped in dew, awaiting, apparently, the completion of daylight. The sky becomes whiter, the dawn, meanwhile, extinguishing the stars; on all sides both vegetation and plants come out in clear relief; the gauzy veil grows thinner and thinner and finally evaporates; their color reappears; they are reborn with the light, and we feel the sweet wonder of creatures surprised to find themselves as they were the previous evening, again to resume their suspended life. The whole gorge is filled with them, while monstrous mountains, on the two sides of this scattered and charming population, rise up like guardian giants in sombre masses indenting the luminous sky with their whitened brows. At length a flash issues from one of the rugged crests; the sudden, dazzling jet pierces the vapor; sections of verdure begin to brighten, the streams glow, and huge antique vines, the domes of the trees, delicate arabesques of clambering shrubs, all the luxuriousness of a vegetation fed by the freshness of eternal springs and by the humid warmth of the rocks displays itself like the attire of a fairy enveloped in her gauze of gold.

No, it is not of a fairy here that we must speak but of a goddess. The fantastic is only a caprice and a malady of the human brain; nature is healthy and stable; our discordant reveries have no right to be compared with her beauty. She is self-sustaining and self-developing; she is independent and perfect, active and serene, and that is all that can be said of her; if we presume to compare her to any human work it must be to the Greek gods, to the august Pallas and the supernatural Jupiter of Athens; she is self-sufficing as they are. We cannot love her, our words fail to reach her; she is beyond our grasp and indifferent; we can only contemplate her like the effigies of temples, mute and bareheaded, in order to impress ourselves with her perfected form and invigorate our fragile being in contact with her immortality. This contemplation alone is a deliverance. We escape from our turmoil, from our desultory and ephemeral thoughts. What is history but a conflict of unaccomplished efforts and abortive works? What have I seen in this Italy but secular gropings of genius circumventing each other, disintegrating faiths and unsuccessful enterprises? What is a Musée if not a cemetery, and what is a painting or statue or piece of

architecture if not a memorial which a passing generation anxiously erects to itself in order to prolong its
waning thought by a sepulchre as evanescent as this
thought? On the contrary before heaven, amidst
mountains and waters, we feel as if we stood in the
presence of perfect and perennial beings. No accident
has befallen them, they are the same as at the first day;
every year the same spring sends forth to them from
copious sources pith and vigor; our exhaustion is restored by their might and beneath their tranquillity our
restlessness subsides. In them appears the uniform
power evolved by the variety and transformation of
things, the great fruitful and genial mother whom
nothing disturbs because beyond her there is nothing.
Then from the soul departs an unknown and profound
sensation; its inmost recesses then appear; the innumerable lines with which life has invested it, its
wrecks of passion and of hope, all the human dross
which has accumulated on its surface is dissolved and
fades away; it reappears in its simplicity; it revives
the instinct of former days, the vague montonous
words which formerly placed it in communion with the
gods, with those natural gods who live in all things; it
feels that all the words it has since spoken or heard are
but confused babblings, a mental concussion, a street
noise, and that if there is one healthy and desirable
moment it is that when, quitting the vexations of its sojourn, it perceives, as venerated sages have said, the
harmony of the spheres, that is to say the palpitation
of the eternal universe.

The road winds up the declivities, and toward Isella,
the mountains become bare and crowded. Walls of
cliff fifteen hundred feet high enclose the route within
their defiles. Their yellow bases, blackened by the
exudations of the springs, their towers, their chaos of
deformed and corroded ruins, seem to be the crumbled

masses of myriads of cathedrals. One vainly recurs to
memory or to his dreams for forms of this kind; you
imagine some enormous trunk hacked by the axe of a
blind colossus whose children, more feeble, afterward
approach with pruning-hooks a hundred feet long and
full of obstinate fury, in order to add other gashes to
the mighty blows of their father. It would require
similar rage and insanity to explain these grand precipitous breaches, these sudden chasms,* these over-
hanging crests and needles, this monstrous wildness of
disorder. Trains of tarnished frost creep about the
hollows, each one melting and then flowing away; thus
on all sides do the streams collect and intersect each
other, at one time sinuous and clinging to the brown
sides, at another scattered in cascades and exposing in
the air their feathery foam. In the distance smoke is
ascending and the torrent fights its way grumbling between the rocky palisades.

We still ascend and the snow glitters between the
peaks; sometimes it whitens an entire declivity and
when the sun shines on it its brightness is so vivid that
the eyes are blinded by it. The defile widens and
sloping fields spread out in their snowy shroud. All,
however, is not barren: armies of larches climb in disorder and with an air of resignation to the assault of
the cliffs; their fresh buds give them a peculiar yellow
dress; a few morose firs spot them with their black
cones; they mount upward in rows among dying trunks
and bodies of mutilated trees and all the ravages of
avalanches; like the survivors on a battle-field they
look as if they knew that they were still to fight again
and were aware of all the suffering that awaits them.
On the summit, near the hospice and village of the
Simplon extends a mournful plateau ploughed with furrows all bedimmed with melting snows like an abandoned, devastated cemetery. Here is the boundary

between two regions and it seems as if it were the boundary between two worlds; the dazzling peaks are lost in the whiteness of the clouds, so that one nc longer knows where the earth ends and where the sky begins.

INDEX.

The Novels of Friedrich Spielhagen.

In uniform style. 12mo, cloth, $2 per volume.

I. PROBLEMATIC CHARACTERS.
Translated by Prof. Schele de Vere.

II. THROUGH NIGHT TO LIGHT, *(Sequel to "Problematic Characters.")*
Translated by Prof. Schele de Vere.

III. THE HOHENSTEINS.
Translated by Prof. Schele de Vere.

IV. HAMMER AND ANVIL.
Translated by William Hand Browne.

V. IN RANK AND FILE.
(In preparation.)

"Such a novel as no English author with whom we are acquainted could have written, and no American author except Hawthorne.—*Putnam's Magazine.*

"These characters live, they are men and women, and the whole mystery of humanity is upon each of them."—*N. Y. Evening Post.*

"Terse, pointed, brilliant, rapid, and no dreamer, he has the best traits of the French manner, while in earnestness and fulness of matter he is thoroughly German."—*Boston Commonwealth.*

"Far above any of the productions of either Freytag or Auerbach."—*N. Y. Times.*

"To Friedrich Spielhagen, comparatively a new-comer in America, must be granted the first place among modern German novelists."—*Boston Post.*

"Vastly superior to the bulk of English novels which are annually poured out upon us—as much above Trollope's as Steinberger Cabinet is better than London porter."—*Springfield Republican.*

"We have no hesitation in pronouncing 'Hammer and Anvil' one of the greatest masterworks of fiction, in any language, of late years."—*Ev. Mail.*

"Everywhere one traces the hand of a master, and this work (Hammer and Anvil) alone would be for any man a title to enduring fame."—*Liberal Christian.*

"Like Auerbach, he is a subtle and profound thinker, and possesses that rare gift in a modern novelist, the ability to plan a story with ingenuity and probability. In tenderness, passion and pathos he seems to us quite unsurpassed by any writer of fiction, English, German or French."—*John G. Saxe.*

Pumpelly's Across America and Asia.

Notes of a Five Years' Journey Around the World, and of Residence in Arizona, Japan, and China. By RAPHAEL PUMPELLY, Professor in Harvard University, and some time Mining Engineer in the employ of the Chinese and Japanese Governments. Royal 8vo, with maps, woodcuts, and lithographic fac-similes of Japanese color-printing. Price, $5.00.

"One of the most interesting books of travel we have ever read. . . . . We have great admiration of the book, and feel great respect for the author for his intelligence, humanity, manliness, and philosophic spirit, which are conspicuous throughout his writings."—*Nation.*

"Fresh throughout—fresh in material and fresh in style. . . . . Sensible and racy, full of important facts, and enlivened by entertaining adventures. It is rarely the fortune of a young man to have so good a tale to tell, and rarer still for a young man to tell his tale so well."—*N. A. Review.*

"Mr. Pumpelly's narrative is interesting and instructive throughout. . . . . He makes no attempt at eloquence or fine writing, but his book is often eloquent, and is characterized by that best kind of fine writing which consists in presenting concrete details picturesquely and forcibly, with entire simplicity of statement."—*Atlantic Monthly.*

"It is crowded with entertainment and instruction. A careful reading of it will give more real acquaintance with both the physical geography and the ethnology of the northern temperate regions of both hemispheres than perhaps any other book in existence."—*N. Y. Evening Post.*

"We cannot now recall any recent traveller whose diction is quite as perfect in style, and whose faculty of description so admirably supplements his faculty of seeing. He sees only what we would like to see, and while he does not weary one with tedious descriptions of things which strike only his own attention, he does not fill his landscape with the huge historic objects of the guide-books. . . . Whatever else there is about his book, there is no baldness. It is warm, glowing, human, and luminous through and through."—*Overland Monthly.*

"One of the most fascinating and intelligent books of travels that has ever fallen into my hands, . . . and the next book of travels you buy, let it be this."—*Irenæus (Rev. Dr. Prime) in New York Observer.*

3

Biographical Sketches. By HARRIET MAR-
TINEAU. 8vo. Cloth. Price, $2.50.

There are over fifty eminent persons "sketched" in this volume. Among them are Professor WILSON ("Christopher North"), JOHN GIB-SON LOCKHART, MARY RUSSELL MITFORD, CHARLOTTE BRONTË, SAM-UEL ROGERS, HENRY HALLAM, THOMAS DE QUINCEY, LORD MACAULAY, MRS. JAMESON, WALTER SAVAGE LANDOR, GEORGE COMBE, ALEXAN-DER VON HUMBOLDT, ARCHBISHOP WHATELY, LORD RAGLAN, THE NAPIERS, MISS BERRY, FATHER MATHEW, ROBERT OWEN, LADY BY-RON, JOSEPH HUME, LORD LYNDHURST, LORD PALMERSTON, LORD BROUGHAM, THE EMPEROR NICHOLAS, METTERNICH, KING FREDERICK WILLIAM IV. OF PRUSSIA, THE DUCHESS OF KENT.

"Miss Martineau's large literary power, and her fine intellectual training, make these little sketches more instructive, and constitute them more generally works of art, than many more ambitious and dif-fuse biographies."—*Fortnightly Review.*

"It is as pleasant to read a series of "Biographical Sketches," in which no ambitious attempts at swelling periods or eloquent flights are made, as it is to find none of that indiscriminate laudation which is so generally lavished on the dead, and to be constantly made aware of the presence of a critical judgment, which, if sometimes over-severe, is never knowingly unjust."—*Pall Mall Gazette.*

The Hermitage, and other Poems.
By EDWARD ROWLAND SILL. 16mo. Cloth. $1.50.

Poems, by ROBERT K. WEEKS. 16mo.
Cloth, gilt top. Price, $1.25.

The Legends of the Birds. By CHARLES
GODFREY LELAND. With twelve lithographs, superbly printed in colors, on differently tinted papers; by F. MORAS. 1 vol. 4to, half vellum, fancy boards. Price, $1.00.

Language of Flowers. By Miss ILDREWE.
With an Introduction by THOS. MILLER. Illustrated by colored plates and numerous woodcuts, after Doré, Dau-bigny, Timms, and others. 12mo, cloth. Price, $3.50.

Father and Sons. A Russian Novel. Trans-
lated from the Russian of Ivan Sergheievitch Turgenef, by EUGENE SCHUYLER, Ph. D. 12mo. Cloth.. $1.25.

"Admirable."—*Nation.*
"A novel far better worth reading than most of those which come rom the press, and we are grateful to Mr. Schuyler for the real pleas-ure which his translation has afforded us."—*North American Review.*

4

Auerbach's Villa on the Rhine

Leading literary authorities speak thus of the translation of Auerbach's "Villa on the Rhine":

" For our own part, we prefer the New York Edition : the whole of the first part of it seems nearly unexceptionable ; and afterward, in critical passages, such as Sonnenkamp's confession, where a certain vigor and swing of expression are necessary, it seems to us at once more smooth and more forcible than Mr. Shackford's version."—*The Nation.*

" The translation of the work is thoroughly satisfactory."—*Galaxy.*

The " New York Edition" is the AUTHOR'S EDITION. *A few papers, some of them of no authority whatever, have expressed conflicting opinions regarding the two translations, which have been diligently quoted by interested parties. The above quotations settle the matter.*

Library edition, 2 vols., uniform with " On the Heights," and " Village Tales," $1.00 per vol. ; Pocket Edition, four parts. paper, uniform with the Tauchnitz books, 40 cents per part, or $1.50 complete.

Auerbach's Black Forest Village Tales.

Author's Edition. 16mo, cloth, uniform with the library edition of "The Villa on the Rhine." Price, $1.50.

This is the work which made Auerbach famous. Bayard Taylor says of it in his biographical sketch of Auerbach, prefixed to the author's edition of " The Villa on the Rhine:" These " Villa Stories" are models of simple, picturesque, pathetic narration.... A soft, idyllic atmosphere lies upon his pictures, and the rude and not wholly admirable peasant life of the Black Forest is lifted into a region of poetry.

" In a word, it is one of those rare and wholesome books which the little folks and the grown ones find equally delightful. It is luckily the fashion now to read Auerbach."—*Hartford Courant.*

.... " told with delightful simplicity and naturalness. The engravings are, many of them, very quaint, and admirably illustrate the text. It is on the whole a charming book."—*Boston Commonwealth.*

" Many charming little lyrics are scattered about in these stories, which are rendered with equal simplicity and effect ; and an undertone of German music runs through the whole series."—*N. Y. Evening Post.*

The Annals of Rural Bengal.

By W. W. HUNTER, B.A., M.R.A.S. First American, from the second English edition. 8vo. Cloth. $4.

" * * We have given but a faint sketch of the mass of matter in this volume, the rare merit of which will sometimes only be perceptible to Anglo-Indians unaccustomed to see their dry annals made as interesting as a novel. We most cordially counsel Mr. Hunter, of whom, it is needful to repeat, the writer never heard before, to continue the career he has chalked out for himself."—*Spectator.*

CPSIA information can be obtained
at www.ICGtesting.com
Printed in the USA
LVHW112315171022
730904LV00008B/338

9 783368 125042